COME AS YOU ARE

A GEN X ROMANCE

BLUEBIRD BASIN BOOK 1

JESS K HARDY

Cover art: Aljane Compendio

Cover design: Jess K Hardy

Map by: Jess K Hardy

Published by Pinkity Publishing LLC

PRAISE FOR JESS K HARDY

COME AS YOU ARE

"...the older protagonists are refreshing—and their sex scenes are hot as hell. This is a winner."
- *Publishers Weekly*

"Cozy & sexy. This was a win."
-*KATE CLAYBORN, Author of Love Lettering and Georgie, All Along*

"A charming and heartfelt romance."
-ALICIA THOMPSON, Author of Love in the Time of Serial Killers

"...a hot cider, snow, slobbery rescue dog, fireplaces, cabins with rocking chairs, and mix tapes novel."
-MARIA VALE, author of the Legend of All Wolves series

"I loved this...A very sweet & steamy romance with a very good dog."
-ANITA KELLY, author of Love & Other Disasters and Something Wild & Wonderful

A NOTE TO READERS

Content notes: Addiction, divorce, mourning the loss of a parent, a gaslighting ex, a difficult relationship with a parent.

"Just don't let me fuck up will you
'cause when I need a friend it's still you"

J MASCIS

to all my friends
and to 1991

BLUEBIRD BASIN
RED FALLS, MT
BIG HORN
MEADOWLARK
FRUIT LOOP
MAX'S TERRAIN PARK

GLACIER RIDGE
LITTLE HORN
ROLLERCOASTER

CHAPTER ONE

ASHLEY

There were only so many bills a person could stack on their desk before the pile fell over. Ashley, having reached this milestone twice, started a third pile with the most recent power bill—FINAL NOTICE stamped in bright, incriminating red ink across the front. While making a quick mental calculation of how screwed she and her mother were, her phone buzzed four times, her ex-husband's face blooming onto the screen like toxic algae.

"Ugh," she groaned while Murphy whined under her desk. Reminding herself to change Chuck's caller ID pic to something more appropriate like a snake, or the devil, she put him on speaker. "What do you want?" *Be nice, Ashley. Three-piles nice.*

"What?" Chuck whined even louder than her dog. "Can't I call my ex-wife every once in a while? Aren't we friends?"

Ashley's only response was an eye roll so profound she wouldn't have been surprised if he sensed it all the way on top of his mountain.

"How are sales looking this season?" he asked with the snide confidence of a man who already knew the answer.

She considered bragging that season pass sales were stellar, the best year they'd had since her dad died. But Chuck could always tell when she was lying. This was one of his villain superpowers. "How's Deanna?" she asked instead of answering. "Or is it Tiffany now? I can never keep up."

His laughter oozed like oil. "Jealousy was never a good look on you."

If Ashley had been a cat, she would have hissed. "Why are you calling?"

"You know why, Ash."

"My name is Ashley." Whenever he called her *Ash* she wanted to light something on fire. She hated these calls, loathed them. After their divorce, she and Chuck had barely said a single word to each other for three blissful years—only when necessary and usually about their daughter. It wasn't until he took the job managing Conquest Mountain Resort that he'd started calling once every few months, then once a month. Now the calls came almost weekly. It was always the same infuriating conversation, he'd ask how Bluebird was doing, wait for her to admit the mountain was losing money, then swoop in with an offer to buy her out. Despite how badly she wanted to tell him to go back to the circle of hell from whence he spawned, she never did. If she and Maude Alice couldn't turn things around soon, she might have no choice but to accept his offer.

"Why do you insist on struggling when we could partner up and make Bluebird Basin part of Conquest? Nothing would change. It would still be your mountain to run. But you'd enjoy all the perks of corporate support—"

"Oh please," she cut in. "Perks like ticket price hikes and blackout days? Like making this mountain inaccessible to the community that's supported my family for over forty years? Perks like that? No thanks. Not interested."

"Yeah but your community isn't supporting you anymore, Ash. They're coming here to Conquest. They're supporting me now. You know I loved Max like he was my own father, but his old-fashioned ideas about family ski resorts have made you completely naive."

If she had a nickel for every time he'd called her naive, she'd still hate him for it, but at least she'd be able to pay the power bill.

"Come on." His voice dropped into that cringeworthy, insinuating tone he always thought was seductive when really it was just gross. "I could support you again too, if you gave me another chance. We were so good together."

She stared at her phone like tentacles had sprouted from the screen. After the cheating and the lies, the last word she would ever use to describe her marriage with Chuck was *good*. With her finger hovering over the 'end call' button, she said, "You don't get to talk about my dad, Bluebird is not for sale, and we are never getting back together. Goodbye, Chuck." She mashed the button, snatched her phone off her desk, and was a second away from hurling it at the wall when her mother breezed into her office.

"What on earth?" Maude Alice squinted at Ashley, and then at the phone still poised to fly. "Let me guess. Chuck?"

"Wouldn't be a day ending in 'y' without Chuck reminding me how dire our financial situation is, and how he could ride in on his white horse and save us all." Setting her phone back down on her desk, Ashley tried to calm herself by petting Murphy's belly with her foot. "Do you ever feel like someone put your entire life on a sled and just launched it down a hill? And all you can do is watch it slide away, knowing no matter how fast you run, you'll never catch up to it again?"

Maude Alice frowned. "What an absolutely dismal thought. Thoughts like that will only make your crow's-feet dig in deeper, which is the last thing you need. Happiness is a choice, Ashley. You just have to choose it. Like me. I'm ecstatic, and my skin has never looked better."

Evidently her mother had been listening to her podcasts again. "Never mind."

"But funny you should mention our finances. I have something for you." Beaming proudly down at her, Maude Alice set a document on Ashley's desk. "I think this might be the best idea I've ever had."

Suspicion mounted. Maude Alice's best ideas had a spectacular track record of ending in epic shouting matches and ballooning credit card debt.

"What's this?" Ashley asked. Reading over the first page of the document, she blinked, rubbed her eyes in case her middle-aged vision was failing her, and looked again at what appeared to be an employment contract between Bluebird Basin and some place called Little Timber Sober Living Home. "Tell me this isn't what it looks like."

"It's what it looks like," Maude Alice replied without remorse.

"Terms of employment include..." Ashley muttered, skimming the contract. "Drug tests? Parole officers?" Her voice ratcheted up with every word. "Mother, have you lost your mind!"

Startled by her outburst, Murphy bolted out from under her desk.

"Oh, she scared you, didn't she?" Maude Alice crooned, petting the Saint Bernard behind his ears. She peered up at Ashley, a silver brow arched. "Of course I haven't lost my mind. I'm innovating."

Even though frigid air streamed in through the cracked window across from her desk, Ashley's blood boiled. "I know things are bad, but they aren't *this* bad!"

Ignoring her, Maude Alice spread the contract out on the desk, running a manicured finger along the terms. "Look how cheap they are. All they want is minimum wage, lodging in the staff cabins, and they'll need ski lessons. We'll save a fortune if we hire these men instead of college kids."

Doing the math quickly in her head, Ashley couldn't deny the savings would make it much easier for them to make payroll, something they'd barely been able to do all last season. And it wasn't like college kids were crawling out of the woodwork to work at Bluebird anymore, not with Chuck's mountain offering wages they could never compete with.

Ashley rubbed at her temples, her head pounding while she studied the contract again. "It says here that some of these men have criminal records. Some of them have served time. Recently. And you're telling me they don't even ski?"

"I'm sure at least one of them skis," Maude Alice said thoughtfully. "Or boards."

When Ashley looked up again, she found her mother fighting a grin. "This isn't funny. We aren't doing this. We aren't hiring addicts and alcoholics who just got out of prison and who don't even know how to ski!"

"*Recovering* addicts and alcoholics," Maude Alice said. "And you're overreacting. Once you meet the owner, you'll realize how right I am. Look alive, dear. He arrives in," she checked her watch, "ten minutes."

"What!"

"You have a meeting with the owner, Matthew Madigan, at 10:00 a.m. sharp."

"Since when? It's not on my calend..." Glancing down at her desk calendar, Ashley spotted one word written in fresh ink and very tiny print at the corner of today's date: *Madigan*. "Did you just write this today?"

"No, I wrote it yesterday."

Grinding the heels of her palms into her eyes, Ashley said, "Does this Mr. Madigan have a background too?"

"Madigan, actually. He goes by Madigan."

She dropped her hands so she could give her mother an unobstructed scowl. "I'm not calling him that. It's not a real name. It's a pirate's name. And I asked you a question."

Straightening the picture of Davis at her high school graduation on Ashley's desk, Maude Alice said, "He may have a record, but he's on the up and up now. He's got quite the story, actually."

"You've scheduled a stranger with a criminal record to come and meet with me in ten minutes," Ashley waved a hand over her insulated overalls, "in my snow bibs?" She felt suddenly like her office was growing, or maybe she was shrinking. Maude Alice had an uncanny ability to produce both sensations.

"We both know you're at your best when you're set back on your heels."

Ashley gritted her teeth so hard a molar squeaked. "I'm at my best when I'm prepared and presentable. I'm at my best when I don't have to tell a criminal named Madigan— Seriously, what the hell kind of name is Madigan, anyway?"

"*It's Irish*," came a deep voice from the hallway. Bright blue eyes, a salt and pepper beard, and the broad-shouldered man who owned them peeked in through the door. "I'm early," he said apologetically. "I can come back."

Ashley's heart thumped hard enough to bruise a rib. Chuck's call, the contract, and now this big, bearded man in her office... Everything was happening too quickly, control slipping out from under her like rapidly melting snow.

"Don't be silly, Madigan. It's wonderful to see you again." Maude Alice strode across the room, giving him a kiss on the cheek like they were the best of friends. "This is my daughter, Ashley. She'll be the final signature on our contract."

Mr. Madigan, with his broad cheekbones and thick brows and million-dollar smile, nodded at her. "Nice to meet you, Ashley." He held out his hand, and when she took it, he gripped hers firmly and said, "And I'm not a criminal."

Her throat seized as she shook his hand once, quickly letting it go because her palms were itchy and awkward, and she was worried they might start sweating. "Oh, I didn't—"

"I *was* a criminal." A corner of his mouth quirked under his beard. "But that was years ago. Now I'm pretty much a glorified camp counselor for other addicts and ex-criminals."

Ashley wanted to bury herself under the floorboards. "I'm sorry, Mr. Madigan. I didn't mean... It's none of my... Um, please, sit." She waved him over to the chair on the other side of her desk.

Pulling off his snowcap with tattooed hands—the word HOPE inked across his right fingers and FEAR across his left—he revealed thick, dark brown hair that curled at the ends, strands of grey sprinkled in around his temples. His eyes were a piercing, crystal blue, like the lakes in Glacier National Park. Ashley thought he might be older than her, but not by much, maybe late forties, early fifties.

When he noticed Murphy, his face lit up. "Whoa, check out that dog! He's huge!"

"That's Murphy," Maude Alice told him.

"Hey, Murphy." Dropping gracefully to his knees, he scratched Murphy's head. "How's the big man?"

"Murphy is a very expensive and very pathetic excuse for a rescue dog." Maude Alice crossed her arms over her chest. "He seems to like you, though. If you want him, Madigan, he's yours."

"Mother!" Ashley blurted out. Then, catching herself, she insisted in a quieter, more composed tone, "The dog is not for sale. And he'll make a perfectly fine rescue dog someday. He's still only a baby."

"How old?" he asked, making kissy faces at the dog.

"Almost three," Maude Alice answered on her way to the door.

"Like I said, he's only a baby. He just needs some time to develop, some patience and understanding."

"What he needs is to start earning his keep," Maude Alice countered.

Ashley's nostrils flared, irritation swelling like a mushroom cloud until Mr. Madigan said, "I think you're right, Ashley. He'll come around." Staring deeply into Murphy's eyes, his voice went soft. "Some of us just take a little longer than others, isn't that right, buddy?"

Apparently no longer controlled by her brain, Ashley's head tilted longingly to the side while she came unacceptably close to sighing at the way Murphy stared back at Mr. Madigan, like he finally felt understood. But if Ashley wanted to sigh about Mr. Madigan's soft voice and kind words—not that she did—she could do it later. Right now she needed to focus.

"Well, I'll leave you three to it," Maude Alice said while Murphy licked Mr. Madigan's cheek. "Good luck, Madigan," and then, under her breath, "you're going to need it."

CHAPTER TWO

ASHLEY

Ashley stared hotly after her mother. For what felt like the thousandth time since she'd passed Ashley control of the mountain, Maude Alice had overstepped her bounds and undermined her. And now she'd left her alone to deliver bad news to a complete stranger all done up in a flannel and jeans, looking like some ruggedly gorgeous REI model while he canoodled with her dog.

"Mr. Madigan," she started.

"Most people call me Madigan." Finally taking the chair across from her, he settled his cap into his lap, letting his denim-clad legs spread. Murphy sat down next to him so they could both stare at her.

"Mr. Madigan," she repeated, clinging to the life raft of professionalism in the open ocean of his blue eyes. "I apologize that my mother made you think we'd be interested in your, uh..."

"Men," he supplied.

"Right, men," she managed weakly. "You see, Bluebird Basin is a family mountain."

"That's great. Lots of my guys have kids."

"That's not what I mean. We can't have criminals—"

"Ex-criminals," he clarified. "And they don't all have records."

"I understand," she said as steadily as she could. "I still don't think it's a good idea for them to work here."

Sitting back in his chair, he closed his tattooed fingers over the threadbare armrests. "Can I ask why not?"

"Because I don't know them. And because... Well, because they're..." Her throat went catastrophically dry.

"Addicts?"

She grabbed the water bottle off her desk and downed its contents in several loud gulps. Wiping her mouth with the back of her hand, she said, "I don't want to seem unsympathetic or close-minded, but I'd be lying if I said that wasn't part of it." With the calm, compassionate way he looked at her, she couldn't help but feel like she *was* being unsympathetic. But she wasn't. She was only being practical. "Besides this is a ski mountain, and it says in the contract that you'll need ski lessons. So I'm assuming your men don't ski."

He took a deep, patient breath in through his nose and let it out slowly through his lips, his hand abandoning the armrest to burrow into Murphy's scruff. "I have ten men who need jobs, and three of them can ski. Maude Alice told me not to mention the boarders, but two board."

Ashley stiffened. "Why did she tell you that?"

"She told me you hated boarders."

Closing her eyes, beseeching the backs of her lids for patience, she clarified, "I don't hate boarders, no matter what my mother told you. I just..." *can't stand my philandering, opportunistic, boarder ex-husband.* "It doesn't matter." She pulled her hair over a shoulder, wrangling the conversation back on track. "We'd have to train the other half of your men, then?"

"Yes," he said, serene as a cow lying in a bed of summer grass. "But aren't there positions on the mountain that don't involve skiing? One of my guys was a cook. Another is a diesel mechanic."

That snagged her attention. They'd been trying to find a diesel mechanic to help maintain their archaic chairlift engines for years. Her mechanic, Shannon, did the best she could, but she wasn't a diesel expert. Still, what if news got out? What if hiring these men made them lose kids? Families? The only demographic they still hadn't forfeited to Conquest.

"I'm sorry," she said, standing her ground, "but we could lose skiers if they knew crimin—*ex*-criminals," she self-corrected, "were putting their kids on the chairlifts. I don't mean any offense to you or your men, but after the last few years we've had, it's too risky."

"I don't think you'd lose any skiers," he said while Murphy grumbled, thumping onto the floor to curl up around his boots. "Attitudes towards addicts and ex-cons are changing. Red Falls has been very supportive of my home and the men who live with me. And either way," he paused, frowning at the spot of drool Murphy left behind on his thigh, "it's really not."

"Sorry about that," Ashley said, handing him a tissue. "And what's really not?"

When he leaned forward to take the tissue, some mouth-watering mixture of cedar and spice leaned with him. "Thank you." While wiping the drool from his thigh, he explained, "I mean, it shouldn't be all that risky, using my men. Some people from town might recognize me up here—"

"I don't doubt that," she mumbled, and when his brow rose sharply in response she blurted out, "because you're so bi— Tall!" She'd almost called him big. "You're so tall, I mean. And you have all of those..." Her hand gestured vaguely in the air.

"Tattoos?" he suggested, his brow inching even higher as he caught her staring at the black and grey waves rising above his shirt collar to crest onto his neck.

"Right. I just meant that you might be memorable." Heat soared up her throat, leaving bright red patches in its wake she was sure. "Because of the tattoos."

If he noticed her flushing meltdown, he didn't let it show. "Word might get around that the men working on your mountain are from Little Timber," he admitted. "There's not much I can do about that. But if it does, it won't come from us. One of the stipulations of the contract includes providing the men with as much anonymity as possible. No camera crews, no uplifting news articles, no publicity stunts, for their protection."

"*Their* protection?" Ashley said. "What about *our* protection? What about the kids who ski here?"

His smile was unfairly genuine, like Mr. Rogers grew a beard, took a bunch of steroids, and spent six months covering his body in ink. "None of my guys are violent offenders, no sex offenders, no arson or larceny. They're all clean and drug tested weekly. They're just guys who fell off the edge, and now they're trying to climb back up. We lost our contract with the paper mill when it closed down, and while I do have other offers for their employment this winter, we all thrive best when we're outside," he glanced through the windows at the peaks rising beyond them, "with beautiful things to look at." Turning back to face her, he asked, "Don't you agree?"

Like a porcelain doll being tipped back and forth, she could only blink blankly at him.

"And I'd love for the guys to learn how to ski. It's important for recovering addicts to have hobbies."

"It is beautiful here," she said at length, her gaze gliding along the sweep of his brow, down the sharp line of his nose, over the long, thick column of his throat. "But it's also hard work in conditions that can be harsh and unforgiving. Are they all aware of this?"

Those intensely blue eyes gleamed. "Sure they are. These guys are hard workers, and a lot of us have had to live out in the elements at least once in our lives."

"I see," she said, not really seeing, not really having a clue. "They aren't violent?"

"No, not at my home. You have my word on that."

Even though she couldn't deny that Mr. Madigan was nailing his sales pitch, she was still wary. This was just such a typical Maude Alice move, risky and impulsive and everything that made Ashley lose sleep at night. But with how dismal season pass sales had been so far, less than half of what she'd projected... "I can't believe I'm even considering this."

His big hands rose into the air. "I feel like I need to apologize. I really didn't realize I'd be springing this on you out of the blue today. That's not the way I usually like to conduct business. Why don't you take some time to think about it, read through the contract, talk it over with Maude Alice?"

Ashley bit her tongue. If she'd been given the chance to talk this over with Maude Alice, there'd be no contract to read.

"Here." He slid his business card across her desk. "After you think it over, you can call me. I mean—" the faintest pink blush crept above his beard "—my number and my email are on the card if you want to talk more about this. You could call, or email. Email is good. Why don't you just email?" He might have been stammering, and Ashley might have found it more charming than she'd wanted to.

She picked up his card. *Matthew Madigan, Owner and Administrator of Little Timber Sober Living Home. Red Falls, MT.*

"Thank you, Mr. Madigan. I'd appreciate having some time to think about this."

"Well, that's better than a no," he said with a resigned grin. "But I should probably let you get back to work." Pushing himself up to his feet, he extended his hand toward her again. "It was nice meeting you, Ashley."

There was something about the way he said her name. She'd never particularly liked her name. It was too conflicted, too hard yet soft at the same time and in all the wrong ways, just like she was. Like her name was some gigantic, self-fulfilling prophecy. But when he said it, the way it rolled smoothly off his tongue, it sounded quiet, easy.

Shaking off the sound of her name on his lips, she shook his hand firmly and said, "Goodbye, Mr. Madigan."

He nodded, pulled his cap down over his head, gave Murphy one last scratch under his chin, and strode through the door.

Thumping her forehead onto her desk, Ashley let a long and frazzled groan seep out of her.

"Oh, one last thing," he said, sliding back into her office.

She shot to her feet, her heart shooting into her throat. "Yes?"

"I like those," he looked her up and down, "*things* you've got there."

Had she fallen asleep? Thumped her head on her desk so hard she'd given herself a concussion? "Things?"

"Yeah, those overall, snow things. They look warm, and I should probably get some for the guys if you sign the contract. What are they called, and where can I find some?"

What *were* they called? She couldn't remember. Were they called snow things? That didn't seem right, but she couldn't think of anything else to call them. She was a second away from telling him she thought they might be called snow things when Maude Alice rounded the corner and said, "*Bibs*, Madigan. The word my daughter is searching for is *bibs*."

"Thanks, Maude Alice," he said, and then, glancing at Ashley, "I hope I have a reason to order some."

As soon as he left for real, his footsteps trailing off down the stairs, Maude Alice leaned against Ashley's door with a self-satisfied smirk and said, "See? I was right, wasn't I?"

Staring through the windows at the mountain she loved, at the bunny hill where her dad had taught her to ski, the empty slopes she hoped would be filled with happy skiers in a few short weeks, then turning back to the stacks of bills on her desk, her phone sitting beside them, hearing Chuck's voice echo in her head, she knew what she had to do.

"The only thing you're right about, Mother, is how far I'm willing to go to save this mountain." Only this time, Ashley wondered if she was finally going so far she'd never be able to turn back.

CHAPTER THREE

MADIGAN

WET SNOW MADE THE STEEP, winding road leading down from Bluebird Basin so slick Madigan worried he might leave finger-shaped dents in Lydia's steering wheel. Feathering the brakes, he squinted through the fat flakes hitting his windshield even with his wipers on high. Which on Lydia, his '77 Suburban, was just barely fast enough to justify their use. Narrow, hairpin turns and steep drop-offs aside, he knew his nerves had more to do with the woman than the road.

He'd turned whatever charm he could muster up to eleven, but ever since he'd left Ashley's office he couldn't help feeling like he'd blown it. She was not impressed with his proposal, or with him. At all. Maude Alice had been an easy sell when they'd met for lunch the other day, when she'd warned him—in what he recognized now as an epic understatement—that Ashley might be more difficult to convince. *No kidding.*

He'd let his nerves get the better of him, he realized as his back tires lost a bit of traction around a turn. Mainly because he really wanted this job for his guys, but also because there was something about Ashley that knocked him off balance. She was smart and gorgeous, a fatal combination to his cool these days. But she also had this irresistibly classic thing going for her that reminded him of actresses in the 80s when curly hair and wide eyes and pointy noses were the style, like a no bullshit Goldie Hawn.

Finally turning onto the highway after inching down the last switchback off the mountain, he released his death grip on the steering wheel and popped in a cassette tape, cranking the volume so Shane MacGowan could sing to him about a woman with brown eyes.

"How'd it go, Boss?" Kevin asked, sitting next to Clay at the big kitchen table, both men cradling steaming mugs of tea in their hands. "Did you get us a new gig?"

Hanging his coat on one of the hooks lining the hallway, Madigan said, "I mean, it could have gone a lot worse."

"That doesn't sound very promising," Kev mumbled, his knee shaking under the table like an excited dog, the way it had since his release to Little Timber about a month ago.

"She's mulling it over," Madigan said on his way into the kitchen. "Thinks it's risky. But she didn't say no."

Clay eyed him thoughtfully. "She has some preconceived notions about addicts, I take it?"

After pouring his own cup of tea, inhaling the spicy peppermint steam, Madigan took a seat at the table. "She just wants some time to think it over."

"Of course she does," Clay said, reasonable as always. "It's a pretty big decision whether or not to let hardened criminals loose on your mountain."

"Hardened?" Madigan cocked a brow at the stout, older black man whose thick stubble sported only a few more grays than his own beard.

Clay smirked. "You know, public urination, stealing from children. Hard stuff like that."

"Hey!" Kev chimed in indignantly. "I had to piss, and the cops were on my ass. And that kid's bike was just sitting there in the yard." He shook his head. "Kid needed to learn to be more careful with his stuff anyway."

"Thankfully you were there to teach him that lesson, huh, Kev?" Madigan ribbed. Kev was a good-looking white kid, early twenties, curly blond hair, clear blue eyes, and somehow still tan even in a Montana winter.

"Exactly," Kev said. "Anyway, did you at least *try* to be nice to the owner? What's her name?"

"Ashley." Madigan had never known an Ashley before. He liked the name. He liked saying it. *Ashley*.

"Were you at least nice to Ashley? Or did you go all Mad Madigan? All grumbly and growly, storming out dramatically into the snow when she didn't sign right away?"

"Mad Madigan?" He slid his eyes to the side. "Kevin, have you been Googling me?

"Maybe." Kev shrugged. "It's not my fault you used to be a famous rock star dreamboat."

"Well, knock it off. Of course I was nice to Ashley, and I don't growl. When have you ever heard me growl?"

Holding his arms stiff at his sides, Clay said, "My name's Madigan." His voice was low and gruff and mocking. "I'm a great big, bearded grump. Now make your beds and do the dishes!"

"I don't sound like that."

Clay and Kev shared a look while they sipped their tea.

"I gave her my card. She's supposed to call. Or email," Madigan said, wondering if she actually might call, and what her voice might sound like over the phone if she did—soft and smokey like whiskey-soaked cotton... "How's the kid?"

"Hasn't left his room," Kev said. "Just lying on his bunk, staring at that picture."

Madigan picked up his mug. "Rough deal, that one. Has anyone tried talking to him today?"

"I offered him leftovers from Thanksgiving dinner," Clay said. "He wasn't interested."

After swallowing a gulp of almost painfully hot tea, Madigan said, "All right, I'm going in."

"Go easy on him, Boss. He's going through it."

"Hell, Kev. What do you think I'm gonna do? I'm actually a pretty nice guy."

Raising his mug back to his lips, Kev muttered, "Tell that to the last guy who didn't make his bed."

Madigan knocked on the open door. Even though he didn't allow any closed doors in Little Timber, he always knocked before he entered. "Hey, Sam. How's it going?"

"Fine," Sam replied shortly, curled onto his side facing the wall, his feet dangling off his bunk.

Madigan remembered when he'd been as skinny as Sam, as frail, like a stiff wind would scatter him into a million pieces. "Wanna talk?" he asked, taking a seat on opposite bunk. "The first week out can be hard." Especially a first week that had included Thanksgiving. A Thanksgiving Sam spent alone, staring out the window, waiting for family who never came.

"No." Sam pulled his knees up close to his chest, staring at a picture pinned to the wall.

Madigan made out the shape of a woman with long brown hair, a golden tan, wearing a yellow sundress. A little girl stood in front of her, maybe five years old. It was a picture of Sam's wife Izzy and his daughter Sara. The prison staff had told Madigan that Sam had spent much of his sentence like this after he finally kicked—quiet, somber, alone in his bunk, staring at that picture. It's certainly how he'd spent the last week at Little Timber. Madigan didn't think Sam had said more than ten words since he'd picked him up at the state prison.

"I'm sorry they didn't come yesterday, Sam." In his experience, there was little point in beating around the bush with recovering addicts.

"I said I don't want to talk, all right. So just fuck off, okay."

Madigan sniffed, then covered one of his hands with the other, pushing on his knuckles until they popped. "Sure, I'll leave you alone. But there's no swearing here."

Sam finally rolled over. "What?"

"No swearing. House rules."

He sat up on the side of his bed. "You're fucking kidding me."

Shaking his head, Madigan said, "Afraid not. And since you've sworn twice now, you've just earned yourself bathroom duty."

"What the fuck, dude? You *just* told me I couldn't swear. How the fuck was I supposed to know?"

And *hell* if this kid didn't remind Madigan of himself thirty years ago. Just salty and pissed off and convinced it was him against the world. "Rules are posted right there." He tilted his head toward the door where the 'House Rules' were written clearly in black Sharpie on white poster board. "It's not my fault you're too busy staring at that picture to notice your surroundings. And now that you've broken the swearing rule four times, you've got bathroom duty all week."

"That's fuc—" Sam gritted his teeth. "That's messed up. I haven't done anything to anyone since I got here. I don't deserve bathroom duty."

"It's not really up for debate. This isn't a democracy, it's a sober living home. I'll get you the bucket."

"Wait, what bucket?" Sam's brows pulled together, his hands wringing in his lap.

Madigan felt only mild guilt for meting out the punishment—typically reserved for infractions far worse than swearing. But he knew firsthand that after spending your entire sentence beating yourself up, it could be a relief to have someone else do it for you for a change. And with a bathroom used by ten men waiting for him, Sam was definitely about to get his ass kicked. Hopefully so thoroughly he might even get some real sleep tonight. "Follow me and find out."

After showing Sam the ropes of cleaning Little Timber's bathroom, then helping Kev and the other guys do the dishes after Clay made a ridiculously good stir-fry for dinner, Madigan called lights out and retreated to his room. Sitting in his chair, he clicked on his desk lamp and pulled his guitar out of its case, parking it in his lap.

It'd been years since someone had called him Mad Madigan, and hearing the nickname again felt a little like seeing a ghost. While strumming out a string of random chords, not quite a song, memories of his life in the band emerged from the shadows, the fame, the women, the drugs. The friends he'd lost. The friends he hadn't spoken to in decades. Those few golden moments buried under six feet of rubble.

His fingers moved over the strings more deliberately as he played the opening chords to one of the Makers' biggest hits, "Shine Bright." He rarely played those old songs anymore, but something about today, about Kev using his nickname, Sam curling up defensively on his bunk, had made nostalgia rear its sentimental head.

Just when he reached the chorus, his ass buzzed. Setting his guitar down, he pulled his phone out of his back pocket. The number wasn't one he recognized, but he always answered his phone in case it was one of the guys who'd stayed at Little Timber in the past, or someone new who needed his help now. Flipping the phone open, he tucked it between his shoulder and his ear. "Madigan," he said, rubbing his eyes.

"Hello, Mr. Madigan. This is Ashley. Ashley Cooke. From Bluebird Basin. We met this morning, if you remember. In my office."

He wanted to respond, but she wouldn't let him get a word in.

"On the mountain. The ski mountain. I should have just emailed," she muttered, probably to herself. "I'm Maude Alice's daughter."

Thinking she might finally be finished introducing herself, he opened his mouth when she said, "Are you there?"

"I'm here." He liked the quick and nervy way she talked, like if a lightning bolt could speak. "Just waiting for my turn."

"Oh, right, well..."

He took the opening. "Hello, Ashley. Of course I remember you. How are you?" Leaning back in his chair, he settled a hand behind his head.

"I've finished reading over the contract, and I have a few stipulations I'd like to add."

He sat forward again. Was she actually considering signing? "Okay, shoot."

"The men will need to be drug tested twice a week instead of weekly."

It would cost him a bit more, but it was doable. "Done. What else?"

"You can stay in the staff cabins," she continued, her soft, husky voice brushing against his ear, "but only the men. No visitors in the cabins."

"Some of the men have wives, partners, children. Weekends are typically open for scheduled visitations."

He could practically hear her wheels turning. "We'll have to look at visitations on a case-by-case basis. But we can't have people we don't know staying in the staff cabins. I hope you understand."

"That's fair." He could iron out the kinks on this issue once they got up there, once she got to know the guys and realized they weren't coming to wreak havoc on her ski hill.

"And Maude Alice and I reserve the right to terminate the contract at any time. This is nonnegotiable."

He'd included a term in the contract requiring two weeks' notice of termination, except in the case of breach of contract—if any of the guys failed their drug tests, didn't show for their shifts, or caused any damage to her property—but he'd figured that was a long shot anyway. "That's not ideal, but if it gets us the job, I'll agree to it."

When she took a slow, deliberate breath, Madigan couldn't shake the feeling she was still trying to convince herself that signing the contract wasn't completely bonkers.

"Hey," he said, hoping to ease her mind. "I know this is a big deal. It was obvious when I met you and Maude Alice that you both love your mountain. I know working with me and my men might feel like a risk."

"It *is* a risk, Mr. Madigan. But considering the situation the mountain is in, it's a risk we're willing to take."

He nodded dutifully even though she couldn't see him. Somehow he felt like he was back in school and dangerously close to getting booted out of class by one of his teachers. Just one wrong word... "No risk, no reward, right?"

There was a sharp sound over the line, like maybe she'd slapped her hand over her forehead. "Opening day is in two weeks. How soon can your men start?"

He couldn't keep the smile from spreading across his face. "Just as soon as I buy the guys some of those adorable snow bibs."

"Oh my god," she muttered.

Pump the brakes, Romeo. "You won't regret this, Ashley. I promise."

"I hope you're right," was all she said before she ended the call.

CHAPTER FOUR

ASHLEY

Sleep eluding her, Ashley paced back and forth until Maude Alice thumped on the wall separating their rooms and shouted, "It sounds like Radio City in there! Go to bed!"

Maude Alice could sleep through a tornado. But Ashley, who'd inherited her father's busy mind, thought too much. Would the men from Little Timber be difficult to work with? What would her dad have thought of the decisions she was making? Would he be disappointed in her? Would she end up having to sell to Chuck?

She'd spent the last week preparing the staff cabins, organizing job roles based on the list of the men's skills and training Mr. Madigan had provided her with, making schedules and coordinating with the seasonal staff she'd be keeping on. She felt as ready as she ever would for the men's first day, but every time she closed her eyes, the familiar crush of grief pressed in. They would never have wound up in this position if her father was still alive. She wouldn't be fending off Chuck's offers left and right, fighting with Maude Alice every day, struggling to keep collections off their asses. Signing employment contracts with flannel-wearing strangers.

Crossing her room, she stared at the picture of her parents hanging on the wall. They were standing in front of the mountain with their skis in their hands, their goggles resting on their foreheads, their cheeks rosy, smiles huge. The picture had been taken the day her parents had bought Bluebird, and they both looked so young and happy. Tracing Max Cooke's bulb nose with her finger, grateful once again that she'd inherited Maude Alice's nose instead of his, Ashley wanted so badly to talk to him. She wanted to tell him what was happening just like she used to when she was a kid, when they'd catch last chair at the end of the day, talking on the chairlift about everything and anything. When he'd tell her everything would be okay, no matter how bad things seemed. But he was gone. He was gone and she was on her own.

Climbing back into her bed, she pulled her covers up to her chin and watched the moonlight cut across her walls until the sun chased it away.

Staring nervously out a window in the dining hall, Ashley watched the road leading up from Red Falls, waiting for Mr. Madigan and his men to arrive. When her phone buzzed, she yanked it out of her pocket like it was a bomb about to explode.

Davis: Good luck today, Mom. Grandma told me about the men from the sober living home. Why didn't you tell me? Are you avoiding me? Do you need me to come? I don't need to stay in Missoula over break. The lab is quiet and things with Patrick are weird anyway. Love you. Miss you.

Ashley typed out a perfunctory, *Sorry, sweetie. Just got busy and it slipped my mind*, even though this was nowhere close to the truth. Ashley purposefully hadn't told her daughter about hiring the men from Little Timber because she knew Davis would feel obligated to leave school and come help out at Bluebird over the winter. Evidently, Maude Alice had gone ahead and told her anyway. *No, you don't need to come. What do you mean by weird? Is everything okay? Love and miss you too.*

Davis: I don't know. Patrick just never does anything and he's always in a shitty mood. Will you call me later?

Ashley: I will, promise. Please don't tell your father about our new hires. He's exhausting enough as it is.

Davis: I won't say a word. I'm proud of you, Mom. This is very forward thinking for you. And Grandma told me one of the men is a total smokeshow. Madigan or something? Sounds like a sexy pirate.

Clapping her hands together on her way into the dining hall, Maude Alice shouted, "Here we go!"

"Christ, Mother!" Ashley hissed, fumbling her phone. "Are you trying to give me a heart attack?"

Maude Alice gasped in feigned surprise. "Did my daughter just deign to speak to me again? Mark the date! That was a world record Ashley Cooke Silent Treatment."

"I wasn't giving you the silent treatment," Ashley insisted, even though she hadn't said more than a few words to her mother since Mr. Madigan had left her office over a week ago. Considering that Ashley's adoption of silence as her preferred defense mechanism came directly from her mother, Maude Alice shouldn't be surprised. After all, she was the one who'd decided unilaterally there were things, *people*, they wouldn't talk about anymore. "I've just been busy getting this mountain ready."

"Whatever you say, dear."

Taking in Maude Alice's outfit—a cashmere sweater, skinny jeans, tall grey boots, her silver, shoulder-length hair appearing freshly trimmed—Ashley said, "You look nice today."

"I thought I'd try to look my best for our new employees." Maude Alice's brow arched. "You obviously didn't see the need."

"Wow. Thank you for that vote of confidence." Ashley thought she looked just fine in her faded denim jeans and checkered button-down shirt and muddy work boots. *Shit*. Maybe she should change.

"There they are!" Maude Alice cheered, clapping her hands

together again as a Suburban drove into the parking lot, rumbling and sputtering while it slowed to a stop below the lodge.

Too late to change now.

Twenty feet below them, Mr. Madigan hopped out of his truck, scratching his beard and laughing breezily at something one of the other men must have said. Ashley's nerves had driven her to the point of insomnia, yet here he was, laughing like he didn't have a care in the world. Why couldn't she be breezy? Why was she so on edge all the time? When her mother shook her head again at her appearance, Ashley realized she didn't have to look very far for the answer.

While the men piled out of Mr. Madigan's Suburban—brown with wood grain trim and looking older than she was—Ashley pulled on her lower lip, realization slapping her hard across her face. She was not the woman for this job. She'd never broken a single rule in her entire life, law abiding to a fault. She didn't drink, had never smoked a cigarette, hadn't even gotten a traffic ticket. There was no way these guys would listen to her.

"What a crew." Maude Alice grinned, not at all overwhelmed or insecure, two emotions Ashley was fairly certain her mother had been born without.

"Yep," Ashley said, still tugging on her lip.

Turning to face her, Maude Alice made a *tsking* sound. "Smile, dear. You look angry when you don't smile. You don't want to scare the men off before they've even started, do you? Come now," she fluffed Ashley's hair until Ashley swatted her hand away, "let's go welcome them to their new homes."

Taking a deep breath, Ashley fisted her hands at her sides and considered, however briefly, throwing herself down the stairs.

"MADIGAN, HELLO AGAIN." Maude Alice leaned in for a kiss on the cheek that Mr. Madigan gave her without a second thought, his hand sliding over her lower back.

In some sort of mother/daughter psychic connection that had never existed before, Ashley could have sworn she felt his hand on her own back, warmth spreading out over her skin.

"Hello, Ashley," he said, nodding once in her direction.

Crossing her arms tightly over her chest, she pasted a weird smile onto her face on the off chance she actually did look angry. "Hello, Mr. Madigan."

"Please, call me Matthew." His smile wasn't weird. His smile was blinding.

"Okay. Matthew." She looked up from his lips only to get sucked straight into his eyes. It wasn't her fault. Nothing so blue and intense and sparkling in the sunlight the way they were could exist without being stared at. It was a natural fact, that shade of blue was magnetic. Peeling her gaze from Matthew, she turned to face the men. Ragtag, she thought, was a charitable term to describe them. Jeans and khakis, hooded sweatshirts, and one of them wore a cowboy hat that looked like a dog used it as a chew toy. "You all must be our new employees."

Moving down the line of men, Matthew introduced them one at a time. Jeff, Brian, Mark, Jacob. Names she recognized from the list he'd given her. He called the man with the hat 'Tex,' because of course he did. Tall and rangy Tex, as it turned out, was her new diesel mechanic.

Ashley's attention snagged on the man named Sam. Sam had sandy hair, dark brown eyes, and couldn't have been much older than Davis. His head was down, his narrow shoulders drawn in tight, and he stood a full step back from the others like he wanted to be anywhere but here. Unable to stop herself, she wondered what sorts of things he'd been through to look so...scared.

"This is Kevin." Matthew clasped the second to last man in line's shoulder.

"Nice to meet you Ashley and Maude Alice," Kevin said, speaking fast and loud. "We can't thank you enough for letting us work here this winter. Sorry none of the guys said that yet. It's not their faults. Most of them learned their manners from stray dogs."

Kevin was a handsome blond kid. Watching him laugh through a wide, toothy grin after Tex elbowed him in the ribs, Ashley realized he'd make a fantastic ski lift operator.

Moving to the end of his line of men, Matthew stopped next to a black man who was close to Maude Alice's age if Ashley had to guess, sturdy as a tank and nearly as big. "And this is Clayton."

"Nice to meet you, ma'am," Clayton said after removing his cap, revealing a bald head that glinted in the sun. "Don't listen to Kevin, we're all very well mannered. Well, except for Madigan, but he's a lost cause."

Matthew smiled tightly. "Thanks for that, Clay."

"Clayton," Maude Alice said. "You're the cook, isn't that right?"

"That's correct, ma'am."

Clay had a nice smile, Ashley thought. Great dimples.

Waving a hand through the air, Maude Alice said, "None of this 'ma'am' business. You and I will be working together in the kitchen, so please call me Maude Alice."

"All right." Clay's cheeks turned crimson. "Maude Alice."

After all the introductions had been made, silence fell over the men as they shifted uncomfortably on their feet. Realizing abruptly that they were waiting on her, Ashley glanced down the line of men who'd help either make or break her mountain this season, and said, "Welcome to Bluebird Basin," wondering what the hell she'd gotten herself into.

CHAPTER FIVE

MADIGAN

MADIGAN HAD FOLLOWED behind Ashley all day while she'd oriented the crew to the lodge, the rental shop, the kitchen, the bunny hill she'd teach the men to ski on in the morning, and finally the cabins. She'd been all business, barely allowing herself a single smile, not even when Kev cracked a joke about needing to find a cowboy hat-shaped helmet for Tex. But Madigan understood, she was taking a chance on them. It was a big deal.

The guys had been on their best behavior. They hadn't even thrown a single snowball until Ashley had left them at the cabins and retired to the lodge. A steady hum of enthusiasm had run through them all day. It was a good sign, he hoped.

Popping his head into Clay and Kev's cabin, he said, "These are so cozy. Don't you think they're cozy?"

"Speak for yourself," Kev grumbled half-heartedly, unzipping his duffle bag on his bed. "You don't have to share one,"

"Oh, come on, Kev." Clay unzipped his bag. "We've got more room here than we had at Little Timber. It's like summer camp."

"Busy day, huh?" Taking a seat on their couch, Madigan

scratched his head through his cap. "But I think it'll be good. I think it'll work out. I'm excited. It's exciting, right? Aren't you guys excited?"

Kev and Clay peered up from their bags.

"What's your deal?" Kev asked, his eyes narrowing. "You're all nervous or something."

"It's the blond. Madigan has a thing for blonds."

"I do not have a thing for blonds, Clay," Madigan lied. "And her name is Ashley."

Smirking while he pulled some shirts from his bag and put them in a drawer, Kev said, "From what I've heard, you haven't had a thing for anyone, blond or brunette, for like a million years."

"He's saving himself," Clay said, "in case Kim Gordon finally remembers he exists."

"That is hysterical," Madigan said sarcastically, finding it suddenly too warm in their cabin. "I'm gonna go check on the rest of the guys, but I'm just in the cabin next door so let me know if you need anything."

"Aww, thanks, Dad," Kev crooned. "Can I crawl into bed with you if I have a nightmare?"

Rubbing his knuckles over Kev's curly hair, Madigan said, "You're a big boy now, Sport. But if you do have a nightmare, you can always crawl in with Clay."

"That's right, Champ." Clay held his arms out wide. "I can be your security blanket."

Madigan left their cabin to the sound of Clay cackling after Kev threw a pillow at his face.

AFTER SPENDING the better part of the last decade sharing the living space in Little Timber with ten other men, having his own private cabin felt like the height of luxury. It was small—a couch, a rocking chair, a bed, a kitchen just as big as it needed to be, and a nice sized bathroom—but the vaulted ceilings gave the space some breathing room so it didn't feel cramped. It felt warm, homey, nice.

He turned on the lamp by his bed before starting a fire in the stove. Then he looked inside the cupboards, the small pantry, the fridge, all thoughtfully stocked with foods and drinks he knew the men would appreciate—cold cuts, bread, milk, cheese, peanut butter, hot dogs, pop. There was a bookshelf by the bed filled with National Geographics, skiing magazines, mysteries and romance novels. He knew the guys would like those too, even though they'd probably hide them under their pillows before ever admitting to reading them, except for Kev. He was the type to walk around with a romance novel tucked into his back pocket.

There were other thoughtful touches too, a vase of dried lavender on the table, candles on the mantle above the stove, soft, neatly folded towels in the bathroom, and a hand-painted trail map of Bluebird Basin hung in a wooden frame on the wall. Studying the map, he traced his fingers over Bluebird's twenty or so runs with names like 'Meadowlark' and 'Fruit Loop' and 'Bitterroot Bowl.' His gaze hovered over the lodge at the mountain's base before following the trail leading back to the cabins where, remarkably, he now stood.

Sniffing under his arms—*not bad, but not great*—he unbuttoned his flannel and walked toward the bathroom, halting in his tracks when someone knocked on his door.

"Just a second," he called out. It was probably one of the guys needing shampoo or soap or something. Most of them wouldn't remember their heads if they weren't attached. Pulling open the door, he said, "You forget something?" as an icy blast *whooshed* into the cabin, blowing his unbuttoned flannel open wide. He knew he shouldn't have, but all day long he'd silently wished that Ashley would look at him, just once. Even though she hadn't then, she was definitely looking at him now, her brown eyes moving over his body, dropping to his stomach before skipping back up to his chest, his throat, his face, like a rock over a lake.

"You're... You must be... I should..." Her face had turned as red as his shirt.

Maybe he hadn't completely lost his touch. "Hi, Ashley."

"Um...hi." She said nothing else.

Hooking a thumb over his shoulder, he said, "Did you set up the cabins? They're really great. The guys are gonna love staying up here."

"I did. And I'm glad. That they will," her throat bobbed, "love it."

Catching her checking out the ink over his right pec, he let the corners of his lips tilt. "That's Mary," he said, pulling his shirt back a bit to show her the full black and grey tattoo of his schipperke. "My dog when I was a kid."

"I wasn't..." She jerked her gaze up and over his shoulder. "I wasn't looking."

"Do you want to see any of my others?" His brow ticked up. "I have a lot."

Her eyes slammed shut. "Mr. Madigan, I'm sure that I do not."

The stammering, the red cheeks, she was so adorable he could barely stand it. "Matthew, please," he said. "My dad is Mr. Madigan. Or you could call me Mattie. My parents call me Mattie, but I prefer Madigan."

"Matthew, Mattie," she spluttered, shaking her head. "I wasn't... I didn't mean... This isn't... Oh my god," she groaned, wheeling around and nearly slipping on his snow-covered porch.

He whipped his arm out, grabbed her elbow to steady her. "Whoa, there. Are you okay?"

Slipping out of his grip, she stomped down his stairs. "I'm good. Great. Goodbye. Goodnight, I mean."

"Wait, Ashley. Where are you going?" he asked, buttoning up his shirt while he walked to the end of his porch. "Did you need something?"

"Nope," she said, trudging away from him through the snow, her blond curls trailing down her back under her hat, the puffball on top bouncing in time with her steps. "Just checking that you and the men had everything you needed. Looks like you do. Have everything. You need. Goodnight." Meeting up with Murphy, who waited for her with his tail wagging, she disappeared down the trail through the trees, slipping again at some point judging by the loud snap of a tree limb and the even louder, "*Shit!*"

He wanted to run after her, apologize for teasing her, for doing...whatever it was he was doing. Flirting? Was he flirting? It had all happened so quickly, the last five minutes blurring together like some hormone-infused fever dream. He'd always been direct with women, never holding back when he wanted something or someone. But he wasn't Mad Madigan anymore, spending each night trolling for groupies to keep him warm. He was your Friendly Neighborhood Madigan now—nice, quiet, harmless, even if he had been checking out her ass in her jeans while she'd hurried away from him. Okay, maybe he wasn't completely harmless. But there was something about her, nervy and tense, pure kinetics like one of those balls on a string he'd played with as a kid, flinging wildly in every direction whenever he tried to hit it with a paddle. His mind descending into deplorable, paddle-laden territory, he slapped his cheek. "Get a grip, idiot."

A lot rode on this winter for his guys, for his home, and for Ashley. Moving the operations of Little Timber to Bluebird was a huge risk. If it didn't work out, the guys wouldn't be able to pay their rent, he wouldn't be able to pay the mortgage on Little Timber, and Ashley and Maude Alice could lose a substantial portion of their staff all at once. Even worse, once Bluebird opened it would hardly be the controlled environment he'd fought to maintain at Little Timber. There would be temptations, and he'd have to work twice as hard to keep the men on track. He'd been doing well for a while—mainly because he'd forced himself to remain single and keep his focus on work—but he knew his tendency to ruin things always trailed behind him, lurking like a dealer around the corner, especially when it came to relationships. Despite his weakness for driven, highly-strung, easily-flustered women, instead of running after her into the snow and making a scene, he stepped back into his cabin, shut the door, and took a shower. During which he masturbated.

Twice.

CHAPTER SIX

ASHLEY

The men standing before Ashley looked comically similar in their matching blue snow bibs and apprehensive expressions.

"You mean we'll have to pull ourselves up on that rope?" Clay rubbed a gloved hand over his whiskered chin, staring up the bunny slope like it was Mt. Everest Ashley wanted them to summit rather than a 100-foot-high beginner hill.

"No," she said. "The rope pulls you up. All you have to do is hold on and not fall down."

"That's, like, not possible," Sam said, wide-eyed.

Bumping his shoulder against Sam's, Kevin encouraged, "It's easier than it looks. Trust me."

Finally arriving onto the scene, Matthew cleared his throat, the sound jerking all the guys to attention. He had a way with them, Ashley had to admit. They listened to him, respected him. All he had to do was raise a brow or clear his throat like he just did, and they all fell right into line. Ashley, on the other hand, was still so embarrassed about racing away from his cabin last night she could barely look at him. How long would it take? How many years away from Chuck would have to pass before she regained a single ounce of the self-confidence he'd stolen from her?

Obviously not nervous or embarrassed or lacking any self-confidence at all, Matthew grinned, looking almost rudely comfortable in jeans and a puffy vest over a dark grey sweater. At least he wore sunglasses. It was easier to look his way when his sparkling blue magnet eyes weren't looking right back.

"Easy?" he asked. "Is that right, Kev? Well, hotshot, maybe you should show everyone how it's done." His ribbing diffused some tension, even Sam's shoulders relaxing a fraction, but Ashley squinted down at him because Matthew wasn't on skis. He'd refused to even try on a pair, yet he had the nerve to give these guys a hard time?

"Maybe you should lead by example," she said, her steady tone coming as, quite frankly, a bit of a shock.

A chorus of "*Oohs*," sounded from the men, one "*Sick burn*," and then Clay made everyone laugh when he said, "Yeah, Madigan. Did you forget your skis in your crib?"

Sucking on a tooth, Matthew raised his sunglasses up to nestle in his hair. And there they were, *magnet eyes*. "I don't ski."

Kevin made a massive fart noise.

"Interesting." Ashley turned back to the men. "Please raise your hand if you also don't ski."

Five of the men raised their hands.

"And yet here you are, in your gear, willing to learn." Peering back down at Matthew, she arched an accusatory brow.

"I think you've made your point, Ashley," he said over the men's snickering. While he stared at her with an expression that was somehow indignant and amused at the same time, he snapped open the camping chair he'd brought with him, settled it onto the snow, and took a seat. "But as much as I'd love to join you, I am here in a purely supervisory capacity."

"You see what we have to deal with?" griped Brian, a tall and friendly middle-aged man with dark eyes and light brown skin.

Rolling his eyes, Matthew screwed the top off his stainless-steel thermos and inhaled the steam. "Mmm," he murmured, the sound breaking some law of physics so it could rumble through her bones. "Maude Alice makes a mean cup of joe."

"Not cool, Boss. Super not cool," drawled Tex, looking awkward in a helmet instead of his cowboy hat.

Regardless of how Matthew was choosing to spend his time this morning, Ashley was impressed that all ten men had shown up for their lesson today, even though several of them would work positions that wouldn't require them to be out on the slopes. There was a camaraderie with these guys that she appreciated. A ski hill crew was a lot like a family. When you worked outside during a sub-zero blizzard or rescuing skiers off a broken-down lift or digging them out of a snowslide, you had to have each other's backs in order for everything to run smoothly.

There was nothing *smooth,* however, about helping the men grapple with the rope tow. Skis flew, bodies hit snow, men grunted and face-planted, some emerging with snow-covered beards. Despite all the bumps and bruises, laughter rang through the air. Even Sam chuckled at one of Clay's more spectacular wipeouts. Matthew, on the other hand, was having way too much fun watching from the comfort of his chair, pointing at the men's flailing falls, throwing his head back and howling at the sky. His laughter, warm and deep, stirred the hairs on the back of her neck like a magnet roving over a sea of tiny iron filings.

Even though she'd never seen such an uncoordinated group of humans, pride radiated through her. The men never gave up, they never quit, and they were all quick to help each other when they could. Eventually, after nearly half the day had slipped away, every single one of them made it up the rope tow to the top of the bunny hill. Now she just had to teach them how to get back down without killing themselves.

"Pizza? You want us to make pizza?" Clay asked, staring at his skis with a perplexed expression.

"Not quite," Ashley said. "You make a pizza slice *shape* with your skis. See, right now the way you're standing, your skis run parallel to each other like french fries. Keep them like that and you'll go too fast. But if you make your skis look like this—" spreading her heels out, she pointed the tips of her skis together, making the snowplow shape every new skier had to learn if they ever stood a chance of stopping by any method other than falling "—you can control your speed. Try it."

Almost immediately, Tex and Jacob crossed their tips, lost their balance, and fell onto their butts. The noonday sun beat down, and after helping Tex and Jacob back up onto their skis, Ashley stripped off her coat and tied it around her waist. Pulling her shirt away from her chest, she glanced downhill at Matthew, still sitting in his chair, waving up at her with one hand while petting Murphy who'd emerged from the lodge to sit beside him with the other.

Shifting her attention away from the J. Crew photo shoot below her, she rolled her shoulders and addressed the men. "The first thing to remember when you start skiing is that you don't actually want to ski down the hill."

"We don't?" asked Clay, switching his skis from *pizza slice* to *french fries* and back again.

"The bottom of the run is your destination, but skiing is less about the destination and more about the journey. When you ski, at first anyway, you want to take your time. You want to be a snake." She made an S shape with her hand through the air. "You want to ski *across* the hill, then turn and ski back. Becoming a good skier is all about turning. It's all about control."

"Ma'am," Tex said, "we're addicts. We suck at control."

When the other men laughed, she laughed too. "That's okay. Learning control when you're on skis is a process for all of us. Nobody gets it right away. The important part is to keep trying."

They nodded solemnly. Then, one by one, they looked down the mountain, their brows furrowing deeply like how they'd do on this bunny hill would be a commentary on how they'd do for the rest of their lives.

"I think I misspoke," she said, wanting to lift some of the weight she felt settling over the men. "The most important part is to have fun. Skiing is really fun. I promise. Control is just the thing that lets you have fun without getting hurt."

"Jeez, Ashley," Kev said with a sweet, crooked smile that would have stolen her breath when she was in her twenties. "I'm getting that put on a bumper sticker."

"How'd it go out there?" Maude Alice asked as Ashley dragged her wrecked body into her office. "I watched through the window. Thought I might have to call the paramedics after a few of those tumbles."

Ashley fell into her chair while Murphy thumped to the ground, sprawling out in a patch of sunlight under a window. "Surprisingly well, actually. A handful of them are pretty good skiers," she paused, "and boarders."

"Will wonders never cease?" Maude Alice said with a healthy dose of sarcasm. "You wore out my cook. Poor Clayton hobbled into the kitchen to borrow an ice pack and reschedule his training. He looked like he'd been wrestling a bear."

Ashley grinned, remembering one of the big man's particularly impressive wipeouts. "He definitely took a few hits. But he did great. You might have some competition for him. He'd make a sweet liftie."

Maude Alice was aghast. "Like hell he would. I need help in the kitchen, and you have plenty of bodies out there to run the lifts."

Pulling off her boots, Ashley groaned as she wiggled her toes.

"I couldn't help but notice that Madigan didn't ski today."

Ashley eyed her mother warily. "He did not."

"And you let him get away with that? That's not like you."

Squeezing her eyes shut, she reached for the water bottle on her desk. "Mother, what Matthew does or doesn't do is not my concern."

Murphy grumbled.

"Even the dog knows that's a lie," Maude Alice said. "But whatever you say, dear. Chuck called."

Ashley coughed on her sip of water. "Again? What did he want this time?"

"You know what he wanted."

"How much?"

"Nowhere near enough." Maude Alice studied her nails, painted a pretty, dusty rose. Ashley used to paint her nails, before the divorce, before she started running Bluebird, before any polish just wound up chipped and worn after shoveling snow or working the chairlifts all day.

Burying her face in her arms, Ashley said, "Why won't Chuck leave us alone? How many times do I have to tell him Bluebird isn't for sale? It's harassment." Her voice became quiet, small. "He was the worst mistake I ever made."

"He won't leave you alone because he wants you back and can't have you. And he wasn't a mistake, without Chuck we wouldn't have Davis. Have you talked with her recently?"

"Yesterday. She texted." Ashley raised a brow. "You told her about our new hires?"

"I did."

"I really wish you hadn't. I don't want to worry her. She has enough on her plate already."

Maude Alice set her hands on her hips. "You need to give her more credit. She's a grown woman, and you're still babying her."

"It's not babying, Mother. It's called parenting."

With a dismissive sigh, Maude Alice said, "If you say so."

Ashley wanted to tell her mother that she wouldn't know good parenting if it slapped her in the face, but she didn't have it in her. Besides, arguing with Maude Alice never accomplished anything other than widening the gap between them. "I'm going to go take a nap before dinner."

"Good idea. You're an insufferable grump when you're tired."

Biting back a retort, Ashley snapped her fingers. "Come on, Murph. Us 'insufferable grumps' need to go sleep it off."

On the way to her bedroom, she caught a dark shape through the window. At the bottom of the bunny hill, his snowcap sitting slightly crooked on his head and his hands stuffed into his pockets, Matthew stared up the slope, kicking at the snow.

While she scratched Murphy's head, an idea popped into hers. There was no way around it, Matthew Madigan intimidated her. She didn't think he was purposefully trying to intimidate her, but with her mother's overbearance, her father's death, and Chuck's rampant infidelity, it was an easy thing to do these days. She didn't want to be intimidated, though. She wanted to be strong, confident, someone her mother could no longer crumple with a few choice words, someone Chuck couldn't push around so easily. Someone Davis could finally look up to.

If today had taught her anything, it was that there was one place she still had some belief in herself, on the snow. Maybe if she could get Matthew on skis, she could shake her nerves and gain enough confidence to at least be able to talk to him like a normal person. She wasn't sure if he'd go for it. He'd been pretty firm on his no skiing stance. But there was something in the way he looked up at the bunny hill as the sun sank toward the trees that made her think he might actually say yes.

CHAPTER SEVEN

MADIGAN

Kev straddling Clay's back and kneading his muscles was not something Madigan thought he'd see today. "What's going on in here?" he asked, stepping inside their cabin.

"I'm broken," Clay mumbled into his pillow. "I broke my back, and my neck, and my ass. Everything."

Madigan had to press his lips together not to laugh. "Kev making it all better?"

Leaning forward to dig his elbow into the muscles running along Clay's spine, Kev said, "Somebody is awfully smug over there considering the only thing he did all day was hold down his chair."

"That's not true," Madigan countered. "I also laughed. A lot. My sides still hurt."

Turning his head toward Madigan, Clay said, "Face it. You chickened out."

Madigan scoffed, brushing off the truth of that statement while he sat on their couch. He grinned when he spotted the romance novel splayed face down on Kev's nightstand.

Kev and Clay, still in the same position on Clay's bed, stared at him in an accusatory silence.

"Fine," he yielded. "You win. I chickened out. Happy now?"

Climbing off Clay's back, Kev said, "Yep." Then he walked into the kitchen to grab a Sprite from the fridge. "Group tonight?" He popped open the can. "I'm feeling antsy."

"You're always antsy," Clay groaned, rolling over onto his back.

Madigan shook his head. "Not tonight. You all need a rest. But I do have something special planned for tomorrow morning that will definitely help with the antsiness."

Sitting up on the edge of the bed, Clay tilted his head. "When you say 'morning,' you mean?"

"Dawn."

"Ugh, you're a sadist!" Kev moaned, pretending to weep into his hands.

Madigan shrugged. "That's nicer than what Sam called me."

"Did young Sam earn himself bathroom duty again?" Clay asked.

"That he did. But it kind of seemed like he thought it was worth it."

"*I'm* thinking it might be worth it," Kev grumbled. "Dawn? Seriously?"

"Relax. Eat some dinner. Get some sleep." Madigan stood, zipping his coat up. "I'll see you both bright and early."

On his way back out into the snow, he could feel Kev flipping him off behind his back. Probably Clay too.

After an early dinner of chicken noodle soup and a PB&J, Madigan threw two logs into the stove, then he knelt to light a fire. Just as he struck the first match, someone knocked on his door.

"Who is it?" he shouted, hoping he could get away with not having to stand right back up. Once he assumed a kneeling position these days, getting out of it took some doing.

"It's Ashley."

Arthritic knees forgotten, he popped right up and walked to the door. "Hey, Ashley. What can I do forrr...youuu?" The words slowed on their way out of his mouth when he noticed the pair of skis in her hand, the hopeful look in her eyes, and the mischievous twist of her lips. He squinted at her, and then at Murphy sitting next to her, excitedly wagging his tail. "Why do you have skis? And why are you both looking at me like that?" Madigan was no stranger to interventions. This felt like an intervention.

"I've been thinking about something. If you want to stay in these cabins, you really need to know how to ski."

He frowned. "Why?"

"Because of the fire hazard."

"Come again?"

Leaning the skis against his doorframe, she flipped her hair off her shoulder and said, "If there's a fire in your cabin, you'll need to be able to get out fast. And in the heart of winter, the snow out here can get so deep that the only way to get out fast is to ski out."

"I see." He crossed his arms over his chest. "Interesting. And why would there be a fire in the middle of winter?"

She pointed to his stove, currently flameless. "Because those can be very dangerous."

"The wood stove?"

"Yes," she stated firmly. "And if one of these cabins goes, they'll all go."

"Has this happened before? This catastrophic, wood stove-induced, multi-cabin structure fire?"

"Very nearly," she replied.

"That must have been terrifying."

"Oh, it was. And the one person who couldn't ski, tragically, died."

"How devastating." Leaning forward, he said in a quiet, conspiratorial voice, "Ashley, I think you might be lying to me."

"What? I'm not lying," she insisted weakly.

"I. Don't. Ski," he reminded her. "Do you want to come in? It's cold out here."

"I saw you staring up at the bunny hill," she said, not moving.

Trying not to fixate on the fact that she'd been watching him, he said, "There was a pretty bird flying around up there. Like a hawk or an osprey. Maybe an eagle."

She wasn't buying it. "Matthew, I would like to teach you how to ski."

His throat seized. "Um, no thank you?"

She smiled at him. It was a small smile, but it was enough to raise the temperature outside by at least twenty degrees. "I'm serious," she said. "I need your help with something."

"What could I possibly help you with that involves skiing?"

Gesturing toward her dog, she said, "Murphy is supposed to be a rescue dog, only he's terrible at it. I don't have the time to work with him, but with your men busy all day, I figured you might have some spare time on your hands."

This was one hell of a backfire to his attempts to cozy up to her dog. "I'm not a dog trainer, and I don't ski. I'm clearly the worst person for this job."

"It's really not that hard, skiing or training Murphy. Plus, he likes you. See?" She pointed at Murphy again, his tongue lolling out of the side of his mouth while he gazed lovingly up at him.

"That is not my fault."

She made her voice soft, devastatingly sympathetic. "This isn't a punishment, Matthew. You'll be living on a ski mountain all winter. I don't think I could handle it if you spent the entire season up here and never learned how to ski. You'd miss out on so much."

"Like what? Broken legs and head injuries? And it's all so," he shuddered, "high."

"It is a mountain. They tend to be high." Reaching down beside her, she picked up a pair of ski boots he could have sworn weren't there a second ago, like they'd sprouted magically out of the snow to taunt him. "Here's what I propose. Every afternoon, I'll give you ski lessons. I figured you wouldn't want to look silly in front of the guys so—"

"What makes you think I'll look silly?" he said, reluctantly taking the boots from her and holding them over his chest like a shield.

"Did you watch the guys today? It's inevitable. I mean, Clay alone." She laughed, actually laughed. He'd never heard her laugh before, and it was like if sunshine could make noise. "I think he left a permanent impression of his face on the bunny hill."

"Exactly. Clay is a mess tonight. Why would I want to do that to myself? I can't help the guys if I'm laid up in bed with a broken neck." He stood up straighter, believing this line of reasoning to be ironclad. "That's what I'm here for, to help these guys get back on track. Not to go barreling down a mountainside with toothpicks attached to my feet."

Her eyes, big and brown and suddenly filled with compassion, saw straight through him. "I think you might be scared."

"I'm absolutely scared," he admitted evenly. "What's your point?"

Angling her chin toward the word 'FEAR' tattooed across the fingers of his right hand, she said, "You just don't seem like the kind of man to let a little fear hold you back. But maybe I'm wrong. If you really don't want to learn to ski, I won't push you. In fact, I'll never bring it up again."

"Good." He felt completely off kilter, like the tides had turned on his teasing her with his tattoos and bare chest last night. Like he was on her playing field now, running around in circles trying to figure out the game. He had to admit, he kind of dug it. "Thank you."

"Okay, then. Good night, Matthew." She reached out to take the ski boots back.

He hugged them tighter to his chest. "Wait. Don't go yet." He really had zero interest in learning how to ski. She wasn't wrong, the entire notion of skiing terrified him, the loss of control, the heights, the speed... But he really *did* want to spend more time with her and, he realized grimly, this might be his best chance. "We could do these lessons after hours?"

She nodded, her expression brightening. "We can start on the bunny slope. Then, when you're ready, we can try the chairlifts."

"Chairlifts?" *Hell no.* "You mean those rickety metal benches attached by wire hangers to moving strings of tinsel?"

She blinked at him, several times. "Wow."

"I'm sorry, but anyone willing to get on one of those things has a death wish." While touring with the Makers, he'd spent entire nights wandering alone through some of the seediest neighborhoods across the globe, fending off knife-wielding drug dealers and baton-wielding cops, and he'd still rather do that again than ever ride on one of those catastrophes.

"We'll need to work up to chairlifts," she said. "Got it."

"If I agree to this, and I'm not saying I am," he clarified when the smile curving her lips pretty much made his decision for him, "but if I did, when would we start?"

Her eyes lit up, glowing like honey, like caramel, like eight million other delicious things. "How about right now?"

CHAPTER EIGHT

ASHLEY

Even though the sun had dipped behind the mountain, there was still plenty of light to ski by. Or stand around by, since that's about as far as they'd gotten.

"You'll have to put the skis on first. It's much harder to ski without them."

"Haha," Matthew fake-laughed, staring down at the skis, then over at the rope tow, then up the mountain, then back to the skis. "I think this was a bad idea."

In truly unfortunate timing, a massive boom shook the trees.

"What was that?" he shouted, assuming a defensive stance, his arms flying out wide, eyes enormous. "Are we under attack?"

She snorted. "No, we're not under attack. That's just Mace, my ski patrol manager, setting off avalanche bombs. You'll hear them sometimes, usually followed by cheering because bombs going off means we have good snow. Right now we're only running tests."

"You cheer for bombs?" He stared anxiously into the trees. "That's pretty punk rock for a sport where people wear one-piece neon snowsuits."

Pressing her smile briefly between her teeth, she said, "Let's get you into your skis. We'll order your neon snowsuit later. Here." Carefully, she stepped toward him, feeling a little like she was stepping dangerously close to a fire or a volcano or the sun. After demonstrating how to clip in using her own ski, she lined his ski up for him and said, "You can hold on to me for balance, if you want."

His hand, when it closed over her shoulder, felt exactly as big and as warm as she thought it would. Not that she'd been thinking about his hands. Not that his hands had secured a starring role in her dreams last night or her fantasies in the shower this morning. He was trying to be gentle, but she wanted to tell him it was okay, he could lean on her, put more of his weight on her, for as long as he wanted to. "Good job," she said instead when he clipped his boot into the first ski, wondering why her hormones had suddenly decided she was worth more than a second of their time. "Now try the next one."

Picking up his other boot, he only managed to move it an inch off the ground before his ski slid forward. "I can't do it. It's impossible."

"You watched all the guys do this earlier today. Did it seem impossible to them?"

"Yes."

Inching even closer to him, so close she could not only see but also *feel* the way their breaths tangled, clouding in the air around them, she said, "You're going to slide a little. The thing is, you kind of have to commit to getting that second ski on. No half-measures. Pick your other foot up, jam your toes in the bindings, and slam your heel down hard."

"Hard?" His lips quirked while Murphy panted beside him. "How hard?"

"Um.." she swallowed the flustered lump trying to rise in her throat, "fairly?"

With a quick thrust, he clicked the heel of his boot into place. "You're right." His brows waggled. "You do have to do it hard."

She could have sworn the snow around her feet hissed, melting and evaporating into steam.

"So what's next? Do I move them like... *Umph!*" There was a slip and a thump, and then Matthew was on his side in the snow.

"No." She smiled down at him. She liked him down there, floundering and helpless and nowhere near as intimidating as he was while on his feet. He looked almost cute. "You don't move them like that."

"Apparently not," he grunted, trying to sit up and going nowhere. "I think I'm stuck." Rolling onto his back, he watched in baffled silence as his left ski flopped to the side, his tips facing opposite directions. He peered up at Ashley then let his head fall back into the snow. "This can't be right."

Kneeling next to him, she said, "Definitely not right. This is a good lesson though."

"On what?" He propped himself up onto his elbows. "How to fall?"

"Not on how to fall. On how to get back up *after* you fall."

His grin was a solar flare. "Ashley, that's something I've been working on for decades."

Bumping into her chest like a kitten rubbing its head against her ribs, her heart purred. Doing her level best to ignore the sensation, she talked him through rolling onto his side and aligning his skis. Then she held out her hand.

He studied her outstretched hand, her arm, and finally her eyes. "When I've fallen up there," he pointed his chin up the hill, "you might not be around to help me up, right?"

"That's true," she answered.

"Then how do I get up by myself?"

It took a while, twilight's deep grey staining the sky, but eventually he dug his edges in, shifted his weight, and pushed himself back up onto his skis. When he looked at her, sweating and red-faced, he smiled.

Chuck would not have smiled, she realized, a little shaken. After this type of embarrassment, a moment like this where she was stronger and he was weaker, Chuck would have screamed at her, hurled his gloves angrily into the trees, and stormed back into the lodge to ignore her for the rest of the night.

"Ashley, are you all right?" Matthew asked her, his brows pulled tight, his smile slipping away.

"I'm fine," she said. "Just cold."

He wiped snow off his pants. "Me too. I think that was good for the first lesson, don't you?"

"You don't even want to try the rope tow?"

Grimacing at the rope like it was made of snakes, he said, "That's a solid no. Besides, I've got an early meeting with the guys tomorrow, and I'm already worried I won't be able to move when I wake up." When he tried to pull his boot out of one of the bindings, shaking his still-attached ski above the snow, he frowned up at her. "How do these things come off?"

Moving behind him, she placed her hands over his shoulders and said, "Like this," into his ear, stepping down on one of his heel levers. After he pulled his boot free, she walked around him to stand at his side. "Once you progress to skiing with poles, you can use the pole to push the lever down. For now, hold on to me while you try to stomp down on the other lever."

He did as asked, his hand heavier over her shoulder this time. "So I just...stomp on it?" With a clunk, his other boot popped free.

"That's it." Standing so close to him, his blue eyes locked onto hers, his warm, minty breath brushing over her cheeks, she could almost imagine what it would feel like to kiss a man again. A man who wasn't her ex-husband. A man with a salt and pepper beard and full, pink lips. A man who—although he wasn't technically an employee—was close enough to one that she should absolutely not be imagining kissing him. Backing away a step, she asked, "What do you and the men meet about, if you don't mind me asking? Is it like rehab, or a support group? Are you a counselor?"

After bending over to pick up his skis, he stood and said, "No, I'm not a counselor. I used to have a counselor come to the center once a week for the guys. But—" there was a heavy pause "—it didn't work out. The only thing I've got going for me is that I've been stuck where a lot of these guys are currently stuck, and I've found my way out. They usually have a lot to unload, a lot of feelings to sort out. I think my most important role is to be a good listener, support them, and try not to judge them. You'd be amazed how much they need that."

She wasn't amazed. What she was—imagining having someone in her life who wanted to listen to her, who'd let her talk her feelings through without judgment—was jealous. "I see," she said. "So tomorrow morning they'll be talking, and you'll be listening?"

His laughter was a low, resonant rumble. "No. Tomorrow morning we will not be talking. We'll be doing something much more," he smirked, "*strenuous*."

"Oh, strenuous, right. That sounds...really great." Why couldn't she speak? Her face was hot. Was she turning red? Did she look like a lobster? She needed to go splash water on her face, maybe take a cold shower. "Well, have fun with the, um," she gestured vaguely in the air, "strenuousness."

"I don't know if *fun* is the right word. But it'll be memorable."

A sudden, powerful desire to fall into his handsome, smirking face and bury her fingers in his beard took possession of her, like if she stayed there with him for one more second she would no longer be fully in control of her actions. Overwhelmed by the intensity of her...urges, she broke away, pivoting back toward the lodge while whistling for Murphy to follow.

"Hey! Wait!" he called after her, then he grunted. "How the hell do you walk in these boots? I feel like a robot."

When she turned back around, she found him stumbling toward her, looking exactly like a robot. Despite herself, she burst into laughter. "Pro tip?"

"Please," he said, lurching to the side.

"It's easiest to walk on your heels when you're in ski boots."

Giving it a try, he said, "Huh, you're right, like a little blond genius." Eating the distance between them—her heart thumping in time with each crunch of snow under his boots—he said, "Where should I store them? The boots and the skis?" He looked down at his boots. "And these might be hard to get off all by myself."

While it was true she'd been distracted ever since Matthew had hopped out of his truck and insinuated himself into her daily routine, there was one thing she knew without a shadow of a doubt. She should *not* follow him back to his cabin, sit at his feet, gaze up into his eyes, and help him take off his boots. *No way.* This mountain was her life, this winter her last chance to prove she could keep it running without her dad. Even if the air seemed to crackle and spark between them, even if she'd never felt anything quite like it, that's all it was, only sparks. Sparks could be ignored, stomped out.

She couldn't lose focus. Losing focus could mean losing the mountain. And then, aside from Davis, she'd be left with nothing but a smug ex-husband and her own crushing inadequacy. Chuck had made her feel inadequate for too long already. She wouldn't let anyone or anything make her feel that way again. "There's a ski rack on the wall beside the door of your cabin, and a place for your boots by the stove. Just undo the clasps and push them off. The boots, that is. It's a piece of cake." Retreating from Matthew's amused expression, she nearly tripped over a mound of snow. "You'll figure it out."

"Thank you for the lesson," he shouted after her, but she'd already turned back around, marching for the safety of the lodge, her boots stomping out any lingering sparks one by one.

"WHERE HAVE YOU BEEN?" Maude Alice asked, sitting alone at the table in the dining hall where they usually ate dinner together. "I had to eat by myself, and you know how I hate eating alone."

Ashley wasn't sure how much she wanted to share with Maude Alice about where she'd been and who she'd been with, but there was a 99% chance her mother had been watching them through the windows anyway. "I've started teaching Matthew how to ski."

"You have?" Maude Alice said, slowly setting down her fork.

"Could we please not make a big deal out of this?" Ashley asked even though it was futile.

"When do I ever make a big deal out of anything?"

"Are you being serious right now? Where should I start?"

"Oh, please." Maude Alice huffed dismissively. "You're just too sensitive."

Ashley closed her eyes, allowing them to stay that way for three solid seconds while she took a steadying breath. *You're too sensitive* was Maude Alice's favorite insult, her tried and true shot across the bow. Like being sensitive was some unforgivable offense. Like caring about things, allowing things to upset her, allowing things to make her feel anything but perfectly happy all the time was an incontrovertible character flaw. "I'm going to have Matthew train Murphy. He has the time, and Murphy likes him. Maybe he'll have better luck than we've had."

Maude Alice shot up from the table, a smile bursting across her face. "I think that's a wonderful idea!"

"I'm not really looking for your endorsement, Mother."

"What has gotten into you tonight?" she asked, wounded. Because that's how it always went. Maude Alice pushed her buttons, Ashley bristled in response, and Maude Alice acted hurt, making Ashley feel like an asshole.

"Nothing. Sorry. I just need a bath."

"What you *need* is to get laid."

"Mother!" Ashley cried, horrified.

"How long has it been? Since Chuck?"

"We are *not* talking about this." She tried to walk away, but Maude Alice moved to stand in front of her, squinting like a thin but impassable wall of scrutiny.

"It *has* been since Chuck, hasn't it? Eight years, Ashley? Eight!"

Whipping her head around, even though she knew they were alone, Ashley hissed, "Please keep your voice down."

"*I've* had sex more recently than you have."

"What? When? With who?"

"It's with *whom*, dear. And it was with—"

Holding up a hand, Ashley said, "Never mind. I don't want to know."

"Do you even have a vibrator?" Maude Alice asked. "Because I have a spare that I haven't used yet and—"

"For the love of all that's holy, I am begging you from the depths of my soul, please stop talking." Twisting to the side, she narrowly slipped past her mother's barricade.

"You don't want any dinner?" Maude Alice asked after her. "I made chicken. It's quite good."

"In a shocking turn of events, I seem to have lost my appetite." Climbing up the stairs, Ashley couldn't help but wonder if walking away from people was the only thing she was good at anymore.

CHAPTER NINE

MADIGAN

He thought they'd made progress yesterday, but Madigan still couldn't understand why Ashley was so nervous around him. Had he become intimidating in his old age? He used to be good with women. When he was in the band, he only had to wink at a woman in the crowd and she'd be waiting for him backstage after the show. But that was an entire geologic era ago. Trying to impress Ashley now felt like trying to swing a rusty gate—loud and obvious and anything but smooth.

He'd been single for so long he figured he'd probably stay that way until he was playing bingo in a nursing home. Women and drugs, sex and getting high, they'd always gone hand in hand for him. It was hard to separate the temptation for one from the temptation for the other, even after all these years. Being alone had made his life easier, simpler. Why was he so intent on trying to complicate things now? Why had he spent last night lying on his bed, imagining Ashley's brown eyes slipping down his chest? Or her smile that rarely showed itself, but when it did nearly took him out at the knees? Why was he fantasizing now about how soft her skin might feel under his rough fingertips, or the way the firelight in his cabin might dance across her naked body?

He shouldn't be feeling this way. He shouldn't be having these thoughts about her at all, let alone first thing in the morning, in only his boxer briefs, surrounded by ten other men also only in their underwear. In the freezing cold snow. But five slow breaths in downward dog had a tendency to empty his mind to its most basic preoccupation. And right now, Ashley was that preoccupation.

"Are we staying in down dog all morning?" Clay grunted, his knees bent while he struggled to hold the inverted V position.

"One more breath," Madigan instructed. "Let the blood running to your head strengthen your resolve." If only his head was where his blood was running. "Let yourself examine this discomfort, study it, observe it, *feel* it. Experience this discomfort without judging it, without feeling like you need to change anything about it." Was that what was doing? Was he judging his own emotions? Not letting himself feel them? Not giving himself a chance to grow?

"My feet are numb," Sam groused. "How am I supposed to *feel* anything when I'm freezing to death?"

"On an out breath, step forward with your right foot, then your left, then slowly roll back up, one vertebra at a time until you're standing."

"I can't, Boss! My back's broke!" cried Tex, stuck hanging over at his waist.

"Someone please help Tex stand up," Madigan said calmly, standing in mountain pose with his arms at his sides, shivering. The guys weren't wrong. He'd better wrap this up before everyone's parts got frostbitten.

"Holy shit."

Whirling around at the familiar voice behind him, Madigan threw his hands over his scantily clad junk and said, "Ashley?"

"There's no swearing allowed," Sam said smugly. "Madigan's gonna give you bathroom duty."

"Bathroom duty?" she repeated, her gaze darting from one man to the next before landing again on Madigan. "What's bathroom..." She closed her eyes for a long blink and muttered, "Never mind," while shaking her head. "What are you all doing out here?"

"Snowga," Kev answered, flexing his abs and flashing that too-bright smile that Madigan knew got the kid into nothing but trouble. "Leave it to Madigan to invent yoga in the snow."

"Snowga? In your underwear?" While the rest of the men either blushed or laughed or both, Ashley threw a hand over her eyes, her cheeks flaring red. "I'm sorry. I didn't mean to interrupt your...snowga."

"Did you need something?" Madigan asked. When she peeked through her fingers to look at him again, his pecs twitched, an entirely involuntary response to having a woman's eyes on his body. At least he was pretty sure it was involuntary. He worked out a lot—yoga, hiking, weights, and now chopping wood. At first he did it to make his physical pain match his emotional pain, and to take his mind off his cravings. Then it became one of the few things that made him feel good. Now it was pretty much habit. He didn't necessarily exercise to make himself look good, but he also didn't mind that benefit. Especially not with the way Ashley's eyes fixed briefly on his chest.

Clearing her throat, she said, "Maude Alice and I made breakfast for everyone. So, come on over whenever you're," she swallowed, "finished."

"Breakfast?" Brian rubbed the back of his neck. "That sounds a heck of a lot better than turning into a human popsicle."

Trying for the least intimidatingly smile he could muster, Madigan said, "We'll be right over. Thank you."

"Um, no problem. I'll just be leaving now." And then Ashley took her gaze and her red cheeks and spun on her heel, making a beeline for the trees.

Kev strolled up to stand beside Madigan, both men watching her go. "You make her nervous, Boss."

"I do not," Madigan insisted. "I don't make her anything."

"She's, like, running away from you."

"She's running away because she's cold. And she just walked in on eleven half-naked men doing snowga."

"The thing is, though, she was only staring at *one* of those men."

Making sure to catch one final view of her before the trees swallowed her up, Madigan said, "No she wasn't. Mind your own business."

"Dude, she looked at you like you were a slice of cake."

"No, not cake." Clay chuckled. "Madigan's more of a blueberry muffin."

"I am *not* a muffin," Madigan protested, running a hand in front of his inked, toned chest to prove his anti-muffinness. "You take that back."

"You're right," Brian said. "Muffins are too squishy. What about a Snickers bar?"

"Kettle corn?" Tex said.

"I am not a food item!" Madigan cried. "I am a human being."

"Debatable," Sam mumbled.

Rolling his eyes, Madigan said, "Had enough yet? Anyone else want to have their fun at my expense?"

The men stifled their laughter, but none of them said another word.

"Good, now go get dressed. And if I hear one single blueberry muffin joke during breakfast, we're packing up and moving back to town."

"Is that a threat or a promise?" Sam asked, then ducked to avoid at least five snowballs hurled at his head.

"Wow. You guys really like muffins, don't you?"

Madigan had already called upon all ten years of meditation training to maintain his cool. But Ashley pointing out the fact that every man at the table, aside from him, had piled at least two muffins onto their plates required the adoption of an entirely new mantra: *I will not throttle these guys right here at the breakfast table.*

"Especially blueberry," Kev said, hiding his grin by taking another bite.

Eyeing Tex as he inhaled a muffin whole without chewing, Maude Alice said, "I'm glad we made so many."

"Thank you for making us breakfast."

Madigan turned toward the quiet, thin voice. *Sam.* Sam said thank you for something. Sam said words to other people, nice words. He wanted to give the kid a hug.

"Of course, Sam," Maude Alice said.

"Do you have the recipe for these muffins?" Clay asked. "My grandchildren would love these."

Maude Alice tapped the table next to Clay's hand. "Meet me in the kitchen after breakfast, and I'll gladly pass it on to you."

"Tex." Ashley's voice tickled the hair along Madigan's arms. "My maintenance manager, Shannon, will be arriving later tonight. You'll be working closely with her, so I'd like to introduce you in the morning."

Tex tipped his hat. "You just tell me when, and I'll be there, Ms. Cooke."

"Do you know what I'd like?" Maude Alice leaned forward, resting her elbows on the table, steepling her fingers. "I'd like it if you would all take turns telling us a little about yourselves. Where you're from, what you did for a living, and how you wound up at Little Timber."

Madigan coughed on his coffee while the men—and he would have laughed at the irony if he could breathe—coughed on their muffins.

"Mother!" Ashley gasped.

"What?" Maude Alice said, innocent as snow. "I'm curious. Aren't you curious? I think it would be a nice way to get to know everyone better."

"People aren't curiosities," Ashley whispered harshly as the coughing at the table quieted down.

Although Madigan agreed with Ashley, he didn't think Maude Alice meant any harm.

"How about this?" he said, drawing wary looks from some of the men and vigorous head shakes from the rest. Sharing war stories, he knew, was not usually something addicts enjoyed, and certainly not something he would ever pressure the guys into doing if they didn't want to. But he thought he might be able to meet Maude Alice halfway. "Let's go around the table and introduce ourselves, say where we're from, and anything beyond that is completely optional. I'll go first."

The men relaxed, relieved breaths exhaled all at once around the table.

"That would be lovely. Thank you, Madigan," Maude Alice said graciously. Ashley still looked mortified on their behalf, but then Maude Alice asked, "Would that be all right with the rest of you? I didn't mean to make you feel uncomfortable."

Slowly, color returned to Ashley's cheeks. Exactly, Madigan thought, where it belonged.

The men nodded and then, suddenly, all eyes settled on him. Nerves sparked in his stomach, heat prickling up the back of his neck as anxiety pecked at him. But he wanted to set a good example for any of the guys who felt like coming forth. So he girded his loins, sucked in a breath, and said, "My name is Matthew Madigan. I grew up outside of Olympia, Washington. My parents and three brothers still live there, but I moved to Montana fifteen years ago because I wanted a fresh start. There were too many memories in Washington." He considered telling them he was in a famous band, but it felt like preening, and the last thing he wanted was for the men to feel like he was showing off. "I was a musician before I was sent to prison for using and selling drugs, mostly heroin. Now I run Little Timber." There, quick and easy. No big deal, even though his heart knocked like a fist against his ribs, determined to beat itself out of his chest.

Ashley and Maude Alice sat as still as mice, unblinking, their mouths partway open. Brian snorted at the end of the table, probably at their shocked expressions.

"Thank you," Ashley said softly. "Thank you for sharing that with us."

He nodded, the thought crossing his mind that maybe she'd been wondering about him. He doubted she'd ever met an ex-con before he walked into her office. Maybe she'd been imagining all sorts of things he might have gotten locked up for. For better or worse, now she knew.

"You bet," he replied airily, pretending he didn't feel a substantial weight rising off his shoulders. That was the thing about a past, no matter how many times he'd talked about it or processed his life and his choices, it was still his past. It came with him everywhere he went, hiding and revealing itself with every new person he encountered. He made a mental note to talk to the guys about this feeling later, to let them know it was common and okay to feel weird about it.

"My name is Clayton Briggs," said a deep voice to his right.

Madigan wanted to clap Clay on the back in gratitude for stepping up next, but he didn't, not wanting to embarrass him.

"I'm from Billings, and I have one son who still lives there with his wife and my three grandbabies. I'm an alcoholic." He ran a hand over his bald head. "This isn't my first stint living at Little Timber, but this is without a doubt the most interesting of my stays with Madigan. Strange the way things work out." He smiled at Ashley, and then at Maude Alice. "I'm real happy to be here at Bluebird."

"And we are so happy to have you, Clay," Maude Alice said with an unguarded, genuine smile Madigan hadn't seen on her before.

One by one the men introduced themselves, Jeff, Jacob, Tex, everyone offering up their names, former occupations, where they grew up, occasional details about their families. So far, everyone else had chosen to remain silent on their pasts. And then it was Sam's turn.

He sat stiff as a fencepost next to Ashley, his fork gripped tightly in his hand, his knuckles turning white around it. Madigan expected a quick introduction from the kid, maybe just his name. Maybe nothing at all, which would have been fine.

"I'm Sam Bailey," he said, his eyes glued to his plate. "I've been unemployed for a while, but I used to work at Lost Creek Bank in town."

Madigan sat back in his chair, bringing his coffee mug to his lips, expecting Sam to be finished.

"I'm a drug addict. Meth. I have a wife and a daughter," Sam's voice cracked, "and I miss them every single second of every single day."

The devil himself could have risen from the floor pitchfork-first and Madigan would have been less shocked. There was a small movement out of the corner of his eye, Ashley's hand reaching across the table toward Sam's, stalling out, returning to her cup of coffee. Her reaction, the distressed look on her face, her concern, struck Madigan like a kick to the ribs.

"Thank you, Sam," she said.

Keeping his head down, Sam nodded.

"Your turn, Ashley." Maude Alice's lips pursed expectantly. "It's only fair."

With her jaw clenched, Ashley met Madigan's stare for a moment, then she looked down into her coffee. "All right. My name is Ashley Cooke. I have one daughter. Her name is Davis, and she's studying biochem in Missoula. I don't have any siblings. I love to ski. I love this mountain." Her chin rose. "My father, Max Cooke, bought Bluebird when I was a kid. I've lived my entire life up here with him and Maude Alice, until he passed away a few—"

"And you all know me," Maude Alice cut in sharply, rising to her feet and placing her napkin onto her plate. "I think that's good for introductions. You should probably go out for your lessons now since there's a cold front coming through this afternoon."

Madigan had seen—and employed—plenty of deflection tactics in his day, and this one was textbook. Whatever Ashley was about to say about her father, Maude Alice wanted none of it. He watched Ashley withdraw, almost shrinking into her chair as an iron wall of tension slammed down between where she sat and where her mother stood.

"Sounds good," he said, trying to lighten the mood. "After the snowga, the guys have had plenty of cold already today."

"My toes are still numb," Brian weighed in, doing his part to restore the peace. Madigan nodded at him, a silent thanks.

With a smile as close to a flat line as it could get while still being a smile, Ashley pushed back from the table. "Well then, let's get started."

Clay winced. "More rope tow?"

She shook her head, and it seemed to shake off some of her tension. "Not today. Today you're graduating to the bunny lift."

CHAPTER TEN

ASHLEY

Against a snowy, vanilla orange sky, Matthew stared at the rope tow, squinty and suspicious like he still expected it to wrap itself around his neck and squeeze.

"It won't bite," Ashley told him, rubbing her neck which was stiffening up after her lesson with the rest of the men this morning. There had been fewer wipeouts today, but she'd still helped haul plenty of the guys out of the snow when they'd fallen trying to get off the chairlift.

"It will too," he argued. "Didn't you seen the guys' bruises?"

Ashley hadn't noticed any bruises on the other men this morning when she'd interrupted their snowga. In point of fact, she hadn't noticed any of the other men at all. She'd only noticed Matthew. And she'd been *re*-noticing him over and over in her mind all day. He had more tattoos than she'd realized, the dog on one pec, a four-leaf clover on the other, a full sleeve of waves flowing down his right arm. There was something intricate over his left hip she hadn't quite been able to make out, and it was significant, how badly she wanted to know what it was.

"Is everything okay between you and Maude Alice?"

The topic shift was so monumentally tectonic, she nearly stumbled. "What?"

"I couldn't help but notice there was some tension this morning."

Someone without eyes or ears would likely have noticed the tension between her and her mother at breakfast, but most people wouldn't have the nerve to just ask her about it right in the middle of the bunny hill. "It's personal. And you're stalling."

"Sorry," he said, flinching away from the rope after barely touching it with one of his gloved hands. "I just thought you might want to talk about it. Sometimes it's good to talk about things."

Not in my family, she thought. He might be right, but the last thing she felt like doing today was talking about Maude Alice, especially not with him. It wasn't that she thought he wouldn't be understanding; she suspected the opposite. But she liked spending this time away from the lodge, away from her mother, just away from all of it. That's probably why she liked spending time with him so much. He was like...a respite. "There's nothing to talk about. Just grab the rope. You're worse than my kids."

"I thought you only had one kid."

She laughed. "The kids I teach to ski. You can do this. Grab the rope." She normally wasn't this pushy during lessons, but the temperature was dropping rapidly, and she was cold. Also, the snowflakes landing delicately onto his dark eyelashes one at a time like a dusting of powdered sugar made her feel alarmingly woozy.

"But I want to know more about you," he said quietly, surrounding the rope with his gloves and letting it slide between them. "Why does this thing have to go so fast?"

"You're dallying. Bend your knees, lean back, and hang on."

"Did you just say 'dallying?' Will a horse-drawn carriage come by to pick us up later for tea, Milady?"

Ashley usually hated being teased. Chuck always made fun of her, delivering endless insults under the infuriatingly benign umbrella of 'it was only a joke.' But the way Matthew teased her, like he was teasing himself too, like they were in on the joke together, she didn't mind it. She might have even liked it. She might have even felt like teasing him back. "Spoken just like a dallier."

"I'll have you know that I am not, in fact, a dallier," he said. "I really do want to know more about you."

She stomped feeling back into her numb feet. "Once you've skied down this hill, we can talk all you want. But now, just close your fingers and—"

"Whoa!"

After hiking over to the heap of Matthew lying on the snow, she helped him untangle his skis and stand back up. "Good," she told him. "That was good. Now try again."

Eventually, like a timid, musclebound snail, he let the rope pull him up one inch, and then another. And then he froze.

"This is one of those things that's easier than it looks. It just takes some getting used to. I know it's intimidating, but all you have to do is trust the rope."

"Trust the rope," he repeated, squeezing until the rope jerked him up another few inches. When he let go again, she moved in behind him, bracing him with her hands so he didn't slide backwards on the steeper part of the slope.

"Trust the rope. Trust yourself. You've got this."

"Ashley," he said, his voice rumbling through her hands pressing into his back. "There's something about you, the way you talk to the guys, and to me. You keep making me feel a certain way."

If she pulled her hands away now, he'd likely lose his balance. But it suddenly felt too intimate standing this close to him, supporting his weight.

Turning his head just enough to give her a glimpse of his profile, his wry smile, he said, "I wasn't entirely sure what it was, until just now. It's strong. You make me feel strong, even when I'm scared of a little rope. You make the guys feel strong too. I think it's because you're so strong, so confident out here. It radiates from you. Has anyone ever told you that before?"

Nobody, in fact, had ever told her that, or anything even resembling that. Chuck thought she was a pushover, and she was when she was with him. Maude Alice thought she was uptight and emotional. Davis thought she was a workaholic. Her dad had thought she was perfect just the way she was. But nobody had *ever* told her she was strong.

When he squeezed the rope again, enough to pull away from her, she stepped out from behind him. "You're doing great," she said, rubbing at the warm, aching spot that had emerged in the middle of her chest. "I'll meet you at the top."

"What if I fall down again?" he called after her when she started hiking up the hill.

She could hear the rope whizzing through his gloves as she waved a hand over her shoulder. "You'll get back up. Because you're strong too."

He didn't fall again, and after another five minutes of starts and stops, of grunts and something that sounded like an impossibly deep squeal, Matthew summited the bunny hill.

"That sucked," he said. "Who invented that torture device? Jigsaw?"

She laughed, then shivered.

"Are you cold? You're cold, aren't you? Why don't we pack this up and start over again tomorrow? I'll just take my skis off and hike down."

She shook her head. "Even if it gives me hypothermia, you are skiing down this hill tonight."

His blue eyes twinkled in the dying light, his smile skewing crooked. "Told you. Strong."

Rubbing at her chest a second time, she showed him the pizza slice, the french fries, and once he had both down, she walked beside him as he carved across the bunny hill in the widest snowplow she'd ever seen anyone pull off.

"You can go a little faster," she told him.

"Don't rush me, woman," he said, making his snowplow even wider around a turn.

"Okay, but your quads are going to be worthless tomorrow if you keep this up. At some point you're going to have to let go."

A nervous laugh rushed out of him. "Letting go is one of those things that usually gets me into all kinds of trouble."

They'd stopped in the middle of the hill, staring at each other, the moon cresting the mountains and covering them in a muted blue light.

"What kind of trouble could you possibly get into between here and the bottom of the hill?"

His head tilted, his eyes crinkling at the corners. "You really don't want me to answer that."

Yes, actually, she kind of did want him to answer that. She'd never met anyone like him before. He was open, like a book waiting to be read. He didn't hide behind any pretense. He was unapologetically himself. He thought she was strong, and now he was just watching her, waiting for her to say something. It was all just...too much.

Wheeling around, her pulse whipping itself into a frenzy, she walked straight down the hill, trying not to trip, trying to push down the hope that his eyes were on her, roving over her body.

"Is this better?" he shouted to her down the hill.

When she turned back around, watching his blue silhouette glide over the snow, his snowplow narrower, turns more graceful, she realized he had very nice balance, probably from all that snowga.

Just when she shouted, "Looking good!" a mass of brown fur and panting breaths galloped past her. "Matthew!" she warned. "Incoming!"

He barely had a chance to brace himself before Murphy ran straight up to him and jumped, knocking him back with his huge front paws. Hiking back up the hill, Ashley found Matthew on his back, laughing while Murphy made a meal of his face.

"Murph! Get off!" she shouted, pulling Murphy back by his collar. "I don't know what's gotten into him."

Rolling to his side, Matthew pushed himself up, wiped snow off his butt, and said, "Trouble spots trouble, ain't that right, Murph?" Matthew winked. The dog barked. Ashley, with significant effort, did not sigh.

Letting Murphy go, she watched as the dog trailed behind Matthew, both making lovely turns all the way down the hill.

"I think you might be a natural skier," she told him when they all reached the bottom.

"Really?"

"Yeah, you have good balance, and excellent control over your body." She blanched. That came out wrong. She could feel it the second the words passed her lips, like they carried an electrical charge and now they were just out there, buzzing erratically between them.

"You have no idea," he replied, his smirk landing somewhere in the syrupy space between her belly and her spine.

"Oh," she managed, removing her hat, yanking off her mittens, unzipping her coat.

"Ashley?" He looked mildly concerned. "How much are you planning to take off?"

Wilting from embarrassment or desire or something she couldn't even name, she shoved her mittens into her pockets. "Lesson's over. You did great. See you tomorrow."

"Wait," he said. "I actually have something I wanted to talk to you about."

She groaned inwardly, feeling like she really couldn't handle any more stomach flutters or warm, aching chest spots. "What's up?"

After a deep and measured breath, he said, "Christmas will be here before we know it, and I know you said you were worried about visitors, but the guys wanted me to ask you again now that you know them better."

This was an impromptu ice bath over her blazing libido. Why had she taken off her hat? It was freezing out. "I see," she said, hating that she had to be such a hard ass. "But once we open, it gets very busy up here, very quickly. The guys will all be busy too. And even though they will get them, I don't take any days off during the season. I don't want to keep the men from seeing their families, but I won't have time to deal with people we don't know staying in the cabins."

"I know that," he said quickly. "And you wouldn't have to worry about a thing. I would set up and monitor all the visitations. I wasn't thinking of any overnight guests either, more like a gathering. Dinner maybe? In the dining hall?" He glanced to the path leading back to the cabins, his brow furrowing. "The holidays can be hard when they're alone."

He seemed so sincere, like making sure the men got to see their families was just as important to him as it was to them. "I think that's a really nice idea," she said, feeling herself soften. "I'll talk to Maude Alice about it tomorrow."

On an enormous, relieved exhale, he said, "Thank you."

"But I want you to do something for me." She felt a little guilty about leveraging this moment in her favor, but this would be good for him too. At least she thought it would.

When his eyes narrowed, she couldn't help but wonder how used he was to making compromises, giving and taking. It was probably unavoidable in his line of work. "Okay," he said warily.

"I want you to ride the bunny lift with me tomorrow."

With a low hum and a wry smile he said, "That's dirty, Ashley. Really dirty."

Maybe it was dirty, but this wasn't the first time she'd resorted to shady tactics to get a boy to ride the chairlift with her. Back when Chuck was the hottest boarder on the mountain, she'd employed all sorts of tricks to get him to notice her. That was before he'd convinced her to marry him even though she'd caught him cheating on her with Mary Williamson in the rental shop. Before he'd systematically worn her down with non-stop criticism and judgments until she'd nearly vanished. Before she'd finally kicked him out after trying everything she could to get him to stop cheating, because she hadn't wanted Davis to have divorced parents. Before she'd wasted so much of her life on a bad marriage.

Matthew's face, his smile, glowed as bright light flooded the bunny hill. While they both turned toward the parking lot, Ashley gritted her teeth at the familiar truck sloshing through the snow. The pickup came sideways to a stop, taking up two parking spaces, its engine idling while Chuck opened the door and jumped out.

Shielding her eyes from the obnoxiously bright headlights her ex hadn't bothered to turn off, Ashley grumbled.

"What have we here?" Chuck asked, walking onto the hill like he already owned the mountain. "Night skiing?"

His familiar, pretentious drawl spiked her blood pressure. Moving a step closer to Matthew as Murphy growled, low and menacing, Ashley muttered, "Think of the devil and the devil appears."

CHAPTER ELEVEN

MADIGAN

Madigan's hackles rose. He'd developed a finely tuned douchebag meter over the years, and it was pinging off the charts at this man suddenly up in their faces.

"Chuck," Ashley said, not quite a sneer but not too far off either. "What are you doing here?"

This Chuck person looked exactly like a Ken doll—swoopy blond hair, cartoonishly big blue eyes, a jaw that could crack walnuts. He wore a bright red Eddie Bauer puffy coat and khakis so crisply pleated they looked ironed.

Holding up a pie tin in his hands, the Chuck person said, "I was just in town and stopped by Glazed and Confused to get one of Mira's chocolate pies Maude Alice loves so much."

A muscle in Ashley's jaw jumped. "Of course you did." She took the pie from him. "So you'll be going then?"

"Who's this?" Not waiting for an answer, the douchebag extended his hand toward Madigan. "Chuck Thompson. And you are?"

"This is Matthew," Ashley answered.

"Madigan, actually. Everyone," he flicked his eyes to hers, "*else* calls me Madigan."

She bit her cheek, and he wondered not for the first time what was keeping her from saying his name, and how he could persuade her to change her mind just so he could hear it from her at least once.

"Madigan?" Chuck said, the insipid laughter seeping out of him snapping Madigan's attention back to the present moment. "What is that, Scottish or something?"

Scratching his beard, a sharp contrast to Chuck's clean shave, Madigan said, "Irish."

Chuck scoffed. "Like there's a difference, right? Irish, Scottish. It's all the same."

"How incredibly incorrect," Madigan replied flatly.

"Matthew is part of my crew this year. He's coming on in," Ashley paused, like she was trying to come up with something plausible, "management."

"What's he managing? The bunny hill?" Chuck's pompous guffaw made Madigan's hands ball into fists.

If they'd met like this thirty years ago, Chuck would already be unconscious. But that was Mad Madigan. Friendly, mature, civilized Madigan didn't just knock random guys out anymore when they looked at him wrong. Forcing his hands open again, he replied, "Yes, Chuck. I am managing the bunny hill."

After covering her smile at Madigan's sarcasm, Ashley said, "Thanks so much for bringing the pie for Mom. Drive safe."

Instead of leaving, Chuck took a step closer to her. Madigan tensed instinctively.

"Did Maude Alice tell you about my last offer? Did you give it any consideration? WinterMass is getting..." He glanced down at his boots for a split second, long enough for Madigan to glimpse a chink in his entitled armor. "They're very motivated to acquire Bluebird."

"For the last time, Chuck," her voice was low, resolute, and sexy as hell, "Bluebird is not for sale. And if you come up here one more time with some pathetic, insulting offer—"

Raising his hands, he said, "All right, all right," with a condescending lilt. "Calm down, Ash."

Her shoulders snapped tight, the anger radiating from her alerting Madigan to the fact that he should never call her *Ash*.

"Don't tell me to calm down," she pushed back.

"Come on. It's just business. It's nothing personal. But you never could tell the difference between the two, could you? If you could, you probably wouldn't be in the predicament you're in now."

Madigan could practically hear Ashley's internal screaming as she gritted out, "Goodbye, Chuck."

"Fine, I'm leaving." Chuck's nod toward Madigan was cursory. "It's been a pleasure, MacDonnell."

"It's Madigan."

"Whatever, bud," Chuck said, running his fingers through his angel-fine baby hair.

Even though this Chuck person might be a friend of Ashley's, although Madigan doubted it, nobody called him *bud* and got away with it. Especially not some blue-blooded, sanctimonious prick.

But then Ashley said, "You need to leave, Chuck. Now."

Madigan was a big fan of this version of Ashley, bold and badass and standing her ground.

It was hard to tell in the flat light, but Madigan thought Chuck's face had turned as red as a brick wall. "You should really reconsider my offer. It might be the last one you get." And with that thinly veiled threat, he turned around and marched back to his truck. There were two snowboards slotted into a rack on top of Chuck's jacked-up F350, and Madigan no longer had to wonder why Ashley didn't like boarders.

"Are you all right?" he asked her while they watched Chuck peel out of the parking lot.

After blowing out an exhausted breath, she said, "I'm fine."

"So, Chuck, he's...?" He let the question hang in the air while Chuck's taillights faded into the distance.

"Chuck was my husband for sixteen years," she said softly, like she was admitting some terrible secret. "We've been divorced for eight, only he keeps conveniently forgetting that fact."

Puzzle pieces clicked into place. Ashley's shock when he'd told her he thought she was strong, her need to run away from their conversations whenever she started to get uncomfortable. Madigan knew guys like Chuck Thompson, and they made miserable partners, more concerned about status than connection, always the first to tear someone else down just so they could feel superior. And he highly doubted the douchebag ever gave her a single decent orgasm. "That explains a lot," he said under his breath.

Spinning toward him in a whirl of indignation, she said, "What do you mean by that? What does it explain, exactly?"

"Nothing. I didn't mean anything," he said, backpedaling as quickly as he could. "He just seems like a jerk, that's all. And you're really going to make me ride the chairlift tomorrow?" He gave her his puppiest of puppy dog eyes, trying to change the subject before he had to explain his assumption that her ex-husband had been terrible in bed.

"I think you can handle it. Why? Don't you?"

"Me?" Madigan pointed at his chest. "Absolutely not."

He didn't know from experience—having never been married or in any type of long-term relationship—but he'd seen over and over how a visit from an ex could derail an entire day for his guys. He felt no small sense of accomplishment that she was smiling at him now, even if it was still so sad he would have jumped onto the chairlift with her in the dark just to make her happy again.

"You'll keep me safe tomorrow, right?" he asked, flirting a little but also seriously concerned.

The moonlight glinting off the foil covering Chuck's pie made her eyes sparkle. "I guess we'll just have to wait and see."

CHAPTER TWELVE

ASHLEY

SHANNON'S BOOTS stuck out from under one of the ancient machines they used to groom the cruising runs while she banged away at something metal, swearing like a sailor.

Ashley knocked twice on the groomer's door. "She giving you a hard time?"

The short, sturdy woman who'd worked for Bluebird for as long as Ashley could remember—first for her dad and now for her—slid out from under the machine, wiped a grease-stained hand over her forehead, and said, "She's a stubborn bitch."

Tex snorted on Ashley's right side while Kev laughed nervously on her left.

Frowning at Ashley's companions, Shannon scrunched up her nose under her cap. "You the men from Little Timber?" She squinted at Tex. "What's with the hat?"

Pulling off his ratty cowboy hat and holding it to his chest, Tex said, "Name's Tex. Nice to meet you, ma'am."

"Tex is the diesel mechanic," Ashley explained. "And this is Kevin. He'll be working with Mace."

Shannon got to her feet and brushed her hands off on her coveralls. "Really," she said, walking up to Tex while looking him up and down. "You don't look like much of a mechanic."

Ashley had to give her that. Tall and wiry with slightly buck teeth, even without the hat Tex looked more like a cowboy than a mechanic.

"Well, not professionally," he clarified. "I grew up on a farm. We had lots of tractors and couldn't afford to pay anyone to fix them when they broke down. What my daddy taught me about diesels he learned from my grandaddy. And what my granddaddy knew he learned from my great-grandaddy. I'm not fancy." He ducked his chin. "But I've never met an engine I couldn't fix."

Ashley didn't know how Shannon would respond to the notion of working with a recovering addict, family taught farm hand. Shannon was a highly organized, no bullshit kind of woman, and Ashley couldn't shake the feeling that she constantly compared her to her father and found her lacking. She highly doubted this situation would improve Shannon's estimation of her.

Her dark brows pulling together under her short, black hair, Shannon said, "I could use some help with the diesels, I guess." Ashley's shoulders dropped in relief. "Work starts at six a.m. every day. It's cold, hard, and we don't stop until the work's done. Can you handle that?"

Tex nodded. "Yes, ma'am. Sounds just like the farm."

Climbing back under the groomer, Shannon said, "Good. Then make yourself useful and get me that torque wrench on the counter."

"Yes, ma'am!" Flipping his hat back on, Tex nodded, tugging on the brim even though Shannon couldn't see him.

Ashley and Kev walked out of the garage just as Shannon said, "Thanks. But if you call me ma'am again, you're fired."

"I've always wanted to do something like this, helping people, doing something good for once in my life." Kev hadn't stopped talking since they'd left the garage. "I can't thank you enough for giving me this chance, Ashley. I won't let you down. I promise."

Since he was such a strong boarder, and by far the most personable of the group, Ashley decided to cross train Kev in liftie duties as well as helping Mace on the ski patrol. "Mace is one of the best, Kevin. Just listen to him, do what he says, and you'll do great, okay?"

"I will. I swear I will," Kev said, buzzing with excitement, reminding her of a golden retriever—friendly, willing, and like if he'd had a tail it would be wagging.

They found Mace in his office on the main level of the lodge, clacking away on his laptop, probably ordering supplies for the season. Ashley knocked on the door. "Hi, Mace. Good to see you back."

Bouncing up from his chair, Mace shook Ashley's hand and said, "I'm so stoked to be back. Summer camp was legit the worst!"

"Bee stings and Band-Aids?" she guessed.

Mace rolled his sea green eyes. "All day long."

"Hey, I'm Kevin," Kev said, holding out his hand, introducing himself before Ashley got the chance.

"Hey, Kevin." Mace shook Kev's hand excitedly. In his mid-twenties with curly copper hair and fair skin dotted by freckles, Mace was a naturally happy person with a smile that brightened up every room. Positioned as she was between Kev and Mace, Ashley felt a little like she was standing directly in a shaft of sunlight. "I'm so jazzed to have some help this winter," Mace said. "Ashley said you were a pretty good boarder, too."

"I don't know about that." Kev mussed his blond curls. "I used to board a lot as a kid, but I'm pretty rusty."

"No worries. I'll take you out so much you'll shake off that rust in no time flat."

"Thanks, man." Turning back to Ashley, Kev said, "This is just awesome!"

When Ashley opened her mouth to agree, Maude Alice interrupted her, shouting down from the top of the stairs, "Ashley, have you seen my dog?"

Blowing air loudly through her lips, Ashley said, "Well, gentlemen, I guess I have to go find Murphy. Are you all right here, Kev?"

Mace placed a hand on Kev's shoulder. "He'll be great."

Kev, not seeming entirely comfortable with Mace's overly friendly gesture, stepped out from under Mace's hand and said, "I saw Murph over at Madigan's cabin this morning. You might find him there."

"I should have guessed," Ashley sighed. "I think Murphy might be cheating on me."

"Well," Kev's smile was sly, "Madigan is kind of irresistible, don't you think?"

"Wh...what?" Ashely stammered "No, I don't think. I mean, sure he's charming but..." She retreated toward the stairs, seeking an immediate exit from this conversation. "He's not—"

"Ashley, wait. Look out!"

Mace's warning came a second too late as Ashley bumped into a stack of ski poles leaning against the wall, sending them crashing to the floor while she jumped out of the way. After Mace and Kev helped her pick up the poles, she grabbed her coat, hat, and slightly wounded pride, and went on the hunt for her dog.

"Here you go, Murphy." Matthew's deep voice wended through the trees. When she reached the clearing to his cabin, she found him kneeling in the snow, holding out a black T-shirt for Murphy to sniff.

"I'm freezing," came a muffled shout from a mound of snow on the other side of Matthew's yard. "This is abuse. I'm calling my parole officer."

"Hush," Matthew said. When he turned back to re-focus his attention on Murphy, he noticed Ashley standing at the edge of the clearing.

"What are you doing?" she whispered.

Murphy whined when he saw her, jumping to his feet, his tail wagging eagerly behind him.

"Shhh," Matthew whispered back, the afternoon sun bright on his smiling cheeks. "You'll distract him."

Wincing, she mouthed, "Sorry."

Taking Murphy's big head between his equally big hands, he said, "You can do this Murph. You just have to concentrate." He brought the shirt up to Murphy's nose again, letting the dog get a good long sniff. "Someone is hurting out there and we need to help them. Help me find them, okay?" His tone, warm as a fireplace, loosened Ashley's skin around her bones. Rising to his feet, he scratched Murphy under his chin. Then, flinging a pointed finger out toward the trees, he instructed, "Go! Go search!"

Ashley waited, anticipating the same reaction she'd gotten from her dog since the first day she'd started training him herself, and then when Maude Alice had tried her hand, and finally when the outrageously expensive private trainer had worked with him for a week and declared him untrainable: bored, motionless panting. Instead, amazingly, the dog leapt up, galloping toward the mound where some poor unfortunate soul had been buried in the snow.

"Unreal," she whispered. Maybe Matthew had some sort of natural dog-whispering affinity. Or maybe even animals found him irresistible.

"Good boy!" Matthew praised while Murphy buried his nose into the mound of snow, pulling back a blanket to reveal Sam's disgruntled face. "You found him! You found the skinny, grumpy young man who was hurting and lost!"

"That's...not...funny," Sam managed while being bombarded by Murphy's enthusiastic face licking. "Can I get up now?"

"Yeah, yeah," Matthew said, sinking down onto his knees in the snow, lavishing Murphy with pets and praise and treats from his pocket while Sam struggled to his feet.

Emerging from the trees, Ashley said, "I can't believe he did that. Murphy, maybe there's hope for you yet."

"There's always hope." Matthew scratched Murphy behind his ears, but his gaze cut toward Sam. "For all of us."

"Can I go now?" Sam's lips were tinged blue, his teeth chattering. "I can't feel my...anything."

"Sure, Sam. Thanks for your help today. You did great."

"Like I had a choice," Sam grumbled, but there was an unmistakable quirk to his lips when he patted Murphy's head on his way back to his cabin.

After planting a big, loud kiss on Murphy's snout, Matthew stood, beaming so brightly she had to fight the urge to shield her eyes. "Hi, Ashley."

A shiver sprinted down her neck. What was it about the way he said her name? She was in for a long winter if she couldn't hear him say her name without having a full body meltdown. "Hi."

"Did you need something?"

Did she need something? Probably. But what was it? Her mind went blank, her thoughts composed of nothing more than a dull, resounding, "Uhhh," until Murphy, *bless him*, barked at her. "Oh, Maude Alice sent me out to find Murph. She likes to nap with him sometimes in the afternoons."

"Far be it from me to stand between a woman and her napping partner," he said, pulling his hat off to run a hand through his hair, leaving it tousled and messy.

Her toes curled in her boots. "You did great with Murphy."

"Thank you," he said, still beaming.

"See you later for our lesson?"

Without warning, he unzipped his coat, revealing the black thermal base layer clinging to his pecs for dear life. "Wouldn't miss it. Even though I'm pretty sore from yesterday."

Her attention still glued to his chest, she pulled absently at her lower lip and said, "Maybe you just need to do more of that snowga."

His pecs gave a barely perceptible flex, but she perceived it, all right. She perceived the *shit* out of it.

"Maybe I should. Maybe," another flex, "you should join me."

Wrenching her gaze up from his chest, she met his eyes. They brimmed with amusement.

"Hi," he said, smirking. "Happy you could join me up here."

"Oh my god." Her entire body locked up, her nervous system refusing to function except for whatever part of it regulated her body temperature, which was skyrocketing. "I was just *staring* at you."

"You were."

"I'm sorry."

"I'm not."

When she yanked off her hat, his smirk graduated to a grin. She really needed to stop taking off her clothes around him. "I won't do it again."

Backing away a step, he said, "I didn't mean to make you feel bad about it. I..." He cleared his throat. "I like it when you look at me."

She pulled her hair up off her neck, desperate for cool air. "You shouldn't, though. I mean...*we* shouldn't."

"We shouldn't," he repeated slowly. "Shouldn't what? We shouldn't look at each other?"

"No," she said with significantly more resolve than she felt. The truth was, she liked it when he looked at her too. At her age, she didn't really get looked at anymore. There were friends who smiled at her and laughed at her jokes, employees who listened when she talked, like what she was saying was important. But there were no *looks*. No lingering stares or secret glances, no sensation ghosting over the back of her neck that someone might be imagining what she looked like without her clothes on. She hated to admit it, but with every passing year she felt more and more...invisible. She was the boss, the mother, the daughter, the ex-wife. But when was the last time she was the object of anyone's attention? When was the last time she felt desirable? Matthew's eyes, his *looks*, they made her feel desirable.

But there was more to life than being desired. There were things like determination and success, professionalism and respect, honoring her responsibilities. Important, serious, *adult* things. Still, she couldn't deny the pull she felt toward him, the incessant way her thoughts turned to him. What she needed, she realized, were some ground rules, some impenetrable, indestructible boundaries. Everything would be better, easier, less uncomfortably warm once she nailed those into place.

"We should definitely not look at each other."

"Okay." He crossed his arms over his chest, staring quizzically at her. "What about talking to each other? Can we still do that?"

"Of course we can talk to each other," she said, fanning her face with her hat. "Just not about snowga or getting into trouble or how strong you think I am or—"

"You don't want me to tell you that you're strong?"

She did. She really did. But she also didn't. She needed to make him understand, but how when she barely understood herself? "I need to focus on the mountain. *Only* on the mountain. Bluebird is struggling, and I can't get distracted."

"And you think I'd be a distraction?"

An enormous one, she thought while two genuinely concerned grooves sank between his brows. "My dad," she began, unexpected emotion stinging her eyes, "he loved this place. This mountain was everything to him. And then he died and..." She paused, pulling herself together. "I can't let him down. I can't fail. If Chuck ends up with Bluebird, I'll never forgive myself."

"Ashley," Matthew said, his forehead smoothing out while something like anger flickered in his eyes, over the muscles in his jaw, "it's okay, I understand. And you're right, we both need to focus. You've got the mountain, and I've got the guys."

Blowing out a breath as the vice around her chest eased its grip, she said, "Exactly."

When Murphy whined, leaning into Matthew's thigh, he scratched the dog's head. "It's gonna be hard, though," he said, his eyes still locked on hers. "Not looking at you. Not telling you all the ways you impress me. Not thinking about you in ways I probably shouldn't."

Her knees wobbled. She didn't dare tell him it would be a struggle for her too, to keep herself from melting like an ice cream cone whenever he did something nice for one of the guys or revealed some deep stroke of insight into her tense and tangled life. To ignore the way her skin buzzed when she thought he might want to touch her, maybe cup her cheek or slide his hand behind her neck. To stop wondering what the weight of his body would feel like pressing her into her mattress...

"We'll just have to try harder," she warbled, wishing she could scoop up some snow and pour it down her pants without looking weird. "It's just like you told Murph, there's always hope. For all of us."

When his chin tilted up toward the sky, the deep, bellowing laughter that burst from his chest stretched her out from one end to the other, uncoiling her like a rusty spring. "All right, Ashley Cooke." He extended his hand to her. "Here's to trying harder."

Shaking his hand firmly then letting it go, she said, "We're both mature adults. It can't be that hard to keep things professional, can it?" And to her credit, she almost believed it.

CHAPTER THIRTEEN

MADIGAN

"I CAN'T. I thought I could, but I can't do it." Fear, white and electric, crackled through him. "It's too high."

"This one doesn't go very high," Ashley said, staring up at the bunny hill chairlift beside him. "We keep it low to make the kids feel more comfortable."

"Can we bring the dog?" he asked, grasping at straws. "I'd feel safer with the dog."

She shook her head. "He hasn't been trained yet. He might jump off."

I *might jump off,* he thought miserably. "Do I really have to do this?"

"Of course you don't. But," she smiled, a bright and sunny thing under the overcast sky, "how else will you train Murphy to ride the lift if you can't ride one yourself?"

Sneaky, but she had a point. He really liked training the dog. He liked the heavy, concrete feeling of having a goal to work toward. He knew the guys appreciated this feeling too, that was why this gig was so important to him. Already the men were relaxing, coming out of their shells, talking more, joking around more. Even Sam.

As much as he hated to admit it—and he really, really hated it, like stomach flu levels of hate—Ashley had probably been right about cooling their jets. They both had too much riding on this season to start doing...whatever it was they might have been starting to do. He should know better anyway. No matter how powerfully he was drawn to her, the timing was off. Maybe, for him, the timing would always be off. "Okay, fine. Let's just get this over with."

They'd brought Brian along to run the lift. Madigan figured he was the safest of the men to witness this debacle, the most likely not to give him hell or tell the rest of the guys how much of a scaredy-cat he'd been.

"You've got this, Boss," Brian said. "Just sit back when the chair comes around and let it sweep you up. You'll be fine."

"That is perfect advice, Brian," Ashley said. "You're gonna be an excellent liftie." She flashed this proud, delighted smile that Madigan found immensely difficult not to get lost in. But he was trying harder now, no looking, no lingering, that was the deal.

"I can't believe I'm doing this," he said, shuffling forward to line up for the next chair, his heart clambering into his throat.

"Just get ready to reach back for the bar," she told him.

"It's going so fast." His chest heaved, his lungs burning, heart hammering. "Can we slow it down?"

"It's already as slow as it goes. You're going to be fine. Trust me." And then she squeezed his arm. "You can do this."

Every molecule, every atom, every electron that had ever existed converged at the spot where her fingers pressed into him. When the chairlift hit his legs, lifting him into the air, he barely even felt it. But then she let him go just as the chair lurched, swinging back and forth while yanking them higher and higher up the slope, a slope that seemed to extend, stretching out to infinity in front of him. He slammed his eyes shut, sucking all the air he could into his lungs.

"The swinging will even out soon," Ashley said. "Are you all right?"

How could she be so calm? "I'm fine," he said through gritted teeth, his eyes still shut tight. "This is great. Super fun."

Lowering the safety bar—which he grabbed onto with both hands —she said, "Open your eyes. It's a short ride, and a beautiful evening."

Slowly, cautiously, he cracked one lid, and then the other. The sun just barely skimmed the peaks of the Pintlers, a few stars twinkling beneath a crescent moon. But Ashley's eyes, more gorgeous than anything he'd ever find in the sky, glowed sunset gold while they stared into his.

"Beautiful," he agreed, wondering if her cheeks had been that red before they'd gotten on the lift. He didn't think so. Before he could study the shade of her flushed skin, deciding whether it was more of a rose or a cherry, she faced forward.

"I've noticed the men call you Boss," she said. "Do you make them call you that or...?"

"No. God no," he said, laughing.

"Why do they call you that then?"

Loosening his death grip on the safety bar, he said, "It started a few months after I'd opened Little Timber. I'd driven to the prison to pick up a new resident named Huge Harvey. The name was no joke, Harvey was enormous, bigger than Clay and as rough as anyone I'd ever met. After he hauled himself into Lydia, he turned to me and said, 'So, how's it gonna be, Boss?' In prison, it's what we call all the guards. *Boss*. But Little Timber isn't prison, so I reminded him that he was out, that he didn't have to call me Boss because I wasn't his boss. He squinted at me with these bloodshot grey eyes that looked like they'd seen everything—and I've seen a lot, but they'd seen more— and he said, 'I mess up with you, I go back to prison, right? So even though you think you ain't, you're still the boss, Boss.'"

"Damn," Ashley said, grimacing.

"He was right though," Madigan admitted. "It put me in my place, reminded me what my responsibilities were. And the nickname stuck. I've been Boss ever since. I still talk to Harvey every few months. He lives in Dillon now, runs an animal shelter."

"Does he still call you Boss?"

"Every time," Madigan said, then the chair lurched, flipping his stomach. "So what's the story with Chuck?" he blurted out, the need to distract himself from the vibrations rumbling through the seat and into his balls as they passed under one of the towers overriding the part of his brain that normally kept him from blurting out random questions about a person's ex.

She only frowned at him, deeply.

"That came out of nowhere. You don't have to answer that."

When she shrugged, he could almost hear the bricks stacking up into a wall around her. "There isn't much of a story, nothing groundbreaking. Chuck and I met in high school and got married a few years after graduation. We had Davis, our daughter, shortly after. The marriage wasn't good, but he loved Davis, so I stuck it out even though he was unfaithful. Until I couldn't anymore."

"I'm sorry," Madigan said, sensing the pain hiding between each of her words. She said they'd been married for sixteen years, and that was a long time to be stuck trying to make it work with a cheating, narcissistic prick.

She shrugged again. "Things happen. I've realized that life hardly ever works out the way you think it will. Sometimes better, sometimes worse, but it rarely gives you what you expect."

"That," he said, "is very true. And now Chuck's trying to buy the mountain from you?"

Turning to face him again—her cheeks definitely rose, not cherry—she said, "The worst part is, every year it gets harder to say no to him. We are in the worst financial position we've been in since my dad died. As much as I hate to say it, this winter is probably our last chance to keep from having to sell to Chuck and WinterMass."

"What's WinterMass?" Risking a glance down at the snow moving underneath his skis—which after a lifetime of terrible ideas might have been his worst—he shut his eyes to keep the world from spinning.

"It's a conglomerate of ski resorts owned by a small group of super rich people. It's the death of mom-and-pop ski hills like Bluebird." She blew out a breath, a cloud rising from her lips. "Selling out to Chuck and WinterMass would be the worst possible scenario I could ever imagine for Bluebird. It would be my biggest failure. My dad, he'd..." Her eyes misted, and he hoped it was just the bite in the air. If she started crying, he didn't know what he might do. Wipe her tears away with his thumbs? Kiss her forehead? Cuddle her in tightly to his side? He was pretty sure all three would easily violate their 'no looking' policy.

"Not what he would have wanted?" he guessed.

"No." Her voice was firm, her eyes, thankfully, not filling with tears.

Even though he dangled twenty feet in the air, this grounded him. If there was one thing he understood, it was the fear of failure, so much that he'd gotten the word tattooed across his fingers. "So this is a make-or-break season for you and Maude Alice?"

"We're here," she said instead of answering while she raised the safety bar. "Tips up."

"Tips up?" he said, his stomach plummeting to land somewhere in his left boot. On one hand, he realized as the unloading ramp loomed, he'd made it through an entire chairlift ride without throwing up or panic-jumping to his death. On the other, he still had to figure out how to get off. What would happen if he couldn't? Would he have to ride the lift all the way back down? All by himself?

"That's right," Ashley said. "Raise your tips."

Wrenching his skis up perpendicular to the ground, his tips pointing toward the sky, he asked, "Like this?"

"Um, not quite," Ashley said calmly, but he detected an air of *I'm-trying-my-hardest-not-to-laugh-at-you* in her tone.

While the chairs in front of them whipped around, sucked into the roundabout and spat back out to swing mercilessly back down the hill, Madigan reexamined every life choice he'd ever made that brought him to this moment.

"Level your skis out a little," she told him. "Let the chair push you at first and just ski forward. Don't worry about turning. Just ski straight ahead and snowplow to a stop. You've got this."

No, he did not have this. He didn't have anything close to this. "Okay," he ground out, his eyes shut tight.

"Matthew, open your eyes! You need to see to ski!"

Not reacting fast enough, he grunted as his skis slammed into the snow, pitching him forward. While he flailed, his arms windmilling helplessly, the chair crashed into his butt on its way around the turn, launching him forward, tangling his skis and twisting him around, sliding him directly into Ashley's path. Somehow her hips wound up clutched between his hands, his biceps straining to give her a soft landing right on top of him.

Her gasp, her parted lips only inches from his, her eyes gilded by the setting sun, he felt himself stir underneath her. It had been a very long time since he'd had a woman in this position, and his response to her body on his was pure muscle memory. He ached to brush back the curls falling forward to curtain her face, to taste her lips, to feel the softness of her mouth. Desires he hadn't allowed himself to feel in years shot like fire through his veins—longing, lust, need, hunger. Squeezing her hips, feeling her body mold to his, he whispered her name while he watched her eyes move across his face, down his nose, settling on his mouth.

"I think this is looking," she said on a shaky breath.

"No." He slid his hands down her hips, barely an inch, barely enough to feel the subtle rise of her ass. "This is *staring*. And I couldn't stop if I wanted—"

"You okay up there, Boss?"

Madigan groaned as she slid off him. *Thanks a lot, Brian.*

Fishing her walkie out of her pocket, she pushed the button and said, "Just a little tumble. We're good."

While the planet spun at two times its normal speed, he propped himself up on his elbows. This thing with Ashley, the sensation of having her on top of him, it was more than simple attraction. There was something there, something that pulled on his spine, urging him back to her. What she'd just told Brian was right, they *were* good. Or maybe they could have been good if things were different.

Pushing herself back up onto her skis, she held out a hand, her cheeks indecently flushed. "Little hairy for a minute there, but you made it."

Smiling ruefully, he said, "Story of my life," while he took her hand, wishing he could keep it there at least for a little while, nestled inside his.

CHAPTER FOURTEEN

ASHLEY

After pulling up the most recent report of season pass purchases, Ashley buried her face in her arms.

"Oh, it can't be that bad," Maude Alice said, picking at the duct tape holding Ashley's cracked office window together.

"Unfortunately, it can." They'd been barely limping by since Max died, but with this forecasted to be a stellar snow year, Ashley had held out hope for a last-minute bump in pass sales. It hadn't happened.

"You worry too much. Everything will work out, it always does."

Ashley exhaled through her nose, dragonlike. Just once, just one single time, she wanted to be the optimist. But Maude Alice always stole that spot from her, forcing her to be the ever-present, Negative Nancy voice of reason. "I don't think it's a good business strategy to rely on everything miraculously working out, Mother. We need a plan. We need something to bring in new skiers."

"I might have some ideas," Maude Alice said. Ashley didn't like her ambiguous tone, but before she could inquire as to what sort of *ideas* her mother had, Maude Alice asked, "Are you going skiing with Madigan again this afternoon? You've been spending quite a bit of time together. I'm not sure if you've noticed, Ashley, but Madigan is a very handsome man. You have been spending a great deal of time with a very handsome, very single man."

Even though she could still feel his strong hands wrapped around her hips, still see his eyes staring deeply into hers, she was absolutely *not* discussing any of it with her mother. "I haven't noticed because I am a professional. And I don't know if we're going skiing today. We all have a lot to do before opening tomorrow."

"Of course, dear," Maude Alice said, rising to her feet and walking toward the door. "A storm is coming through tonight and it might get windy up there. If you do by chance go out with very handsome, very single Madigan, please be careful."

"When am I ever not careful?" Annoyance prickled under Ashley's skin. Maude Alice was the reckless one. She was the one who ducked ropes, poached slopes, and had never worn a seatbelt a single day in her life

"You're right, daughter. You're always careful." Maude Alice's smile was wistful. "But hope springs eternal."

"Is EVERYTHING ALL RIGHT?" Matthew asked. "You're quiet this evening."

There was, Ashley knew, something about riding chairlifts that tended to open people up. When she used to ride the lifts with her dad, she'd talk to him about everything under the sun while the trees slipped past. And later, watching the same magic work on Davis as a teenager, conversations flowing between them during a time when getting more than three words out of her in an entire day had been a miracle. Even though sitting so close to him made her nerves spark like a lighter being flicked, over the last few days, riding with Matthew, she'd felt the same. It wasn't easy, opening up when she'd had a perpetual CLOSED sign hanging from her neck since her divorce. But with Matthew listening quietly beside her, hearing her in a way she'd forgotten she could be heard, paying attention like her thoughts and feelings were important to him, opening up didn't feel so daunting. With him, she didn't have to be on guard or looking out for traps or second guessing every word that wanted to come out of her mouth in case it might start a fight. With him, she could just be...herself.

"I'm fine," she said, pushing her snowcap back out of her eyes. "Just something Maude Alice said today really got to me." *You're always careful.* Like it was a condemnation, the worst thing a person could be. If she was overly cautious, it was only because she had to be. It was only because her mother wasn't.

"Hmm," he murmured, staring straight ahead, his hands clutching the safety bar on their second trip up the big lift to the beginner and intermediate runs. "Do you want to talk about it?"

Did she? The thought of discussing Maude Alice exhausted her, like she didn't have the stamina, like her ability to explore and express her feelings about her mother had been beaten into submission and was now so atrophied from disuse it was completely dysfunctional. "I don't know."

"Can I tell you something, then? Something I've noticed?"

When she turned to face him, her heart tripped, stumbling over its next few beats. He always looked good, unfairly handsome, but today... The man was gorgeous. He'd trimmed his beard, and his blue coat reflecting in his blue eyes made them glow like neon. Two days had passed since she'd been on top of him, and his eyes were still all she saw whenever she closed hers. "Is it a bad thing?"

He laughed. "No, it's not a bad thing."

"Okay," she agreed cautiously. Since their *incident*, since his warm, hard body had become her own personal landing pad, since his growled, "No, this is staring," had made her realize that words could be delicious, leaving their sweet taste in a person's mouth for days, they'd been behaving themselves. Back to business. Focused. In fact, they hadn't even talked about the incident once. Maybe, she wondered while her brows crowded together, it hadn't even happened at all. Not the way she remembered it happening, his eyes staring so hungrily into hers she might have let him devour her completely if Brian hadn't interrupted them.

"I spend a lot of time," he said, derailing her train of thought, "probably too much time, paying attention to the people around me. It was something one of my therapists suggested I try after I got clean, to help focus my mind on other people rather than only on myself and my own needs. It helped a lot then, and now it's just something I do without realizing it. People like Maude Alice, people who are outgoing and larger than life and a bit demanding, they can be difficult parents. Intentionally or unintentionally, they can make their children shrink."

All the air in her lungs froze, clinging to her ribs in tiny, sharp crystals. He'd just deconstructed her entire relationship with her mother in two sentences. Had he done this to her as well? Paid attention to her to the point of two-sentence, gut-wrenching analysis? She wasn't sure she wanted to know, so she changed the subject. "When did you start going to therapy?"

"I started in prison, then I stuck with it for years after I got out. Hardest work I've ever done, but it probably saved my life."

A gust of wind brushed over her cheeks while she struggled with how to best word her next question. "Did something happen that made you turn to drugs? If you don't want to talk about this, we can—"

A deep breath expanded his chest. "No, I don't mind. And not really, nothing I can pinpoint. I had a normal childhood, great parents, annoying younger brothers but that's nothing revolutionary. For some reason though, ever since I can remember, I always felt...artificial. Like while everyone else was a real, genuine person living a real, interesting life, I was only playing the part. I thought too much. I was awkward and anxious. But then I swiped a glass of champagne off a tray at one of my mom's work parties and instantly everything changed. I was thirteen years old, and I finally felt real. Booze transformed me into this funny, charming, engaging person, and everyone seemed to like me better when I was drunk." He shrugged. "That's all it took. And then, when I was sixteen, I met heroin and it was all over. She was the love of my young life, especially once I joined the band."

"That's right. You said you'd been a musician."

His lips tipped up. "You remembered."

Doing her best to ignore the way his smirk, his rumbling voice, made her belly float up toward her chest, she asked, "You were in a band?"

Sucking on a tooth, he answered, "I was."

"What kind of band? Like a rock band?"

"Uh, yep," he admitted sheepishly, pink rising into his cheeks. "Like a rock band."

"Local?"

He might have groaned, or it might have been the wind. "Seattle. In the nineties. We were...kind of a big deal for a hot minute."

"Really? Would I know of your band?"

His blush intensified, like someone had bitten a cherry in half and brushed it over his skin. "Possibly. I played lead guitar for the Makers."

Ashley's eyes flared. "Are you serious?"

"Deadly."

She was stunned, gawping like the man sitting next to her had suddenly shape-shifted into someone she'd never met before. "You were in the Makers? *The Makers*, the Makers? Like grunge band, super-famous, MTV megastars..." Her words dried up as images of younger Matthew flooded her mind. She remembered him. He'd been so skinny back then, always hunched over his guitar in their music videos, hiding behind his long hair, rarely showing his face.

"Is there any way we could not make a big deal out of this?" he asked, his head falling forward to rest against the safety bar, his face hidden again.

"Oh," the word came out clipped, like it ran headfirst into a wall, "of course." But her thoughts disagreed. This felt like a big deal, like an enormously gigantic deal. She'd never met a famous person before.

"I'd appreciate that. Those weren't my finest years."

An urge to run her hand up and down his back shook her, making her clench her ski poles more tightly in her hand. "I'm sorry I freaked out like that. It's just...you're a rock star. A real-life rock star. On my ski hill."

Sitting back up, he met her still-excited stare. "I get it, Ashley. I do. But the Makers was a disaster. The years I spent in the band were complete and total chaos. Infighting, parties, drugs, women, more drugs. I don't think I slept for the entire decade. And then, towards the end, it all just got really, really bad."

She remembered watching what had happened to the Makers on MTV News—the lead singer's overdose, the ugly break up, the deaths of so many people in that scene from drugs, people he probably knew, people he might have cared about, loved. "I didn't mean to bring this up today. I really am sorry."

"It's okay." His big shoulders rose and fell. "Had to come up sooner or later. It was such a wild time in Seattle back then. Way too much fame, way too quickly, for people who were never cut out to be famous. I lost a lot of friends when the fame changed them. I lost a lot more to drugs. I'd rolled the dice just as much as they had, maybe even more. I'm only still alive because I got lucky, and I had parents and siblings who refused to give up on me. Before I got arrested, before I got clean, I was not a person you would recognize. I was hard, angry, strung out. I had either stolen from or alienated all my friends. I was alone, homeless, selling drugs on the streets, completely lost. I mean, I know I wouldn't be here," he looked around, pointing at the surrounding mountains, "if I hadn't been there, if I hadn't gone through all of that. But it's always strange meeting fans who remember our music as some of the best times of their lives, when it was some of the worst for us."

Without taking a spare moment to second guess herself, she placed her hand over his. "That sounds really hard."

His thumb pressed gently over her pinky finger. "Understatement. But that's my story. Now you know pretty much everything about me."

She doubted that. "I don't know if this will make you feel any better, but I'm not actually a fan."

He laughed, and it was so charmingly self-deprecating she couldn't help but join him. "What?" she said. "I'm sorry but I never really liked grunge music."

"Ugh," he groaned, still laughing. "*Grunge*. What a stupid, reductive name for such a varied music scene."

"Yeah, but I'm younger than you. Grunge was too heavy for fifteen-year-old Ashley. How old are you, anyway?"

"Fifty-three," he said. "But I'm not falling for the trap of asking you—"

"Forty-six."

He grinned, then squinted at her, considering. "Let me guess, young Ashley was into...Madonna maybe? Or New Order? I know, the Lemonheads. You liked the Lemonheads."

"I *totally* did!" she said. "I haven't thought about them in forever. How did you know that?"

"Easy." He was nonchalant, so effortlessly smooth that he gave her no warning whatsoever to brace herself for what he would say next. "All the smart, hot girls loved Evan Dando. Drove me nuts."

A brisk flurry hit the chair, swinging them from side to side. Matthew gasped, sandwiching her hand between his and the bar, *barely* distracting her from the fact that he'd just called her hot.

"It's okay," she told him. "It's just the wind. Remember, these chairs are designed to swing."

"Would it kill them to swing a little less?" His head angled back, his eyes shut tight, his throat long and bared like a sliver of moonlight she could reach out and touch.

"Prince."

Peering down at her through slitted lids, he scowled. "That's not a very nice thing to say, Ashley. I'm terrified of heights."

She snorted. "I'm not calling *you* a prince. I'm telling you that I liked Prince, and TLC and Mary J. Blige. I liked pop and hip hop when grunge was big. Still do, I guess."

The wind whipped the chair again, snowflakes whirling like embers through the air around them.

He nodded haltingly. "I can see that. Young Ashley dancing in her room to "Ain't too Proud to Beg," maybe rocking a side pony."

"You're making fun of me," she said, feeling his grip over her hand tighten, his cheeks paling as the wind continued to pick up, battering their chair.

"I'm not." His teeth chattered, his jaw clenched. "I love Prince and TLC. And don't even get me started on Mary. Met her once at the VMAs."

"Shut up!"

"It's true."

Just before she could ask him to tell her every single detail about meeting one of her heroes, the chair jerked to a halt, bobbing in place.

"What's that?" He whipped his head around, left to right and back again like a chaotic lawn sprinkler. "What happened? Is the lift broken? Did it break?"

The chair swung and lurched, prisoner to the crosswind now that their forward momentum had stopped.

"It's not broken. This lift just stalls out every once in a while." Pulling her walkie out of her pocket, Ashley said, "Hey, Brian. What's going on down there?"

"Stalls out? Like the motor?" Matthew's voice rose, striking a panicked pitch. "How long? How long does it stall out for? How long will we be stuck like this?"

"*It's the diesel,*" Brian said over the walkie. "*I've called Shannon and Tex. Hang tight.*" But Ashley wasn't paying attention to Brian. She was paying attention to Matthew. "Hey," she said calmly, watching him drag air into his lungs as he ripped off his gloves. "You probably shouldn't take off your gloves. It's cold—"

"I have to get down." He hurled his gloves off the lift one at a time. "I can't stay here like this!"

"Stop!" she shouted when he tried to push the safety bar up. "You can't jump off a chairlift! You'll break your legs!" Fighting with him over the bar, she elbowed him as gently as she could in the ribs and slammed it back down. "Matthew, calm down."

"I can't." He clutched at his chest before unzipping his coat. "I can't breathe." When he struggled against the bar again, panicking, she realized she had to do something drastic or he really was going to jump off the lift, and she'd have to watch him fall.

Grabbing his face, she held it tightly between her mittens. "Matthew, look at me. You will not jump off this lift."

His gaze darted frantically across her face, over her shoulder, down to the snow, his pupils gigantic. "We're stuck. We're up too high. I have to get down!"

"No, you don't. Look at me. Breathe. You need to breathe." It wasn't working. It was like he couldn't even hear her as he shifted in his seat, his eyes closing tight, his chest heaving. She had to find a way in, something to distract him, something...big.

She'd been avoiding it, clinging to this flag she'd planted into the ground to mark some invisible boundary between them, keeping her safely on one side while he remained on the other. But she couldn't strand him now. He was struggling. He needed someone to be with him, to stand beside him. And in this moment, it was hard to remember why that was a place she'd convinced herself wasn't safe to stand.

"Madigan," she said for the very first time, sliding her hands down from his cheeks until they cupped his jaw. "Open your eyes, Madigan. It's okay. It's going to be okay."

His face was as white as the snow gathering on his coat, but when his eyes slid open, focusing slowly on hers, they were clear, his gaze steady. "Ashley, did you just call me—"

"I shouldn't have refused to say it. I don't even know why I did, except that I'm stubborn and scared most of the time. All the time. And you're so—"

"It's okay." Leaning forward until their foreheads touched, he shuddered against her. "I obviously have some fear issues too."

"Are you all right?"

His deep breath silenced the alarm bells blaring between her ears. "I think so. I get panic attacks sometimes. I hate heights. I hate feeling trapped."

Sensing him pulling away from her, she held his face still. "Don't look down, just stay with me. Stay here until we start moving again."

"My hands are cold."

She laughed, a cloud rising between them. "I'm sure they are. You threw your gloves off the lift."

Grasping her mittens—the brutal honesty in his eyes twining tightly around her chest—he pulled her hands down to hold them between his. "Thank you. Thank you for taking care of me."

Ashley had known for a while in a distant sort of way that her heart had become a vault, fortified with brick walls and barbed wire, barricading everything soft and defenseless safely inside it. She'd never meant to close herself off this way, but those were the parts of her Chuck preyed on the most, her self-confidence, her sense of humor, how much she cared about the people around her—which Chuck still insisted was the reason Bluebird wouldn't survive with her at the helm. But while Chuck's words had locked her up, she wondered if maybe someone else's could become a key. When Madigan saw her weakness, and instead of ridiculing her, thanked her for it, something inside her sprang free, bricks tumbling, barbed wire unwinding.

His bare hands rose to cup her jaw, and she felt herself pulled toward him, as inevitable as night pulling the sun behind the mountains. For once, her mind was still, her thoughts quiet. There was only the snow falling, the light fading, and the man sitting beside her. Closing her eyes, tilting her head, she leaned in until the hairs of his beard just barely tickled her parted lips. And then the chair lurched.

"We've got you." Brian's crackling voice over the walkie jerked them apart. *"Hope you didn't get too frazzled up there."*

Frazzled? she thought, her heart thundering. *That was a* hell *of a lot more than frazzled.*

"I'm...sorry about that." Madigan's voice was barely audible over the lift's droning whir. His hands grasped the safety bar again, his eyes fixed on the mountain in front of them.

"It's okay," she said, even though it wasn't okay because she had no idea what, specifically, he was apologizing for. For panicking? For touching her? For looking as warm and inviting as a fire after a blizzard while she'd very obviously almost kissed him? Refusing to ask, she clutched her poles over her chest. She continued refusing to ask during the silent and uneventful remainder of the chairlift ride. She refused to ask while they skied down the hill. She even refused to ask when they said an awkward goodnight and parted ways.

In fact, standing motionless under a scalding spray in her shower, she decided she would spend the rest of her life refusing to ask. They'd gotten carried away, caught up in the moment, but now the moment was over, nothing had really happened at all, and they never, ever needed to talk about it again.

CHAPTER FIFTEEN

MADIGAN

"She finally called you Madigan?" Kev asked, sitting on the edge of his bed, his knee bouncing. "Really?"

"She did." Madigan didn't like to almost-kiss and tell, but he needed to talk. He needed his head put back on straight because ever since the chairlift ride everything from his neck up felt like it had slid sideways.

Standing in the bathroom doorway with a towel wrapped around his waist and steam rising from his recently showered skin, Clay said, "Go on."

"We sort of..." Madigan ruffled his hair. "I don't know. I was a mess, but there was a moment between us. We leaned in, things got very quiet, and we may have," he paused, wincing, "tilted?"

"Tilted?" Kev repeated.

"Tilted," Madigan confirmed.

"Wait," Kev said. "Both of you? Or just you?"

Madigan scoffed. He might have been out of the game for a minute, but he knew a pre-kiss tilt when he saw one. "There was definite tiltage, from both parties."

"Okay, but what angle of tilt are we talking here?" Kev asked, his brow furrowed. "Shallow, like a sample-peck? Or like a full-on, I-want-your-tongue-in-my-mouth," he jabbed his thumb over his shoulder to the book on his nightstand, "romance-book-cover tilt?"

"What in god's name is a sample-peck?" Madigan shook his head. "This was a mistake. Coming here was a mistake."

Walking to the couch where Madigan sat, Clay placed a hand on his shoulder and squeezed. "You had to come here. It's drug test day. Where's my cup?"

Madigan pointed toward the dresser where he'd placed two test cups.

"So what happened after?" Kev asked. "After the tiltage?"

"Brian fixed the lift, we started moving again, Ashley kind of," Madigan's shoulders inched toward his ears, "*jerked* away from me, and then we went skiing. All the way down the mountain. In complete and utter silence."

"Woof."

"Not helpful, Kev." As if he didn't already know how bad it sounded, or how bad it had felt.

After pulling a grey T-shirt over his head, Clay took his test cup from the dresser. "What do you mean by 'silence?'" he asked. "You didn't say anything to her after almost kissing her?"

Madigan racked his frazzled brain, trying to remember exactly what had happened through the fog of Ashley's eyes and lips and breath. "I think I said...something to her."

"What?" Kev eyed him warily. "What did you say?"

Clearing his throat, Madigan admitted in a tight, steadily rising tone, "I think I said, 'I'm sorry about that.'"

"You apologized?" Clay asked, baffled. "A woman almost kissed you, and you said, 'sorry about that?'"

Kev only blinked, his mouth gaping.

Madigan buried his head in his hands. "How bad is it? Don't lie to me. How badly did I mess up?"

After a heavy silence, Kev said, "I mean, I'm not surprised she didn't want to talk to you after that."

"You didn't have a conversation about it at all?" Clay asked, his forgotten test cup clutched awkwardly in his hand. "You just...*apologized*?"

"I get it, okay." Madigan scrubbed his hands over his face before letting them drop to his sides. "It's not entirely my fault, though. I'd just had a massive panic attack, and then there she was right in front of me, helping me, calling me Madigan under the perfect moonlight. And then we tilted, and my brain just short-circuited."

"You had a panic attack?" Kev asked, his expression sobering. "Are you okay?"

Reaching out to clap a hand over Kev's knee, Madigan said, "I'm good. Thanks, Kev."

"I'm curious, though," Clay said thoughtfully. "*Why* did you apologize to Ashley? Why was that your response?"

Madigan shrugged. "Because we're not supposed to be doing things like tilting or sample-pecking or any of it. She has made it abundantly clear she isn't interested in anything other than a professional relationship with me. It's irresponsible, anyway. She's too busy. I'm too busy. We're both too busy."

"Is this, like, something that happens when people get older?" Kev asked, incensed. "You climb into a little box, close the lid, and convince yourself you're too busy to ever have any fun again?"

Both Clay and Madigan scowled at the kid. "Zip it, pup," Madigan grumbled.

"What?" Kev said. "It's true, isn't it?"

"You don't think there's any chance she changed her mind about whether or not she's interested in a relationship?" Clay asked. "People are known to do that from time to time."

"It doesn't matter if she did," Madigan lied through his teeth. "It's a bad idea to get involved right now. We're both—"

"Busy?" Kev suggested, a brow raised in accusation.

"No. What I was *going* to say is that we're both juggling a lot right now."

"So...busy."

Glaring at Kev, Madigan said, "We have responsibilities, and we need to focus on those responsibilities. Responsibilities that include," he nodded at Kev, "you."

"Madigan," Clay's tone reminded Madigan of an exhausted parent, "how long have we known each other?"

"Seven years, I think."

"That's about right. And In all the years I've known you, you have never, not once, kissed a woman. Not even a sample-peck. You live like a monk."

"That's not true." He'd kissed several women, even slept with one. And when he'd inevitably screwed that up, the guys had lost their counselor.

"I thought you might just not be into relationships," Clay said, staring him down. "But I think it's something else, and I think you know exactly what I'm talking about."

"Hello, Sigmund. Funny, I don't remember signing up for psychoanalysis today."

"Someone's deflecting," Kev singsonged, drawing a circle in the air to encapsulate Madigan's face.

"We aren't judging you," Clay said, "but there's a reason you came over here tonight. You need to talk about this. If you didn't, you wouldn't have brought it up."

Madigan knew Clay was right, but his thoughts were so jumbled, his nerves so jangly he didn't even know where to start. "I just... I'm worried. It would complicate things, trying to get something going with Ashley. I don't want to blow this opportunity for you guys."

"Nope, that's not it," Clay said, finally taking his cup into the bathroom, leaving the door partially open behind him because that was the rule. "You may have your own reasons to live the monk life, but don't use us as an excuse. We don't exist for you to hide behind."

This sentiment resonated the same way a sledgehammer resonated after it busted through a wall. Madigan *was* hiding behind the men, behind Little Timber. He'd been hiding behind them for years, focusing all his time and energy on the home and none of it on himself. He looked down at his hand. FEAR. When would it stop driving him?

"Darn it," Clay grunted.

Peering in through the bathroom door, Kev asked, "Prostate again?"

"Enjoy your young prostates, men," Clay said, his voice strained. "You have no idea what's waiting for you."

Kev grabbed his test cup from the dresser before swapping places with Clay. "Well, Boss," he asked through the bathroom door, "what do you think about what Clay said?"

"Would you listen to that?" Clay angled his head toward the sound of Kev taking a leak. "That stream could crack pavement, lucky little turd."

Burying his knuckles into his beard and rubbing, Madigan admitted, "The truth is, I really like her. She's funny and patient. She's determined and focused." *She's so beautiful I never want to look at another woman again for as long as I live.*

"She totally has that uptight, strait-laced thing too," Kev said from the bathroom. "Like the sexy high school librarian."

"Don't talk about her like that," Madigan said, even though he agreed.

"You're gun-shy," Clay said, placing his test cup back onto the dresser. "We all are. We've all relapsed and had to dig ourselves back out. We're all afraid of letting people in because we might end up letting them down."

Memories of his own relapses, of the relapses of the men staying with him which happened so often, yet crushed him every single time, flashed through his mind.

"But someone wise once told us—it might have been you, in fact—that hiding from life is not recovery. The freedom is in embracing life fully, the good, the bad," Clay pointed at Kev, "and the ugly."

Putting his cup back on the dresser next to Clay's, Kev rolled his eyes.

"You've gotten pretty good at accepting the bad and the ugly,"

Clay said, "but sometimes I wonder if you're still afraid to embrace the good."

TRUDGING THROUGH THE SNOW, Madigan couldn't shake Clay's words. He *had* been hiding from certain parts of his life. Quitting drinking and doing drugs had been one thing. Since he didn't need to participate in either of those activities again, he'd been able to cut them out of his life without ever having to learn how to have a healthy relationship with them. Romance, love, intimacy? Those were completely different. After he'd spent years abusing intimacy, he'd cut it out of his life too with no long-term plan of how to work it back in.

Aside from a few failed attempts, he did live like a monk, and he was starting to see what was missing from that lifestyle. She had curly blond hair, eyes like honey dripping through a ray of sunlight, and a laugh that made him want to do nothing but make her happy for the rest of his life just so he could hear it. His life was simple these days, comfortable, safe. But was it good? Had Clay been right? Was he refusing to embrace what could be good for him because of fear? Because of ghosts? What would he tell the guys if they were in his position? What *had* he told the guys over and over again? *Growth is uncomfortable. Clinging to comfort leaves little room for growth. Chase after comfort, and you'll be running in place for the rest of your life.*

As soon as he rounded the corner to his cabin, he slowed, grinning up at the dog waiting for him on his doorstep. "Hey, buddy," he said, climbing his steps while Murphy's entire body wagged. The motion jostled something large and black strapped to his collar. "Whatcha got there?" Retrieving the object—a walkie talkie—from Murphy's collar, he unfolded the note nestled under its belt clip.

Hi, Madigan,

Throwing a hand out, he steadied himself against the cabin door, his name in her handwriting doing some alarming rearranging of his heart and his stomach.

I couldn't get Murph to leave your porch tonight. He's good at sensing when someone needs him. Use this to call me if you want me to pick him up.

~Ashley

The smile shooting across his face, the riot in his chest, *this* was what he'd been missing. *This* was what clinging to comfort had been denying him. "Screw the monk life," he said out loud. Turning the walkie on, he hit the talk button. "Ashley?"

After a moment of empty static, *"Madigan?"*

His heart strained to find its next beat. No matter how many times he'd wondered how good it would feel to hear her call him Madigan, his imagination had failed spectacularly to even come close. He knew he needed to talk to her. He knew he needed to be an adult, take a chance, *be uncomfortable*, and tell her how he felt about her. And he would, just as soon as they got through opening. She was going to be so busy, stressed out about ticket sales and weather and all sorts of other ski mountain stuff he knew nothing about. The last thing he wanted to do was add to her stress with his feelings. He just had to be patient and wait until the time was right. "Thanks for the walkie," he said. "Can I keep Murph? He's right, I do need him."

"Really? He takes up most of the bed. And he snores. And drools."

"Really," he replied, smiling at the walkie. "I'm tired of sleeping alone."

CHAPTER SIXTEEN

ASHLEY

Opening week's attendance had been less than inspiring, but the men had done so well and worked so hard Ashley could almost overlook the dismal numbers. Besides, the storms in the forecast were sure to help ticket sales, keeping locals at home skiing fresh powder at Bluebird rather than making the longer trek to Chuck's fancy Conquest Mountain where they made their own snow and had high-speed quad lifts and fancy hotels with spas and ski-in-and-out chalets...

"You're going to crack your teeth clenching your jaw that tightly."

"I am not clenching my jaw."

"Oh, please," Maude Alice said, joining Ashley at the windows facing the mountain. "I could hear your teeth screaming down the hall. Oh, look! There's Madigan and Murphy." She banged her fist against the glass.

Ashley dug her fingernails into her crossed arms. Even from all the way up in the lodge, she couldn't miss the deep divot sinking between Madigan's brows when he waved up at them. She'd barely seen him all week, too busy with opening, working sunup to sundown, longer hours than she needed to work, longer hours than she'd ever worked in her entire life. Anything to avoid the way her entire body *zinged* like someone tossed a toaster into her bath whenever she was near him. Talking to him on the walkie had been hard enough, but saying words to him in person felt impossible.

She'd almost kissed him. Sure she'd done it to save him from breaking both of his ankles or maybe worse, but that hadn't been the only reason. She'd *wanted* to kiss him. She had wanted to kiss Matthew Madigan since he'd gotten down on his knees in her office and cuddled with her dog. The worst part was, she still wanted to kiss him. She wanted to feel his lips on hers. She wanted to know whether his beard would feel scratchy or soft against her skin. She wanted to know how tiny she'd feel wrapped inside his great big arms. But they hadn't kissed, and then he'd apologized, and now she was floundering.

"It's the dog's fault," she said under her breath, staring down at Murphy who sat at Madigan's side, panting in sublime happiness.

"What's the dog's fault?" Maude Alice asked. "You're too hard on poor Murphy."

"Nothing. And no I'm not. You're the one who's always calling Murphy worthless, not me."

Brushing her off, Maude Alice said, "You have to admit it, the men are working out. You didn't trust me, did you? I don't know why I'm surprised. You never take my word on anything."

Normally this kind of conversation with her mother filled Ashley with poorly contained rage, but it was an unseasonably warm day, and Madigan was only wearing his snow bibs over a white thermal top. His muscles filled out his shirt, his pecs bulging over the bibs, his biceps swelling to strain the fabric of his long sleeves. She'd never been attracted to a man built like him before. Where Chuck was lean, Madigan was thick. Where Chuck was fair and svelte, Madigan was dark and burly. Watching him saunter to the Moonlight lift, clasping Kev's hand and pulling him into a hug, smiling that sunshine-lives-in-his-mouth smile, she wondered if maybe she had no idea what her type actually was. Maybe it wasn't as clean-cut as she'd always thought. Maybe it was beards and flannels and tattoos and a heart so big she could hear it beating through the window.

She needed to talk to him. She needed to grow up, get her shit together, stop letting her insecurities dominate her life, and tell Madigan how she felt. Even if it terrified her.

"Ashley? Are you there?" Maude Alice snapped her fingers in front of Ashley's face. "Hello?"

"What? Of course I'm here," she huffed. "Don't be ridiculous. I take your advice all the time."

Maude Alice scoffed.

Peering through the window again, Ashley stared up at the pristine blue sky that had no idea of the chaos coming for it. She felt a sort of kinship then, with the sky.

Maude Alice sighed. "The calm before the storm."

"Let's hope so, anyway," Ashley said. A storm was always a wild card when it came to skier and staff safety, but they really needed the snow.

"I went out earlier, and the snow is lovely today. Will you and Madigan catch last chair? I noticed you haven't skied together much this week."

"I don't know." Maybe she should catch last chair with him. She could talk to him on the lift. It was always easier on the lift.

"Are you two in a fight?" Maude Alice's brow twitched. "Lover's quarrel?"

"Jesus, Mother!" Ashley hissed, blood rushing hot into her cheeks.

"What? I see the way you look at each other. You can tell me, you know."

"No, I can't. Because there's nothing to tell, and even if there was, it would be none of your business."

"Why?" Maude Alice threw her hands into the air. "Why is your life none of my business?"

"Because it just isn't. It's my life, and who I do or don't ski with is my business, and—"

"Will you two ever stop arguing?"

Doing a literal double take, Ashley blinked, rubbing her eyes to focus her vision on the young woman standing in her doorway who couldn't possibly be, "Davis?"

"Hi, Mom."

"What are you doing here?" Ashley tried to say, but Maude Alice's bluster drowned her out.

"Davis! What a wonderful surprise!"

"Hi, Grandma!" Davis said, her arms stretched out wide so that Maude Alice could crowd between them. Because, somehow, Maude Alice always managed to steal the first hug.

"Why are you here?" Ashley asked. Davis was supposed to be in her lab working. She was supposed to be in Missoula, getting her degree, living her own life far away from the stress and worries of Bluebird Basin. "Did you come for the weekend? *Just* for the weekend?"

Once Maude Alice let her go, Davis leaned in to kiss Ashley on the cheek and muttered, "Subtle, Mom. Really subtle." And then, like a moth to a flame, Davis's gaze slid to the window where Kev and Madigan were still standing by the lift, laughing about something. "Whoa," Davis whispered, wide-eyed. "Who is that?"

"Which one, dear?" Maude Alice asked. "The blond or the beard?"

"Davis," Ashley interrupted, or tried to anyway but Davis's attention was glued to the window. "What are you doing here? Does Chuck know you're here?" The last thing she needed was Chuck getting pissed at her over a Davis visit he didn't know about.

"The blond, although the beard is gorgeous too," Davis said, ignoring Ashley completely. "Who are they?"

"Our new employees," Ashley said. "And they have names."

"I'll bet they do." Davis arched a brow, her bright blue eyes glossy in the sunlight.

Grabbing Davis by the shoulders, Ashley physically spun her

away from the window and demanded, "What. Are. You. Doing. Here?"

Davis sighed. "It's not a big deal, so don't freak out."

"What's not a big deal?" Ashley asked, freaking out.

"Calm down, Ashley," Maude Alice cut in. "Let her speak."

"Don't tell me how to raise my daughter," Ashley snapped.

"Ugh! Can we just, like, not do the family feud thing right now? It's nothing, honestly. Enrollment is down or something, and the lab had to make some cuts."

"What kind of cuts?" Ashley asked.

With her lips pressed into a thin, resigned line, Davis flicked a hand down her body. "Staffing cuts. *Me* cuts. As in me no longer being employed by the lab."

"Oh, honey," Ashley said, rubbing Davis's arms. "I'm so sorry."

Davis shrugged, her mouth pinching in the corner just like it had since the day she was born. "It's okay. I needed a break from Patrick anyway, and now I can help out over the holidays." She tilted her head toward the window. "And maybe meet blondie down there."

"His name is Kevin," Maude Alice said. "He's very nice."

"What's the beard's name? Is that, what was it, Martigan or something?"

"Madigan," Ashley said tightly. "Matthew Madigan."

Davis's head swiveled toward Ashley. "Madigan," she smirked, "the sexy pirate."

Images invaded Ashley's mind—Madigan in tight pants and tall black boots, his white shirt open and billowing in the ocean breeze, a sword slung low on his hip.

When Maude Alice banged on the window again—startling Ashley so thoroughly she pulled a muscle in her neck—Kev and Madigan looked back up at them, that furrow reclaiming its spot between Madigan's brows. His gaze shifting between Ashley and her daughter, he mouthed, "*Davis?*" while waving.

Ashley nodded, and because she couldn't help herself, she smiled at him.

"*Ahh*, I see how it is," Davis said, staring at Ashley, nodding meaningfully.

Ashley stopped smiling.

"Well, since I'll be here for at least the next few weeks, why don't you introduce me to Kevin?" Davis winked at Ashley. "And the sexy pirate too."

CHAPTER SEVENTEEN

MADIGAN

Sprawled out on his bed, staring up at a knot in one of the wooden beams spanning his ceiling, Madigan wondered how he'd botched this whole thing with Ashley up so badly. He'd given her all the space he could without moving to another state, but even while she'd introduced him to her daughter, she'd barely said a word to him. It was the apology, had to be. Clay was right. What kind of idiot reacted to almost getting kissed with an *oops, sorry*? An idiot who'd probably never get kissed again, that's who. If his bandmates could see him now, they'd laugh his pathetic ass all the way back to 1991.

While he sighed deeply, his phone, trapped underneath him in his back pocket, buzzed. Pulling his phone out, not at all surprised to see the name on the caller ID, he flipped the phone open and said, "Hey, old man."

"Hey there, Mattie. How's life?"

Just hearing his dad's deep voice improved his mood. "The service up here is spotty, so we might get disconnected," he said, hauling himself up to sit on the edge of the bed.

"Yeah, yeah," Conor said. "I had a feeling about you, so I had to call. What's going on?"

After all they'd been through—the drugs, the fighting, the stealing, and then the arrests, the apologies, the enduring, unconditional support Madigan never believed he deserved while he recovered—his dad now had some sort of psychic connection to his moods.

"It's nothing. I'm fine."

"You can't lie to me, Son. So stop trying. Is it the men? Are you too cold up there on that hill and need a hug?"

Nailed it. "The men are doing great. I think they're having fun here. The work is hard, and they're all so wiped when they get done they're too tired to get into any trouble."

"Nothing like a hard day's work. So what is it then? What's got you triggering my Dad senses?"

Madigan blew out a breath, running his hand through his hair. "There's...there might be...a woman."

Only silence responded.

He looked at his phone before putting it back to his ear. "Dad? Did I lose you?"

"No, I'm here. Just...a woman? A woman for you?"

"I don't know. Maybe? I'm into her, but I'm not sure she's into me."

"Impossible. Ridiculous. Tell me what you like about her?"

Madigan scoffed. "I'm fifty-three years old, Dad. I'm not going to tell you all about my crush." *About how I can't stop thinking about the way her lips tilt up for a split second every time she sees me. Or how she always smells like apple blossoms. Or—*

"Crush?" Conor said with a chuckle. "This is too good. Now I *have* to know about her. Come on, it's not like I'll tell anyone. Except for your mother. And maybe your brothers."

"Don't you dare."

"I'm kidding. Spill."

Flopping back down onto his bed, Madigan groaned, "I can't believe I'm doing this."

"Believe it. Let's start with her name."

"Ashley. Her name is Ashley."

"Ooh, good name."

"Dad, come on."

Conor laughed. "What? It's true. Keep going."

"Well, she's gorgeous."

"Obviously."

"She's completely out of my league."

"Doubtful."

"She's smart and competent, and she's so great with the guys. But she's... There's something..." The words tripped on their way out of his mouth.

"I'm listening," Conor said calmly. "No point in keeping it all inside. It'll come out eventually, one way or another."

Pushing through, because his dad was right, he said, "She's really busy." He rolled his eyes at himself. *Dammit, Kev.* "I mean she's got a lot of responsibilities. She's put together and dedicated and driven and—" chewing on his lip, he forced himself to admit the doubt and insecurity that had been haunting him for weeks "—and I don't think I'm good enough for her."

"There it is," Conor said with a sigh.

"Yeah," Madigan agreed, both relieved to finally have it out there, but also indescribably frustrated that he was here again, feeling ashamed and inadequate and unworthy of anything good in his life.

"Listen, I understand why you feel this way. I do. But someday you're going to have to let this go."

"I'm not sure I know how."

His father's inhale was lengthy, his exhale even longer. "I may not know much, but I do know that hiding from relationships isn't sustainable. Denying yourself love isn't sustainable. Living your life for everyone around you instead of for yourself isn't—"

"Sustainable," Madigan finished for him.

"And here's the kicker, if you keep insisting that you're not ready to have a healthy romantic relationship, you'll keep believing you're not good enough for one either."

"Ow," Madigan said, grunting from the impact of this massive parental gut punch of truth.

"So, when are you going to tell Ashley how you feel?

"I'm not sure. We're not really talking right now."

"Why? What did you do?"

"*I* didn't do anything," Madigan insisted. "But *we* almost had...a moment."

"A moment? What kind of moment?"

"A, um, near-kiss moment. That I apologized for, for some idiotic reason."

"That is...unfortunate," Conor said, and Madigan could hear him wincing. "Let me guess, ever since your post-near-kiss apology, you've been pretending the moment never happened? She's been avoiding you, and you've been letting her?"

Frowning, Madigan muttered, "I mean..."

"You need to tell her how you feel."

"But what if—"

"You need to tell her how you feel, even if she isn't ready to hear it. Even if she might not feel the same, which seems highly unlikely," he added under his breath. "Life is risk, Mattie. Embrace it."

"That's easy for you to say."

When his dad spoke again, his voice was heavy, weighed down by well-worn sadness. "It's *not* easy for me to say, believe it or not. I know risk. Your mother and I risked so much when we called the police on you. It was the most difficult decision we've ever made."

Madigan closed his eyes, reminded yet again that he'd been the cause of so much pain and heartache. "I'm sorry, Dad." He'd apologized to his parents a hundred times at least, but it was never enough. There was no enough.

"I know you're sorry. Your mother and I know in the deepest layers of our souls how sorry you are. I am hereby, right this second, releasing you from ever having to apologize to us again. The point I am trying—poorly—to make, is...that life...is..." The rest of his sentence broke up into random, staccato syllables.

"What's that, Dad? I can't hear you?"

"Take a risk, dammit!" his dad shouted, the connection improving. "You've earned it. And you won't mess anything up, trust me. You're far too careful for that."

He almost laughed. Somehow in the last two decades while trying to change his selfish, self-destructive, Mad Madigan ways, he'd over-corrected and become a hesitant, timid hermit. "Are you sure?"

"I am 100% positive. You are the best man I know, Mattie. I've never been prouder of anyone than I am of you and what you've accomplished. But if you tell your brothers I said that I will deny it to the grave."

Hot tears stung the backs of Madigan's eyes. "Thanks, Dad."

"Anytime."

"You're both the best men I know!" his mother shouted from what sounded like a different room. "What are you two talking about, anyway?"

"Gotta go, Mattie. Your mother's making lasagna."

"Oh, man. You're killing me." Laurie Madigan's lasagna was legendary.

"I'd tell you how amazing it smells, but even I'm not that big of an asshole. Now go and tell Ashley how you feel so I can get some sleep without wondering if you're having a mid-life crisis."

"Tell Mom I love her."

"Just your mom?"

Madigan wiped his eyes with the back of his hand. "I love you too, Dad."

"That's more like it."

After holding his phone briefly to his chest, he flipped it shut at the exact same time Brian threw his door open.

"Boss, you gotta come," Brian panted, his eyes wide.

"What is it?" Madigan started to ask, but the echo of men shouting at each other through the trees answered his question.

"They've been at it for fifteen minutes," Brian told him as they hurried to Tex and Sam's cabin. "Figured I ought to come get you once I heard glass shattering."

Madigan gritted his teeth. Everyone had been getting along so well, and now the guys had broken something. Something that belonged to Ashley.

"Thanks, Brian," he said, mounting the cabin steps. "I'll take it from here." After knocking on Sam and Tex's door once, he barged inside.

Sam stood stock-still in the kitchen, Tex tense and heaving across the room, a lamp shattered on the floor between them. Sam's face was red and wet. Tex's fists were clenched at his sides.

"What the hell is going on here?" Madigan demanded.

Whipping a finger out at Sam, Tex said, "He called me an inbred redneck. A stupid, worthless, inbred redneck! And then he threw a lamp at me. He's lost it, Boss!"

"Sam?" Madigan asked the kid trembling in the kitchen. "Is this true?"

Tears streamed down Sam's narrow face as he held something up in his hand. "He spilled his Coke on my picture. It's fucking ruined. It's all I had of them. It's all I had you, dumb fucking hick!"

"Fuck you, asshole!" Tex spat. "It was an accident. Maybe you should try moving on with your life instead of spending every second staring at a picture of a family who doesn't want you back anyway!"

As Sam burst from the kitchen, Madigan grabbed Tex's shirt and yanked, shoving the tall man down onto the couch while he thrust an arm out to hold Sam back, positioning himself directly between them.

"Calm down!" he roared over the men who were too busy shouting at each other to care about his attempt to play referee. "Sam, back off! BACK OFF! None of this is worth breaking your parole over!"

Sam retreated a step, but fire burned in his eyes. Madigan had been waiting for Sam to blow, and it was almost a relief watching it happen now, seeing some sort of emotion break through the kid's stony, apathetic surface. Keeping his eyes locked on Sam's, Madigan asked, "You calm, Tex? You cool?" over his shoulder.

"Getting there," Tex replied, his voice strained. "Need a minute."

"Good enough," Madigan said, pushing Sam back into the kitchen until the counter separated the men again. "Stay," he instructed with an outstretched hand, then he stepped back into the main room, kneeling by the wall so he could clean up the pieces of Ashley's broken lamp from the floor. "Come on, guys. Why'd you have to break her stuff?"

"Sorry, Boss," Tex said, coming to his senses.

When Madigan looked at Sam again, the kid was hunched over, his face buried in his hands, his shoulders shaking. "It was all I had."

Screw the lamp. Pushing himself up to his feet, Madigan walked into the kitchen, grabbed Sam by the shoulders, and pulled him in tight. Sam struggled at first, pushing ineffectively against Madigan's chest. Eventually he relented, his skinny arms dropping to his sides, that picture still clutched in his hand while he cried in Madigan's arms.

"I'm sorry about your picture, Sam," Tex said with a tremble in his voice. "I'm sorry about what I said. I shouldn't have said any of that."

"I'm sorry too," Sam said, stepping out of Madigan's arms and wiping his eyes. "Sorry I threw the lamp at you, Tex. I just...fuck." Fresh tears filled his eyes. "I miss them so much."

Standing between two grown men crying, Madigan felt his own eyes mist over. It never failed. "All right," he said, blinking hard. "Both of you, on the couch."

Sam joined Tex on the couch, and they stared up at Madigan, waiting anxiously for the fallout of their altercation. Giving them all a chance to pull themselves together, Madigan mulled over his options. There was always bathroom duty. Giving them shifts in the kitchen so Clay could sleep in for once was an enticing idea. Chopping firewood would put them in their places, with the added benefit of wringing them out physically. But in the end, Madigan settled on the punishment he knew would make them the most uncomfortable, and probably be the most helpful.

Sitting on the edge of Tex's bed, Madigan leaned forward, resting his elbows on his knees. "Remind me, Sam. What is rule number seven of the Little Timber code of conduct?"

Sam pulled a face. "How the fu—"

Tex cut him off, saving him from saying another swear word. "We don't hurt each other, physically or emotionally."

"Correct." Madigan nodded. "Followed by rule eight, which is?"

"We don't call each other names," Tex replied.

"That's right. And now I will be adding an eleventh rule: We don't break our host's stuff."

Sam groaned.

"You both have broken three rules tonight, four if you include the swearing. As your punishment, you both have to say four nice things about each other. Out loud. Right now."

"Come on, Boss," Tex protested. "Give us a break. Can't we just have bathroom duty or something?"

Grinning at this confirmation that he'd chosen the perfect penalty, Madigan said, "If you're going to act like kindergartners, you will be treated like kindergartners. Sam, you go first."

Sam opened his mouth, then closed it again, his eyes pleading with Madigan to take mercy on him.

"And you have to face each other," he said, not taking mercy on anyone while he took each man by a shoulder and angled them toward each other.

Sam's jaw was tight, but he accepted his fate. "Fine. I like your hat, Tex. It's...classic."

"That's good," Madigan said. "But let's see if you can dig a little deeper with the next one."

Looking up at the ceiling, Sam moaned. Tex and Madigan only waited. Realizing he wasn't getting out of it, Sam looked at Tex again. "You have a nice smile. It always feels genuine. You're good at cards. And you're a great listener. There. That's the best I can do."

"Nice job, Sam," Madigan said proudly. "That wasn't so hard now, was it?"

"Whatever," Sam grumbled, crossing his arms over his chest.

"Your turn, Tex." Madigan sat back, waiting for some similarly kind but ultimately superficial statements from Tex.

"Sam," Tex said, pushing his hat up a bit so he had a clearer view of the kid. "You have the biggest heart of anyone I've ever met. You love your family so much it makes me wish I had one of my own. You do things you think nobody notices, like spending extra time helping the freaked-out kids on the bunny hill and making sure all the cabins are stocked with toilet paper and towels, so Ashley doesn't have to do it herself. I notice these things. You're a really thoughtful and caring person."

Madigan hadn't noticed these things Sam had been doing at all. He'd had no idea. No matter how many years he'd been doing this, helping addicts, the ways the men grew once they were finally clean never ceased to amaze him.

"And I am so sorry I ruined your picture. I was careless. It was hurtful, and I didn't mean to hurt you."

Sam's shoulders dropped from their post beside his ears. "It's okay, man. I know you didn't mean it."

Standing from the bed, Madigan said, "Good job, guys. I'm proud of both of you. Now I'm going to leave so you two can hug it out, and I can get overly emotional in the privacy of my cabin. See you in the morning."

After stoking the fire in his stove until it roared, Madigan considered making dinner. But after riding the emotional roller coaster of coaching two grown men through their feelings, he needed fresh air more than he needed food. And he really wanted to hear Ashley's voice.

Scooping the walkie off his dresser, planning to hail her once he got back outside, he grasped his doorknob. When he pulled the door open, his feet glued themselves to the floor. Her cheeks rosy from the cold, her eyes wide with shock, Ashley stood with her hand frozen in a fist poised to knock.

"Madigan?" she said, a little breathless as her head tilted. "Are you okay? Have you been crying?"

Good lord. This was just what he needed, for the woman he was desperate to impress to realize he'd been crying. "No, I haven't been..." He was too embarrassed to even say the word. "I just got something in my eye, a bug or something."

"A bug? In December?"

"Weird, right? Are you here about the lamp? I'm so sorry about that. The guys, they just—"

"Lamp?" She frowned. "What lamp?"

"Tex and Sam had an argument, and one of your lamps was a casualty."

Her lips twitched, hinting at a smile so sweet he could almost taste it. "Is that why you were...why you got a bug in your eye? Over a lamp?"

He couldn't help but laugh. "No," he said, even though it wasn't entirely true. "Well, sort of, I guess. It's complicated. I'll buy you a new lamp tomorrow."

"You don't have to do that. I have plenty."

After a silence that grew heavier with every passing second, he asked, "Are you here looking for Murph?" As if on cue, Murphy lumbered up onto the porch to sit by her side. Gazing up at Madigan, panting loudly, the dog barked. "I guess not."

"He's looking for you, actually. He wouldn't stop whining, just waiting by my door like he was expecting..." She shook her head, soft, blond curls spilling over her shoulders. "He doesn't want me tonight. He wants," she cleared her throat, "you."

She was nervous, stammering, and considering the raw emotion still making his chest ache, painfully tempting. "I was just about to call you," he said, holding up the walkie talkie.

"You were?"

"Yeah." He might not know how she felt about him, but this thing between them, this pressure in his chest whenever he thought about her, he couldn't ignore it anymore. "I wanted to talk to you."

"Oh," was all she said. She wasn't making this easy on him, but that was okay. He never trusted anything that came easily.

Digging his bare toes into the wood floor, he said. "We haven't really talked since we almost—"

Her gaze dropped to her boots.

"And that's probably my fault," he added quickly. "I should have talked to you. I should have checked in to make sure we were all right. But now I'm worried." He took a hesitant step toward her. "Ashley, did I do something wrong?"

Backing away, her spine going stiff, she said, "You didn't do anything wrong. It's just... I'm just... I don't..." Her voice wavered, her chin quivering. Something was wrong.

"Is everything all right? You can talk to me if you want to. I'm a good listener."

"I'm fine," she said tightly, and he could feel her shutting down. "I'm sorry. I shouldn't have come here. Goodnight, Madigan."

"Wait," he called after her, but she didn't stop, racing down his stairs while Murphy whined on his porch like he wasn't sure what to do. Not entirely sure what to do himself, Madigan shouted, "Ashley, wait!" running after her into the snow without even putting on his boots.

CHAPTER EIGHTEEN

ASHLEY

On her way to Madigan's cabin, she'd felt brave, ready, intent on telling him she had feelings for him. But then his eyes were red and swollen, his voice deep and gravelly, and all her brave words evaporated like mist. Even though the trees hovered in front of her, waiting to swallow her up, she knew by the demanding footsteps crunching at her back that he wasn't going to let her hide this time.

"Ashley! Stop!"

Forcing her feet to stop moving, she stared into the trees. She was so afraid to turn around, to look at him while having to admit she was too much of a coward to tell him how she felt.

"Why do you keep running away from me?" His voice was right behind her, so close she thought she'd only have to lean back, and he'd be there.

Fisting her hands, she made herself turn around while keeping her eyes glued to her boots. "I'm not running. I'm not...anything." She noticed his feet. "Madigan, you're barefoot."

"Doesn't matter," he said, almost a growl. The hairs on her arms shot for the sky. He took a step toward her. She stepped back the same distance. "Look." He pointed at her continuing retreat as evidence. "Running."

"Fuck," she groaned.

"What did I do wrong? Whatever it is, I'm sorry. I'm sure we can work it out, but you have to talk to me."

"I can't," she confessed on a pained exhale. He hadn't done anything wrong. He was perfect. *She* was the galloping disaster. "You didn't—"

Reaching out for her, he slid his hand onto her cheek, his thumb brushing softly over her skin. "You are so beautiful. Do you have any idea how gorgeous you are?"

The earth shifted on its axis. She hadn't been told she was beautiful in so long, she'd resigned herself to living out the rest of her days never hearing it again. It was too much, his soft touch, his even softer words. She didn't know what to do with the emotions storming inside her because she wasn't like him. She couldn't just cry or reach out or take that last step that would finally bring them past this space where it felt like a mountain range separated them. "I can't."

His hand dropped from her face, leaving a patch of icy cold in its place. "What do you want?"

She didn't have an answer. Or maybe she had too many answers. "I don't know. I just... I have to go."

"Christ, Ashley." His tone bit at her. "And I thought I was hiding."

"I am *not* hiding," she insisted, even though she was, even though she'd dig herself a hole in the snow right that second if it would make her heart stop pounding.

Devouring the distance between them until he towered over her, the furnace-like heat pouring from his body, he said, "You *are* hiding. We almost kissed on the chairlift. That happened, Ashley. And I have been trying to talk to you about it. I would have tried harder, but you've been avoiding me, and I didn't want to upset you. Or maybe," he straightened, his brows sliding together, "maybe you regret it.

Maybe I've just got this all wrong. If that's true, I'll deal with it. But you need to tell me."

Even with him this close, in her space, warming her through her coat, she still couldn't stop trying to hide. It was like some invisible force pulled at her arms and legs, covering her mouth, wrapping around her chest and yanking her toward the trees. "I haven't been avoiding you. I've just been busy."

Inhaling sharply through his nose, he said, "Right. Okay. Enough." Then he turned on his heel and started off toward his cabin.

"It's true though!" she shouted at his back.

Wheeling around again, his hands out at his sides, he begged her, "Just tell me what's going on. Tell me what I did wrong, and I'll fix it. Tell me to leave you alone. Tell me to never talk to you again. Tell me you're not into me. I'll believe you, but you have to talk to me."

She bit her lip hard enough to hurt. She wanted to tell him. She wanted to tell him everything. She wanted to tell him that she couldn't stop thinking about him, that she'd never met anyone so thoughtful and caring and humble in her entire life. She wanted to tell him that he was beautiful too, more beautiful than the evening sun hitting the mountains and turning them every shade of pink. But she couldn't. The massive, looming, unforgiving wall she'd erected to protect herself after all of Chuck's lies and betrayals stood between them, and no matter how hard she tried to knock it down, it wouldn't budge. She'd built it too strong. "I want to. But for some reason I can't."

"You can," he said softly. Not giving a shit about her wall, he stepped so close to her his breath mingled with hers, brushing warm over her lips. "I know you can."

"I...don't want to run from you," she said haltingly, staring at his chest. "I don't. But I don't know how not to."

His fingers eased under her chin, tilting her face up until she met his eyes. "I'm not that scary, am I?"

"No, you're not scary at all. I'm just... I'm a mess."

"You're not a mess," he said with such compassion it made her eyes sting. "You're just being careful. But maybe we could be careful together. I want to be careful with you, as careful as you need me to be." Slowly, barely moving, he leaned toward her. Even though he gave her all the time in the world to run away again, this time she didn't. She couldn't.

When his lips touched hers, warm and soft, the coarse hairs of his beard brushing against her skin, she wanted nothing more than to sink into him. She wanted to slide her hands over his chest, feel his heart beating under her fingertips, find out if it drummed in time with hers. She wanted to lose herself, to wrap her legs around his waist and let him carry her to his bed and take her until she forgot her own name. But he didn't know her, not really. He thought she was smart and capable and intriguing. He didn't know that she was actually cold and closed off and broken down. He didn't know she was lonely and so sad sometimes it scared her. If he found out, if he really got to know her, he wouldn't want her. Just like Chuck hadn't wanted her.

Breaking the kiss, she covered her mouth with her hand, trying to hold the feeling of his lips on hers for as long as she could.

His breath was ragged, his chest heaving. "I see."

What did he see? How much of her shattered insides had he noticed?

"Look, Ashley. I'm a grown man. As much as I want you, it's obvious you don't want me back. I get it. I'm just sorry it took me so long to figure it out."

"Wait," she blinked, "what?" He thought she didn't want him? It was absurd. She felt like her desire for him, her *need* for him, was written all over her body in embarrassingly obvious bright, flashing neon. "That's not—"

"It's fine. I'm sorry I misread," he shook his head, "this entire situation." And then he turned away from her again, his bare feet crunching through the snow as he walked back to his cabin.

"Wait," she said, stumbling after him. "Don't go."

"I'm not going anywhere," he said, still walking away from her. "I'll be right here."

Was this how it had felt every time she'd walked away from him? Cold and miserable? "Wait," she said again, pleading while she followed him up his stairs, through his door, into his cabin, closing the door behind her. What had she done? He'd offered to help her crawl out of her shell a hundred times, and she'd shot them all down because of what? Fear? Because of Chuck? Was she really that damaged? "Wait, Madigan. I'm sorry. I'm not good at this. I got scared. Please, wait—"

He spun around, the frustrated sound tearing from his throat freezing her in place. "I *have* been waiting."

"I know," she breathed. "I know you have. But it's not you."

"What do you mean?" His voice was dark as night.

"I mean, it's not you." Her heart slammed into her ribs, her labored breath scorching her throat. "I've been terrible because I know you've been trying. I know I've made you wait."

"And I'll keep waiting for you." He stepped toward her, crowding her against his door. "If there's a chance at all, I'll keep waiting. But you must feel it." His eyes blazed into hers. "You have to know how hard it is for me, staying away from you. Every day, every minute it gets harder. Because I want..." He bit his lip. "Ashley, the things I want."

"Wh...what?" she stuttered as his gaze dropped to sear a meandering line from her stomach to her breasts, her neck, her throat. "What...kind of...things?" Was she still speaking words? English words? She couldn't tell.

Slowly, he placed his hands on the door, one on either side of her head. "I want so many things." The rumble of his voice spiked her heart rate into the stratosphere. "I want to know how soft your hair feels against my cheek." He leaned in close, angling his head, his nose pushing her hair away from her neck. "I want to brush my lips over your skin, right here." His warm breath over the place where her shoulder met her neck blurred her vision. "I want to kiss you, here."

The barest ghosting of his lips just behind her ear made her eyes roll up behind her lids. "I want to touch you. I want to taste you. But most of all, I really want to fuck you."

Her lungs seized, resulting in what was probably a terribly awkward gasp. She didn't care, because he wanted to fuck her. He wanted to *fuck* her. "You don't swear," she whispered, the clean cedar and spice scent of him invading her senses, forcing her to bury her nose into his curls and sniff, no better than her dog. "You never swear."

There was a small, breathy laugh against her neck, and then his entire body slumped, tension draining. His forehead rested briefly on her shoulder before he pulled away from her, removing his hands from the door. "I swear plenty," he said, sitting heavily on the edge of his bed, scrubbing his hands over his face. "I just never swear in front of the guys. When you live with a bunch of men, it's nothing but swear words day in and day out if you don't set some boundaries."

Boundaries. Was that why he'd left her standing there plastered to his door like a wet towel and hyperventilating? Because of boundaries? It was what she'd asked him for, wasn't it? It was how she'd been keeping him at arm's length. But she didn't want him at arm's length anymore. She wanted him at hand's length, breath's length. And she needed to tell him that. "Madigan..."

"I came on pretty strong there. I'm sorry."

"Sorry?" she repeated, peeling herself from his door.

He ran a hand through his hair. "I have some issues when it comes to intimacy."

"Issues?" Having apparently lost the ability to do anything other than repeat whatever he said, she took a wobbly step toward him and asked, "What kind of issues?"

Staring up at her, his blue eyes peering cautiously through a forest of long, dark lashes, he said, "I used to fuck a lot. Too much."

Her mouth fell open, the skin on the back of her neck shrinking rapidly. "Oh," she said, and then in a further attempt to impress him with her vast vocabulary, "that's...interesting."

"Being in a famous band had made it easy, but I was out of control. Sex went hand in hand with the drugs for me. I quit fucking around the same time I kicked everything else. I've been tested, though," he added, "multiple times. I'm negative for everything." Wiping a hand across his brow, he added, "Miraculously."

With another step, she edged closer to him. "You quit sex?"

He nodded. "More or less."

"When's the last time you—"

"Years." He scratched his beard, the coarse salt and pepper hairs rasping against his knuckles. "It's been years. I had a short-lived thing with the counselor I'd been using at Little Timber, but that didn't end so well. Nothing since then."

"For me too." The words came out funny, too high. She cleared her throat. "It's been years for me too, if you were wondering. If you'd thought about it." Somehow she'd gone from not being able to speak to not being able to shut up. "Just so you know my...sexual recentness." Nonsense. Nothing but nonsense coming out of her mouth.

Reaching out for her hand, he hooked his finger around her pinky. "Even then, even when I tried with that other woman, it hadn't felt right. I hadn't felt ready. But now, with you, it's so different. With you, I feel ready. And even though it terrifies me to say all of this out loud, I need to tell you how I feel. I need to tell you that I am really, really into you."

She stared down at him for a long, speechless moment. She'd been so caught up in her own fears and insecurities, she hadn't stopped to think about his. She hadn't stopped to think that maybe she wasn't the only one of them who felt nervous or apprehensive about intimacy and romance. But of course she wasn't. They weren't in their twenties anymore. They'd both lived entire lives. They'd both loved and lost and been hurt in their own ways. They'd both taken risks and made mistakes they were still paying for.

Watching him while he watched her, feelings she'd been pretending weren't real, or at least weren't okay for her to feel—comfort, trust, desire, affection—rose to the surface the way they often did when he was near. Only this time, she didn't shove them back down. She let them pour over her because she realized, in some soul-deep way, that when she was with him, she was no longer alone. She also realized, in this long moment, that she was still wearing her coat. With the fire blazing in his stove and his hand now closed around hers, heat prickled over her skin. She wanted to take her coat off, but with how close she was to him, how intently he watched her, taking off a single stitch of clothing in his cabin felt like an invitation. But maybe she wanted to invite him. Why couldn't she just invite him?

"Hey," he said softly, probably noticing the distressed look on her face. "If you're not ready for this, it's okay. This isn't an ultimatum. I just need to know if there's a chance."

When he tried to take his hand from hers, she panicked, grasping it and holding on tight like she'd get swept away if she let him go. "You were right when you said I was being careful, because that's what I do. I'm careful. I'm careful because I'm always worried that if I'm not, if I let down my guard for five seconds, I'll get tricked again. I'll be made a fool of again. I'll have my heart broken again. But I don't want to be careful anymore, not with you." Steeling her nerve, she admitted, "All those things you said, everything you want, I want those things too. I want," she closed her eyes, took a breath, then forced herself to look at him, "you. I want you." With those three words suspended in the air between them, she pulled at her coat collar, her head spinning, her vision blurring. "God, I am so fucking hot right now."

His brow jumped. "You can say that again."

Her laughter was a decibel shy of hysterical. "I mean my coat. The stove. It's really hot in here."

"Ah, I think I can help." Reaching up for her zipper, his expression achingly sincere, he said, "I haven't felt anything even close to the way I feel about you in so long. Excited, nervous," he pulled the zipper tab down, one tooth at a time, each inch lower making her knees tremble, "*hungry*."

Her trembling intensified.

"I shouldn't have apologized when we almost kissed. I should have been honest and told you that I'd wanted to kiss you. I should have told you that I've thought about kissing you since the first time I laid eyes on you, that I think about you all the time, and that even though we both know starting something is risky, to me you're worth it." After pulling her zipper all the way down, he slid her coat off her shoulders and placed it on the bed beside him. "You're worth the risk."

All at once her heartbeat slowed, the tension in her muscles melting as she slipped into the space he opened for her between his knees. She slid her hands over his shoulders while his slid up her thighs to rest on her hips. "I have an idea," he said, his fingers hooking into her belt loops. "What if we go slowly?"

"What do you mean?" she asked as he tugged her closer.

"Slow, as in unhurried, as in the opposite of fast." Contrary to the sentiment, he pulled her so close his lips hovered only an inch from her stomach, the warmth of his breath seeping into her skin. "What about a date?" He opened his mouth, took her shirt loosely between his teeth, then pulled back until the fabric slipped free. "Dinner?"

Dinner? What's dinner?

"Ashley?" His lips pressed into the would-never-be-flat-again swell of her belly. "What do you think?"

She couldn't think. There was no think. There were only her fingers threading into his hair. "I haven't been on a date in years," she said, doing everything she could to not sound like all the blood in her entire body had just rushed between her legs. "Like a dress-up date?"

The softest kisses peppered her belly. "I was thinking casual."

"Casual. Casual is good." Chuck always went for fancy. Fancy clothes, fancy cars, fancy restaurants. Fancy affairs. "I like...*uhn*—" while she'd been trying to speak, he'd nosed her shirt up, his lips brushing over the skin just below her belly button nearly making her fall over "—casual."

With a mournful sigh, he pulled back, letting her shirt fall back down into place. "Friday night?" When he stared up at her, amusement tangled with the firelight in his eyes.

"Sure," she somehow managed to say, even with some level of coherence. "Friday sounds good."

"Perfect. Then it's settled." When he leaned back away from her, she felt his loss like a string tugging at something deep inside her, urging her to follow him. Was it over? She didn't want it to be over, not yet. But then he stood from the bed, and in one fluid motion he picked her up, slung her legs around his waist, and set her down on top of his dresser. He might have even growled while he did it, but she couldn't say for certain, every single sound in the cabin devoured by her pounding heart and the blood roaring in her ears.

"Madigan," she wheezed, "what are you—"

Grasping her ass, he yanked her forward until she ran up against him, thick and hard and thrilling. "Before you leave me, I have to kiss you. A real kiss. I'll die if I don't."

She started to say, "Okay," but her mouth had barely formed the 'O' before his lips crashed into hers, one of his hands riding up her back to cup her neck, his other hand pressing into the small of her back, holding her in place against the firm ridge of his cock.

When he squeezed her neck, tilting her head, when his tongue slid along her lower lip, her restraint snapped like a twig between his hands. She moaned, hooking her ankles behind his hips, sliding her hands up his arms, her fingers tracing his tensed muscles through his shirt.

His tongue slipped between her lips, and she opened her mouth for him, losing herself in the sensations of being held so tightly, being kissed like the world was ending. Being desired. She'd dreamt about kisses like this, when she was sixteen, lying in her bed, her fingers exploring her body. When she was twenty, wondering why kissing Chuck never felt like this. When she was deep into her marriage, so convinced she'd missed her chance, that she'd never have any real passion in her life. She'd been so phenomenally wrong.

Madigan was all passion, all heat. His beard brushing against her lips, the confident, unyielding way he held her, she'd never felt anything as primal as this kiss. His tongue caressed hers, tasting like mint and snow. Then his lips left her mouth to trail hungry kisses over her cheek, her jaw, down the column of her throat which she bared fully to him. She was so turned on, so out of her mind, so completely undone by his strength and his lips and his hands that her hips rocked and tilted, grinding helplessly against him. Groaning against her neck, he started moving in time with her, their bodies in perfect sync as he drove himself over the seam of her jeans in slow, mind-numbing strokes that made his dresser bang into the wall behind her.

She leaned into his pressure, sliding her fingers into his hair and tugging as his mouth found hers again. His hand slipped beneath the hem of her shirt, ghosting up her ribs to cup her breast over her bra, his thumb running across her peaked nipple. In an unfortunate and entirely unwelcome moment of clarity, she realized if they kept this up much longer she'd come, right here, fully clothed, in his arms. She'd come hard and be unable to hide it. And they didn't want that. They wanted to go slowly.

"Stop," she said somehow. "Madigan, stop."

He pulled away, his eyes dazed, lids heavy, his lips so red and wet they should have been illegal. She was panting, but so was he.

"That kiss," he said, his gaze tracing her lips. "I've never..."

"I had to stop. Otherwise I might have—"

"Me too," he said. "And I haven't come in my pants since junior high."

She laughed, a tight, nervous chuckle. But then her laughter grew, rising from her belly. Because what in the hell just happened?

"Ashley, are you laughing at me?" Even though a blush tinged his cheeks, his grin was enormous.

"No. Well, yes. Maybe. I think I'm laughing at both of us. I'm laughing at..." She gestured between them, feeling completely disheveled as she noticed his shirt—which she'd apparently tried to remove because it rode halfway up his abdomen, revealing defined abs decorated in ink, the trail of dark and silvery hair leading into his jeans, a trail she wanted to follow with her fingertips, her lips, her tongue...

"You shouldn't look at me like that," he said, his abs flexing as he pushed into her again. "Not if you want to get out of here without coming in your jeans."

Before she caved and wound up telling him, "Okay, why don't we do that," she pulled his shirt back down, pressing it flat over his stomach, trying to keep her fingers from lingering too long between the hard ridges of his muscles.

When she looked up at him again, he smiled down at her and said, "That wasn't slow."

Gripping the edge of his dresser to keep herself from gripping him, she smiled back up at him. "No. It wasn't."

He took one of her hands in his, brought her knuckles to his mouth, and just as she felt the brush of his lips against her skin, a single paw scratched loudly at the door.

"I should probably go," she said reluctantly.

With a deep breath, he lowered her hand. Then he grasped her hips again, slid her off his dresser, and set her feet onto the floor. "You probably should. But I'm keeping Murphy tonight. If I can't sleep with you," a corner of his mouth tipped up, "at least I can sleep with him."

The way her heart cartwheeled into her ribs made her wonder, at least for a second, if she was having some sort of cardiac event. While she rubbed at her chest, he sank to a knee in front of her, holding her boots in place so she could step into them. "This is a little weird," he said, rising to his feet again so he could help her back into her coat.

"What's weird?" she asked, her breath catching as he started pulling her zipper up slowly.

"Even though all I want to do is take them off, it's kind of hot helping you put your clothes back on."

She had absolutely no response to that.

When the zipper reached just above her breasts, he released the tab and said, "Thank you, Ashley." There was that earnestness in his eyes again, that vulnerability that was a thousand times sexier than any wry glance or sultry stare. "Thank you for not running away from me tonight."

How did he do that? How was he so hot she nearly combusted one moment, then so sweet and tender the next it made her want to wrap him inside her arms and never let him go. "Madigan, I don't know what to say."

Grasping the front of her coat in both hands, all fire again, he said, "Don't say anything." And then he yanked her close and kissed her one last time.

CHAPTER NINETEEN

MADIGAN

"Yo, Madigan, what planet are you on today?" Clay asked, his eyes narrowed.

"Huh?"

"Kev asked you a question."

Madigan scrubbed his hands over his face before he scanned the men packed into his cabin for group, all of them staring at him, waiting. "Sorry, guys. I haven't been sleeping great." This was an understatement. He'd spent the last several nights grinning up at his ceiling, his hands behind his head, his heart fluttering. He couldn't shut his brain down, couldn't stop thinking about the little things. How soft her hair was and the way it smelled like apple blossoms. The patch of freckles over her nose that he'd never noticed before and wondered if it spread out in the summer to cover her cheeks. The way her brown eyes had tiny flecks of green in them that could only be seen at kissing distance. He'd seen her every day since the best kiss of his life, catching her secret smiles, her flushed cheeks, the way she pulled her hair over her shoulder, giving him an unobstructed view of her neck. Not going to her, not sweeping her up into his arms and kissing her right there on the hill in front of god and everyone had taken every ounce of self-control he possessed. But maybe tonight. Maybe tonight he could kiss her again.

"There it is again," Kev said, pointing at Madigan's face, at the embarrassingly dopey expression Madigan made himself tamp down. "What is up with you? It's not just lack of sleep. You're, like, off in dreamland." After Kev and Clay both peered at him meaningfully, Kev raised a brow and said, "Be here now. Right, Boss?"

"Sorry, you're right." The guys needed him here, present for them. They hadn't had group since they'd moved up to the mountain, and he was sure they all had some decompressing to do. "Would you mind repeating your question, Kev?" he asked, taking his mug of coffee from the kitchen counter and raising it to his lips.

"I asked, what should a person in our position do if they think they might be interested in another person. Like, romantically."

Inhaling coffee directly into his lungs, Madigan coughed.

"I mean, I know I'm not ready for anything serious. I've only been clean for six months. But shoving all my feelings down doesn't feel right either. What's the answer?"

Madigan took a moment to scratch his beard, hoping to come off as contemplative rather than completely caught off guard by the same question he'd been asking himself for weeks.

"Well, Kev," he began, trying his hardest to dig deep into his countless years of therapy and AA meetings and...more recent experiences to say something not only helpful, but also hopeful. "It's different for everyone, I think. A lot of it depends on how good you were at relationships before you started using."

Most of the men groaned, some laughed.

"Right." Madigan nodded. "Most of us weren't very skilled in this arena. It might take us a bit longer. It's not my intention to put limits on any of you, and aside from staying clean, I'm not sure it's healthy to put too many limits on ourselves anyway."

"So, I should go for it?" Kev asked.

Madigan tried not to frown at Kev's eager expression. *Go for what? For who?* Had Kev met someone up here? "I think honesty is good, patience is even better. Relationships can complicate the already complicated path to recovery. But they can also help because having support from someone you care about is a wonderful thing." He noticed Sam's head turn abruptly toward the window, his jaw clenching as he stared distantly at the snow blanketing the trees.

"The danger," Madigan continued carefully, "comes in relying on that support for your own progress in life. Once we rely on someone or something else to get us through the day—"

"Then we're right back where we started," Sam said to the window.

"It's a risk. That's the risk of relationships for people like us." His father's words echoed. *Take a risk, dammit!* "But life *is* risk, right? I have no idea why we're here on this planet, but I don't think it's so we can tiptoe cautiously through our years and die alone and comfortable because we hid everything that made us human away in some prison of our own making. Because we were scared of messing up, of hurting the people we love again." He knew these words would resonate with the men, especially Sam, but he couldn't help wondering if he'd said them for himself as well. "All we can do is try to be open and honest. Don't hide who you are and what you've been through. It's obviously up to the other person if that's something they can handle, or something they even want to handle. Because, let's face it, we can be a lot to handle."

"Speak for yourself, Boss," said Brian, who was still happily married. Quiet laughs surrounded him.

"And most importantly," Madigan said, reminding himself as much as them, "take everything slowly. Like glacial levels of slowness. There is no rush, and if something doesn't feel good to you or if your old cravings or your antsiness or whatever your triggers are start clawing their way up to the surface, talk about it. Go to a meeting if that's a thing that works for you. Talk to your friends. Find a good therapist. Call me," he said, clapping a hand over his chest for emphasis. "I am always here for you guys. Always. There are so many options available to help you continue to live your lives, to help you go through good times and bad times and boring or painful or exciting times, all of it." He swung his arms out wide. "Everything, even intimate relationships, without using or drinking again."

"I know I'm risking bathroom duty by saying this." Tex's eyes were big and sincere, his hat off and in his lap. "But that was really damn beautiful."

Madigan had already changed his shirt twice after sweating through his deodorant. He'd never been so nervous. After taking the steps up to Ashley's office two at a time, he turned the corner and froze as two Ashleys stared up at him from Ashley's desk, both wearing equally amused expressions.

"Hi, Davis, Ashley," he said, smiling at mother and daughter, spitting images of each other.

"Hey, Madigan." Davis's lips quirked as her gaze swept over him. "How's the pirate life?"

Glancing at Ashley, he raised a brow and replied, "Smooth sailing so far?"

"Yo ho ho," Davis said. "I might be into your first mate, by the way."

Record scratch. "Come again?"

"Kevin. He's hot."

Kev's question during group suddenly made sense. What had those two been up to? "Kev? Really?"

Nodding slowly, Davis said, "Absolutely."

Ashley gazed imploringly up at the ceiling, and Madigan could only share the sentiment.

"Where are you two going anyway?" Davis asked.

"I made reservations at Scotty's. I hope that's okay."

Davis gasped. "How did you know that was Mom's favorite restaurant, you absolute charmer?"

"He's taking her to Scotty's?" Maude Alice asked, crowding into the room behind him. "You're pretty good at this whole 'wooing' thing, Madigan. Not that I thought you wouldn't be."

"Hello, Maude Alice," he said, his shirt feeling suddenly too tight, the room too hot. He pulled off his hat and ruffled his hair.

"All right," Ashley said, rising to her feet, saving him from sweating through a third shirt. "I think that's enough interrogation for one night." Watching her grab her coat from the rack near the door, Madigan stumbled back a step. She looked stunning tonight in dark jeans with tall brown boots, her golden hair trailing down the back of a pale pink sweater that looked soft enough to pet. "There's still meat-loaf in the fridge. Don't wait up." Then, mercifully, she took Madigan by his arm and ushered him from the room.

"Should we take Lydia?" he asked on their way to the parking lot.

"Who's Lydia?"

"My truck."

"Of course it is," she said with a sideways grin. "Sure, let's take Lydia. You probably won't believe this, but I hate driving in the snow."

"That is a bit ironic for someone who owns a ski hill."

When they reached Lydia, he opened the passenger door for Ashley, closing it again after she climbed in. Once he slid into his well-worn spot in the driver's seat, he turned toward her. He liked the way she looked in his truck. Ashley had such a classic beauty, and he always thought Lydia was one of the most classically beautiful things he'd ever seen.

"I like her," she said, running her fingertips over the dashboard.

"Me too. I like her a lot." Unspoken words lingered between them as they stared silently into each other's eyes.

"We should get going," she said, breaking the silence. "It might snow later."

"Yeah," he said, gazing at her lips, wanting to kiss her again so badly the desire scared him a little. Instead of trying to kiss her, instead of rushing to satisfy his urges, he took a breath, blew it out, and started Lydia up.

CHAPTER TWENTY

ASHLEY

"Should we listen to the radio?" Ashley asked, her hands clasped in her lap. Now that they were alone in his truck, his clean, spicy, delicious scent filled her with a nearly overwhelming desire to bite him, not that she'd ever bitten a man before. But what was it? His soap? Detergent? Beard oil?

"Unfortunately the radio doesn't work," he said, his eyes pinned to the road. "But the cassette player does."

"Cassette player?" She gasped in feigned shock. "Is Lydia a time machine?"

The lights from Lydia's console illuminated his grin. "Welcome back to the 1990s. There's a thing of tapes under your seat, although I'm not sure you'll find anything you like."

Reaching under her seat, she pulled the cassette case out by its frayed leather handle. When she grasped the zipper and pulled, she did feel like she was in the 90s, getting ready to rifle through her girlfriends' tapes during spring break road trips, or sift through Chuck's tapes while hiding her constant disappointment in his obsession with Rush and Toby Keith. Praying not to see any Toby, she opened Madigan's case, realizing instantly that she shouldn't have worried.

The tapes were a goldmine of everything Madigan—Bowie, Primus, the Velvet Underground, Tom Waits, PJ Harvey, Bonnie Raitt. *Sweet mercy*, the man listened to Bonnie Raitt so often she'd earned a coveted space in his only-30-cassette-holding case. She could almost see him, cruising down the highway in Lydia, belting out "I Can't Make you Love Me" at the top of his lungs, maybe with a single tear rolling down his cheek into his beard. Scanning his tapes, running her fingertips over their smooth plastic covers, she pulled one out and gave it a shake. "You like the Psychedelic Furs?"

He nodded—a big, enthusiastic rock star's nod. "Oh, yeah. 'Love My Way,' are you kidding me?" And right there before her eyes and with this rich, soulful, underwear-incinerating voice, he sang her the first verse of one of the greatest songs ever written.

"You have a gorgeous voice," she said unevenly, pressing her knees together to soothe the heat pulsing between her thighs.

"Thanks," he said while she slipped *Forever Now* into the cassette player. "I used to sing backup for the Makers, but I kind of destroyed my vocal cords with cigarettes and booze. I don't sing very much anymore."

What a shame, she thought, but kept it to herself.

They only had enough time for a few songs to play before they reached town and he parked in front of Scotty's. But Ashley could have stayed in Lydia with him all night, listening to music, making out in the backseat, letting him go to second base, maybe third. Instead, when he came around to her side of the truck and opened her door for her, she took his outstretched hand and held it all the way into the restaurant.

"I KNOW you've been worried about sales," he said after the hostess sat them at their table. "How are things looking so far?"

Spreading her napkin out in her lap, she said, "Better than the last two years thanks to the good snow this season. But it's still nowhere close to what I'd hoped for. I don't know if it'll be enough."

"Enough to keep from having to sell to Chuck?" Candlelight flickered in his eyes, making them glow cobalt against the dark grey Henley clinging to his chest and shoulders.

"Right," she said, hoping he couldn't hear her stomach growling because Scotty's always smelled amazing, like garlic and basil and fresh baked bread. "We haven't done well since my dad died. He was the heart and soul of Bluebird. He had a spirit that drew people to him, to the mountain. Maude Alice and I try, but we just don't have it."

"When did your dad pass away?"

Sliding her salad fork a bit to the side, she said, "Three years ago. He had a stroke, and just when he was starting to take steps again he got something called aspiration pneumonia. And then he was just gone, in less than a week. He was only sixty-seven years old."

"I'm so sorry, Ashley."

She'd heard these four words so many times since Max had died, leaving her completely unmoored. But it was strange the way she knew in her bones that Madigan really meant them.

"Thank you," she said, trying to smile but not quite getting there. "It also doesn't help that our main competition has more money and resources than we ever will."

"Chuck's mountain?" he guessed. "What was it called? Kumquat or something?"

"Conquest," she corrected with a laugh.

"So close," he said, snapping his fingers.

"My dad always wanted Bluebird to be an affordable mountain so that skiing would be accessible for anyone from Red Falls who wanted to try it. We have locally sponsored scholarships for low-income families, outreach programs for struggling kids, free specialized equipment rentals for people with disabilities, even low-cost daycare during the winter. All these things would vanish if we sold out to Chuck."

"Let me guess, he doesn't care about this kind of community outreach?"

"He does not," she said with certainty. "Chuck thought my dad was a bleeding-heart idealist who was intent on running Bluebird into the ground."

"Interesting. What did your dad think of Chuck?" he asked

A small thrill rushed through her at the realization that she'd been waiting for someone to ask her this question for years. "My dad thought Chuck was a status-obsessed asshole who never cared about anyone other than himself." *God,* it felt good to say that.

"Your dad sounds like he was my kind of guy."

A smile tugged at her lips. Her dad had tolerated Chuck because she'd married him, and because he was Davis's father. But she'd always known he couldn't stand him. While she stared at Madigan across the table, an entirely new type of grief settled under her ribs, dull and aching. Max would have liked him, and she was sad they'd never get to meet.

"How close do you think you are to having to sell?" he asked after taking a sip of his water.

"If sales don't turn around, I don't know how we'll avoid it much longer. What we need is something to draw in more families and bring new people to the sport. That's Bluebird's sweet spot. We may not have fancy spas or heated chairlifts, but we're a great mountain for kids and normal people who can't afford $200 lift tickets."

"There are heated chairlifts?" he asked, genuinely stunned. "Seriously?"

"Yep. Some chairlifts even have digital screens and carry eight skiers at once."

His jaw hinged open, his eyes adorably round. "Wild."

"Bluebird won't ever be able to compete with those types of frills. But I keep feeling like there has to be something we can do to bring in skiers, something creative and inventive."

"Hmm," he considered, running his knuckles over his beard, his HOPE tattoo disappearing and reappearing under the thick, coarse hairs she could still feel tickling her cheeks. "Do you have anything in mind?"

She shook her head. "All I know is that it needs to be something big. I'd love to build a terrain park to bring in younger skiers and boarders, but we don't have the time or the money to make that happen."

"Have you ever thought about an event?" His fingers twirled his glass of water on the table. "Like a concert?"

"A concert?"

His shrug was a little too jerky to be nonchalant. "A big enough concert could bring in new skiers *and* money. I know a lot of musicians, friends who've offered to help Little Timber out in the past and would probably dig the chance to support a local family ski hill being threatened by big corporate money. We could call it a fundraiser. We could," he cleared his throat, tugging nervously on his collar, "even make it a yearly thing to support an ongoing partnership between Bluebird and Little Timber. If that's something you and Maude Alice think you might be interested in. If not, that's totally fine. No pressure. It was just a thought."

Ashley hadn't really let herself consider a continued relationship with Little Timber, or with Madigan after this season. But she could see how it might go, new men to train every year, new opportunities to introduce people to the sport she loved, more ways to support Red Falls and the surrounding communities, more time catching last chair with him, laughing with him on the slopes, kissing him in his cabin.

"Or not," he said when she'd gone too long without responding. "I shouldn't have brought this up. You probably want to see how this season plays out before even thinking about bringing us back next year. It's just that the guys are loving it so much and—"

"Madigan, no," she cut in. "It's not that. I've just never really thought about—" *you and me and a future together* "—a concert. It's a great idea, but I don't know the first thing about planning something like that."

He sat back in his chair, the tight lines between his brows relaxing. "If you're interested, I can take care of the rest. I'll make some calls and see what I can put together and when."

Ashley was about to ask how much he thought putting on a concert like that would cost her when a tall, beautiful young woman with dark brown hair falling almost to her waist stopped at their table and said, "Madigan?"

Blinking up at their server, Madigan said, "Izzy?"

"What are you doing here?" the woman named Izzy asked, her shoulders stiff while her gaze darted around the restaurant, like she was looking for someone she didn't want to see. "Is he—"

"We're just getting dinner," Madigan said, his hand raised, his tone reassuring. "Just the two of us. I didn't know you worked here. I really didn't."

This, Ashley thought, was a strange conversation. Who was this woman and why would she care where Madigan went for dinner? Was she the counselor he'd had a fling with? Couldn't be, she was too young. *Could it?* Either way, the tension snapping tight between Madigan and this woman made Ashley feel like she was intruding, like she should go to the bathroom, give them some privacy. But Izzy was also there to take their order and leaving now seemed rude.

After a moment of uncomfortable silence, Izzy set her jaw and said, "I just started last week."

"That's great." Madigan's smile seemed to settle Izzy's nerves, the tension in her shoulders fading.

"Thanks." Izzy tucked a strand of silky hair behind her ear. And then, as if finally noticing there was someone else at their table, she looked at Ashley and said, "Sorry, um, would you two like anything to drink?"

"Izzy," Madigan said, "this is Ashley Cooke. She owns Bluebird Basin, where we're working this winter."

Izzy's lips turned down. "He's working at a ski hill? He can't even ski."

"He learned," Madigan said, his eyes flicking toward Ashley. "Ashley taught them."

And then she understood. Izzy knew one of the guys. Maybe she was a friend, a sister, a girlfriend, a wife. Either way, Ashley was definitely intruding.

"Should I step away for a minute?" she asked. "So you two can talk?"

Madigan didn't say a word, leaving the verdict up to Izzy.

"You seriously taught Sam how to ski?" Izzy asked her.

Without thinking, Ashley brightened and said, "I did. Sam is so great. He's one of the best bunny hill lifties I've ever had, just fantastic with the kids."

Izzy went stiff again, Madigan winced, and Ashley felt like she'd just somersaulted into a minefield.

"Is that so?" Izzy said, squaring her shoulders as her left eyebrow floated toward her bangs.

"She doesn't know," Madigan jumped in. "Izzy, she doesn't know any of the men's histories. You know I never share that information."

"I'm feeling really lost here," Ashley admitted, her palms sweating. "Did I say something wrong?"

After a moment, her edges softening a fraction, Izzy said, "No, you didn't say anything wrong. It's just that I'm Sam's ex-wife. And while I'm happy he's good with your kids, it would have been nice if he'd spent more than five minutes in the last five years with his own daughter."

One time, in fourth grade, Ashley fell from the monkey bars and lost her breath for what felt like an eternity. The sensation of Izzy's words slamming into her chest was nearly identical. "I'm so sorry," she said, because what else was there to say? She'd unknowingly stumbled into a conversation, a world, she knew nothing about. The only thing keeping her from trying to apologize herself into a hole in the ground was Madigan's hand taking hers, his thumb brushing softly over her knuckles.

"Izzy," he said evenly, "I'll have a Coke." He seemed so unruffled, so calm, like he'd had conversations like this one a thousand times.

And maybe he had. "And Ashley will have," he paused, a corner of his mouth pulling tight, "beer? Wine?"

"Water," she said. "Just water. Thank you, Izzy."

Izzy's expression—conflicted and apologetic and far too exhausted for someone so young—made Ashley want to stand up, pull her into her arms, and hold her for as long as it took to make it go away. Which, of course, was something she couldn't do.

"I'll be right back with your drinks," Izzy said shortly before she walked over to the bar.

"Shit." Ashley felt awful. "I wish I hadn't said any of that."

"You didn't do or say anything wrong," Madigan said, squeezing her hand then letting it go. "This is just the way it goes sometimes. If I'd known Izzy had taken a job here we would have gone somewhere else."

"I hope I didn't upset her. But I don't see how I didn't."

"It wasn't you." His big shoulders rose and fell. "It can be hard. I meet these guys, and now so do you, in a very different stage of their lives than when they did the most damage to the people around them. My job is to help them start over, even if they're still surrounded by the pieces of all the things and people and situations they broke when they were using. Even if they have to learn how to live the rest of their lives holding those broken pieces close, knowing they might never be successful in putting them back together again. Sometimes the damage they've—*we've*," he corrected, "caused makes moving on hard for everyone involved." He glanced at Izzy who was waiting for their drinks at the bar, her back turned to them, her arms crossed tightly around her waist. "Sometimes the people we hurt don't want to be a part of our new lives, and we can't blame them for that. Just because we may find a way to forgive ourselves, it doesn't mean anyone else has to forgive us too, or even has to listen to our apologies. With addicts, with our loved ones, it can get," he scratched his beard, his lips pressed tight, "complicated. Especially when kids are involved."

"I might not know much about addiction, but I can understand that part of it at least," Ashley said. "Davis took it hard when I finally left Chuck. Barely spoke to me for weeks. But Chuck has never once apologized to me for cheating, for lying, and I expect he never will. He'd have to admit he did something wrong first. But even if he did, even if hell froze over and Chuck Thompson realized he did me wrong, I'm not sure I'd want to hear his apology. I'm even less sure I'd believe it."

Cracking his knuckles, Madigan said, "First of all, Chuck's a prick."

Her snort was loud enough to turn the heads of an older couple a table over.

"You're right, though," he said, "sometimes it's just too late. But sometimes..." He looked at Izzy again, his brows sliding together. "Sometimes there's still a chance. I really hope Sam gets that chance."

"Me too," Ashley replied quietly as Izzy returned to their table to drop off their drinks and take their orders.

Much later, after they'd finished their meals and were contemplating dessert, Madigan asked out of nowhere, "So, only water?"

Ashley tilted her head. "What do you mean?"

"You only ordered water tonight." He toyed with his knife. "Did you just do that for me or..."

She thought she might know where this was headed. "No, I didn't do that for you. I just don't drink."

Abandoning the knife, he blinked at her and repeated, "You don't drink," slowly and carefully like the words were in a language he'd just learned how to speak.

"I never really have. I don't drink. I don't do drugs. I am a very boring woman."

He only stared at her, his lips parting.

"What?" Now she was nervous. "I thought you'd be okay with me not drinking—"

Abruptly, his head fell forward, landing on his folded arms. "I was so worried about what I'd do if you were a drinker, since we've never talked about it. It's so much easier for me to spend time with people who don't drink, safer." When he looked up at her again, he did it with a smile. "I probably should have asked you about this before, but I'm so relieved right now."

Reaching out for him, she interlaced her fingers with his, wishing they were alone so she could walk around their table, crawl into his lap, and run her fingers through his curls.

"Maybe we should skip dessert," he said, looking up from their clasped hands. "I can think of other things I'd much rather eat."

Her eyes bulged, she audibly gasped, and she might have even screamed if they weren't in such a public place.

"Sorry," he grimaced, "old habits. Slow, right? We're taking things slow. *Slow, Madigan,*" he muttered, shaking his head.

"Right, slow," she agreed, her heart pounding furiously inside her chest because talking with him, feeling the warmth of his hand intertwined with hers, savoring the way he looked at her tonight like he really was hungry for her made her want only one thing.

And it had nothing to do with slow.

CHAPTER TWENTY-ONE

MADIGAN

In an ironic twist, Madigan felt drunk, higher than the time the Makers played that festival in Prague and he'd partied obscenely hard with the lead singer of Starflare for three straight days. Leaning against the cold tile of the bathroom wall, he tried to steady himself, feeling like the restaurant was inside a snow globe and someone had just given it a good, hard shake.

He needed a break, a moment to calm himself, take some deep breaths, and pull his head out of the clouds. It all felt too damn good, being with her, talking with her. Conversation flowed too easily, sparks so bright he could almost see them floating through the air with every little touch, every time their eyes met, that moment when she'd let her foot slide up against his. He was trying very hard not to be scared by how good everything felt with her when the bathroom door flew open, a pretentious blond douchebag with a popped collar bursting in.

"Madigan, isn't it?" Chuck said, his chest puffed out like he was prepared to fight a bear.

"That's right," Madigan replied, leaning back slightly from the urinal. "And you're Chuck. I'd shake your hand but..." He glanced down to where he'd unzipped his pants but hadn't taken himself out yet.

"I appreciate that." Chuck's laughter was this overly friendly farce he'd probably honed to perfection during soul-sucking executive lunches and golf game sales pitches. "So, you're here with Ashley?"

"That's right."

"For work?" His beady blue eyes narrowed. "Or pleasure?"

Madigan's hackles rose. "Well, Chuck, I'm not sure that's any of your business."

"Look, bud." Chuck's composure snapped as he bared his perfectly straight white teeth. "I know Ash better than anyone. I know her *inside and out,* if you catch my meaning."

"Pretty hard to miss," Madigan ground out, his internal temperature rising. "But if you really knew her so well, you'd know she fucking hates being called Ash."

"What? She doesn't hate..." Chuck's jaw clenched. "That's not the point. Whatever you think is happening between you and Ash—"

"—ley," Madigan said, fighting a smirk at the angry vein that popped out in the middle of Chuck's forehead.

"I'm sure a lowlife loser like you probably thinks you've hit the goldmine with her, but you've got another thing coming. She's obviously just decided to slum it with a townie this winter."

"Slum it?" He struggled to keep his temper on its leash, but even Friendly Neighborhood Madigan had his limits. "You might want to think long and hard about what you say next, friend."

"I'm *not* your friend," Chuck sneered. Madigan had to give it to him, he had a real flair for stating the obvious. "I know who you are. I know all about you and the criminals you've brought to Bluebird. I'm sure this is all very exciting for Ash, but she's always been naive, too trusting. Once I get her to realize who you *really* are—nothing but a washed-up, has-been, lowlife loser—she'll come running back to me."

Staring up into the light fixture above his head long enough to burn an afterimage into his retinas, Madigan sighed deeply. There was no exceptional mystery to the Chucks of the world, and he'd sized this one up the second he'd watched him jump down from his enormous truck. Chucks were entitled, selfish, narrow-minded, and most importantly, outrageously insecure. He wasn't proud about starting a literal pissing contest in the bathroom at Scotty's, but he needed to bring this conversation to a screeching halt before he did something he'd truly regret.

Reaching into his pants, he pulled himself out, aimed at the urinal, and said, "I'm sure you're right, Chuck. But unless you're in here to go to the bathroom too, I gotta say it's feeling a little weird having you watch me take a leak."

Chuck's gaze slid to the single urinal next to Madigan, and then to the two empty stalls behind him, and then, comically, down to his own pants. His nostrils flared.

"Didn't plan this one out too well did ya, *bud*?"

"This isn't over," Chuck said, stepping awkwardly back toward the door. "She'll be back with me by the end of the season. She'll be back, and you and your men will be gone."

Madigan really hated being threatened, but he especially hated being threatened when his dick was in his hand. And this was, regrettably, not the first time this had happened to him. Regardless, he was committed to making sure this would be the first time he wouldn't shove someone's head into the nearest toilet bowl over it. He wouldn't even let his volume rise a single decibel over his normal inside voice when he said, "Fuck off, Chuck," and started to piss.

The vein on his forehead bulging to an alarming size, Chuck spun on his heel and yanked the bathroom door open so hard it slammed against the wall. And then he was gone, leaving Madigan alone to wonder if anything the asshole had said was true.

"Did you see Chuck in there?" Ashley asked when he returned to their table.

"I did. He's a delight."

"Shit. I'm sorry, Madigan. He took your seat once you left, and after I told him to leave he marched into the bathroom. Are you okay?"

"I'm fine," he lied, his blood still hot, muscles primed, insecurities screaming. He scanned the table. The plates had been cleared and two mints sat on top of a signed receipt. "Did Izzy already bring the check?" Had Ashley paid the bill? Did she think he couldn't afford it? Could this night get any worse?

"She did. Chuck paid our tab."

Apparently it could. "He paid for our dinner?"

Ashley's expression was painfully apologetic. "He did it before I could stop him." She took Madigan's hand, which he hadn't realized had curled itself into a fist. "He's trying to intimidate you."

As much as he hated to admit it, Madigan *was* intimidated. Chuck's bullshit had wormed its way under his skin. He didn't have Chuck's money or squeaky-clean appearance. He didn't run a fancy ski mountain or own a $60,000 truck. He hadn't saved a penny of the money he'd made as a rock star. All he had were dwindling royalties, Little Timber, and Lydia. And the worst part was, he really thought he'd moved on from letting anyone else make him feel this inadequate. Not only was he pissed at Chuck, now he was pissed at himself too.

"Madigan," she said, working her fingers into his closed fist. "He's a terrible person. The worst. You know I can't stand him, right?"

As her thumb brushed over his, he forced himself to hear her. Was Chuck Thompson the kind of man whose opinion he wanted to put any stock in? Was this two-timing ass worth ruining their night over?

Holding her hand, Madigan stood from his chair and walked around the table. Maybe he was out of his depth. Maybe he wasn't good enough for Ashley. But he'd be damned if he'd let Chuck ruin their date. Tugging her up to her feet, he said, "That makes two of us. Let's get out of here."

They drove home slowly, creeping up the winding road back to

Bluebird at a snail's pace, listening to music, holding hands. After a while, even Chuck's bathroom tirade slipped from Madigan's mind. All he could think about, all he *wanted* to think about, was Ashley's voice when she started singing along to the Furs, the way her fingers slid in and out of his, over the back of his hand, over his tattoos, like she was getting to know his skin, his veins, his bones. Like just holding his hand wasn't enough. By the time they reached the parking lot, he was so turned on he could barely see straight.

Throwing Lydia into park, he reached over, unfastened Ashley's seatbelt, and said, "Hi," while staring at her lips.

"Hi," she said in this breathy way that stiffened his cock in his jeans.

He brushed her hair back off her shoulder, letting his fingers trail over the skin along her neck. "We're home."

Her gaze sank to his mouth, her tongue peeking out to wet her lips, her body leaning toward his, and, *thank fuck,* he was going to kiss Ashley Cooke again.

He stayed still at first as her lips pressed softly against his. It thrilled him, waiting to see what she would do, feeling how she wanted the kiss to unfold, letting her surprise him when her fingers slid into his hair and curled, with the unbearably sexy noises she made as she yanked him closer and opened her mouth for him. But when she pushed him back into his seat and crawled into his lap, he couldn't stay still for another second.

Cupping her neck with one hand while she rocked her hips into his, he slid the other under her sweater, thanking the sliver moon for the dark night. When he pulled the cup of her lacy bra down, freeing her breast, he brushed his thumb over her nipple and she broke the kiss, her head falling back as the most phenomenal moan rose from her throat. She had small breasts, sensitive nipples, his favorite combination. He had to see them.

Pulling her sweater up just enough, he dove inside, letting the soft, stretchy knit fabric enclose him in a cocoon with her skin, her heaving chest, her perfect breasts. He kissed the sacred notch at the base of her throat, feeling her heart beating wildly under his lips, and she whimpered. When he moved to the side, sliding the strap of her bra off her shoulder, guiding her nipple into his mouth, she rocked against him so hard he almost lost it. He knew they were supposed to be taking things slow, but he also knew she needed something from him. The entire drive up had been mind-melting foreplay, revving him up until he was redlining. If she felt even a fraction of the frenzied desire thrumming through his veins, she needed to come. And he refused to leave her unsatisfied.

With his tongue circling her other nipple, he brought his fingers down to the button of her jeans and waited there. Either she'd stop him, or she wouldn't.

"Ashley?" he said around her nipple tugging gently on the button when she didn't push his hands away.

"Yes," was all she said in reply. It was all he needed.

Making quick work of her button and zipper, he slid his thumb down between her jeans and her underwear. He wanted more, he wanted skin, he wanted to slip his fingers between her folds, slide them inside her, but not tonight. Tonight was already out of control enough, and even though slow had left the station, he was still at least trying to be good. But the dampness that met his thumb as it moved down her seam, making him imagine how soft and warm and wet she'd feel if he just inched that strip of fabric to the side, made him growl, sucking her nipple back into his mouth with a little more force.

She gasped, holding his head tight to her body through her sweater, her hips bucking against his hand, and he was in heaven.

Moving his thumb back up, he found the swollen heat of her clit. When he pressed down, her entire body shuddered. He wanted to tease her, take his time, draw this out for as long as he could. But right now, with the way she grasped at him, the way her heart thundered under his lips, teasing wouldn't be fair. With a few brisk circles, she came quickly, beautifully. He pulled his head out from under her sweater just in time to watch the orgasm take her, her eyes closed, lips parted, head thrown back as he pressed and circled until he could tell she'd had enough.

Kissing her bared throat, he slid his hand out of her jeans to zip and button her back up. He arranged her bra straps into place, then he pulled her limp body into his arms. When he cracked the window, letting the cold night air in to clear Lydia's steamed-up windshield, she whispered, "That wasn't slow," into his ear.

With a smile she couldn't see, he said, "Requesting permission to raise the current speed limit."

"Granted," she said, the hairs along his arms stirring as she laughed into his neck.

CHAPTER TWENTY-TWO

MADIGAN

Madigan spent the last week helping the guys and working with Murphy during the day, skiing with Ashley in the afternoon, and kissing her until their lips were bruised in the evenings. They still hadn't gone much farther than they had in Lydia and his restraint astonished him. Maybe all the yoga and meditation he'd been doing hadn't only helped his mental clarity. He felt more in control of his body, his needs, his desires, than he ever had before with a woman. Sure, he wanted her so badly he'd fucked his fist about twenty times in the last three weeks, but despite what the guys loved to say about him, he wasn't a monk. He was just a man. A man who hoped he'd been patient long enough to at least get to see Ashley without any clothes on. And today, he had a solid plan today to aid in that endeavor. But first things first.

He'd spent the morning making some long overdue calls to his bandmates, his friends in other bands, and his contact in Red Falls to see about securing a permit for a possible concert at Bluebird. Every single person he'd called, the lead singers of Chaining Jane and Gravel, the manager for Starflare, his bandmates, had all agreed ecstatically to travel to Montana in the heart of the winter to put on a concert for a tiny ski mountain, and for Little Timber, and mostly, he knew, for him. It was enough to make him tear up not once, not twice, but thrice.

He'd saved his last call, and likely his fourth crying jag, for Cole, the Makers' drummer, and his best friend.

"Mad, how the hell are ya?" Cole's booming, bearhug of a voice put an immediate smile on Madigan's face. "It's been too long."

It really had, over a year. "Good, man. I'm good. How are you?"

"I am amazing. I became a grandfather last week."

"No kidding?" Leaning back in his rocking chair, Madigan hooked his hand behind his head. "I didn't even know Becks was expecting." Cole had one daughter from his long and tumultuous relationship with the lead singer of Asyd Nancy. Since they'd finally called it quits—at least Madigan was pretty sure they had—Cole was the only man Madigan knew who'd been single as long as he had.

"Six-pound baby girl. Ten fingers, ten toes, and a set of lungs like you wouldn't believe."

"Takes after her grandfather then," Madigan ribbed. "Nobody howled at the moon like you."

"Hey, I'm not the one who blew out his vocal cords during a screaming match with the guys from Refuge," Cole shot back.

Laughing out loud, Madigan said, "I'd almost forgotten about that show. Those new wave Brit shits poured beer all over our amps. They deserved what they got."

"Mad Madigan in their faces and three broken guitars, if I remember correctly."

"I might have gone a little overboard," he admitted, squeezing the back of his neck. Most of the time Mad Madigan felt far away, like an entirely different person he'd only known in passing. But sometimes, like today—planning this concert and the other little trick he had up his sleeve for Ashley, when excitement and mischief thrummed through his veins—Mad Madigan felt as close as his own beating heart. Considering how much of his adult life he'd spent trying to forget about his past, having his other self come out of hiding like this weighed on him. Mad Madigan was wild. Mad Madigan was selfish. Mad Madigan ruined everything. He really didn't want to ruin this.

"We all went a little overboard back then," Cole said, a colossal understatement. "What's the occasion? Haven't heard from you in an age."

Madigan spent the next ten minutes telling Cole about Little Timber's move onto the mountain, Bluebird's struggles, and his plan for a concert fundraiser in mid-January.

"Are you shitting me? Of course I'll be there," Cole said brightly.

A relieved sigh breezed through Madigan's lips. Including Benji, the singer from Stone's Throw who'd fronted the Makers during their last tour, and Lou, their reclusive base player, Cole signing on meant the entire band was on board. He'd been fairly certain Cole would be down, but he also knew that Cole, just like all the other musicians, had responsibilities now, families, brand new grandchildren. They were busy living lives.

"It sounds like a blast from the past, and you know I'd give you the shirt straight off my back if it meant helping Little Timber. But—" Cole's voice took on that knowing tone that always meant Madigan was about to get called out "—I can't help but wonder if there's something else at play here. I mean, if your nervous ass is ready to climb back on stage, this must be a big deal. You wouldn't be keeping something from me would you, Mad?"

"No way," Madigan answered unconvincingly. "I'm an open book, Cole. You know that."

Cole snorted on the other end of the line. "You lie like a rug. But I won't pry. You'll tell me when you're ready."

They talked for a few more minutes, catching up before Cole had to go help Becks with his granddaughter who was wailing bloody murder in the background.

"She really does have some lungs."

"Told you." Cole laughed. "She's like a fire alarm."

"Take care, Cole," Madigan said. "I'll be in touch with the details."

"You do that. Can't wait to see you, and to find out what, or *who*," Cole insinuated, "has finally convinced you to play again."

Madigan wasn't sure why he decided not to tell Cole about Ashley. It seemed like pressing his luck somehow, talking about something he wasn't even sure was a thing yet, especially with how badly he wanted it to be a thing. And with what he had planned for Ashley today, he needed all the luck he could get.

MADIGAN'S FATHER had mastered the art of performing small and secret romantic gestures, little thoughtful acts that always made Madigan's mother melt, and were likely responsible for all three of his younger brothers, and probably himself, coming into existence. Channeling his dad, Madigan carried the box holding the new window and his tools up the lodge steps and crept quietly into Ashley's office while she was in town running errands. He'd barely settled himself under the cracked window when—

"Good morning, Madigan."

With a mighty yelp, he shot back up to his feet, fumbling his hammer in his hands.

"Don't hurt yourself," Maude Alice said, entering the room with an easy authority.

With a hand over his galloping heart, he said, "You startled me."

She stared at him, her hands on her hips, obviously waiting for him to explain his presence in Ashley's office.

He pointed at the window. "I noticed it was cracked a while ago, and I—"

"You can change out a window?" she asked, appraising him with a skepticism that felt uncomfortably close to judgment. He supposed he deserved the look. He was trying to get into her daughter's pants, after all.

"Oh, yeah. I worked in construction for years. Kept me busy after I got clean. You don't think she'll mind if I fix it, do you? I thought it could be like," he scratched his head, "a Christmas present."

Madigan had always considered himself a good judge of character. But when Maude Alice crossed the room to rise onto her toes and kiss him on his cheek, she caught him so completely off guard he froze, his arms awkward at his sides, the hammer still clutched in his fist.

"Don't worry, dear, your secret is safe with me. And no, she won't mind." Peering up at him, clear-eyed, she said, "Chuck couldn't fix a loose screw. I'm rooting for you, Madigan. You're good for her." Backing away a step, she straightened her sweater and added, "Ashley has a hard time letting people in, especially her mother. I hope she lets you in. She deserves some happiness." She raised her chin. "I suspect you do as well."

Madigan watched silently as Maude Alice strode from the room. He knew first-hand how complicated relationships between fathers and sons could be. But mothers and daughters, he realized, needed an entirely different word. Complicated didn't even touch it.

Turning back to the window, he peered down at Bluebird's base spreading out below him. He smiled at the families and college students and retired couples arriving to ski, at Sam helping a toddler onto the rope tow, at his guys running the lifts, all of them laughing with sun on their cheeks. And then there was Kev, leaning against the chairlift control shed, very obviously flirting with a cute young blond. *Of course.*

Yanking up the window, Madigan stuck his head out and shouted, "Yo, Kev! Get a ladder and come give me a hand."

Kev jumped, looking caught, before scampering over to the tool shed. Spinning around, Davis looked up, flashing Madigan a wide grin and two big thumbs up.

Madigan laughed quietly to himself as an odd mix of emotions moved through him. He was proud of Kev for shooting his shot with Davis. He was also deeply concerned the kid was in way over his head and might end up getting his heart broken.

"My job isn't to keep them from getting hurt by life," he reminded himself, because he always had to remind himself of this. His first instinct was to shelter the men who stayed with him, but that wasn't what they needed. They needed to be brave and resilient, and nobody ever got brave without being allowed to make some mistakes. Even if this mistake had BAD IDEA stamped all over it.

Ninety minutes later, however, working feverishly with Kev while they struggled to install Ashley's window before she got home, he realized Kev wasn't the only one of them in over his head.

CHAPTER TWENTY-THREE

ASHLEY

ASHLEY HOPPED out of her truck, grinning from ear to ear because the weather was mild, it was a perfect blue-sky day, and her lips were blissfully swollen from kissing Madigan for hours the night before. They still hadn't done much more since their date, but it wasn't for her lack of trying. Despite what he'd said in Lydia about raising their speed limit, Madigan still wanted to keep their pace slow. So that's what they'd been doing, making out, touching each other over their clothes, grinding against each other like horny teenagers. It was the best kind of torture, but at this point the intensity of her sexual frustration could power a small city. She needed to see his body, to touch his skin, to make him feel—

"Ashley! Hey, Ashley!"

Wheeling around, she spotted Sam walking toward her from the bunny hill, pulling off his cap. "Hi, Sam," she said, hoping her highly inappropriate thoughts weren't painted all over her face. "How are you?"

Too busy worrying at his cap in his hands to even look at her, he said, "I'm good, thanks. Um, do you have a second?"

"Sure. How's life on the bunny hill?"

"It's really great, but that's not what I wanted to talk to you about." After studying his hat for a long moment, he finally looked up. "Madigan told me you met Izzy last week."

Ashley's heart skipped a beat. "We didn't know she worked at Scotty's. I swear."

"Oh, totally," he said, waving her off. "I was just thinking... I was wondering, um, how did she look? I mean, is she doing okay? Did she still seem...mad at me?"

Sam was so much happier these days compared to when she'd first met him, and she didn't want to ruin that for him. She also didn't want to say anything Izzy might not want Sam to know. This, Madigan's world, these men's world, all felt suddenly, staggeringly complicated. "I couldn't say for sure, Sam." She bit her cheek when his eyes met hers, pleading. "But maybe. Maybe she's still upset."

His shoulders sank. "I figured. I'd just hoped..." He shook his head. "I don't know what I hoped."

"Maybe she just needs more time," Ashley offered.

"Maybe," he agreed stoically. "I invited her up for Christmas, but I doubt she'll come. I really fuc— I really messed everything up."

"I'm sorry, Sam." It wasn't enough, but it was all she could give him as she watched him make his way back to the bunny hill, shaking it off as he high-fived a little shredder before helping her zip up the rope for another run.

JUST AS ASHLEY walked into her office, her phone vibrated, four sharp buzzes. *Chuck. Shit.* She'd completely forgotten to tell him Davis was in town. Pulling her phone out of her coat pocket, she sat at her desk, accepted the call, and said a preemptive, "Don't yell at me."

His voice was sickly sweet. "I'd never yell at you, Ash. When have I ever yelled at you?"

She scoffed loud enough that he'd hear it. He'd yelled at her plenty, but Chuck's favorite type of aggression was much more subtle, comments on her appearance, withholding affection, making sure to knock her down a peg if she ever felt even the tiniest bit good about herself. "Davis is here. Did she tell you she was coming?" Since his tone was overly friendly, Ashley figured he wasn't calling about their daughter. This was just his weekly sales pitch.

"She did not," he replied stiffly. "I thought she was working over the break."

Ashley groaned because she knew, somehow, Chuck was going to make this her fault. "The lab made some cuts. She's hoping they'll pick her back up next semester."

"I told you both she should have gone to Montana State. Those liberal hippies in Missoula—"

"You're very wise," she said on an exhale, just wanting this conversation to be over. "She decided to stay and help us out here at Bluebird over the break."

"I don't know that I'm comfortable with Davis spending that much time with convicts. Why don't you just partner with me so we can keep our daughter safe and I can hire you some workers who aren't criminals?"

Although Ashley could still hear Chuck's gratingly condescending voice coming from the phone she'd lowered slowly onto her desk, she wasn't paying attention to her ex anymore. She was paying attention to her beautiful, brand-new, duct tape-free window.

"Ashley? Are you there? Are you even listening to me?"

"I'll call you back," she said, ending the call with zero intentions of calling him back at all. Instead, she swiped her walkie off its charger, walked to the window, and pushed talk.

"Did you fix my window?"

Madigan responded quickly with, *"Do you like it?"*

Running her fingers over the frame, she imagined him sneaking up to her office to put the window in while she was gone. She had no idea he'd even noticed it was cracked. "I love it."

"Merry Christmas, Ashley."

Where Chuck's voice had made her blood run cold, Madigan's melted her bones beneath her skin. Throughout their entire, lengthy, worthless relationship, the nicest thing Chuck had ever done for her was taking out the garbage that one time she'd had the flu. She hadn't even had sex with Madigan yet, and with this single act he'd shifted her world on its axis, redefining everything she thought she knew about romance. Her office had been cold, *she* had been cold for so long. But he was always warm, and now, with this window, he'd brought his warmth to her. She pressed the talk button again. "This is the best present. Thank you."

After a moment, he said, *"Do you think you might ever want to spend the night? Not sex or anything, but just like a sleepover?"*

She nearly dropped the walkie. "You want to have a sleepover?"

"I do."

"When?" she asked.

"Tomorrow? Christmas Eve pajama party at my place?"

She bit back a squeal. "I'll have to ask my mom first, but—"

"No, you will not!" he barked.

Laughing, she said, "Yes. I'd love to have a pajama party with you."

"Good. We can head over here after decorations."

They'd planned to decorate the lodge tomorrow afternoon, just like they did every year as far back as she could remember. But thanks to Madigan, this was the first year she was actually looking forward to the tradition since her dad died. "Thank you again for the window."

"It was my pleasure."

Clutching the walkie to her chest, she spun around in a full circle.

CHAPTER TWENTY-FOUR

MADIGAN

Raising a suggestive brow at Ashley, Madigan pinned a sprig of mistletoe above the ski rack in the lodge, wanting nothing more than to walk to her, pull her into his arms, and dip her into one of those dramatic, old-fashioned movie kisses.

When she winked at him and mouthed, "Later," he accidentally crushed the plastic ornament clutched in his other hand.

Davis, hanging lights over the door next to him, turned her head at the *crunch*.

"So," she said, sidling up to him, "you and my mom, it's getting pretty serious, huh?"

He inadvertently crushed another ornament, continuing his apparent Godzilla-like quest to reign terror on cheap Christmas decorations. "These things are so fragile," he said guiltily, tossing the plastic bits into a nearby trashcan.

Davis laughed with Ashley's laugh, with that same smokey fullness. "It's okay, Madigan. You don't need to be nervous around me. I'm stoked for my mom." Wrapping her fingers around his arm, she pulled him into a corner. "But you *really* pissed off my dad. What did you say to him?"

Davis had just reeled him into deep, uncharted waters. He was no relationship expert, but even he knew that talking to Ashley's daughter about her ex-husband was off limits. "Nothing," he said. "I didn't say anything to him."

"Listen, I love my dad, but he's got, like, zero chill when it comes to my mom."

"I've noticed," he mumbled.

Davis's expression softened. "I know he wasn't a good husband, but he's always been a good father. My mom doesn't realize this, or doesn't care—which is totally her right, I guess," she added. "But my dad is under tremendous stress at Conquest to be successful, and to squash every ski hill in the surrounding areas. That's why he keeps trying to buy Bluebird from Mom. He'd rather acquire Bluebird for WinterMass and try to keep it running than see it go out of business, which is what his bosses want. He really thinks he's trying to be the nice guy here."

Madigan was dubious. "He's trying to be nice by harassing Ashley and pressuring her into selling her beloved family mountain to him?"

Davis shrugged. "In his mind, that's the situation. His life has gone to total shit since Mom kicked him out. He's stressed, miserable, and lonely. All he wants is for her to take him back, and he's used to getting what he wants. So just...be careful."

Still uncomfortable talking about Chuck without Ashley present, Madigan deflected, leaning toward Davis with the crooked grin that had gotten him out of more than one tight spot. "I'm always careful."

"Niiice," she said, nodding slowly. "I can definitely see why Mom is feeling you. 10/10 swoon factor. You must have *killed* when you were my age, just fended off tail left and right I bet."

He stared at her, speechless. He might not be the smartest man in the world, but he knew when he'd been out-manned—or out-womanned, as it were—in a fight, so he did the only smart thing he could and whipped out his little white flag. "I like your mom, Davis. I like her a lot. I might have gotten off on the wrong foot with your dad, but I'd rather not start World War III here. So if you have any advice for me, I'd actually really appreciate it."

With a sigh, she told him, "Stay out of his way. He's pretty shrewd when it comes to getting what he wants. Although," she reconsidered, "anyone who stands between him and Mom is technically in his way, so you may be screwed no matter what you do."

Fantastic. "Thanks, Davis. I feel much better now."

Patting his arm apologetically, she said, "I'll do what I can."

"What were you two talking about?" Ashley asked, joining him under the mistletoe after Davis walked away.

"Oh, nothing much," Madigan said, wishing he could slide his arm around Ashley's waist, bury his nose in her hair, and breathe deep. "Just that apparently Chuck doesn't like me, which we both already knew."

"Hmm," she murmured while watching Davis string more lights right next to where Kev was busy tacking up a string of garland.

"It's weird after getting divorced, having a child who still loves this person you can't stand."

He edged closer to her, enough to wrap his pinky finger briefly around hers. "I've never thought about it that way."

Looking up at him, she asked, "Do you have any children, Madigan?"

Ho boy. He winced. "None that I know of?"

"Oh my god." She palmed her forehead. "Seriously?"

"I told you I used to fuck a lot," he whispered. "I always tried to be safe, but there were times when I'd been so completely gone, I had no idea what I'd done. I reached out to everyone I could remember being with after I got clean, but there were probably a lot of women I couldn't—"

"I get it," she said, cutting him off. "I mean I don't *really* get it, but," she took a breath, "I'm trying not to judge."

"Look, I may not have kids," he said, "but I do have the guys. I feel parental toward them, at least I think I do. I care about them. I worry for them. I feel responsible for them. I'd do just about anything for them if they needed me."

"It's a lot, right? Having a kid is not what I thought it would be. It's like you instantly feel responsible for another human being's happiness, even though you know you have barely any control over it."

He thought about his own parents, how they must have felt watching addiction swallow him up whole. "You are *completely* right about that."

"Davis, she has this man in Missoula, and I don't think he's good for her." Ashley crossed her arms over her chest while they watched Davis and Kev thread garland under the dining hall counter. "She has to find her own way, but it's not always easy to watch. I know she'll be okay. I just don't want her to make the same mistake I did."

"And what mistake was that?"

Turning to face him, she reached up to straighten the collar of his flannel and said softly, "Marrying the wrong man."

He leaned toward her, close enough that when he whispered, "I think I should get away from you," his lips brushed over the shell of her ear.

"Why?" Her shaky exhale hit him straight in the dick.

"Because we're standing under mistletoe, and I really want to kiss you."

"Tonight, though, right?" she said, her body inching closer to his. "Pajama party?"

"Absolutely." Pulling away from her, he bent over and picked up his box of ornaments. When he stood again, he winked and said, "I'll go down on you first, then later I can braid your hair."

CHAPTER TWENTY-FIVE

ASHLEY

After meeting with Maude Alice to go over the state of their outdated rental inventory and discuss their plans for dinner with the men and their families tomorrow night, Ashley stood under a stream of scalding water and set about *preparing* herself. This shower wasn't any normal shower. This was a pre-possible-sex shower. It involved loofas and shaving cream, scrubbing and exfoliating and shaving all the way up. There was lotion and more scrubbing and an extra dose of conditioner because Madigan liked the way it made her hair smell like apple blossoms.

After the shower, she dried her hair, shaved her mustache, plucked the ten or so random hairs that sprouted stubbornly from her chin ever since her hysterectomy, put on a tiny bit of blush and lip gloss, then she looked at herself in the mirror. Even though he'd said tonight was only a sleepover, after years of scarcity—and if he was willing—she was absolutely going to have sex. With Madigan. Tonight. She was even wearing her best set of matching, somewhat sexy lingerie.

"Hey, gorgeous. You coming soon?"

She certainly hoped so. Grabbing her walkie off her sink, she clicked talk and said, "Almost. Why, do you miss me?" She set the walkie back down to fluff out her hair.

"Of course. I miss you whenever you're not with me."

The smile she saw in her reflection made her look ten years younger. "I think you might be the most romantic man I've ever met."

"Plus," he continued, *"I have a massive erection, and I don't know what to do with it."*

She laughed at herself. "Just devastatingly romantic."

"I aim to please."

"I'll be right over."

Throwing on her coat, she almost tripped practically jumping into her boots. After hooking her backpack filled with PJs and clothes for tomorrow over her shoulder, she raced out into the snow and down the path toward his cabin.

"Hi there," he said after he opened his door.

"Madigan." She stared at him, slack-jawed as the fire in his stove crackled in the distance. "You aren't wearing any clothes."

Frowning down at his body, he said, "That's not true. I'm wearing underwear. It's a pajama party, so I figured I'd go ahead and get into my pajamas. Although, to be honest, I usually sleep naked."

"Of course you do," she murmured, entranced by his big shoulders and his pecs and his abs and those V-shaped muscles that cut down from his hips, pointing like an arrow to the bulge in his boxer briefs. And then there were his tattoos, the dusting of soft, pettable hair covering his chest and belly.

Opening the door wider, he stepped out of the way. "What? Don't you?"

"Ah, no," she said, peeling her eyes from him long enough to walk inside. "I sleep in fleece pajamas, knee-high socks, and usually a hoody."

"You're like a mummy!"

She set her backpack on his couch. "I get cold. I don't churn out 5,000 BTUs all the time the way you do."

Walking up behind, her whispered into her ear, "Yeah, but you like my BTUs."

She turned, reaching around him to squeeze his ass, bringing her chest to his. "You do have really cute BTUs."

Breaking the rhythm of their banter, he paused, gazing tenderly into her eyes. "Are you okay? Now that you're here, are you sure you still want to sleep over?"

Had she ever been so sure of anything before in her entire life? But sleeping over with him wasn't the scary part. Putting herself out there, telling him what she really wanted tonight, that was what had tied her stomach in knots all day. Because he might not want the same thing. He might not be ready. He might say no to her, reject her, make her feel stupid and embarrassed and small. *He wouldn't do that,* she told herself, breathing through the fear. He wasn't Chuck. He was good. Madigan was good.

Staring at his chest, calling forth the bravery of her ancestors and the trees and the mountain and anything else charitable enough to help her push out the words, she said, "I know you said we didn't have to, and we don't if you don't want to. But I would—" closing her eyes, she blurted out the rest like she was ripping off a band-aid "—I would very much like to have sex with you tonight if you're okay with—"

Suddenly he swept her into his arms, whisking her up off the floor. While his mouth found hers, the rasp of his beard brushing over her cheeks, she wrapped her legs around his waist as he carried her to his bed and laid her down as gently as if she was made of glass. He didn't speak, and neither did she, because everything was just absolutely happening while he undressed her, releasing the buttons of her shirt one by one, his eyes boring into hers as he slowly slid her shirt open.

"You're absolutely sure about this?" he asked while he unbuttoned her jeans, sliding the zipper down, kissing the exposed skin just below her belly button.

"Y...yes," she managed, slipping her fingers into his hair, her heart a wild thing in her chest.

"Good." He tugged, peeling off her jeans and placing them on his dresser. Standing at the foot of his bed, he stared at her, his gaze traveling up her thighs, making her skin tingle. He smiled at her matching lingerie, navy lace with tiny satin bows. They were nice enough, but she was sure he'd seen nicer. The way he looked at her though, his eyes dark and heavy-lidded, the way he licked his lips, he made her feel better than nice. He made her feel sexy.

His attention roved from her belly to her breasts, her throat, up her neck until his eyes met hers. "Ashley, you are so fucking gorgeous." Not giving her a chance to feel embarrassed or try to deny the compliment, he climbed up her body until he towered over her, his broad shoulders eclipsing most of the room from her view, his hand sliding up her inner thigh.

She let her head fall back to the pillow when he leaned down, his lips closing around her nipple through her bra. Her back arched when his hand reached the apex of her thighs, cupping her, the heel of his palm pressing into her. Glancing down at him again, she watched him pull her bra cup down with his teeth. He kissed her exposed breast, sucking her nipple into his mouth. The image of his lips on her skin and the muscles of his shoulders rolling above her made blood rush hot between her legs. When he shifted her underwear to the side, sliding two fingers up and down through her slickness, settling them at her opening, her hips tilted toward him, her body begging him to push into her.

Instead, he pulled his hand away and raised it up to her other breast, using the lubrication he'd gathered between her legs to tease her nipple, moving his fingertips in slippery circles over its sensitive surface.

"That feels so good," she breathed, trying hard not to grind against the leg he'd slid between hers. She didn't want to seem too eager, too needy, but her restraint was a frayed rope about to snap.

Raising his head, he grinned at her. "I might not be good at a lot of things. But this? This I am fucking *great* at." As if to prove his point beyond a shadow of a doubt, he slid down her body, hooking his fingers into the thin band of her underwear and pulling them off. Finding the strip of damp lace from how wet he'd already gotten her, he held it up to his nose and inhaled deeply, moaning appreciatively. It was the single most erotic moment of her life, his face buried in navy lace, his eyes locked onto hers until they fluttered closed like he was in ecstasy. No matter what happened between them after tonight, she would, she knew, keep those navy panties forever.

Tossing the sacred panties over his shoulder—where they landed right on top of her jeans—he kissed her right thigh, her left. Then, settling on his belly between her legs, he kissed the swollen, throbbing bud of her clit.

"Madigan," she gasped. The last time she'd had a man's head between her legs had been before Davis was born. Chuck didn't like going down on her, so it almost never happened. Sinking into the deep, slippery sensation of Madigan's tongue gliding slowly over her sensitive skin, she realized it might as well have never happened. Because whatever Chuck had tried to do with her so long ago had felt nowhere near as good as this.

With his fingers splayed wide on her belly, Madigan's hand pushed down, holding her in place while his tongue traced her opening, up along one side, and then the other. When it slid inside her, she left the confines of her body. He thrust his tongue in and out of her, tasting her, fucking her, pulling out to roll and flick the slippery tip over her clit. The sensation was so intense it was almost painful. She whined. She whimpered. She tried not to grind against his face, but it was nearly impossible.

His hand on her belly pushed her down even harder, holding her still while the rest of her body threatened to float off the bed. He rolled his tongue over her clit again, slow and firm, warm and wet, while his finger teased her opening.

"Please," she begged him, desperate to have his finger inside her.

"What do you want, Ashley?" he asked her, blowing a stream of air onto her sensitive skin, making her gasp. "Tell me what you want, and it's yours."

Refusing to feel embarrassed even though insecurity lurked just behind the bright pleasure rolling through her entire body, she whispered, "I want your finger inside me."

Finally, and so slowly she had to fight not to scream, he slid his thick finger inside her, pressing up toward her front wall. "Like that?" he asked, blowing on her again.

"Yes."

He slid his finger in and out, his tongue flat and pressing into her clit. The pressure was mind-numbing, enough to keep her right on the edge of climax but not enough to push her over.

"Please," she begged again, almost frantic, losing control in a way she didn't think was possible anymore. Her hands fisted in his sheets as he pushed a second finger inside her.

"Does that feel good?" he asked in between soft licks and feathering kisses.

"Yes." Was there a word stronger than yes? *Hellyes? Fuckyes?*

"Does this make it better?" His other hand, releasing its pressure on her stomach, slid up her chest, his finger and thumb pinching and rolling her nipple between them.

"Oh, god, yes. Yes! Fuckyes!" she shouted, louder than she'd ever been in bed. She might have felt self-conscious about her volume if she wasn't so busy riding his fingers while his tongue flicked, his lips closing around her as he sucked her over the edge. Pleasure, hot and unrelenting, barreled through her, forking like lightning from her belly to her back, blazing down her legs to spark into her toes. She was breathing so hard she felt dizzy, her fingertips going numb while he licked and sucked and moaned against her until she had to push his head away.

He bit her inner thigh, a tiny pinch. Then he smacked her clit once, hard, making her jump as the sting of pain and burst of pleasure spiraled through her until her vision went hazy. The smack was so unexpected, so exactly what she needed but didn't realize she could ever have that a part of her misfiring brain wondered if she'd imagined it. If it wasn't for the sweet, hot burn his fingers left behind, she might have convinced herself she had.

He'd wrung her out, tensing and relaxing every muscle in her body, leaving her heavy and warm and expanding, spreading out, losing the boundaries of herself as she sank deeply into his mattress. When he climbed back up the bed, brushing her hair back off her sweaty neck, kissing her forehead, her nose, her lips, she couldn't even open her eyes to look at him.

"Can I make love to you? I need..." His soft curls brushed over her cheek, his forehead resting against her shoulder. "I need you. I need to be inside you."

She said the only word that came to mind. The only word she knew anymore. The best word. "Fuckyes."

CHAPTER TWENTY-SIX

MADIGAN

ASHLEY WAS PURE, unadulterated sin lying on his bed, breathing hard, her lips wet and parted, cheeks rosy with a post-orgasm flush. He'd missed this. He'd missed blissing a woman out so hard she needed a minute or two to come back online. Cherishing them with every touch, every kiss, every lick. *Every slap.*

He winced. That might have been a little too much for his first time going down on her, but he couldn't help himself—the way she'd squirmed underneath his mouth, her hand pushing his head away like she couldn't take another second, her pink, swollen skin...

"Ashley," he said, running his nose up the side of her neck, kissing a line back down. "Are you ready?"

When her eyes finally cracked open, her lips tilted into a smile. "Almost."

Rolling her to the side so he could unclasp her bra and take it off, he told her, "Take all the time you need," while praying silently she wouldn't need long.

When she extended her arms over her head, stretching her entire body out long, her pert tits pointing straight up toward the ceiling, he thought he might be dying.

"That was amazing," she said.

"*You're* amazing," he replied, kissing her neck, her chest, the swell of her breast.

Reaching her hand down between them, running her palm over his painfully hard erection through his underwear, she said, "I want to see it. I want to see you."

"You do?" He pushed his throbbing cock into her hand.

"I've felt you." She stroked him again. "But I haven't seen you."

Brushing his lips over hers, he said, "Your wish is my command." Then he scooted to the end of the bed, stood up, and turned to face her. He felt surprisingly self-conscious, stripping naked in front of her while she watched him carefully, almost studiously, like she might take notes, maybe make a quick sketch. *Just do it,* he told himself. *What's the worst that could happen?* Throwing caution to the wind, he leaned forward and slid his boxer briefs down over his erection, kicking them off to the side.

She didn't say a word, her eyes ratcheting wider and wider.

"What?" He glanced down. He wasn't huge by any stretch, but women had always appreciated his dick. It was nice and thick, straight as an arrow, and just long enough. Had it changed so much over the years? "Is it bad?"

"No, it's not bad," she said distantly, staring transfixed at his cock like it was a hypnotist's watch swinging between his legs. "It's," her throat worked through a swallow, "very nice. You have a very nice dick."

"It'll get the job done," he said, his swagger returning little by little as he took himself in hand and stroked himself in front of her.

"I'm...sure it will."

Her pulse bounded above her collar bone, her pupils blown, her eyes still glued to his hand and his cock and the bead of moisture gathering at his head. Letting go of himself, he crawled back onto the bed, hovering over her body. He kissed her again, deep and slow, then he rose up to kneel between her legs. When he leaned over to fish a condom out of his nightstand drawer, clamping the wrapper between his teeth to tear it open, she said, "You don't need that."

He lowered the condom. "Come again?"

"We've both tested negative, right?"

"Yeah, but what about the other thing? It's not too late for you to get—"

"I've had a hysterectomy. Nothing to worry about there."

The condom dropped from his fingers, landing on the bed with a soft thud. "That is the single hottest thing any woman has ever said to me."

She laughed, scraping her nails gently along his thighs. "I'm sure that's not true."

"Oh, it is. Believe me. But," he frowned, "I've never been bare with a woman before, at least none that I can remember." At this admission, an old, deep fear pushed its way to the surface. What if the sensation of being inside her without a condom after not having been inside a woman for so many years made him start craving sex in an unhealthy way again? Or, and more likely, what if he only lasted for two pathetic thrusts? "I don't know—"

"You can use a condom if you want to," she said. "It's not a big deal. Whatever makes you comfortable. I just want you to be comfortable."

She was concerned about his comfort. *His* comfort. Something, some feeling, some emotion that had lived tight and guarded inside his chest unfurled, spreading out warm beneath his ribs like sunlight. He knew she liked him, that they had a connection. But whether she shared any of the emotions that surged through him whenever he looked at her, touched her, thought about her, he had no idea. He knew he should have asked her how she felt about him already, made sure his heart would be safe in her hands. But there was no way in hell he was going to bring it up now. He was just going to cross his fingers and make love to this gorgeous, willing woman until she moaned his name in that way he couldn't get enough of. And hope that he truly was ready for this, for sex, for intimacy. That was enough to worry about for one night.

"I'm good. No condoms," he said, grinning down at her. "But do you need anything? I've heard after a person's had a hysterectomy they can need lube."

Grinning back up at him, she said, "Sometimes, since the surgery. But," she took his hand, settling it between her legs, letting him feel how wet she still was, "not tonight."

Taking full advantage of the invitation, he slid two fingers inside her, making her gasp. "Definitely not tonight," he said, sliding back out. He took himself in hand, rubbing his head up and down between her folds, covering himself in her slickness. "Are you ready?"

She nodded, her eyes locked onto his in this intimate game of trust. He wasn't going to look away, not until she looked away first, not until he was fully seated inside her. Slowly, he pushed into her, and it was like sinking into heaven.

"Hmmmm," she murmured, biting her lower lip, which was a thing she did whenever he made her feel good, he knew. Because he knew some things about her now, about her body and what it liked. But he wanted to know more. He wanted to know everything.

Sliding out a little, he pushed back in, deeper and deeper with each small thrust until he bottomed out. Lowering himself onto his elbows just to be closer to her, to feel her body under his, he asked, "Does that feel good?"

"Yes."

"How do you like it, Ashley?" He slid slowly in and out of her.

"I... I don't know," she said, her eyes falling closed at his leisurely pace. "It's only ever been one way. With Ch—"

"You mean He Who Must Not Be Named in Bed?" Madigan said, thrusting into her a little harder. "Let me guess, it was quick, boring, then over before you even got close?"

With her eyes still closed, she nodded.

"Well, let's find out what you like. Do you like it slow?"

She answered by way of hooking her heels behind his slowly rolling hips, pulling him closer.

"Maybe you like it deep."

Her fingernails dug into his shoulders as he pushed as deeply into her as he could.

"Or maybe," he said, pulling back a little, sliding his head along her front wall, "you like it shallow."

"Shit, Madigan," she said, her breath picking up.

"That's it, isn't it?" Her body was so warm and soft, and without a layer of latex between them, he felt every nuance of her, every soft ridge, every wet, gripping muscle. He wasn't going to last long, but he'd last long enough. Or at least he thought he would until she tipped her hips, rocking in time with his thrusts, pulling his head down, guiding his mouth onto hers. He was, he realized as he kissed her fiercely while working tirelessly at her G-spot, coming dangerously close to Chuck-ing the entire thing up.

No fucking way. He'd hold out. Even if it literally killed him, he'd hold out. But he had to be deeper. He needed to be all the way inside her when she came. He needed to feel her muscles closing all around him. After a few more strokes over her G-spot, her moans growing louder with each pass, he drove into her, making her cry out. Moving his hips in a steady rhythm, he held his body up so he could bring his hand between them and press his thumb over her clit. In an instant, her breathing changed, speeding up as her fingers wrapped around his neck, her legs squeezing his hips.

"Are you going to come again? Are you getting close?" he asked, even though he knew.

"Ah, ah," she cried, one for each thrust, "yes!"

Distract yourself, old man. Think about bee stings, the dumpster at Little Timber on garbage day, leprechauns...

Since this pace was working for her, he didn't dare change a thing. Even though he was rusty, he still knew exactly what to wait for, the cues from her that he should move faster, thrust harder, push deeper.

There. Her teeth sinking into her bottom lip again, that moan that sounded like pain and pleasure all rolled into one. And mercifully, *there*, those devastating sighs, her breaths quick and harsh until finally it was time to give her everything he had. A bead of sweat rolled between his shoulder blades as he drove into her, hard and fast and relentless.

Dropping his mouth to hers, he kissed her, swallowing her moans while his entire life force trickled over his skin, through his veins, converging at the base of his spine. In three more thrusts, three more circles of his thumb, she came apart beneath him, her walls clamping down, squeezing, milking, jerking his orgasm out of his grip until he had no choice but to let go.

CHAPTER TWENTY-SEVEN

ASHLEY

"MADIGAN?" She tapped his shoulder after coming out of her post-coital haze. He'd rolled most of his weight off her, but she couldn't move the arm still pinned underneath him, and her fingers were starting to tingle. "Are you asleep?"

"Nope," he mumbled into her neck. "I'm up. Did you want to go again? Might take me a minute or two... but..." His voice faded, slurring, becoming adorably less and less coherent with each word.

Nudging him over just enough to free her arm, she sat up and rolled her head from side to side. Her core still thrummed, vibrating with the aftershocks of two of the most intense orgasms she'd ever experienced. But every other part of her body felt deeply relaxed, even her skin, even her hair. It was official, she was about to turn forty-seven, and she'd just had, hands down, the most phenomenal sexual encounter of her life. This was not something twenty-year-old Ashley would have imagined in her wildest dreams.

When she stared down at her naked body, she looked different somehow. Her nipples were pink, her breasts full, her curves—even the ones she didn't particularly like—glowing in the firelight. Her body had become a utilitarian thing since her divorce, since the last half of her marriage if she was being honest. Something she barely looked at and only touched when necessary or after reading a good romance. Bathed in flickering firelight, after having Madigan inside her, taking his time with her, wringing every last bit of pleasure out of her he could, she thought she didn't look half bad.

Turning her head to examine the naked man sprawled out beside her, his eyes closed, his breathing slow and steady, she thought he didn't look half bad either. Actually, he looked unbelievable, like his sole purpose on the planet was to satisfy women and look unbelievable afterward. Not wanting to wake him, but not able to leave him alone either, she leaned over to kiss his shoulder. The yellow and orange firelight danced over his skin, over his broad, tattooed shoulders, his long back, his perfectly round ass. But the fire was waning, the warmth in the cabin giving way to a slight chill. Scooting forward, she tried to make her way to the foot of the bed only for a thick, strong arm to slide across her waist and pull her back.

"You're not leaving me, are you?"

She snuggled back down, stretching out next to him. His face was smushed into his pillow, his one visible eye only halfway open. She ran her fingers over the ridge of his cheekbone. "No, I'm not leaving. But the fire needs wood."

Rolling up onto his side so their bodies aligned, he slid a hand along her outer thigh, over her hip, his fingertips ghosting up her side until his hand settled over her breast. "I think I fell asleep."

"You did."

"Sorry," he said, the sweetest, sleepiest smile on his lips.

"You worked hard. You definitely earned some rest."

He laughed, as low and deep as the ocean, his post-sex laugh.

"Was it good for you?" he asked, his eyes opening enough to find hers.

She wanted to tell him the sex had been phenomenal, transcendent, life changing. But even after all they'd just done together, her nerves crept back in, her fear that if she said too much, went too far, gave him too much of herself, he'd end up not wanting it or finding something wrong with it. *With her.* "It was really good," she eventually said, disappointed in herself because why couldn't she just tell him how she felt?

His thumb sweeping over her nipple swept her thoughts and fears out of her mind, at least for the moment. "Well," he murmured, "you know what they say?"

Covering his hand on her breast with hers, feeling the way his fingers moved while he worked her nipple between them, she said, "No. What do they say?"

He hummed softly. "Once you go thick, nothing else does the trick."

She snorted. "Nobody says that."

"Yeah, but they should." Lifting his hand from her breast, he brought her fingers to his lips and kissed them. "You stay put. I'll get the fire."

While she watched him slide off the bed and walk to the stove, kneeling to start feeding logs into the fire, something in the corner of his room caught her eye. She'd never noticed before, a silver, rectangular box.

Leaning forward, she squinted, trying to make out the shape in the low light. "Is that a boombox?"

Stoking the flames, he said, "Sure is. Dual cassette. Perfect for making mixtapes."

He made mixtapes. This man who sang to her and said the sweetest things and fucked her like she'd special ordered him made mixtapes. "Perfect," she agreed, staring at his long back and strong shoulders as he worked at the fire, wondering if he'd ever make a mixtape for her.

When he stood again, wood snapping like fireworks behind him, he turned to face her. He must have known how good he looked to stand before her so easily, completely naked, covering nothing up. He must have known how sexy—

"Ashley," he said, his voice light, "are you staring at my dick?"

Shit. Heat flamed her cheeks, and her first inclination was to cover her mouth, her eyes, anything to hide her desire from him. But he wasn't hiding. He was only standing there, waiting, watching her with his arms at his sides, his cock swelling. No fear, no games, just Madigan. Maybe she didn't have to hide either.

Pushing herself up to her hands and knees, she crawled to sit on the edge of the bed, sliding her legs wide so he could stand between them. "Yes." She peered up at him through her lashes. "I was staring at your dick."

He gazed down at her, and his openly aroused expression was a gift. His boldness made her bold. His confidence made her confident. His honesty made her feel safe to say things to him she'd never say to anyone else.

His fingers slid over her jaw, his hands tilting her face up toward his. "I've been so afraid of this, of intimacy, for so long"

"Are you still afraid?" she asked, turning to kiss his palm.

"No." He smiled. "Everything feels different with you."

Her eyes on his, she wrapped her hands around his hips, running her fingers over the firm curves of his ass. "But you can't really say that."

"I can't?" His brows pulled together. "Why not?"

"You can't say everything is different with me yet, because we haven't *done* everything yet."

His erection bobbed. "We haven't?" he whispered, his hands leaving her face to gather her hair up into a ponytail. "What did we forget?"

Leaning forward, she took him in her hands and kissed the tip of his cock. "Lots." When she licked the bead of moisture from his slit, he closed his eyes, sucking in air through his teeth.

Pushing him back a step so she could sink to her knees in front of him, she thought briefly about the last time she'd given a blowjob and how much she'd hated it. She'd known Chuck had been cheating, and she'd been trying anything to make him come back to her. He'd barely gotten hard in her mouth and definitely hadn't finished there. It was embarrassing, uncomfortable, and about the farthest thing from sexy she could possibly imagine. But everything *was* different with Madigan, because this was sexy. His hands holding her hair back out of her way, his eyes closed, abs tight, the sounds coming from his throat as she slid the tip of her tongue along the underside of his shaft, she'd never felt sexier. She gripped his base, gentle but firm, holding him steady while she licked a broad circle around his head before taking him into her mouth.

"Ashley," he groaned, letting go of her hair with one hand to cup her cheek, running his thumb over the corner of her mouth where it stretched around him. "So good. You feel so good."

Grasping his hips, she took him in as deeply as she could, bobbing her head, wanting to make him feel as good and as desired as he'd made her feel. Actually, *god help her*, wanting to taste him, to swallow every drop of him. And she hated the taste of semen. But Madigan's, his tasted sweeter somehow. His was delicious.

"I'm close," he strained to say, tugging on her hair, trying to pull out of her mouth.

Shaking her head, she dug her fingers into his hips and held him tight, wanting him to finish right where he was. When he came, fisting her hair, his entire body flexing as he thrust into her mouth so deeply her eyes watered, she swallowed all of him, relishing every grunt and groan and curse that flew from his mouth. After he was done, she pulled back, kissed his belly, and stared up at him with a triumphant grin.

His breath ragged, chest heaving, he gazed down at her in utter gratitude. "Thank you."

"My pleasure," she replied, running her hands up the backs of his thighs.

"You get to be my age and kind of worry that you'll never get another blowjob for the rest of your life."

Sitting back on her heels, she said, "I'm honored to have put that worry to rest. But now that we've gotten all that out of the way," she tilted her head, "is this the part where you braid my hair?"

His barked laughter echoed through the cabin. "I'm actually pretty good at braiding hair."

"Why am I not surprised?"

Holding out a hand to help her up to her feet, he pointed his chin toward her bag. "Did you want to mummy-up first? Or," his gaze swept down her body, licking at her like the flames from the fire, "will you let me keep you warm tonight?"

She pressed her lips into his chest, right over his heart, and said, "I think you know which one I want."

Without another word, he hoisted her up into his arms, carried her back into bed, and kissed her slowly, deeply, pressing her into her pillow with such blind passion she could have kept at it with him all night, no matter how exhausted they'd be in the morning. But eventually they pulled apart, and she rolled onto her side while he slid in behind her, notching himself into place like he'd done it a thousand times, like it was where he'd always belonged.

Stop, she told herself. *Don't overthink this. It was just great sex. Really great, really hot, really...surprising.*

"Madigan?" she asked, remembering something.

"Yes?" he said, his sleepy voice rumbling through his chest where it pressed against her back.

"Did you...*smack* me earlier?"

Burrowing his face into her hair, he squeaked out a tentative, "Maybe?"

She fought back a smile, pulling his hand up to snuggle it under her chin. "That's what I thought. I liked it, in case you were wondering."

"Well, you know, sometimes you have to remind a pussy who's boss."

Their bodies shook as they laughed together until heavy paws thundering up the cabin steps interrupted them.

"I thought you left him with Maude Alice?" Madigan whispered into her ear.

"I did," she whispered back. "He must have escaped."

"Why do I feel like we're in trouble?" he asked as a single, booming, pissed-off bark shook the cabin.

"Probably because we are," she grumbled. Slipping out from under his arm, she padded toward the door. Getting ready to turn the doorknob, she warned, "Brace yourself." And then one hundred and fifty pounds of snow-covered dog charged through the door, launched onto the bed, and slobbered all over Madigan's laughing face.

The last thing Ashley remembered before drifting off to sleep was Madigan's warm body curled around hers, his face buried in her hair, and Murphy sprawled out long across their feet, snoring like a bear.

CHAPTER TWENTY-EIGHT

ASHLEY

Music roused her, the strumming of strings, notes rising and falling in a soft melody. Her eyes slid open, her vision focusing on countless sparkling motes of dust as they danced inside a ray of sunlight streaming through the window.

"Good morning, beautiful." His voice was quiet, far away.

Memories filtered in through the haze. She was in Madigan's cabin. She'd spent the night. They'd finally had sex, and it had been amazing. At some point while she slept, she'd rolled onto her belly. Still in this position now, completely naked, she wished she could be comfortable like this. But she felt his eyes on her, and the temptation to cover up overwhelmed her. Reaching down, she patted the bed, trying to find something to throw over herself.

"Don't you dare," he sang along with whatever song he was playing. "I'm not finished watching you."

His voice had a depth and richness to it, a little gravelly but with a pure, honest tone. He was a rock star, a famous musician, and he was serenading her. She stopped searching for the sheet.

"You'd better still be naked too," she said into her pillow, hiding her face in the soft down.

"Fully dressed. This is just what you get for sleeping in."

Whipping her head around, she was about to give him hell when she realized in a moment of stunned silence that he had not told her the truth. Sitting in the rocking chair next to the bed, Matthew Madigan wore nothing but his guitar and a smile.

"You're so sexy," she told him, watching the muscles of his forearm shift and ripple while he strummed, his long fingers pressing into the frets.

When he sang again, "I know you are, but what am I?" breaking into a soulful falsetto, a shiver raced across her neck.

"It's true," she said, appreciating him the way an art lover might appreciate a beautiful painting. "You're magnificent."

He didn't look up from his guitar. "That is, ironically, what Madigan means: *magnificent*."

"It is not," she said, smiling.

"You're right." He smiled back at her, pausing his strumming long enough to point at his Mary tattoo. "It means *little dog*."

"Little?" She scoffed. "Not very fitting, if you ask me." Of all the adjectives she might choose to describe him, 'little' would be last on the list. He was big, strong, thick, and she wanted to feel those big, strong, thick arms around her again as quickly as possible. Crawling off the bed, she took his guitar from him, set it down carefully in its case, and assumed its place in his lap.

The hand that had been strumming strings slid up her thigh, the one that had cradled the guitar's neck rose to cradle hers.

Staring into his eyes, smoothing his beard down with her fingers, she whispered, "Play me an encore?"

Sex in a rocking chair was surprisingly sensual. Cradled in his lap, her back resting against his chest, one of her hands looped behind his neck, the other grasping his arm so she could feel his muscles pulse and flex while his fingers played between her legs, she came for hours, days, millennia. Until she leaned forward, braced herself on his knees, and rode him so hard her legs shook, his fingers digging into her hips and his grunted, filthy words making her come a second time.

Sometime later, as he kissed up her neck to that spot right behind her ear that always made her shiver, he whispered, "Merry Christmas, Ashley."

She couldn't explain it, but her smile faded, that shiver turning suddenly into something cold and heavy that sank over her shoulders, prickling along her skin like frozen mist. In that instant, held in his arms, she knew with utter certainty that she would never, ever have another man as good for her as he was. But she didn't really have him. He was temporary. *This* was temporary. He'd leave when the season ended, and after that?

"Is everything okay?" he asked, his arms loosening around her. "You're shivering. Are you cold?"

Turning to the side in his lap so she could rest her head against him, she said, "I'm fine, just tired."

His sigh expanded his chest. "Me too. I guess that's what we get for fucking-while-old instead of sleeping."

She laughed, ignoring the emotion stinging her eyes. "Who are you calling old?"

"You're right. Just me." He tucked her head under his chin. "With you, I'm practically a cradle-robber."

After a quiet moment watching slants of morning sunlight move across his cabin while he rocked her back and forth, she decided it hurt too much to wonder how long she'd be able to feel his arms around her like this. Instead, even knowing how much pain and loss she'd feel once they were gone, she decided to enjoy them fully while she could. "Merry Christmas to you too, Madigan," she said, placing her hand over his heart. "I hope you get everything you want."

Pulling her in close, he kissed her head and said, "I'm pretty sure I just did."

CHAPTER TWENTY-NINE

MADIGAN

MADIGAN HAD JUST CLOSED his eyes when someone knocked rapid-fire on his door, making Murphy bark and Ashley catapult from his lap, leaping back into bed and diving under his blanket.

"Who is it?" he growled at the door, thinking that at this hour somebody had better be dying or on fire.

"It's Ashley's mother. And watch your tone, young man."

Sitting bolt upright, Ashley called out, "Mother? What are you doing here?"

"I need to come in," Maude Alice replied. "It's important."

When Madigan looked at Ashley, her eyes went round as acorns as she shook her head at him and mouthed, "*No.*"

He grimaced. He didn't want to upset Ashley, but the last thing he wanted to do was piss off Maude Alice. Making his choice, accepting his fate, he shouted, "Just a second," before mouthing, "*Forgive me,*" back at Ashley.

Throwing on a pair of jeans and a T-shirt, feeling Ashley fuming behind him, he grasped the doorknob. He'd planned to pull the door open a crack, tell Maude Alice they'd be right out, and apologize profusely to Ashley afterward. But the instant he turned the knob,

Murphy barged past him, shoving the door half-way open with his sizable, furry bulk before galloping out into the snow.

"Good morning, Maude Alice," Madigan said, trying to save his ass by stepping out onto his porch and closing the door behind him. "What can we do for you?"

"Well," Maude Alice said, looking him up and down, her eyes squinty, "don't you look...*refreshed* this morning."

Ashley had been right. He shouldn't have opened the door. "Thanks, um, you too." Running a hand through his bedhead, he shivered because he was an idiot standing outside barefoot in a short-sleeved shirt on Christmas morning in Montana. "Cold out here, isn't it?"

"I need my daughter. I have a surprise for her. Ashley!" she shouted past him. "Get up!"

At that precise moment, Clay, Kev, and Sam walked by his cabin, all three men shaking their heads at him while they took in the scene of their hastily dressed leader standing with the mother of his brand-new lover on his porch. Kev mimed a knife cutting across his throat, his tongue lolling out of the side of his mouth.

Gritting his teeth, Madigan flipped them the bird down by his hip where he hoped Maude Alice wouldn't notice.

"Go away, Mother," Ashley grumbled through the door. "I'm busy."

Arching an insinuating brow at Madigan, Maude Alice said, "I can see that." And then a bit louder, "But I'm not leaving until you come out."

Ashley groaned, and when she cursed harshly, Madigan saw unmistakable hurt flicker in and out of Maude Alice's eyes.

"We'll get up," he told her. "Just give us a minute."

Patting his arm, she said, "Thank you, Madigan. You know, I'd hoped spending more time with you would have put her in a better mood. I think you need to work harder."

He opened his mouth, then closed it again, choosing silence as his best, and probably only, defense.

Ashley stomped through the snow in front of him, the view of her perfect ass in her jeans almost making up for how cold he was. Whatever it was Maude Alice wanted to show them, he sincerely hoped it was worth every second he could have been spending naked with Ashley this morning. When they came to the clearing at the base of one of the beginner runs on the far side of the mountain, Ashley slammed to a halt so quickly Madigan almost ran into her.

"Holy shit," she whispered, her hand flying to her chest.

All the men, along with Shannon, Davis, and Mace, stared down at them with huge smiles, standing in front of the last in a line of three massive jumps.

Ashley's head turned slowly toward him, fire blazing in her eyes. "Did you know about this?"

He took a step back so he didn't burst into flames. "No, I mean, not really." He could tell it was the wrong thing to say the moment the words left his lips.

Squaring off with him, her voice deadly calm, she said, "What do you mean, not really?"

"Last week Maude Alice asked if she could borrow some of the men to move some equipment, but I had no idea that this was what they were doing. I swear." He lowered his voice. "Is this a bad thing? It seems kind of cool."

With a fake smile plastered onto her face for the crew, Ashley gritted out, "Yes, it's a very bad thing. I'm going to kill her."

"So," Maude Alice said, walking down from the jump she'd been standing proudly in front of, "what do you think of your Christmas present?"

"What do I think?" Ashley's voice was so quiet Madigan could barely hear her. "I think you've lost your mind. Why, Mother? How?"

"We worked all week, very early and very late every day," Maude

Alice said, her shoulders pinned back, her hands on her hips. "We wanted to surprise you."

Taking in the rest of the run, Madigan finally noticed the other pieces of equipment they'd installed alongside the jumps. He didn't know anything about terrain parks, but it seemed like a lot.

"Rails, boxes, a wall ride!" Ashley hissed. Stepping into Maude Alice's space, she demanded, "How much did this cost?"

"Calm down, Ashley," Maude Alice said, dismissing her concern with a flick of her wrist. "This is what credit cards are for, isn't it? Bluebird needed something big and exciting." She threw an arm out to the side, sweeping over the run like Vanna White. "What's more exciting than a terrain park?"

Ashley's nostrils flared, her jaw muscles flickering. "What credit cards, Mother? We don't *have* any credit cards. All of ours are maxed."

"I opened a new one," Maude Alice replied airily. "Stop giving me that look, daughter. It's fine."

If Madigan knew anything, it was when something wasn't fine. And this situation, this surprise terrain park, was far from fine. Standing between Ashley and her mother, he felt suddenly like he was a wall separating two armies about to charge headfirst into battle.

"We cannot open another card," Ashley bit out. "I've been busting my ass trying to restore our credit rating. This will completely ruin all the progress I've made. How could you do this without talking to me about it first?"

Glaring at Ashley, her expression as icy as Ashley's was searing, Maude Alice said, "You're making a scene. All these people worked very hard to build this park for you. Why are you always so ungrateful?"

Madigan sucked in a breath. This was a direct hit he felt in his own gut, and all he wanted to do was get Ashley and Maude Alice away from here, take them somewhere private to work this out before they brought the entire mountain down. "Why don't we go talk about this inside," he suggested.

"There is nothing to talk about," Ashley stated with finality. "All of this goes back tomorrow."

"I'm afraid that's not possible," Maude Alice said, regaining her composure. "It's non-refundable once installed. You worry too much, Ashley. You'll see. This park will bring in enough money to pay for itself in just a few seasons." And with that, Maude Alice walked away, clapping her hands at the crew and shouting, "She loves it!"

With a strained, exasperated noise, Ashley spun around and started marching back toward the lodge.

Madigan rushed to join her. "It'll be okay," he said. "I think she was just trying to help." Words poured out of his mouth, and he couldn't make them stop. "Maybe she's right. Maybe it will pay for itself in—"

Wheeling on him, she snapped, "Are you kidding me right now?" Her gaze was ferocious, her words razor sharp. "This will not be all right. I'll have to spend the entire day fixing this mess, and you think she was only trying to help? Oh, I get it." Her laughter was humorless. "Poor Maude Alice, right? Her daughter is *so* mean to her, and she's never done anything to deserve it."

His hands rose in equal parts surrender and self-defense. "You're right. I'm sorry. I just thought that with the money we'll make from the concert, you'd be able to pay this off soon—"

"I don't have time to wait for some stupid concert!"

He recoiled, surprisingly hurt. "I'm sorry. I didn't realize it was stupid."

"That's not what I meant," she groaned. "Or maybe it is. I don't know. I don't know anything right now except that I need to find out how much she spent and figure out how to pay it back."

Turning away from him again, she stormed back to the lodge. Only this time he didn't follow.

CHAPTER THIRTY

ASHLEY

PACING BACK and forth in her room, Ashley chewed on her thumbnail. She'd spent the rest of the morning into the afternoon digging through Maude Alice's office, finding receipts, tallying costs for the equipment, calculating the additional payroll because there was no way she'd let anyone who'd worked on the terrain park at Maude Alice's bidding go unpaid for their time. After she'd added everything up, she'd nearly screamed.

The damage was astronomical, Thousands of dollars they didn't have and couldn't recoup quickly enough to make the minimum monthly payments on their maxed-out credit cards—including the new card Maude Alice had opened that Ashley would have to pay off and close immediately if she hoped to keep their barely rehabilitated credit score from tanking. If they ever hoped to be approved for a loan to buy new groomers or replace broken lifts parts or develop the downhill mountain bike course she'd been dreaming about opening someday so the mountain could have steady revenue all year long. Even with the possible proceeds of the concert she'd unforgivably called stupid, after this stunt, they'd be lucky if they could cover payroll next month. Bluebird Basin was already a sinking ship, and with this terrain park, her mother had just kicked a hole in the hull and hurled their last bucket over the side.

When she walked into Maude Alice's office again, her mother was sitting at her desk. Closing the door behind her with a snick, Ashley said, "Mother," trying to keep her voice under control, "please tell me what in the hell you were thinking!" Her control didn't last long.

Continuing to rifle through some random papers, Maude Alice said, "I did something nice for you and for the mountain. We'll get more boarders in now, don't you think?"

"Boarders can't board at a closed mountain," Ashley ground out. "We can't afford this."

When Maude Alice's eyes rolled, Ashley's jaw clenched. "Money, money, money. That's all you ever care about."

"Because, Mother, you put me in charge of the money when you asked me to take control of the mountain. Believe me, I am more than happy to give that control back to you if that's what you want."

"No, dear. You're doing a wonderful job with the mountain."

"You're making it impossible for me to do any kind of job with the mountain!" Ashley cried, her blood boiling. Glancing frantically around the office, she tried to find something to smash, only spotting a small Christmas tree decoration made from wire and tinsel on a shelf that would probably hit the wall with all the satisfaction of a feather.

"I wanted to surprise you." Maude Alice shrugged in a display of wounded innocence.

"Don't you dare play the victim," Ashley said. "Don't you dare make me the bad guy. I am not the bad guy just because I refuse to run this mountain into the ground. Dad would be furious with what you just did!"

Hurt and rage twisted Maude Alice's features as she rose slowly to her feet. "What did you just say?"

This was a fight they'd danced around since her dad died, but this time Ashley refused to hold anything back, letting three years of pent-up frustration pour out of her like a bubbling, toxic river overtaking its banks. "Dad wanted this mountain to survive. It was everything to him. If I didn't know better, I'd think you were sabotaging me. I'd think you wanted me to have to sell the mountain to Chuck."

"You take that back," Maude Alice snapped, her voice hoarse with an emotion Ashley hadn't heard in so long it made her mother sound like an entirely different person. "I *love* Bluebird. I would do anything for this mountain. You're the one terrified of taking any risks. You'd watch us slowly drown before you'd ever risk grabbing for a branch."

Ashley reeled, the words colliding with her chest so hard she stumbled back a step. "I am *not* terrified of taking risks. I'm just realistic. And I'm not so obsessed with being the center of attention that I ignore the consequences of my actions. I don't live my life pretending I'm not aware that my need to be the biggest personality in the room makes everyone else around me shrink!" These were Madigan's words coming out of her mouth because he'd been right. But there was so much more, and it all forced itself out of her. "I'm not the one so scared of my feelings that I've spent the last three years pretending that my husband, my daughter's father, never even existed!" Her voice broke, angry tears filling her eyes.

Maude Alice's gaze was lacerating. "You have no idea what you're talking about. No idea, you selfish child."

"Then tell me!" Ashley cried. "Tell me why we aren't ever allowed to talk about him? I need to talk about him. He was my dad, and I miss him—"

Maude Alice's hands slammed down on her desk. "But he was *my* husband, and he left me! He left me all alone!" As swiftly as this honesty roared out of her, it retreated, curling in on itself. Sitting again, Maude Alice gathered the papers on her desk, shutting down just like she did every single time Ashley tried to bring Max up.

She'd never change, Ashley realized. Never. "You're right, Mother. I *don't* understand. I will never understand how pretending someone never existed is easier than letting yourself or your daughter miss them."

Humming quietly to herself, Maude Alice leafed through her papers like Ashley wasn't even there.

SLAMMING her door so hard her pictures rattled, Ashley stood alone in the middle of her office, awful, irate words echoing between her ears. She wanted to run back outside. She wanted to inhale bitingly cold air and hold it deep in her lungs until they burned. Instead, because she had a mountain to run and a legacy to protect, she yanked her phone out of her back pocket. Knowing she only had one option to get out of this mess—even if it was about as nuclear as an option could get—she pulled up his contact.

Collapsing onto her chair, she leaned forward, resting her forehead against the cool wood of her desk. When she looked up again, the window Madigan had replaced stared back at her. *He's been through so much worse than this,* she thought, remembering how terrible she'd been to him earlier. She hadn't meant to blow up at him, but it was like she'd morphed into someone angry and frustrated and so exhausted from trying to keep their head above water there was little humanity left in them. Madigan hadn't deserved her anger, and all she wanted to do now was find him and apologize. But she couldn't, not yet. First she had to make this call.

"Ashley Thompson, as I live and breathe," Chuck said into her ear.

Snapping the pencil on her desk in half, she said, "It's Cooke, Chuck. Haven't been Thompson since you decided to bang half the town."

"Ouch," he said gamely, always weirdly turned on whenever she gave him hell. "You're salty this afternoon. It's Christmas, maybe you should lighten up."

After muting the call to shout, "Fuck!" at the top of her lungs, she unmuted and said, "This is going to be hard enough as it is, so I'm just going to come right out and say it. I need money."

Silence descended over the line. "I see," he eventually said. "Is it Davis?"

"No," she replied stiffly, "it's Bluebird."

When he scoffed, she could almost see his expression, the impertinent quirk to his lips, his furrowed brow, that way he looked at her like she was so disappointingly dense. "Bluebird? The mountain I'm trying to buy from you?"

"Yes, we're in trouble."

"Let me get this straight, you want me to bail you out so you can keep the mountain I'm trying to acquire? That's pretty rich, Ash."

A shudder tore up her spine at the word 'acquire,' like Bluebird was a strip mall or a gas station. "Yes," she replied, her grip on her phone tightening. "Maude Alice made some purchases we can't cover. I need ten thousand dollars, and I know you're good for it. I can pay you back next month—"

"Of course I'm good for it. You should see my portfolio right now. It's criminal."

She had no doubt it was. His scruples were about as honorable as his views on extramarital affairs. "Will you help me or not?"

"Depends. Are you still seeing beardo? What was his name again? Mulligan?"

"What does he have to do with anything?" she asked, sitting up straighter.

"I don't like him. If he's going to be hanging around your mountain, I'd rather not throw good money after bad. Just being honest."

"It's a loan." *Asshole.* "You'll get your 'good' money back. And he has nothing to do with it."

"You know, I wonder what your skiers would think if they knew you had addicts and criminals helping their precious, innocent children onto the chairlifts."

"Chuck," she warned.

"One call to the paper. I think that's all it would take, and we'd be having a much different conversation right now. So tell me, are you still seeing him?"

Ashley knew what he wanted. He wanted his ego stroked. He wanted to know he was in control, just like he did throughout their entire marriage. He wanted to know she was alone and miserable without him. It was limitless, how much she hated him, but she needed his money, and she wouldn't let him hurt the men. What she was about to say made her stomach cramp and her mouth go dry. But as the walls closed in, she couldn't see any other way out.

"No, there's nothing going on with Matthew," she said, pushing past the tremor in her voice. "There never was."

"Didn't seem like that at the restaurant. You wouldn't be lying to me, would you? You have ten thousand dollars on the line here."

Blinking hard, she forced back the tears and the rage at having to lie about the one thing she never wanted to lie about. This one good, beautiful part of her life she didn't want Chuck to touch. "We had a fling, that's it. It didn't mean anything." The words cut like glass.

"Good. I'll wire the money to you today. But you owe me."

"Thanks, Chuck," she said, dropping her phone onto her desk before running into the bathroom and throwing up into her toilet.

CHAPTER THIRTY-ONE

MADIGAN

MADIGAN HADN'T SEEN Ashley since the morning's disaster, spending the entire day out with Murphy on the back side of the mountain running some drills Kev found online for training ski rescue dogs. He'd felt miserable all day, trying to ignore the voices in his head telling him he'd already ruined everything. *It wasn't me*, he kept attempting to convince himself. She'd been angry at Maude Alice, and he'd responded in an unhelpful way. It would be okay. Once they talked it out, once Ashley calmed down, everything would be okay.

"Merry Christmas, Madigan," Clay said, nodding at him on his way back to his and Kev's cabin. "You heading to the lodge?"

"Merry Christmas to you, too. And yep," Madigan replied, toeing at the snow, "just going to see Ashley."

Clay's right brow ticked up. "You two seem to be getting pretty heavy."

Not expecting this conversation today, Madigan looked around at the ground, the trees, the sky while trying to figure out how to respond. "I don't think—"

Clay raised his hands. "If you don't want to talk about it, that's fine. But I just want you to know that I'm here if you do."

Did he want to talk about it? Maybe he did. He was holding a lot inside these days, and he knew that never ended well for him. Dropping his chin to his chest, he admitted, "I'm a goner. It's bad."

Clay chuckled. "We figured."

"That obvious, huh?"

"Just a little. Also, Kev and I thought we heard moaning coming from your cabin last ni—"

"No." Madigan shook his head. "We will not speak of this."

Clay laughed so hard his belly shook under his coat. "Fair enough. Good luck over there, though." He glanced back toward the lodge. "The kitchen shift was rough. I spent most of the afternoon just trying to get Maude Alice to cheer up." He splinted his belly with his hands. "And eating way too much of this chocolate pie she likes, but it was the only thing that made her feel better. Whatever happened between them today, it wasn't good."

Madigan frowned, staring up at the lodge, wondering what he was about to walk into. "Thanks for the heads up. Is your son coming to the Christmas party tonight?"

Clay grinned. "Bringing the grandkids too."

"That's great, Clay. I'm happy for you."

His expression sobering, Clay asked, "How worried should we be about Sam?"

Madigan sighed. "We might need to circle the wagons if Izzy doesn't show tonight."

"He's come a long way," Clay said with conviction. "It'll be hard, but he'll make it."

"I hope you're right." Madigan sighed. "I'm going in. If I'm not back in an hour, send help."

After an enormous yawn, Clay said, "If I'm still awake, I'll come running."

Madigan took the steps two at a time, the way he always did when he knew Ashley waited for him at the top. Striding through the dining hall, he smiled at the Christmas decorations, the tables set up for the families coming for dinner, the mistletoe still hanging innocently on the wall. He spotted Mace behind the food counter, shoveling a huge bite of what must have been the same chocolate pie Clay and Maude Alice had been eating into his mouth. When he waved at the red-haired kid, Mace waved a jittery, nervous hand back at him.

As soon as he rounded the corner to Ashley's office, he heard her clipped voice. Whoever she was talking to, he hoped it wasn't Maude Alice. He didn't want to jump into that hornet's nest before he'd had a chance to apologize and make sure he and Ashley were okay. Peeking into her office, he found her sitting at her desk, alone, on the phone. Not wanting to intrude, he backed out again and waited in the hallway.

"He has nothing to do with it," he heard her say through her teeth. And then she said something that made his spine snap straight. *"Chuck."*

Was that piece of shit harassing her again?

"No," she said sadly, sounding so defeated it made him want to punch through the wall, but then, *"there's nothing going on with Matthew. There never was."*

His heart stopped beating. It just...stopped.

"We had a fling, that's it. It didn't mean anything."

"Yo, Boss? What's wrong? Where are you going?" Kev shouted as Madigan thundered past him down the lodge stairs.

There's nothing going on... A fling... It didn't mean anything... Matthew... Not Madigan, but Matthew.

"What's up with him?" he heard Kev say to Davis, and then he heard nothing but his boots crunching through the snow and his blood rushing in his ears.

Had what Chuck told him in Scotty's bathroom been true? Had Ashley just been looking for a meaningless winter fling? He remembered the way she'd looked at him this morning, the anger and annoyance in her eyes that he'd thought had been aimed at Maude Alice, but maybe he'd been wrong.

He felt sick, his arms and legs shaking when he stumbled up his stairs and threw open the door to his cabin. Pacing back and forth in front of the empty stove, pulling on his beard, he tried to put everything together to make some sort of sense of what he'd just heard. It didn't take long for him to realize how this had happened. He'd developed feelings, let himself be vulnerable, and had forgotten to do the one thing with Ashley that he'd always told his men to do. Communicate.

They'd never talked about their relationship or defined it in any way. He'd been too scared he'd find out the connection between them that meant so much to him, meant less to her.

Like he just did.

He couldn't stop hearing that familiar voice in his head, torturing him, telling him, *You're not good enough. You'll never be worthy of a woman like her. Stop pretending you're anything more than a used-up junky.* Then he saw Ashley marching toward his cabin through his window. Her hands were fisted at her sides, her mouth moving like she was talking to herself, arguing already. His blood quickened, that old, well-worn instinct to fight first and ask questions later rearing its ugly head.

She climbed his steps and opened his door without even knocking. "You would not *believe* the day I've had," she said, ripping off her hat and tossing it onto his dresser.

"Oh, I think I have a pretty good idea," he replied darkly, his arms crossed, legs spread wide. He was ready. He didn't know what for, or how bad things were about to get, but he was ready.

Pulling up short, she squinted at him, her eyes darting from his crossed arms to his wide stance, settling uneasily on his scowl. "What's up with you?"

He should probably be an adult and just ask her why she'd said those things to Chuck. But the sound of Chuck's name in his mind made him want to break everything in his cabin with his bare hands. "Have any interesting phone calls today, *Ash*?"

"Ash?" She looked at him, confused, like they'd never met before. "You don't call me Ash. What are you even...?" And then, there it was, the wide eyes, the guilty, open mouth. *The recognition.* "Oh my god," she whispered. "You heard me?"

"I was coming to see you and yeah, I heard you. What the hell, Ashley? Was this all just a joke to you?"

"Madigan, please," she said quickly, her eyes pleading as she reached out for him. "It's not what you think,"

He held her off with an outstretched hand. "Explain to me how it's not what I think. Explain to me why you just told your ex-husband that I mean nothing to you. Was Chuck right? Are you just slumming it this winter? Fucking the help for a cheap thrill?"

"What?" She staggered back a step. "You can't be serious."

"Why not? This seems pretty serious to me, Ashley."

"Of course I'm not fucking you for a cheap thrill! I can't believe you'd even think that. What kind of a person do you think I am?"

He wished he could back down just a little, but there was too much fire in his veins, and he couldn't control what it burned. "Maybe I have no idea what kind of person you are. I mean, we barely even know each other."

Her mouth falling open, she sucked in a breath. "That's not true. I made a mistake but—"

"So being with me was a mistake?"

"No! You're putting words in my mouth."

Stepping forward until he loomed over her, he said, "I didn't put any of those words you said to Chuck in your mouth. You did that all by yourself. And now you need to tell me the truth. You owe me that much at least."

Her demeanor changed in front of his eyes, like a sudden storm blowing in. He thought she'd looked caught when he'd first confronted her, guilty. But ever since he'd started in on her, she seemed more devastated than anything. Now, with her gaze slashing across him and her hands landing on her hips, she just looked pissed. The fire inside him finally guttered as a sensation like a hole opening up beneath his feet overcame him.

"Of course I owe you. I owe everyone these days. Why should you be any different?"

"Wait," he said, softening bit by bit as she hardened into stone.

"No, you wanted an explanation about why I said those things to Chuck, so I will give you an explanation. Since Maude Alice decided to spend thousands of dollars we don't have on a terrain park we can't afford, she left me with no other choice but to call Chuck and beg him for money. Because Chuck is a complete and total asshole, he used the call as an opportunity to threaten your men and the mountain. I had to tell him something to keep him from sending reporters up here. And because I don't care one bit what he knows about my life, and I just need his stupid money to save my mountain, I lied and told him we weren't together. It was awful and terrible, and I will never forgive myself for it because I really, really care about you." Her eyes misted, shining like amber. "And I never want to hurt you, but I've hurt you anyway."

His mouth already made the shape, so he went ahead and uttered a profoundly useless, "Oh."

"As far as 'slumming it' goes, let's examine the facts here." She pointed a finger at his chest, the motion sending a single tear down her cheek. "You are the one dedicating your entire life to helping other people. You are the one who meditates and goes to therapy and tries to understand people and does snowga for fuck's sake. You are the one who isn't cold and closed off and so terrified of feeling anything real she sabotages it the first chance she gets." Her voice broke. "If anyone is slumming it in this relationship, it isn't me, Madigan. It's you!"

A gust of wind hit the cabin, snowflakes starting to fall and blow sideways past his windows. He'd messed up. It wasn't entirely his fault, but he'd messed up. "Ashley, I—"

"No, it's too late," she said, spinning toward his door.

Lunging for her, he took hold of her arm and spun her back. "Wait. Please."

"What?" She glared at him, but she didn't pull her arm away.

He didn't know what to say, only that he couldn't let her leave, not like this. He glanced at his dresser "You forgot this," he said, picking up her hat. "It's cold out there, and I don't want you to be cold."

Her tear-filled eyes met his. "But I *am* cold," she told him. "Can't you see that?"

He knew she wasn't talking about the weather anymore. Easing her hat carefully onto her head, letting his fingers run through her curls, he said, "No, that's not what I see at all. Because you are *not* cold. You are warm and caring and compassionate, and I shouldn't have yelled at you. I was just scared. Please don't leave, stay and talk with me."

Her shoulders fell, her entire body collapsing in upon itself as she leaned into him, letting him fold her into his arms.

"Stay with me," he whispered while she trembled against him. "Let's work this out."

"What is wrong with me?" Her voice was hoarse, wrecked by emotion. "I should never have said that to Chuck. Maude Alice and I had just had a fight, and I was angry and bitter, and I just hate having to ask him for anything, let alone money." Pulling away, she looked up at him. "Not a single word of what I said to him was true. I swear it on my life. I know what I said was unforgivable, but I am so—"

Sliding her hat off and tossing it back onto the dresser, he leaned in and kissed her forehead. "It's all right. It's all forgivable, and already forgiven." He said the words, but he wasn't convinced he believed them. Even after all these years and all the work he'd done on himself, it was still so much easier to believe she'd meant those things she'd said to Chuck, to believe he was nothing more than a meaningless fling to her, than it was to believe she was telling him the truth now.

"It's not all right. I hate that I made you feel like you aren't important to me, like what we have isn't important. Because it is." Her trembling transformed into full-bodied shaking as she sobbed, "I just hate who my mother turns me into sometimes. I hate that my dad is gone. None of this would be happening if he was still here. I can't do this alone." Her voice shattered, breaking his heart along with it. "I miss him so much. Sometimes I don't even know who I am without him."

Of course. It was Christmas, and she missed her father. Gathering her up into his arms, he carried her to his rocking chair and held her, stroking her hair, telling her it would be all right, rocking her slowly until her tears finally stopped and the only sounds left were the wind through the pines and the tinkling of snowflakes as they fell onto his roof.

"Are we okay?" she asked, her soft voice against his neck making him shiver.

"First fight is in the books," he replied. "It was a good one too."

Sitting up, she grasped his shirt in her hands and stared deeply into his eyes. "Madigan, I'm so, so sorry."

He cupped her face. "Me too."

"Can we..." Her gaze dropped to his lips. "Can we have makeup sex now?"

With a small laugh, he said, "I don't think that's a good idea."

"Why not?" She slid her fingers into his hair. "I want to make sure we're okay."

"We're okay," he said, pulling one of her hands down to flatten her palm over his growing erection. "I promise. But it's almost six, and there is no way I want our first makeup sex to last only five minutes."

"What?" she shrieked, leaping off his lap like his balls had caught fire. "What time is it?"

He glanced at his watch. "Quarter till."

"Holy shit!" She snatched her hat off the dresser and spun in a full circle, like she couldn't figure out which direction to go. Then she yelled at him, "Get up! We're late!"

Standing from the chair, he repositioned himself in his pants, looped an arm around her waist, pulled her close, and kissed her hard. "We're not late yet. But you're damn cute when you're frazzled."

She grabbed his face, kissing him back. Then she pulled her hat over her head and threw open the door, revealing a snow-covered Murphy sitting patiently on the porch.

"Look! Even Murphy knows we're late!" she cried on her way out. "Come on!"

Patting himself down, he made sure he was still in one piece, which, somehow, he was. Still in one piece. Still with Ashley. And it was still Christmas.

After taking a one-minute shower, he trimmed and oiled his beard then changed into his nicest grey pants and a cream-colored cable knit sweater. Pulling on his coat, he blew out an enormous, relieved, exhausted breath before heading out into the snow.

CHAPTER THIRTY-TWO

MADIGAN

EVEN THOUGH HE and Ashley seemed to have survived their first fight, Madigan's nerve jangled while he climbed the steps to the dining hall. A lot rode on tonight. The holiday visitations had been his idea, and worry chipped away at him. What if some of the families didn't show? What if they did show and fights broke out? Holidays were already hard enough on the men. He needed both hands to count how many times men staying at Little Timber had started drinking or using again between Thanksgiving and New Year's. No matter how many times it happened, it always shocked him to watch people who'd been doing so well get completely derailed by the loneliness and reflection the holidays often brought with them. He only hoped that this big of a Christmas celebration wouldn't set any of the guys off. If it did, he wasn't sure he could bear the guilt, or deal with the fallout. A fallout that wouldn't only affect him and the men anymore, but now Ashley too.

Despite his reservations, he couldn't help but grin when he reached the top of the stairs. Maude Alice and Davis had transformed the dining room into a holiday spectacle. Shimmering silver and gold fabric covered the tables, twinkly lights draped the walls and doorways, and it smelled amazing thanks to the spread of glazed carrots, creamy pearl onions, fresh-baked rolls, and a massive Christmas ham that, *nerves-be-damned*, Madigan absolutely planned to go down on later. *Speaking of going down.*

"Hey, handsome," Ashley said as she walked up to him, a hesitant smile tugging at her lips.

He'd tried to look nice for the event, but Ashley took his breath away. Literally, he couldn't breathe. He put his hand over his heart to make sure it was still beating.

"What is it?" she asked, color dusting her cheeks as she looked down at her dress.

"It's you," he said. "Your dress is stunning." And it was. Thin straps rising over her shoulders, soft black velvet that tapered at her waist before flaring out to just below her knees, strappy black heels he wanted to feel digging into his back. She'd pulled her hair up off her shoulders in a loose twist, soft curls grazing her neck. "You did all this in fifteen minutes?" he asked, awestruck. "Looking gorgeous at the drop of a hat must be one of your hidden talents."

"It's not too much, is it?" She bit her cheek. "I wanted to look nice for the families."

"It's perfect. You're perfect." Her reluctant smile and flushed cheeks made him regret not taking her again in his rocking chair when he'd had the chance.

"You don't look so bad yourself," she said.

Leaning in, he kissed her cheek. "Thank you."

She turned her head toward him, just barely brushing her nose over his neck. "And you smell amazing." Grabbing his arm when he tried to pull away, she stuck her nose into his beard.

"Ashley?" He frowned, glancing around. "What are you doing?"

She inhaled him deeply. "It's your beard oil, isn't it? That smell."

He wasn't sure how, but not one single person in the dining hall seemed to notice the fact that Ashley was currently buried in his beard, sniffing him. "Is it a good smell?"

She hummed. "It's the best smell."

"It's called Man of the Woodlands."

Finally letting him go, she said, "Man of the Woodlands?"

"I'm afraid so."

She sniffed the air one last time. "Doesn't matter. It could be called Man of the Garbage Truck and I'd still want to smell it all day long."

"They actually make an oil called Man of the Garbage Truck. Maybe I'll try that one next."

Glancing toward the window, she said, "They should be here any minute, right?"

He scanned the room, noticing antsy men, their hands wringing in their laps or clenched at their sides. He noticed Sam, sitting alone at a table against the wall. "They should," he replied.

"Do you think she'll come?"

"Izzy?" Madigan guessed. "I hope so, but I don't know. It still feels like a long shot."

"How often do you have to do this?"

"Do what? Wait for families to visit the guys?"

She nodded, chewing on her lip, a crease forming between her brows.

He thought back through the years, so many different men, so much heartache. Some families stayed strong, like his. Many didn't. "Too often, but it never gets any easier. I'm gonna go talk to him."

She squeezed his hand, then let him go. "Good luck."

On his way to the table where Sam sat alone, Madigan grabbed two mugs of hot cider from the buffet table.

"Hi, Sam. Cider?"

"She's not going to come," Sam said, staring at his phone on the table, its screen dark. He'd put on some weight since they'd moved up here. Muscles rounded his angular shoulders and his cheeks had filled out, his face no longer so gaunt and hollow. Despite his resigned expression, despite the anxious way he fidgeted with his phone, the kid looked good.

Madigan set Sam's mug in front of him, then he sat down across the table. "Will you be okay if she doesn't?"

Sam shrugged, his shoulders rising and falling in a hopeless gesture that made Madigan's chest ache. "I guess I'll have to be."

A commotion tumbled up the stairs in the form of two arguing teenage girls. Madigan grinned as Brian raced forward and took his girls into his arms one at a time, kissing the tops of their heads.

Sam turned away, staring glumly through the window again. After a moment, Madigan joined him, watching headlights make their way up the winding road from town as more families arrived.

"You're doing well, Sam. You're doing really well up here."

He looked back at Madigan. "I'm fucking trying, man." He winced. "Sorry, I didn't mean to swear."

Madigan waved him off. "I know you're trying. So do Ashley and Maude Alice. So do the rest of the guys. We see it, I just want you to know that. We see it."

Sam nodded.

Reaching across the table, Madigan covered Sam's hand with his. "If Izzy doesn't come tonight, we are all here for you. We've got your back." He let go of Sam's hand.

"Thanks, Boss." Sam's chin pointed over Madigan's shoulder. "But you'd better go get your girl before Kev snaps her up."

Madigan scoffed. "What girl? I don't have a girl," he insisted, even though he'd already turned to look behind him.

"Dude, give me a break. You two are about a subtle as an earthquake."

Madigan chuckled, watching Kev put the moves on a beautiful blond who was most definitely not Ashley. Sam must not have met Davis yet. "You might be right about that, Sam. But I don't think I have anything to worry about from Kev."

"You sure about that?" Sam said. "I think Kev's gonna get it."

Hearing Davis's laughter behind him, Madigan shook his head and said, "Nah."

"Eyes don't lie."

"Sure they do." He sat back in his chair, interlacing his hands smugly behind his head, watching *his* woman stroll toward them from the other direction. "For example..."

"Gentleman, how's the cider?"

Sam's double take when Ashley walked up to the table was priceless. Then, to Madigan's amazement considering the strain the kid was under, he burst into laughter.

"What's so funny?" she asked, looking down at her dress like she expected to find a stain.

"Sam thought Kev was putting the moves on you," Madigan tilted his head toward the laughing youngsters, "instead of on your daughter." While he might have wished they were being a bit less obvious about it, Madigan was relieved that Kev—who hadn't had a single friend or family member visit him since his release to Little Timber—seemed to be having a happy holiday.

Sam blinked at Ashley. "I'm sorry, but you look... It's like you're sisters or something."

Well done, Sam, Madigan thought.

Gazing down affectionately at Sam, Ashley said, "You are my new favorite person."

"Hey?" Madigan groused. "I thought I was your favorite."

It only lasted a second, but Ashley's eyes flashed wide, and Madigan felt more than heard the way her breath caught. Maybe he shouldn't have said that. He kind of liked the idea of their...whatever it was, not being a secret anymore, but maybe she didn't. Maybe he needed to adjust his expectations, because with how much that barely perceptible tightness in her shoulders made his stomach drop, he wondered if he needed to hold his cards a bit closer to his vest.

"I'm going to go check on the food," she said, smiling at both of them before turning away.

"Smooth move, Boss," Sam said, grinning into his mug of cider.

"Shut up," Madigan grumbled, throwing his napkin at Sam's face the second he lowered his mug.

After most of the food had been eaten and the carols had been sung, what had been a lovely evening started winding down. Clay hugged his son while Maude Alice gave gift bags full of sweets to his grandchildren. Tex shook his brother Will's hand, both men wearing matching cowboy hats, both with matching holes in them. Brian's wife and daughters left loudly down the stairs, and when he turned around after sending the constantly arguing teens off, Madigan thought he almost looked relieved.

While guests continued to file out of the dining hall, Sam stood alone by the window facing the parking lot, still waiting, just like he had on Thanksgiving Day when Izzy hadn't shown.

Walking to his side, Madigan watched the red line of taillights snake down the road. "Sorry, Sam." He wanted to put his arm around him, console him, but he didn't want to make a scene in front of the other guys. "Maybe we can try again for New Year's."

Sam remained silent, his jaw clenched tight, and then one of his hands slammed abruptly onto the windowpane. "Wait."

One single pair of headlights turned into the parking lot, pointing toward the lodge.

"It's her," Sam whispered, barely a breath. "That's Izzy's car. I can't believe it."

Madigan, honestly, couldn't believe it either. As much as he'd hoped she would, he really didn't think Izzy would show. He knew that look in her eyes, that pain. He knew she still held a lot of anger toward Sam, but it was Christmas. And anything was possible on Christmas.

"What's going on?" Ashley said, joining them at the window. "Who's that? Is it—"

"It's Izzy." Sam turned to Ashley, his eyes huge. "Should I go down there or wait up here? What should I do?"

"Oh, no. Oh, Sam." Ashley's strained voice was a fist squeezing

Madigan's heart. When he faced the window again, the world stopped turning.

"Wait! Izzy!" Sam shouted, his fist pounding onto the glass. But it was too late, she'd already turned her red Toyota Camry around, driving back out of the parking lot. "What the hell?" he cried, pounding on the glass again, tears standing in his eyes. "Why is she leaving? She didn't even give me a chance!"

Madigan didn't know what to do. This was so much worse than if she hadn't come at all. How could he fix this? How could he make it right? How could he erase the broken look on Sam's face?

Silence swallowed the room until Ashley said, "No way. Screw this!"

Before Madigan could ask her what she was about to screw, she ducked behind the counter, grabbed a set of keys, and without looking back at him or Sam or anyone else, took off like a bat out of hell down the stairs.

CHAPTER THIRTY-THREE

ASHLEY

ASHLEY HAD ABSOLUTELY no idea what she was doing, only that she had to do something. She had to try. And she hoped she'd grabbed the right damned keys!

Sliding to a stop in her heels in the snow, she shoved the key into the door of the snowplow. "Yes!" she cheered when the key turned, at the same time hearing Madigan and Sam call after her, their shoes pounding down the stairs. She couldn't wait for them, there wasn't enough time. Hauling herself into the truck, she started it up and peeled out, fishtailing over the ice in the parking lot.

Would Izzy think she'd lost her mind? Would she recognize her in the snowplow or freak out that some stranger was driving up on her ass and honking at her? This wasn't safe, the roads were slick, she was being impulsive and probably very stupid. *Oh, well. Too late now.*

Honking her horn and flashing her lights at the Toyota still driving in front of her, she rolled down her window and stuck her head out into the cold night air. "Stop," she shouted. "Izzy, wait! Please!"

When Izzy finally slammed on her breaks, Ashley did the same, careening over the snow-packed road and avoiding a fender-bender by mere inches. Jumping down from the truck, she landed hard, snapping the heel off one of her shoes.

"What the hell are you doing?" Izzy shouted, stepping out of her car and slamming the door. "Are you nuts?"

Ashley grimaced, limping closer to the Toyota. "Sorry. Yes. Maybe," she said, tucking loose strands of her hair behind her ear to keep them from whipping in the wind.

"Did you hurt yourself?" Izzy frowned at Ashley's feet "You're limping."

"Just broke a heel," Ashley replied.

"That sucks," Izzy said. "Those are cute. Or they were cute, I guess."

"I know, right? I don't really have that many shoes and—"

"What do you want, Ashley?" Izzy asked with an exhausted sigh.

Taking a breath, surprised she found oxygen to breathe instead of water considering how far in she was over her head, Ashley said, "Um, I was just wondering why you were leaving before you even had a chance to eat? The ham itself is worth the trip."

"The ham?" Izzy repeated, blinking in disbelief. "You think I scrambled to find a sitter on Christmas then drove all the way up here in the snow for the food?"

Air sailed through Ashley's lips. "Okay. I am not going to pretend to know anything about your life, or Sam's life, or what you've all been through—what he's put you through, I mean," she corrected hastily when Izzy's laser-beam glare singed her eyebrows. "But you came up here tonight for a reason."

"It was a mistake." Izzy shook her head. "I shouldn't have come."

"But—"

"Look, I can't do this. I can't do it again. I thought I could, but I can't. I don't want to hurt Sam, but I just can't be there for him anymore. It's too late. I'm too," her voice cracked, her shoulders sagging, "tired."

Steeling her nerve, giving herself and Sam one more shot,

Ashley hobbled close enough to Izzy that she could speak to her without shouting. "I can't imagine how hard this is. I can only tell you one thing, and this is something I know to be true. Sam is trying. I'm sure he's tried before and failed. I can't speak to that. But he works so hard up here. He shows up every day. He never complains. He takes extra time to talk to the kids who ski here and help them up the rope tow. He makes them laugh. He takes pride in his work here. I know he's not doing this for me, or even for Madigan. And he's definitely not doing it for himself. I know you're tired, but maybe you don't need to be there for Sam right now. Maybe, for once, he can be there for you and your daughter. Because everything he is doing up here, I know in my heart he is doing for the both of you." Tears burned her eyes. "If it's not enough, then it's not enough. But if there is even the smallest chance that you could work some sort of relationship out with him, friends or co-parents or whatever, I am begging you to come back." *Life is so short*, she wanted to say. *Daughters need their fathers*, she wanted to scream. But she didn't say another word.

Letting loose a single, heart wrenching sob, Izzy said, "I can't. I'm sorry, but I can't."

With hot tears streaming from her eyes and freezing to her cheeks, Ashley watched helplessly as Izzy got back into her car, slammed the door, and drove away.

What had she done? What would she tell Sam? How would she tell him that there was no hope left?

Driving back up to the lodge, seeing Sam and Madigan standing by the front entrance waiting for her, disappointment clear in the tight lines of Sam's face, she couldn't hold the tears back. How did Madigan do this every day? It seemed impossible. It hurt so much.

She slid out of the truck and limped over to them on her broken shoe. "I'm so sorry, Sam. I tried. I really tried."

"It's okay," Sam said, brushing the back of his hand over his wet cheeks. "It's just another day. Earning back trust takes time, right Boss?"

After Madigan grasped the back of Sam's neck and squeezed, Sam turned around to make his way back to the cabins alone.

Ashley couldn't watch him go. It was unbearable. Spinning toward Madigan, she buried her face into his sweater.

His arms were warm and strong as they wrapped around her. "You just made a fan for life in Sam," he told her. "He couldn't believe anyone would do something like that for him."

"I didn't do anything, though. I couldn't get her to come back. And," she sobbed, "I broke my shoe."

His hand rising to cradle the back of her head, his lips pressing into her hair, he said, "Welcome to the war."

SHE STOOD BAREFOOT in her dress while Madigan started a fire, still fighting back tears as she thought of Sam and Izzy and their daughter, as she thought of her father. Max would've known exactly what to say to bring Izzy back. He always knew exactly what to say.

Crossing the room, closing his curtains, Madigan stood behind her, sliding the straps of her dress over her shoulders, unzipping her to send the velvet fabric to the floor. "I have something for you," he told her while he unclasped her bra, reaching around her to cup her breasts.

She leaned back into him, sliding her fingers around his neck. "You do?"

"A present." He kissed her shoulder. "But don't get too excited, it's nothing special."

"What is it?"

Turning her around, he hoisted her up into his arms, slinging her legs around his waist before setting her down on the edge of the bed. Then he walked to his dresser, opened the top drawer, pulled out a small, perfectly wrapped box, and presented it to her.

She shook the box against her ear.

Laughing, he rolled his eyes and said, "Just open it, Sherlock."

When she peeled back the paper, she gasped.

"I told you it wasn't much."

"Madigan, it's..." Words failed her because there, cradled carefully in her hands, was a mixtape. He'd made her a mixtape. And on the side he'd written the title: *Catching Last Chair with Ashley.*

He scratched his beard, staring down at his feet. "I tried to pick songs I thought you might like. I had to call in some favors to my tape guy, but I found some—"

"Prince," she said reverently. "And TLC, and Mary!" There was so much to love about the tape in her hands. The Lemonheads, Digable Planets, LL Cool J, Missy Elliot, the Furs. "You remembered the music I like."

Sinking to his knees before her, he said, "Ashley, I remember every single second with you. The first time I met you in your office, the first time I heard your voice on my phone, our ski lessons. But most of all, I remember our chairlift rides. That's when I realized, even during a panic attack, that I was the luckiest man in the world because I was sitting next to you." He nestled between her legs, gazing into her eyes. "Catching last chair with you was how I learned how funny you are, how thoughtful. That's when I first noticed the way your eyes glow when they're reflecting the sunset," he brushed a stray curl of her hair back, tucking it behind her ear, "bright gold with these emerald flecks that twinkle when the light hits them at just the right angle. That's when I realized you were the most beautiful woman I'd ever laid eyes on."

She swallowed the lump rising up her throat as powerful and complicated emotions crowded her thoughts, feelings she hadn't let herself feel trying to escape from the places where she'd locked them up tight. Still holding the tape in her hands, she ran a finger over the song titles, all written carefully in black ink in his sexy slanted handwriting. She recognized the last song, "Shine Bright" by the Makers.

"All the stars in the sky shine dim, compared to you," she recited.

He smirked. "I thought you weren't a fan."

"Everyone knows that song."

"I wrote that song."

"You did?"

He nodded, and she leaned forward to kiss his lips. "It's a beautiful song," she said. "Must have been about someone pretty amazing."

"Oh, it was, but I've gotta admit, it's pretty strange to finally meet the woman you wrote a love song about thirty years after you wrote it."

Her heart stalled mid-beat, then flipped over in her chest to lie down dead on its back. "That is one hell of a line, Mr. Madigan."

"Is it a line if it's true?"

Setting the tape down beside her on the bed, she clutched his face between her hands, whispered, "Thank you," and then she kissed him again, deep and slow, swatting his hand away when it tried to slip inside her underwear. "Not yet, I have something for you too."

"But you're wearing sex underwear," he whined, running his finger over the thin band of the new lacy black underwear she'd bought in town. "You can't come over here wearing sex underwear and expect me not to touch them."

After swatting him away a second time, she hopped off the bed to dig into her backpack, finding the small gift bag she'd stashed inside. Sitting back down on the edge of the bed, she surrounded him with her legs again. "This first, then you can touch my underwear all you want." As soon as she handed him the bag, nerves gripped her. What if he didn't like it? What if he thought it was weird?

Tugging on the strings, biting his lip like a kid unwrapping a candy bar, he reached inside and pulled out the velvet jewelry box. Then he peered up at her through his lashes. "Ashley, are you proposing?"

"Madigan," she groaned, embarrassed and nervous and feeling far too naked. "Come on."

He kissed her quickly, then opened the box. His brows slid together as he pulled out the necklace. "What's this?"

"You don't recognize it?"

He shook his head, spinning the silver pendant back and forth in his hand.

"That," she said, pointing to the depiction of an eagle clutching a smaller bird in its talons engraved into the pendant, "is your family crest. The Madigan family crest."

His eyes whipped up, huge and unblinking.

"I, um," taking her hair down, she pulled it over her shoulder, "I found it online."

Slipping the necklace over his head, holding the pendent up to study it, he said, "You went online and found my family crest?"

He didn't like it. She should have gotten him a scarf or something. "Well," she said, her hands itching to cover herself up, "you like to go by Madigan, so I figured the name was probably important to you, and—"

Pushing her down onto the bed, he loomed over her, ripping his sweater off over his head and tossing it to the floor. The pendant dangled over his chest, glinting in the firelight. "I love it. I love everything about it. I love..."

Silence settled between them, aside from her thundering heart. *What was he about to say? What else does he love?*

"I just realized something," he said, reaching between her legs, hooking a finger into her underwear and yanking them down to her knees. "I never had any dessert tonight." Kneeling at the foot of the bed again, he stared up between her thighs. "And you just happened to have delivered my favorite sweet right to me."

Her head fell back as he spread her apart gently with his thumbs. The urge to open her legs wider for him was overwhelming, but her fancy new underwear kept her knees bound together.

"What's wrong?" he teased, kissing her just to the left, then to the right of where she needed him. "Feeling confined?"

"Fuuuuck," she groaned when he reached up to cup her breast.

"Not quite yet," he purred just above her clit, the movement of his breath making her twitch and pulse as he pinched her nipple gently. "Patience is a virtue."

Her hips rocked, desperate for more pressure and friction where she throbbed and ached for him.

"Ah, ah, ah," he scolded. "All good things to those who wait."

"Did you read a book of proverbs recently or something?" she gritted out.

"Shhhh," he murmured, his lips finally making contact, brushing over her clit. "Less talking, more moaning."

Her eyes fell closed with the first light flick of his tongue. Her jaw clenched with another gentle squeeze of her breast and roll of her nipple. The rhythm repeated itself, his tongue pressing firmly over her clit, then teasing and flicking, his fingers kneading and rolling her nipple between them. But just when she started to feel that familiar, fluttering ache building deep below her belly button, he slowed his pace, lightening his touch.

"What are you doing?" she panted, clutching at his bedspread. "Why are you stopping?"

Peering up from between her legs again, his eyes clear and cunning, he said, "Ashley Cooke, don't tell me you've never been edged before?"

"Edged?" she asked, wiggling underneath him in pure, heated frustration. "What's edged?"

"Well, well, well." An evil, lustful little smirk slid onto his lips. "If this isn't the best Christmas present yet."

CHAPTER THIRTY-FOUR

MADIGAN

He didn't think he'd ever receive another gift as profoundly amazing as her pendant for the rest of his life. Little did he know... He offered up a silent prayer of thanks to all the Chucks in the world for being such undeniably lousy lovers.

"I can tell how badly you need to come," he told her. "And you will, I promise." He flicked his tongue over her bud again, humming when her back arched off the bed. "I can stop if you want me to. Just tell me to stop, and I'll make you come. Or," another slow pass of his tongue, "if you let me, I can give you the most amazing orgasm you've ever had."

Ashley's body responded to him like an instrument, as finely tuned as his guitar. Every touch, every pinch, every lick affected her just the way he wanted it to, winding her up or settling her down. He would have gone bananas over her no matter what, but he found this intensely sensitive and sensual side of her irresistible. And knowing that Chuck had probably never explored her fully, that he'd never taken the time or expended any effort to become an expert in what made her sigh or moan or cry out or beg him to take mercy on her, he couldn't decide if he was ecstatic to be the first man to show her the attention she deserved, or furious she'd gone this long without it.

Waiting until her breathing slowed and her hands released their death grip on his bedspread, he said, "Do you want me to stop?" before kissing her again, ghosting his lips over her sweet, swollen clit. When she hissed and bucked her hips, he pinched her nipple hard enough to hurt. He didn't want to hurt her, ever. But he knew the pain would focus her senses, giving her something to cling to while he kept her balanced on the razor's edge of release.

Her breath shuddered out of her, her legs shaking, straining against her underwear bindings until he thought she might tear them apart. He wondered if this was too much for her, too intense. But then she said, "Don't stop. Not yet."

Victory thrummed through his veins, stiffening his cock and tightening his balls. "That's my girl. When you've had enough, when you have to come, just pull my hair, okay?"

"Okay, okay. Yes."

Dipping his head between her legs again, he slid his tongue through her entrance, making her moan. Her hands left the bedspread to grasp his shoulders, her fingernails digging into his skin, making him have to press his cock into the mattress to dull its throbbing. Rolling his tongue over her clit, up and down and up again, he moved slowly at first, licking her gently, then faster and harder until her rasping breaths transformed into harsh, desperate groans. Until he felt her hot, sensitive flesh twitch under his tongue. Until he brought her so close to the edge he knew one single brush of air would push her over. So he held his breath, letting her body come back down to earth, waiting until her breathing slowed and her legs stopped trembling.

That she trusted him enough to do this to her, that she wasn't pulling his hair yet even though he knew her need for release was overwhelming, made him so hard it caused him physical pain. But as badly as he needed to be inside her, he had to be patient. He wanted her calm one more time before he wound her up again. Kissing her inner thigh, he told her, "You're doing so good, Ashley. So good."

She whimpered, her legs hanging limply off the bed, her chest rising and falling in shallow, panting breaths. He was worried he might be the one to cry uncle first because watching her come down from the edge was so hot he knew if he wasn't fucking her soon he'd explode all over his bed. Once he was sure she was relaxed and ready, he circled her entrance with his finger, slowly, deliberately, and then he slid home.

The sound she made while he eased another finger inside her nearly ruined him. He had to make her come. Now. He couldn't wait.

Pumping his fingers in and out of her, he surrounded her clit with his lips and sucked her right to the edge again. With the noises she was making, the cries and the groans, he knew she wouldn't be able to hold out much longer. When her fingers finally slid into his hair and pulled, he groaned too, so relieved he could barely breathe.

Redoubling his efforts, he palmed her breast, circling her nipple with his thumb while his fingers stroked along her front wall. He licked and sucked her clit until he could feel the orgasm take her, her body clamping down on his fingers, her cries so loud they probably echoed all the way down into the valley.

When she'd finally had enough and pushed him away, he stood, wiping his mouth with the back of his hand and staring down at her. The sight of her, her closed eyes, heaving chest, her knuckle caught between her teeth as pain and pleasure chased each other over her face... He'd never needed anything in his life like the way he needed to fuck her.

"I need you too," she said after releasing her knuckle, like she could read his mind. "I need you now."

Half wild with desire, he pulled her underwear all the way off, threw her legs over his shoulders, and yanked her body down the bed, sliding her straight onto his rock-hard cock. She was so wet, so hot and wet and still pulsing from her orgasm that his first thrust into her nearly made him blackout. He knew she'd be sensitive after what he'd just done to her, so he tried to stay slow and steady, but it was so hard. He needed friction. He needed speed. He needed to take her. He needed to take her and fuck her and empty himself into her.

"I have to go faster, baby. I have to come. I'm... I can't..." *Fuck.* He was dying. He'd edged himself just as much as he'd edged her without even realizing it.

Her hands slid down the bed to find his hips, her fingernails digging in. "I need it too. Don't hold back."

Sinking his teeth into her calf, he drove into her, hard and fast, over and over. Sweat trickled down his chest, the pendant she'd bought him swinging in time with his thrusts as an inhuman growl tore from his throat. The need to fuck, to come, to close his eyes and surrender completely to his body's cravings made icy terror flood his veins. He was disassociating. He needed to take a step back and reel himself in, get himself under control. But he couldn't stop. He couldn't stop fucking her. He. Couldn't. Stop.

When release seized him, primal and unrelenting, he thrust through the final waves of terrible pleasure and collapsed into her arms, cradled against her chest, her legs hooked around his hips, her lips pressing kisses into his hair. He came so hard he saw stars. He came so hard he didn't remember where he was. He came so hard he could have been anywhere, with anyone, just fucking for the sake of fucking. He'd lost control, just like before he got clean. He was disgusted with himself.

"What's wrong?" she said, her hand running over his back. "Madigan, you're trembling."

Sliding back out of her arms, he knelt in a heap at the foot of the bed. "I'm so sorry, Ashley." He shook his head. "I didn't mean to... Please. Please forgive me."

"Forgive you for what?" She sat up, confused. "Hey, look at me."

But he couldn't. He was too ashamed. "I lost control. I just fucking lost it."

Her hands, soft and smelling of flowers, grasped his face. "Madigan, sweetheart. Please look at me."

His eyes rose dutifully to meet hers, because she'd never called him sweetheart before. It sounded like a song he'd heard a million times, but only now learned the words.

"I felt it too," she told him, brushing his damp hair out of his eyes. "I felt wild and out of control too."

"You did?"

She leaned in to kiss his forehead twice, once over each brow, then she pulled him close, holding him against her chest. "I never let go like that. I hold on to everything so tightly, like if I don't, it will all fall through my fingers like sand. But tonight, you helped me let go."

"I never let go like that anymore either. I don't want to be out of control again." She couldn't possibly understand how bad it had gotten, and he'd never tell her. Waking up in strange towns in bedrooms he didn't remember entering, with women he didn't remember meeting. Not having any idea what they'd done, what *he'd* done. Leaving before they woke up and never seeing them again, never seeing them at all.

"You kept me safe," she said. "You never did anything without my permission." Her hand cupped his head, her heart beating a steady rhythm against his ear. "It's okay. It's okay to be wild with me. I'll keep you safe too."

He tried to blink away the tears pooling in his eyes, but they trailed down his cheeks onto her chest all the same.

Kissing his head again, she said, "You were right, by the way. That was without a doubt the most amazing orgasm I've ever had." She rolled a shoulder. "I think I dislocated something."

He laughed, wiping his eyes.

She rubbed his back, soft and consoling. "And we can do plain old boring missionary for a week straight if it makes you feel better."

He'd been so terrified, sliding back into the darkness of his past, and now he was laughing. How had he found this woman? What parallel universe had he fallen into to be allowed to feel as good as she made him feel? He didn't deserve it. He didn't deserve her. "Better make it two weeks," he said, his heart an aching, quivering mess in his chest because they were both laughing now. And because he was certain of something, beyond a shadow of a doubt. He didn't know precisely where he fit in her heart, but no matter what happened between them in the future, she would now and forever have a home inside of his.

Ashley's fingers tracing over his back pulled him from a deep, dreamless sleep.

"When did you get this one?" Her voice was morning quiet, her fingertip running over the curving line of the horseshoe tattoo over his shoulder blade.

"Morning," he muttered into his pillow.

Leaning over, she kissed the tattoo in question. "Morning."

"I got that one right after I got out of prison. Which was," he made his sleepy brain count the years, "twenty-two years ago. I felt lucky at the time, so it seemed fitting."

She hummed thoughtfully. "Lucky to be out?"

Yawning, forcing himself to wake up, he rolled onto his side so he could see her face. The sun rising through the window bathed her in golden light, threading through her blond curls and casting warm shadows over her still naked body. It hurt his eyes to look at her, she was so beautiful. "Lucky to be out, still alive, clean. Lucky to have parents who cared about me enough to get me locked up."

Her fingers running down his arm, tracing over the crashing waves of his sleeve, halted their progress. "Your parents put you in prison?"

"They didn't want to, believe me. But they'd already tried everything else. It was their last chance. It was *my* last chance," he clarified.

"And somehow, despite the odds, it worked. I've been clean ever since. But," he pushed away memories he never wanted to revisit, "it's not a route to sobriety I'd wish on my worst enemy."

"You've been clean for twenty-two years," she said, her finger tracing over a different tattoo now, the knot over his hip. "That's something to be proud of." She met his eyes. "You're hard on yourself, Madigan. Like last night. I hope you're proud of yourself sometimes too."

He would not cry in front of this woman twice in twenty-four hours. "It's hard. I left a lot of pain and destruction in my path. Sometimes it's far away, and I can feel things like pride, happiness, joy. Sometimes it's close and it's...harder."

"When did you get the compass?"

His cock stirred when her fingers moved across his stomach to trace over his compass tattoo. "When I opened Little Timber. For the first time in my life I felt like I knew exactly what I was supposed to do, where I was supposed to go. I didn't want to forget that feeling."

Her hand moved down between them, her fingers wrapping around him, caressing him. "You're so good at what you do. I see it in the men, they look up to you, rely on you. They trust you. You're giving them a chance at a different life. I wonder how many lives you've changed."

"Ashley," he said, "why are you trying to make me cry this early in the morning?" Her smiling face wobbled as tears filled his eyes, his entire future spanning from one corner of her lips to the other.

"Because," she said, her hand still moving over him in smooth, languid strokes. "You're hot when you cry."

He huffed a laugh.

"When did you get the HOPE and FEAR on your fingers?"

"I got those in prison." He closed his eyes when her fingers slid down his shaft again. "When I realized that those two emotions ruled my life, and the trick was figuring out which one of them was in control." Rolling over her, he settled himself between her legs. As she guided him into her, he thought a third emotion might rule him now too. "Two weeks of missionary starts today?" he asked, grinning down at her.

"Who's the lucky one now?" she said, and then she sighed, her head falling back to her pillow, her chin arching up to catch the sunlight as he pushed deeper into her.

I am, he thought. *I am*.

Watching her, her eyes closed, her throat bared with complete trust, words burned inside his chest, words that had grown too big to live only inside him. It was a risk, a risk he knew damn well no man was ever supposed to take while they were inside a woman, but with every thrust of his hips, every moan that passed her lips, he knew he had to try.

"Ashley," he whispered, surrounding her face with his hands, running his thumbs over her cheeks.

"Yes?" She turned her head to kiss his thumb, the sweetness of the gesture making something inside his chest ache like a deep bruise.

"You are the most amazing woman I've ever met. I've never felt like this with anyone before. I don't understand how I even lived before I met you, like my world was in black and white until you showed me color, and now everything just...glows."

One of her legs slid over his thigh, her eyes finding his, her hand reaching up to cup his cheek as her fingers slipped into his beard.

Here it was, the simplest thing. Two people with nothing standing between them. And yet, no matter how hard he tried to push the three words out of his mouth, they wouldn't budge. What if she didn't feel the same? The woman underneath him now was warm and willing, but he remembered the panic flashing across her face when he'd flirted with her in front of Sam last night. When he gazed down at her now, wanting more than anything to take this next step, he couldn't make himself move. Hope and fear raced through him, and he couldn't figure out which emotion was in charge.

"Madigan?" His struggle must have been noticeable. "Where did you go?"

He pulled out, nearly to the tip, then he slid back in. "I'm here.

I'm okay." Words failing him, he did what he did best and made love to her until they were a tangle of limbs and slick with sweat. He knew he was a coward, but he hoped his body told her all the words he couldn't yet say.

CHAPTER THIRTY-FIVE

ASHLEY

Ashley had been slammed all week dealing with the aftermath of a heavy snowfall that ushered in a vicious cold snap. She'd spent every morning detonating avalanche bombs and roping off slide-prone areas on the backside with Mace and Kev after the wind shifted the snow around during the night. Every day she helped Shannon and Tex manhandle the backside lift to keep the bastard running in the subzero temperatures. And every night she limped back to Madigan's cabin after dark, usually so tired all she could do was pat Murphy on the head, curl up into Madigan's waiting arms, and sleep.

The work helped keep her mind off her mother, off Chuck, off Bluebird's financial crisis, but she missed spending time with Madigan when she wasn't sleeping. They'd been on the precipice of something, like they were so close to telling each other how they really felt, how she hoped he felt. But growing up on this mountain, if there was ever a constant force that drove her life in any particular direction, good or bad, it was the weather. This week the weather demanded her attention, so she and Madigan and whatever was growing between them had to wait.

Today, however, the sun was shining, the winds were calm, and after the workday was over, she was going to have a long and uninterrupted evening with him in his cabin doing a hell of a lot more than sleeping.

"Ashley!" Shannon's shout pulled Ashley's attention as the short woman flagged her down on her way past the maintenance garage. "Have a minute?"

"Sure!" Ashley shouted back, skiing toward the garage. "How's the groomer?"

Stepping out into the sun, Shannon pulled her sunglasses from her front coverall pocket and slid them over her eyes. "Hydraulic is shot. How are you?"

"How am... What?" Ashley stammered. In all the years Shannon had worked at Bluebird, she'd never once asked Ashley how she was.

Shannon raised her sunglasses into her hair, squinting against the bright glare off the snow. "Listen, I know we don't talk much about our private lives, but there's something I've been wanting to say to you for a while now."

"You aren't quitting are you?" Ashley asked, panic-stricken. "Please don't quit. Do you need a raise? I don't think we could do anything this season, but maybe next—"

Shannon's hand fell onto Ashley's shoulder. "I'm not quitting."

"Oh, thank god," Ashley wheezed.

Removing her hand, Shannon took a deep breath. "Have I ever told you that my brother is a recovering addict?"

She hadn't even known Shannon *had* a brother. This was something she should have known. Her dad would have known this sort of thing about a member of his staff. "No, I didn't know that."

"I've only reconnected with him in the last few years. I haven't said anything about this because I didn't want things to get weird, but he stayed with Madigan at Little Timber four years ago."

Ashley's mouth felt suddenly like she'd been sucking on an entire bag of cotton balls. "He did?"

Shannon nodded. "Madigan saved my brother's life. I hadn't met him before he came to Bluebird, though. I'm not trying to give you my family sob story here, I just want you to know that you've done a very good thing by taking a risk on these men." She looked down at her boots. "I don't think you realize the impact this opportunity will have on them, on our community. Without Madigan vouching for him, it would have been next to impossible for my brother to find anyone willing to hire him after he left Little Timber. This partnership, the skills the men are learning here, the chance you're taking on them, it's admirable."

Ashley didn't feel admirable at all. She hadn't even considered the far-reaching implications of partnering with Little Timber. Hiring the men had been a means to an end, a mutually beneficial arrangement that improved her bottom line. "I didn't know about your brother," she said. "But I can't take any credit for the men working here. It was Maude Alice's idea."

"Sure it was," Shannon said dismissively, lowering her sunglasses again. "Well, I'm going back to work now, and you can go back to pretending you aren't with Madigan."

"What?" Ashley blanched. Even though she was fairly certain everyone knew they were sharing a bed, she and Madigan still hadn't gone public with their relationship. "I'm not—"

"Not that it's any of my business," Shannon said over her shoulder, walking back into the garage.

Standing in her office, Ashley peered through Madigan's window—which was what she would call the window he replaced for her forever—watching the man himself visit with Kev and Brian at the Moonlight lift while Murphy sat dotingly beside him. She knocked on the window, and when he looked up at her, she kissed her fingertips and pressed them onto the glass.

She had never in her life been so certain about her feelings for someone else, and also so terrified of sharing them. "Ugh," she groaned. "What is wrong with me?"

"That's a loaded question," Davis said, sauntering into her office with a handful of fliers.

"Funny," Ashley muttered, turning away from Madigan's broad shoulders as reluctantly as she might turn away from the slopes on a powder day.

After slapping the fliers on Ashley's desk, Davis sat down in her chair, swiveling it from side to side.

"Are those for the concert?" Ashley picked up a flier. "These are perfect, Davis."

"Funny, that is exactly what Madigan said after I gave him one."

"Oh, really? That's...interesting," Ashley replied enigmatically, setting the flier back on the pile.

Clasping her hands together on the desk, reminding Ashley of a psychiatrist about to render a diagnosis, Davis said, "Mom, can we please stop pretending you aren't crazy about him? It's getting annoying."

"I'm not... We're just friends. He's just a very good friend."

Rising to her feet, Davis walked around the desk, grabbed Ashley's arms, and shook her. "It's New Year's Eve, Mom. It's time for new beginnings. It's okay for you to start over. It's okay to have a new life with a man you are obviously in love with."

Ashley opened her mouth, but when nothing came out she closed it again. It wasn't that the word, *love*, had rendered her speechless. She had so many things to say, about Madigan, about what was in her heart. But when it came right down to it, she was still too scared to say any of them.

"It's ok." Davis rubbed her hands up and down Ashley's arms. "He's a good one, Mom."

Davis was right, Ashley knew. Madigan wasn't Chuck. He would never hurt her the way Chuck had hurt her. He'd never say the things Chuck had said to her, belittle or demean her like Chuck had. Madigan *was* good. But he wasn't the one she feared wasn't good enough. "What if he doesn't feel the same?" she said softly, like saying it loud might make it true. "What if he's not in love back?"

"You have *got* to be kidding me." Davis was incredulous. "That man is so into you it's almost embarrassing. He might as well get a new tattoo across his forehead that says, 'I Love Ashley Cooke.'"

Ashley's chin fell to her chest, a defeated groan creaking its way out of her.

"You deserve this, Mom. You deserve every bit of happiness you feel with him. I know Dad wasn't a good husband. I know he betrayed you in ways you've never told me about."

"Davis—"

"I know he hurt you, and I'm sure you're scared of getting hurt again. But I don't think you need to be scared of Madigan. He is one of the most trustworthy people I've ever met. So trust him, trust yourself, and tell him how you feel."

With a sigh, Ashley admitted, "You're right."

With a satisfied grin, Davis stated, "I know."

Ashley took her daughter's face in her hands. "I don't tell you this enough, but you have grown into the smartest, wisest, most phenomenal woman. And I am so proud of you."

"Aw, that's so sweet," Davis said, taking Ashley's hands from her face and holding them tightly in hers. "And, keeping that in mind, now might be an awesome time to tell you that I'm not going back to school."

"Wait, you're what?" Ashley spluttered. "Hold on a minute. Why?"

"Ummm," Davis began, then she spun around toward the door when Maude Alice popped her head in. "Hey Grandma! It is so good to see you. What's up?"

"We are *not* done here, young lady," Ashley said, but Davis had already tuned her out.

"I'm going skiing," Maude Alice replied stiffly, avoiding making eye contact with Ashley. They'd barely spoken since the terrain park surprise, but it was hard, keeping her anger up. As much as Maude

Alice pushed every single one of Ashley's buttons, she was still her mother. She still hated arguing with her. She still loved her.

Davis perked up. "Can I come with?"

"Of course," Maude Alice said, uncharacteristically reserved considering a Davis request to ski with her would typically send her into stratospheric levels of excitement. "Would you like to join us as well, Ashley?"

Ashley stared blankly at her mother, speechless. This felt like an olive branch, and Maude Alice never gave ground. Was she feeling well? "I'd—"

"She can't come," Davis cut in, winking at Ashley. "She has very important business to attend to with a very sexy pirate."

CHAPTER THIRTY-SIX

MADIGAN

Madigan missed Ashley. He missed her like he'd missed his favorite blanket when he was a kid that time he'd lost it for over a month, like he was never warm enough without her. Even though they'd slept together every night, they'd barely spoken because she'd been so tired. But he missed her. He missed talking to her, skiing with her, staring into her beautiful brown eyes instead of at her closed lids while she slept.

"Boss, you look like hell." Kev's brows slid together when he let Madigan into their cabin. "Trouble in paradise?"

"Zip it," Madigan grumbled, sitting on their couch and running his fingers through his hair, which was a tangled mess.

Pointing a finger at Madigan's chest, right over his heart, Kev said, "You know it's not healthy to keep everything bottled up in there, big guy."

Clay snorted from his bed.

Madigan's only response was to thrust Kev's drug test cup at him.

"Fair enough," Kev said, taking the cup and walking into the bathroom. "But I bet you'd feel a lot better if you talked about it."

Clay rose from his bed, setting a hand over Madigan's shoulder. "He's annoying, but he's right. Better to let it out than keep it in."

"Everything's fine," Madigan admitted. "I promise. Ashley's just been busy, and I'm feeling lonely. That's all."

Clay nodded. "We should have group. It's been a while, and I think we all need it."

"That's a great idea, Clay. I'll set one up for tomorrow." Because nothing, absolutely nothing would stand between him and finally confessing his feelings to Ashley tonight.

"Here you go, Boss," Kev said, setting his cup on the dresser.

After giving Clay his cup, Madigan unscrewed Kev's and dipped the test strip in. He'd performed hundreds of these tests over the years, and he knew all the colors by heart. When Kev's THC band turned dark green, he forced himself to blink twice and look again.

The cabin tilted, his stomach sinking like a brick in the middle of the ocean, like it had miles to go before it hit the ground. "Kev?" he said, raising the strip. "Is there something you need to tell me?"

"Huh?" Kev stared sideways at the strip, frowning. "I don't even know what I'm looking at."

"This," Madigan pointed at the strip, "is a positive test." Despite how many times he'd been through this before, his men relapsing, using, he couldn't believe it. How could he have missed the signs? "Why, Kev? You've been doing so well up here."

Swiping the test strip from Madigan's hand, Kev took a closer look. "This is bullshit. I haven't done anything, I swear."

"Why would you jeopardize this entire winter, Ashley's mountain, even whatever you have going with Davis just to get high?" Was this fallout from the pressure of the Christmas party? Had Kev been more upset than he'd let on that nobody had come to visit him? Madigan had spent the night so worried about Sam and so preoccupied with Ashley that he'd forgotten to check in with Kev.

"Who's getting high?" Clay asked, returning from the bathroom. When he handed Madigan his sample, he caught sight of Kev's test strip. Clay had taken enough drug tests to know the colors too. "Kev?" Clay turned to face his roommate. "What the hell?"

Kev was frantic, his eyes wide, his head shaking from side to side. "I haven't done anything. The test is wrong. It's wrong!"

"Take a seat," Madigan instructed numbly, pointing at Kev's bed while he dipped the test strip into Clay's sample.

"Holy shit!" Kev shouted when the same dark green band popped up on Clay's test strip. "Come on, Madigan. You can't believe this is real."

Feeling like he'd just been hurled off a cliff, he held Clay's test strip up in his trembling hand and said, "I think we've got a serious problem."

AFTER RUNNING tests on all the men, two more, Tex and Sam, popped positive for THC. Madigan was inconsolable. He knew it wouldn't have been hard for the men to find drugs at Bluebird, skiers smoked up on the chairlifts constantly. He just didn't think any of them would actually use while they were here. They seemed happy, thriving, comfortable. How could he have been so wrong? His job was to provide these men with a safe, drug-free environment in which they could find their way to lifelong sobriety, and he'd failed them. He'd failed Ashley. He'd failed everyone, just like he always did.

"Someone fucked us," Sam growled, prowling back and forth in Madigan's cabin, his shoulders hunched like a man spoiling for a fight. "They fucked us, Madigan."

"This is horseshit!" Tex cried.

Gnashing his teeth, Madigan stated as calmly as he could, "There is still no swearing."

"Sorry, Boss," Brian said, looking more nervous and strung out than Madigan had ever seen him, and he'd passed his drug test. "Everyone's just a little on edge right now."

"I'm not sorry," Kev spat, standing next to Madigan's door with his hands fisted at his sides. "Because I am not doing drugs!"

Clay stared at the floor. He hadn't spoken to Madigan since he'd shown him his positive test strip, wouldn't even look at him.

Burying his fingers in his beard, Madigan pulled until his eyes watered. This was not his first instance of multiple failed drug tests at Little Timber, but with every outraged outburst and every impassioned plea, he couldn't shake the feeling that the men were telling the truth. But what could he do? He had to trust the tests—which he'd run twice with the same results. That's what you did in his line of work. You trusted the test. You trusted the test, or you got burned. And he'd been burned before. He'd been the one starting the fires too, swearing up and down to everyone he loved that he hadn't been using so vehemently even he'd started to believe he hadn't relapsed. Even though he had.

"We're leaving the mountain and going back to Little Timber." Bracing himself for the blowback, he added, "Anyone who tested positive and wants to continue to stay at Little Timber will have to test daily, attend daily meetings, and participate in community service at my discretion. For those of you on parole," he swallowed back bile, "I'll have to report the results to your parole officers."

"No," Clay said, breaking his silence. "I'm not going back inside, Madigan. Not over something I didn't do."

"Me neither," Kev asserted, throwing an arm out in Clay's direction. "I mean seriously, Boss. Clay doesn't even smoke!"

Nodding, Clay crossed his arms over his chest. "Can't stand it. All it does is make me sleepy."

"You'll have to drag me back," Sam said. "Izzy will never let me see Sara again if I go back in."

Fear roiled through Madigan's gut. He wanted to believe them, but his head was spinning, his heart pounding, the walls closing in around him. Because whether they were telling the truth or not, right now he didn't have a choice as to what came next. Right now he was stuck. Trapped.

Walking to his door, dread weighing down his steps, he said, "I need to talk to Ashley. Go pack. Once we get back to Little Timber, I'll try to sort this through. But please don't run. If anyone leaves this mountain, there won't be anything I can do to help you."

"Don't worry," Brian said, staring Madigan down. "Nobody's done anything wrong yet, and we're not about to start."

CHAPTER THIRTY-SEVEN

ASHLEY

Bluebird Basin's Facebook page had never blown up like this before, probably because they rarely used it aside from posting snow reports. Ever since Davis started blasting out information about the concert, Ashley had spent at least an hour every day responding to comments and answering questions. According to the concert event page—which Davis dubbed "FlannelFest"—over 1,500 people were 'interested,' and they'd just passed 800 ticket pre-sales. Ashley shut her laptop, about to go tell Madigan the good news when someone knocked on her door.

"Come in," she called out, scratching Murphy's head under her desk while she pulled on her boots. When she sat back up, she found Madigan standing in her doorway, his jaw clenched, face pale, eyes hollow.

"Do you have a minute?" His voice sounded wrong, thin and reedy, his hands clutching his hat so tightly both HOPE and FEAR stretched out over his white knuckles. Murphy slid out from under her desk, but even he seemed to notice Madigan's distress, sitting quietly in place rather than running up to him like he usually did.

"What's wrong?" she asked, rising warily to her feet. "Are you okay?"

His breath came out in a ragged, urgent rush like he'd been holding it in for days. Swaying where he stood, he said, "Not really."

Running to his side, she led him to a chair. "Sit. Lean forward," she instructed, pushing his head down between his knees and rubbing his back. "Breathe."

His shoulders shuddered as he said something, but his voice was muffled by his jeans.

"I can't hear you, sweetheart."

When he sat back up, he stared at the floor, refusing to meet her eyes. "They failed their drug tests."

"What?" she blurted out on instinct, not comprehending. "What do you mean?"

"They failed. The men. They must have found weed somewhere."

"What?" she said again, louder this time, backing away from him. "Weed? When? Who?" All the 'W' questions in the world came stumbling out of her mouth. "Which men?"

He listed names: Sam, Tex, Kev, Clay.

"No, I don't believe it."

"It's true."

She shook her head. They wouldn't have done this. Not Sam. Not Clay. None of them! "Could the tests be wrong? Did you test them again? Test them again."

"Ashley." When he finally looked at her, his brow was creased, tiny, agonized lines radiating out from the corners of his eyes. "The tests weren't wrong."

"How do you know? They wouldn't—"

He reached out, grabbing her hand, his expression so terribly sympathetic she wanted to scream. "They're addicts. This happens."

She yanked out of his grip. "Are they denying it? Madigan, they wouldn't do this."

"Ashley, stop," he said, pleading with her. "You don't understand.

You don't know what you're dealing with. Addicts relapse. We make terrible decisions. We use even when things are going well, even when people are counting on us, even when we have an amazing opportunity land in our laps. Even though it feels personal, it's not. Believe me. It's just how addiction works."

"You're wrong." She knew how ridiculous this sounded, because of the two of them, she was without question the one out of her depth. But she couldn't back down. She just couldn't. She was frustrated, hurt, and so confused her head throbbed. Because what did this mean? What did this mean for the guys? For Madigan? For her?

She could feel him slipping away, shutting down, coldness sweeping in when he was always so warm. It was indescribable, how badly she wanted this not to be happening, how badly she *needed* this not to be happening. How far she'd go to make this *not be happening*. "The tests were wrong. You need to believe the guys! What's wrong with you?"

"What's wrong with me?" he said, his voice rising. "What's wrong with me is that I've been through this more times than I can remember. I've had my heart broken, trust broken, and nearly lost my home because of shit like this. I understand you like these guys. I like them too."

"It's not that I *like* them," she insisted. "It's that I trust them, and I don't understand why you don't!"

"Jesus, Ashley!" He stood from his chair, wheeling on her. The way he looked down at her, the condescension in his eyes, she felt herself getting smaller and smaller, all but vanishing into nothing when he said, "You really are naive."

She couldn't breathe. She could only stare at him, shaking, trying not to cry. Had that just happened? Had he honestly just said that to her?

"Fuck," he groaned, his hands scrubbing over his face. "I didn't mean that. I'm sorry. It's just everything is too close," he yanked on the collar of his shirt, "too much. I just need some space to figure this out."

Space? She would not cry, not until he left. Because that's what this was.

"We broke the contract," he told her. "We're leaving."

Of course he was leaving. That's what the good men in her life did. They left.

"I know we're putting you and Maude Alice in a terrible position, but I have to get the men back to Little Timber. I have to get them somewhere safe so I can try to figure this whole thing out."

When he pulled his hat down over his head, she wanted to rip it off and throw it through his window. She wanted to give it to Murphy as a chew toy. She wanted to beg him to stay. But maybe Chuck was right. Maybe Madigan was right. Maybe she was just a weak, pathetic, naive woman.

"I understand," she said as evenly as she could considering her entire world had just been flipped onto its side, everything she hadn't taken the time and care to secure in place sliding away from her. "When?"

"The men are packing now."

"Now?" Her heart plummeted so fast she grabbed at her stomach to try and keep it from falling through the floor.

He took a step toward her, freezing in place when she stepped back. "I'm so sorry—"

"Ashley!" a frantic, static-filled voice barked over her walkie, making Murphy growl.

"Is that Mace?" Madigan asked, frowning at the walkie.

Swiping the walkie from her desk with shaking hands, she pushed talk. "Mace? What is it?"

"It's Maude Alice," Mace said, breathless. "There was a snowslide on the Bitterroot Bowl. We can't find her."

Shock nearly made Ashley drop the walkie. "Davis was with her, is she—"

"Davis is fine. She's digging with me, but there's too much snow. We need help."

Shoving the walkie into her back pocket, Ashley snatched her coat, not even waiting to see if Madigan was following her down the stairs. She'd never run so fast, jumping into her boots and skis and cutting in on the lift line, Madigan sliding in beside her and Murphy leaping onto the chair between them. Even with Madigan and her dog riding up the mountain with her, Ashley had never felt so alone. Her mother was out there, buried under the snow, freezing, running out of air. And her last words to her had been so cruel, so cold. Refusing to lose both her parents, she willed the chair to go faster with every fiber of her being. But it didn't work, the ancient chair inching sluggishly up the mountain while her heart pounded and her eyes stung.

Eventually, like a monster lurking through the trees, the slide revealed itself, a long and narrow scar of broken snow and ice slashing down the run. The foot of fresh powder that had fallen over of the weak layer of corn snow had made for perfect slide conditions. Which was precisely why Ashley and Mace had roped off that section of the run two days ago. *That woman and her insistence on ducking any rope anyone ever put in front of her!*

Leaping from the chair when they reached the top of the lift, Ashley skied like the wind down to the slide, Madigan hot on her heels. Murphy charged through the snow past them, racing toward Davis and Mace, both on their knees at the far end of the slide.

When Ashley saw the raw desperation on Davis's face, her knees buckled.

"Mom," Davis said through a choked sob when Ashley skied up beside her. "I told her not to duck the rope. I told her it wasn't safe. She wouldn't listen."

Unclipping from her skis, Ashley grabbed Davis and pulled her close. "It's not your fault, honey. It's just the way she is. It's the way she's always been."

Madigan slid to a stop, snapping his fingers at Murphy and shouting, "Search!" Then he ditched his skis and dropped to his knees beside Mace, both men digging and hauling huge slabs of snow over their shoulders.

"Did you see her go down?" Ashley asked as Murphy dove headfirst into the slide, snuffling and digging in the brittle, jagged snow.

"No," Davis said, pulling out of Ashley's arms. "She turned down the run, ducked the rope, and then it was nothing but white and noise."

"Maude Alice!" Mace called out, his voice a dry rasp like he'd been calling out for hours.

"Mom!" Ashley shouted, walking around the bottom of the slide, searching for any signs of movement. "Mom, can you hear me?"

"Grandma!" Tears streamed down Davis's cheeks. "Grandma! Shout if you can hear us!"

Murphy's single, deafening bark was one Ashley had never heard from him before—a short, high-pitched report. Everyone stopped in their tracks and turned toward the dog.

"He's got something," Madigan said, racing to Murphy's side. "What's in there, buddy?"

Murphy sniffed in one spot, then another a few inches away, and then he barked again and pounced, shoving both paws into a mound of snow and ice. Ashley's heart caught in her throat when he started digging, snow flying in a wide arc behind him. His snout dove into the hole he'd made, popping back out so he could thrust his feet into the hole again, digging even deeper.

Ashley and Davis got to their knees, helping Mace and Madigan move chunks of compacted snow away from the area Murphy was focusing on. Abruptly, Murphy backed out of the hole, growling and barking and lurching at the hole like there was a cat stuck inside it.

It wasn't a cat.

"Get me the hell out of here! Get me out!" Maude Alice cried, her voice muffled and cracking. Ashley's mother, who was afraid of nothing, was stuck under four feet of dense snow, panicking, terrified. Pushing Murphy gently away from the hole he'd started digging at again, Ashley peered inside. She couldn't see her mother's face or her coat or her hat, only her hand, her fingernails jagged and torn, the snow around them clawed and tinged pink from trying to dig herself out.

"We will, Mom," she said, her entire body shaking, her eyes filling with tears at that pink snow. "But it's going to take a minute. We'll have to dig."

"Okay," Maude Alice said. "But p-p-please hurry."

Sprawling out on her stomach, Ashley reached into the hole as far as she could. She barely made contact with Maude Alice's fingers, but when she did, her mother's hand jerked to the side, grasping Ashley's tightly.

"Hurry, Ashley. I'm so c-c-cold. And my ankle..."

She snapped. Ashley just...snapped. Ragged sobs tearing from her throat, she dug frantically, raking her fingers through hard, icy snow.

"Ashley." Madigan's voice, his hand on her back, they were the only things keeping her from scraping her own fingers raw digging for her cold, shivering mother. "Ashley, stop. She's okay. Let us help you."

Even after Kev and Brian arrived with shovels and a rescue toboggan, it still took what felt like an eternity of digging to safely uncover Maude Alice. But eventually, while Ashley watched with Davis gripped tightly in her arms, Madigan pulled her mother free of the snow.

"Thank you, Madigan," Maude Alice said weakly, curling against his chest, shivering. As he brushed snow from her face and neck, she asked, "How long was I in there? And why is it so dark outside?" And then she passed out in his arms.

"Mom!" Ashley fell to her knees again in front of Madigan, taking Maude Alice's hands in hers, rubbing her frozen fingers like this would somehow make her open her eyes. "Mom, wake up."

Ripping off his glove, Mace checked Maude Alice's neck for a pulse.

"Grandma?" Davis staggered back a step. "She isn't... She's not—"

"She's breathing. She's okay," Kev said, moving as close to Davis as he could without touching her, everything in his expression telling Ashley that keeping his distance from her was killing him. "She's going to be okay, right Mace?"

"Her pulse is steady," Mace said. "But we have to get her down, get her warm."

After she helped lift Maude Alice's limp body onto the toboggan, Ashley clipped into her skis, turning to follow Mace and Kev as they skied Maude Alice down the run. But then she stalled, unclipped, turned around. Because her daughter was frozen in place, trembling, shaking, watching her indestructible grandmother being hauled down the hill, strapped into a sled, unmoving.

"Davis," Ashley said, pulling her daughter's rigid body into her arms again, squeezing, rubbing her back. "She'll be okay."

"I know," Davis replied, and it wasn't sadness or fear in her voice. It was anger. "I just don't understand. Why is she like this? Why won't she ever listen? Why can't she just...grow up?"

Ashley's sigh when she leaned back to meet Davis's stare was deep and old and tired and necessary. "It's just who she is. Good or bad, she is who she is."

"Yeah, well. Who she is sucks sometimes," Davis said, wiping tears off her cheek. Tilting her chin at Madigan, who hadn't skied down yet, who was staring up at them looking wretched, Davis muttered, "What's up with him?"

Ashley's chest cinched. "Have you and Kev talked today?"

Davis shook her head slowly, suspiciously. "No, we've been busy. Why?"

"Ski down. Talk to him." Ashley glanced at Madigan. "I'll be down in a minute."

After watching Davis go, Ashley studied the hole where Murphy had somehow found Maude Alice. Such a tiny hole in the huge expanse of the slide. So easy to miss. Without the dog, they never would have found her in time, and she would have suffocated down there. They would have lost her. Ashley would have lost her.

"Hey," Madigan said, coming to her side, his eyes locked onto hers, his hands rubbing up and down her arms. "Breathe, Ashley. Just breathe. She's all right."

She hadn't heard him walk up to her. She didn't know she'd been holding her breath. She didn't know she'd started crying. All these things had just happened, like the sun rising and setting, like her arms wrapping around his waist, like her face burrowing into his chest.

"Don't leave," she whispered, squeezing him tighter. "Please."

He held her for a long moment, then he kissed her head through her hat and said, "I'm sorry, Ashley. I wish things were different."

She pulled back, making one last desperate attempt to keep him. "I can amend the contract so you don't have to leave. Please give me a chance. Give *us* a chance."

Emotions went to war on his face—shock, confusion, hope maybe? But then, breaking Ashley's heart into so many pieces it would never beat the same way again, a grim acceptance. She knew what he was going to say before the words left his lips. Another man she'd tried and failed to make stay with her.

"I'm sorry," he said again, taking her hands in his, rubbing her frozen fingers the same way she'd done to her mother, trying to warm her up even though she had a feeling nothing would ever make her warm again. "But I don't have a choice."

CHAPTER THIRTY-EIGHT

ASHLEY

MAUDE ALICE's doctor had come and gone, leaving in a frustrated huff after Maude Alice, awake and stubborn as ever, adamantly refused his recommendation that she go to the hospital. The doctor suggested rest, so that's what she'd been doing, sleeping so deeply—not even stirring when Clay came up to say goodbye—that Ashley wondered more than once if she should ask the doctor to come back.

Leaving her mother's side just long enough to stand at the window in the dining hall, Ashley looked down on the parking lot while Madigan and the men packed their belongings into Lydia. He glanced up at her only once, and when they locked eyes, she held her breath. She knew she'd regret her choice to stay up in the lodge for the rest of her life, but she couldn't make her feet move toward the stairs. She couldn't say goodbye to him. She wouldn't. She was going to figure this out. She was going to get him back.

Returning from saying goodbye to Kev, her eyes red and puffy, Davis staggered up the stairs. Walking right up to Ashley, she nestled into her open arms and said, "Kev didn't do drugs. This is such—"

"Bullshit," Ashley finished for her, stroking a hand over her hair. "I know."

"Are you sure you don't want to go down? They're leaving in a few minutes."

When Ashley shook her head, Davis squeezed her tightly.

THE SUN HAD SET, Davis had gone to bed, and Maude Alice still hadn't opened her eyes. Sitting in a chair beside her bed, Ashley held her mother's hand in hers. Maude Alice's hands had become so frail, her skin thin and delicate, blue veins crisscrossing her knuckles like lines on a map. Even though she knew it was happening in a literal sense, she'd never thought of Maude Alice as getting older, only more stubborn, more stuck in her ways. Sitting with her now, watching her chest rise and fall, staring at the creases etched around her eyes and mouth, she saw it, the years, the age. The impermanence of this person she'd always believed was permanent.

"Please wake up," she whispered, leaning forward to rest her cheek on the back of Maude Alice's hand. They'd spent the last few years silently at odds with each other, never supporting each other, never meeting each other halfway. On a day when they'd all lost so much, at the start of a new year, Ashley knew she didn't want to live that way anymore.

Reaching up to brush strands of soft, silver hair back from Maude Alice's forehead, Ashley said, "I'm sorry, Mom." The words came out hushed and tight, but at least they came out. "I know I'm impossible to please. I know I hold grudges, and I don't forgive easily enough. I know how hard it was for you to lose Dad, and I know how much you miss him." It was easier to talk to Maude Alice while she slept, so Ashley kept going, carefully letting go of the words and feelings she'd been keeping inside herself for three years. "I love you, Mom. You hurt me sometimes, but I hurt you too. I know you love this mountain as much as I do, as much as Dad did, and I am so sorry I said he'd be furious with you. It was a terrible thing to say. Dad would have loved the terrain park." She wiped away a tear before it could slip down her cheek. "He would have taken one look at it and said—"

"'Would you just look at that son of a bitch,'" Maude Alice said through a dry throat, her hand squeezing Ashley's.

"You're awake," Ashley said, wiping her eyes with the back of her hand as quickly as she could before Maude Alice realized she'd been crying. But then she stopped, because maybe it was okay if her mother saw her crying. "How much of that did you hear?"

When Maude Alice's eyes opened, tears made them shimmer. Her voice trembling, she said, "I love you too, Ashley. You're my daughter, my baby. All I want, or have ever wanted, is for you to be happy. I've just done a terrible job of showing it. I'm sorry I wasn't there for you when Max died, or after. I just miss him so much." Now they were both crying. "I don't even know who I am without him. I'm cold and mean and overbearing, and I can't stand it."

Ashley's tears fell onto their clasped hands, her own words, her own feelings echoed back to her. She wasn't the only one who was lost without her father. "I'm sorry I needed to talk about him when you needed to hold him close." She thought about Madigan, about how she couldn't even tell him goodbye today and he was only leaving the mountain. "I'm sorry I never tried to see his death from your perspective. You were right. I was selfish."

"No, you weren't," Maude Alice insisted. "You were grieving, and I couldn't grieve with you. But maybe we can start over, do things differently. I promise to try and talk more, or at least listen when you need to talk. And I promise from here on out to consult you about anything I'm thinking about doing for the mountain."

Ashley nodded, sniffling. "And I promise that I'll listen to you and to your ideas. And we'll do better. We'll be better. But you have to promise to stop ducking ropes!"

Maude Alice laughed, and then she coughed, wincing.

"What is it? What hurts?"

"Everything, dear," Maude Alice replied in such a Maude Alice way Ashley's eyes filled with fresh tears. Pushing herself up, Ashley helping her sit, Maude Alice looked around the room and said, "But where is my hero?"

"Your hero?" Did she mean Madigan? Kev? Ashley wasn't ready to tell her that they were gone. Not yet.

"Murphy!" Maude Alice called out, already sounding stronger because nothing kept her down for long, not even an avalanche. "Where are you?"

Wiggling out from his position half-way under her bed—where he'd been since the doctor had left—Murphy whined, resting his head gently on Maude Alice's arm.

Reaching across with her other hand, she patted the dog on his big furry head and said, "I'm sorry I ever called you a poor excuse for a rescue dog. You saved my life, and just as soon as I can, I am going to buy you the biggest and meatiest bone I can find."

"I'm, um, sorry to interrupt," a hesitant voice said from the door. It was Mace, standing just outside the room. Murphy growled.

"Hush now," Maude Alice said, gesturing with her finger for Murphy to sit.

"Come on in, Mace." Ashley waved him in.

Shaking his head, Mace wrung his hands. "I don't want to come in. I just wanted to say," his Adam's apple bobbed, "that I'm sorry about what happened."

Ashley frowned, confused. "It's not your fault, Mace. We had the run roped off."

"And I ducked it," Maude Alice added, "like a fool."

Mace pressed his lips together. "I know. But I'm sorry anyway. I just wanted you both to know that."

"Is everything all right?" Ashley asked.

He smiled, but it was joyless. "Everything's fine. I'm just glad you're okay, Maude Alice." And then he turned around and walked away.

"That was weird," Ashley muttered.

"It certainly was," Maude Alice concurred, sucking air in through her teeth and clutching at her side when she tried to prop herself up on her pillows.

Helping her lean forward, Ashley positioned three pillows behind her back. "Doc Hanley said you might have a broken rib and you definitely have a sprained ankle. I'll go get you some ice."

"Wait." Maude Alice clutched Ashley's wrist. "Was Clay here earlier? I remember...something. He seemed sad. Did something happen while I was out?"

Ashley took a deep breath, let it out, and then she told her mother everything.

CHAPTER THIRTY-NINE

MADIGAN

KEV'S PAROLE officer's card trembled in Madigan's hand. They'd been back at Little Timber for three days, but he still hadn't been able to dial a single PO's number yet. If he waited much longer, he'd be in bigger trouble than the men. The problem was, nothing about any of this felt right. He didn't feel like a sober living home administrator completing a necessary, if unpleasant, part of his job. Three days removed from the mountain, from the positive tests, three days to work through his shock and disappointment hadn't made him feel any more confident in is decision at all. In fact—while he dropped Kev's card back to his desk—he only felt like a coward, a traitor, and an absolute piece of shit for the things he'd said to Ashley.

All four men who tested positive, on the rare occasion they deigned to speak to him at all, still insisted that they had not been doing drugs. Usually by this point the men would be coming clean, ready to fess up and clear their consciences, ask for help, ask for leniency from the system. Madigan saw no signs of breaking among the guys. In fact, they'd closed ranks, the rest of the men barely speaking to him too, barely making eye contact, giving him shoulders so cold he hadn't taken off his coat since they'd unpacked.

He hadn't spoken to Ashley since leaving Bluebird, since he'd stared up at her through the lodge window and felt his chest cave in on itself. He knew he was just doing his job, keeping Bluebird safe, keeping Ashley safe, but he couldn't shake the feeling that he'd messed up again, that he'd hurt her just like he'd hurt everyone else in his life. Like it was just what he did and would always do. *Hi, my name is Madigan, and I hurt people.*

She hadn't called him, hadn't even come down to say goodbye to him. She probably felt, and rightly so, that she'd dodged a massive relationship bullet when he left. So why did his heart keep trying to convince him he'd given up on the best thing that had ever happened to him without even putting up a fight?

Sitting alone at his desk, he frowned at the plain white walls surrounding him, squinted at the bright overhead lighting, and sighed at how stark and empty his office felt, how cold. He didn't even have a bookshelf or a lamp to create any sense of home, any coziness. There were no romance novels or dried lavender sprigs. There was no roaring fire crackling and popping in the background. Little Timber no longer felt like his home, not the way it used to, not since he felt the comfort of falling asleep curled around Ashley, or the contentment of waking up with her in his arms as the morning sunlight gilded her bare skin.

His head was so full of Ashley, her soft golden curls, her sweet apple blossom scent, how gentle her fingertips felt tracing over his tattoos, that when his phone buzzed on his desk his heart leapt into his throat. He clutched the phone, picked it up, prayed. But it wasn't her.

"Hey, old man," he said, trying to sound chipper and failing miserably.

"Don't you 'old man' me," Conor replied flatly. "What's going on? My Mattie senses have been tingling all week."

"It's nothing. Everything's fine," Madigan lied.

"Nope. Try again."

He ran his hand over his face. "Just a problem with the men. You know how it goes."

"Ah, shit. Mattie, I'm sorry." His dad knew how easily the men who stayed at Little Timber found trouble, as easily as Madigan had when he'd been using. "How bad is it?"

Madigan couldn't give his father any specifics, but he could tell him, "We had to leave the mountain." Saying the words out loud hurt more than he thought was possible.

"You did? Must have been pretty bad then."

"You know I can't talk about it, Dad."

He made a frustrated sound. "I don't need to know the details, Son. But you need to talk. I can tell." And then, after a beat, "How's Ashley taking this?"

"She's fine," Madigan said unconvincingly.

"She's...fine?"

Pulling his pendant out of his shirt, rubbing his thumb over the warm metal, finding it fitting that the only warm thing in his office was the one thing she'd given him, he said, "It's over, Dad. She doesn't want to see me anymore."

After a beat. "She said that to you?"

"She didn't *need* to say it to me," Madigan said, dropping the pendant back down his shirt "We left the mountain days ago, and I haven't heard from her since. It's over."

"So something happened with the men, Ashley asked you to leave, and now she won't talk to you?"

"Well, no. Not...necessarily."

"Explain."

Stifling a groan, Madigan said, "She didn't ask us to leave, but I didn't have much of a choice."

Conor was silent for a moment, and Madigan felt the impact of it, crackling over his neck like lightning about to strike. "She didn't ask you to leave," he repeated, not a question. "And yet you left anyway."

"I have a responsibility to these men, and I couldn't keep them safe up there. Trust me, even though she didn't ask us to leave, she wanted us to."

"So you're a mind reader now?"

"Dammit, Dad. Why are you on my ass over this? I did what I had to do." The way this sounded like utter bullshit even to his own ears was noteworthy.

"Okay, okay. Just stay with me here for a minute," Conor said with exasperating patience. "If she didn't ask you to leave, what did she ask you to do?"

"What do you mean? She didn't ask me to do anything."

"So she let you and the men leave without saying a word? Just waved goodbye and returned to her life as usual. That's awfully callous. Sounds like maybe she wasn't the right woman for you after all."

"That's not what happened," Madigan snapped.

"No?"

"No, she's not like that. She didn't just watch us leave. She tried... She tried to..." He paused, finally recognizing his dad's tactic as the Jedi mind trick it was.

"What did she try, Mattie? Tell me."

Slumping back in his chair, he stared up at the ceiling, accepting defeat. "She said she didn't want us to go. She wanted to try to work things out," he swallowed, "together."

Conor sighed. "Son, you know I love you. But sometimes you are your own worst enemy. When are you going to learn that you deserve a partner in this life? When will you realize you don't have to do everything alone?"

"I don't know," he admitted, fully realizing what he'd done. Ashley had offered to help. She'd begged him to stay and give her a chance, and he'd left her anyway because he hadn't believed her, he hadn't listened. All because of his own fear. *No wonder she hasn't called.* "Why do I fuck everything up all the time?"

"You don't fuck everything up any more than anyone else. It's just that when you do, you go all out."

Impossibly, Madigan laughed.

"Now you just need to fix it."

"It's too late," he said, wishing it wasn't true but knowing it was.

"Really? Or do you think, just maybe, she might be feeling the exact same things you're feeling right now?"

"I don't know—"

"What is she worth to you?"

"What do you mean?"

Madigan could see his father leaning forward, clasping his hands on his desk, staring him down. "What is she worth? What will you risk for her?"

What was she worth? *She's worth everything.* What would he risk? *He'd risk it all.* His dad was right. He didn't care if it was too late. He didn't even care if she felt the same, even though he hoped with every fiber of his being that she did. All he cared about was making sure she knew that he was in love with her. Desperately, madly, and wholeheartedly in love with her.

Standing, Madigan said, "Gotta go, Dad. Call you later." He ended the call, but not before hearing his dad say, "There's my guy."

He didn't have a plan, not even close, but he swiped his keys off his desk and was about to go ask Brian to hold down the fort when Sam opened the door to his office and walked in, followed by Clay and Kev, then Tex, Brian, Jacob, Mark. Soon all ten men stood in his office, arms crossed over their chests or hands stuffed into their pockets.

Taking a step forward, Brian said, "Take a seat, Boss. We need to talk."

CHAPTER FORTY

ASHLEY

WHY HADN'T she taken any pictures of him? Not a single candid, no couples selfies on the chairlift, not even a sneak shot while he'd been sleeping. She kept trying to remember the precise way his eyes crinkled, or how his lips curled into a smile beneath his beard. After three days of not seeing him, not talking to him, not touching him while she listened to his mixtape on repeat with the cassette player she'd dug out of their basement, she just wanted to see his face again, just for a minute. And then she remembered he'd been famous.

Instead of putting out want ads and calling in every favor anyone ever owed her to fully staff the mountain again like she should have been doing, she searched for pictures of Madigan on the web like an infatuated fan. Her eyes stinging because she kept forgetting to blink, she chewed on her thumb, clicking on picture after picture of the twenty-something rock god who occupied her every waking thought, saving her favorites in a file called 'taxes' so nobody would ever think to open it.

"That man was a sex bomb."

Slamming her laptop shut, Ashley spun around in her chair. "Have you ever heard of knocking?"

Davis sat on the corner of Ashley's desk, petting Murphy when he lumbered over and put his head in her lap. "I did knock. You're just thirsting so hard after Mad Madigan you didn't hear me."

"You know his nickname?" Ashley asked. He'd never told her they used to call him that. Maybe he didn't like it. It was probably a nickname he wanted to keep in the past with everything else. But, *damn*, she liked it. *Mad Madigan.*

"I can Google too, you know," Davis replied with a smirk. "Has he called?" The dark circles that had camped out under her eyes for the last few days seemed to be fading away, like maybe she'd finally gotten some sleep last night.

Ashley shook her head, reaching out for Davis's hand. "How are you, sweetie?"

She shrugged. "I'm fine. It's just..." She shrugged again.

"Tell me." Ashley squeezed her hand.

"I know it doesn't matter. I know nobody would ever believe me, but I am positive that Kevin was not doing drugs. And Clay? Sam? I mean, seriously? It's all so hard to believe."

Regardless of how convinced Madigan had been that the men had lied, and that Ashley didn't know what she was talking about, she couldn't convince her brain that these guys would have risked so much to go off and get high in the woods somewhere. It didn't add up, at all. She opened her mouth to agree with Davis when her phone buzzed sharply, four times in a row. *Chuck.*

Murphy snarled.

"Good dog," Ashley said, reaching across her desk to scratch Murphy under his chin.

"What does Chuck want?" Maude Alice muttered, strolling into Ashley's office, recognizing the ringtone. "Haven't we had enough drama for one week?"

"Who the hell knows," Ashley replied. Of course Chuck would get some sort of sixth sense to call her now since she had no staff and probably no concert to raise the money to pay him back for the terrain park, because—and the worst part by far—she had no Madigan. Chuck undoubtedly smelled her misery from miles away, like a shark.

Bracing herself for another offer on the mountain, and for the crushing realization that if they couldn't find a way out of this mess she'd have to take it, she answered the phone.

"Hello, Chuck." Putting the call on speaker, Ashley motioned for Maude Alice to sit down. She'd been feeling better since her near-death encounter with a half-ton of snow, but she was still weak and sleeping longer than usual.

Maude Alice complied, sitting across from Ashley's desk and pulling her sweater tightly around her chest while Murphy trotted over to sit next to her, resting his head on her lap now. He'd been working very hard trying to take care of all three of them over the last few days.

"I've got a surprise for you." Chuck's voice was gratingly chipper.

Davis frowned at the phone.

"Great. You know how much I love surprises," Ashley said sarcastically. After this week, she'd be completely content living out the remainder of her days in a surprise-free existence.

His laughter was pure arrogance. "I heard you lost some staff, so I'm sending you some of my finest. They should arrive later this morning."

Ashley bit down so hard she strained something. He must have heard about the men. Mountain gossip was worse than small town gossip. "That's not necessary," she said. "We've got it covered." This wasn't true, unless by 'covered' she meant working long before the sun came up and even longer after it went back down with Davis, the current skeleton crew staff, and even Maude Alice to keep the mountain open and running. Maybe she was stubborn, maybe she was inflexible, but she refused to ask for or accept any more help from Chuck.

"I hate to say I told you so," he said, his tone conveying how much he actually loved telling her I told you so, "but I knew you should never have hired those men. You just can't trust criminals not to break the law. And finding drugs on a family mountain like Bluebird, that's the kind of story that could put a small hill like yours right out of business."

Slamming her finger into the mute button, Ashley hissed, "How the fuck does he know that?" Only three people knew the men had left because of drugs, and they were all sitting in this room.

Maude Alice shrugged, confused. But Davis wasn't confused, she was furious. Her finger jabbed at the phone. "It was Dad. It had to have been Dad. He framed them. That asshole! YOU ASSHOLE!" she shouted into the muted phone.

"Ashley?" Chuck said, sounding annoyed. "Are you there?"

"Yep," she said after unmuting the phone. "Um, you're right about that. I've definitely learned my lesson. But I gotta go, a, uh, kid just puked in a trash can in the dining hall." Ending the call, she looked up at Davis. "You honestly think he'd do that?"

"Yes, he'd do it," Davis snapped. She held up a finger. "A. He wants Bluebird." Another finger. "B. He hates Madigan." A third finger flicked up. "And C. He'd do anything to win you back. What better way than to turn Madigan into the bad guy, letting Dad swoop in and save the day."

"I agree," Maude Alice said. "He's a sad, pathetic little man."

"But how?" Ashley racked her brain. When had Chuck been here last? Did he pay someone to bring the men drugs? Call her naive, but she still believed the men wouldn't have willingly gotten high. "How did he get them to fail their tests?"

"*I think I might know.*"

Ashley, along with Davis and Maude Alice and even Murphy, turned to look at the man standing in the door.

Holding a drug test strip in his hand, Mace said, "I don't do drugs. But," he looked at the strip, "this is positive."

"What do you mean?" Ashley asked, the room spinning fast enough to make her grasp the edge of her desk.

In the time it took for Mace to tell them about how Chuck found him in his office last week, giving him a few chocolate pies from Glazed and Confused, telling him they were for the "new employees," Ashley nearly broke off a piece of her desk with how hard she'd been digging her fingers into it.

"The only people who ended up eating the pies were Sam, Kev, Clay, Tex, Maude Alice," Mace scratched his copper curls, "and me. I, um, ate one almost all by myself. I know they were for the guys, and I felt really bad about it. But it was so good, and I have a chocolate problem. But afterwards, I felt..."

"High?" Maude Alice asked, a brow raised.

Mace nodded. "I thought I was just getting sick or something. So I slept it off and felt fine the next day. But then, when Kev told me about the drug tests, when he told me which of the guys tested positive, I knew. I knew something had been wrong with those pies, those pies *Chuck* brought here. So I went to the drug store and tested myself." Looking at his test strip again, he said, "Positive for THC." His green eyes, watery and bloodshot, met Ashley's. "He smirked when he gave me the pies, Ashley. He *smirked*."

"That son of a bitch!" Maude Alice shouted, sending Murphy scampering from the room.

"I knew I should have said something right away," Mace said, "but I was scared. I was scared you'd think *I* did it."

"It's not your fault," Ashley said, stepping up to Mace and patting his arm. "You didn't do anything wrong."

"We need to take him down," Davis sneered. "He's gone way too far this time. He will pay for this."

"Honey," Ashley said, worried about her daughter because no matter how much she hated Chuck, he was still her father.

"Don't 'honey' me," Davis pushed back. "He hurt people. He hurt," her voice cracked, "Kev."

Ashley nodded. "We can't just accuse him though, can we? We need proof."

When Mace said, "I, um, still have some of that pie," Ashley smiled.

"Davis?" she said, turning her smile on her daughter.

With her phone already in her hand, scrolling through her contacts, Davis said, "Guess Dad forgot he had a chemist for a daughter with a best friend at the state drug lab."

CHAPTER FORTY-ONE

MADIGAN

Taking in all ten men crowded together in his office, a determined united front staring him down, Madigan set his jaw. Whatever they were here for, they were organized, prepared, and Madigan knew his trip to see Ashley would have to wait. "Gentlemen?" he said evenly. "What can I do for you?"

He wasn't surprised to see Brian taking charge. He was the calmest of the men, the most clearheaded, but his hands were shaking now, his fingers gripping at the seams of his jeans. "We just want you to listen to us." He waived an arm to encompass the men in the room. "Lives are at stake here, marriages, families. Have you called any POs yet?"

"I haven't," Madigan admitted. "But I will, today." He couldn't leave them hanging like this any longer. It wasn't fair.

"The tests were wrong." Brian widened his stance, squaring off. "None of us did any drugs. Nobody has broken their paroles."

Taking notice of the word *us*, even though most of the men standing before him had tested negative, Madigan couldn't help but appreciate the camaraderie. Even so, he drove the heels of his palms into his eyes and rubbed, unable to see his way out of this situation. "Guys, we can't keep going around and around about this."

Brian stood his ground. "You of all people should know how important it is that the punishment fits the crime. There was no crime committed here. If you do make those calls today, you will be ruining the lives of innocent men. And I think you know this. You know something is wrong, otherwise you would have called any of their POs already."

"I did not do drugs," Kev said, stepping forward with a vibrating intensity like he couldn't stand to stay still and silent for another second.

"Neither did I," said Tex, taking his hat off and holding it over his heart. "I swear on my mother."

Sam stepped forward next, his hands open at his sides, pleading. "Izzy let me talk to Sara on the phone last week. And after, Izzy actually talked to me for ten whole minutes. Do you honestly think I'd throw that all away so easily just to smoke weed? *Weed*, Madigan? Please. If I was gonna relapse, it wouldn't be with fuck— with weed."

"We know you've been burned before," Brian said. "We know that addicts lie and manipulate and relapse. We've all done it, but this is not what's happening here."

"Then tell me, what is happening?" Madigan implored. "Please someone explain it to me because I don't know what to do here."

"We were framed," Kev said. "Someone gave you a bad set of tests or slipped us something."

"Come on, Kev. Who would do something like that?" Madigan couldn't even imagine someone stooping so low. It didn't make any sense. "Who would want you to fail your drug tests?"

"A selfish, insecure, snake of an ex-husband. That's who."

At the sound of her voice, Madigan shot to his feet, nearly tipping his chair over behind him. "Ashley?"

When she walked into his office, it was like the sun returning after weeks of non-stop rain. But her arrival was so sudden it barely felt real, and if it weren't for the men's shocked expressions as they parted to make way for her, he might have thought he was making her up, his mind finally breaking under the unrelenting stress of the last few days. "What are you doing here?"

"I'm sorry to interrupt your—" she looked around at the men and frowned, probably noticing the tension in the air, so thick Madigan felt like he could reach out and grab a handful of it "—meeting, but I think there's something you all need to know."

SITTING AT HIS DESK, his nerves racing, Madigan stared wordlessly at Ashley. She sat perched on the chair across from him, leaning forward, whether to get closer to him or to make it easier for her to get up and leave, he didn't want to guess.

The men had filed out to process what she'd just told them, and the chorus of their outbursts—confused shock followed by pure, poorly restrained rage and countless broken Little Timber rules—had finally faded into quiet murmurs in the background.

"Are you all right?" she asked carefully. "You look..."

She didn't need to finish the thought. He knew how he looked because he wasn't all right. "I don't think so," he told her. "I didn't trust them. I didn't believe them. They kept trying to convince me, and I refused to listen. I would have sent some of them back to prison."

"You couldn't have known." Her hands were clasped in her lap, and he wished they were sliding into his. "You did exactly what you were supposed to do."

"What I was supposed to do," he repeated softly. "No, what I was *supposed* to do was protect them, support them. And I failed. I failed them. I failed Bluebird." He forced himself to meet her eyes, no matter how badly it hurt. "I failed you."

"You didn't fail me," she told him. "And you didn't fail them either. None of this is your fault."

He'd seen it before, felt it before, this deeply compassionate side of her. But right now he hadn't earned it, not even close. "Ashley, you don't under—"

Jerking up straight, she cut him off with a raised hand. "If you tell me that I don't understand one more time, I'm going to scream. I understand plenty."

He winced. "I'm sorry. You're right." When she rose to her feet, panic rattled him because he knew she was about to leave. He'd insulted her, belittled her again, and she was going to leave him.

But instead of turning toward the door, she walked around his desk, his heart thumping in time with every step she took. Swiveling his chair to face her, he kept his hands glued to his armrests despite how badly they ached to reach for her. He didn't know what was happening. He didn't know if he was allowed to touch her anymore. He watched her, transfixed as her hand rose slowly from her side. When her fingers slid over his cheek, he shuddered.

"It's not your fault," she repeated. "I don't blame you. The men don't blame you. The only person blaming you for this, is you." Stepping between his legs, she raised her other hand so that she held his face between them. "If this is anyone's fault, it's mine. I'm the one who married that conniving asshole."

"If I ever see him again," he said with barely concealed fury, "*I'll* be the one going back to prison."

"At least you'd have Maude Alice and Davis to share a cell with."

Gazing up at her, sliding one of his hands over hers, curling his fingers through her fingers, he let the words rush out of him, admissions, confessions. "I've missed you. I shouldn't have left. You offered to help, and instead of letting you, I called you naive because I was so scared I'd ruined everything, that if I'd stayed I would have only made things worse. So I ran. When I should have trusted you, when I should have listened to you, when I should have tried, I ran. I'm sorry, Ashley. Please tell me I didn't fuck this up for good. Please tell me there's still a chance for us."

Letting go of his face, she took his right hand in hers, brushing her fingertips over his knuckles, over his FEAR. "You didn't ruin anything. I was scared too. I was scared for the men, for Bluebird. I was scared of getting hurt again. But mostly, I was scared of losing you." Taking his other hand, she traced over his HOPE. "But maybe we can stop being afraid now. Maybe we can stop running. Maybe we can let go, start over, and move on together. I was wrong when I told you that being with you was worth the risk. Because you," she kissed the H, "are not a risk. You are my heart."

"Ashley," he whispered as he reached for her, sliding his hand over her hip. When he pulled her into his lap, when she wrapped her arms around his neck, when her apple blossom scent surrounded him, he knew she was right. He had been running. He was still running, from his past, his fears, from ghosts. From a future with her where he might be truly happy, a future his fear kept trying to convince him he wasn't ready for and didn't deserve. Holding her, breathing her in, he decided right then and there that this would be the last day he'd let fear rule his life. *What the fuck does fear know anyway?* "Where do we go from here?"

Pulling away, she smoothed down his ruffled beard and said, "Well, I'm severely short-staffed. Any ideas where I might find some people looking for work?"

He blinked at her. "You want us to come back?"

"Madigan," she said, shaking her head, "I never wanted you to leave in the first place. Of course I want you to come back."

"Can I kiss you?" He thought his heart might stop beating if she said no, but then her lips brushed over his while her fingers slipped around his neck, and nothing else mattered. Not his guilt or his failures, not even Chuck. Nothing mattered but this moment with Ashley in his arms as he cradled her neck, deepening their kiss, wondering how on earth he'd ever thought leaving her had been the right thing to do.

"Ugh, get a room," Kev mumbled from the doorway, his voice jerking them apart.

"We're *in* a room," Madigan growled. His irritation faded fast because there was a smile on Kev's face, something he hadn't seen in days.

When Sam and Clay joined Kev in the doorway, Madigan tried to help Ashley off his lap, worried she might feel uncomfortable having three grown men staring at them. But she looped her arms around his neck, leaned in, and stayed right where she was.

"Told you we didn't do drugs," Sam grumbled, his arms crossed tightly over his chest until Kev elbowed him in the ribs. "Ouch, dude," Sam spat, rubbing his side.

"Don't be a dick, Sam," Kev said. "It wasn't Boss's fault."

"No, Sam's right," Madigan said. "I knew something was wrong, and I should have trusted you, or at least listened to you. But I didn't, and I'm sorry."

"It's all right," Clay said, even though Madigan could tell that nothing was all right, not yet. Whether this situation was his fault or not, he'd broken Clay's trust by not believing him. After how long they'd known each other, he wouldn't be able to heal this fracture overnight.

"Thank you for fighting for us again, Ashley," Sam said, staring at his shoes.

Welling up, her eyes shining, Ashley cleared her throat. "You're welcome, Sam. But I'm afraid the fight hasn't even started yet. Chuck still thinks he got away with this, and once we all get back to the mountain—"

"You're letting us come back?" Hope beamed brightly in Kev's eyes, hope for the job, the redemption, or just to be near Davis again, Madigan couldn't say. Probably all three.

"If you're all willing to come back, we would love to have you." Ashley's voice wavered. "You're the best staff we've ever had."

Needing to be closer to her, to let her know how much her support of him, of the men, and of Little Timber meant to him, he closed his arms around her waist, buried his face into her hair, and slid his nose up the side of her neck.

"Seriously," Sam said. "We're standing right here."

"I noticed," Madigan muttered against her neck, making her shiver. "Why don't you three go tell everyone else to get packed. Ashley and I would like some privacy."

Once the men left, he leaned back and met her stare.

Smiling at him, she said, "Why didn't you tell me they called you Mad Madigan?"

He burst into laughter. "Where did you hear that?"

"I needed to see you while you were gone, so I googled you." She bit her lip. "You were a very sexy man, Mad Madigan. You still are, and I've missed you so much."

Cupping her jaw, pulling her close and kissing her like it was the last thing he'd ever do, he realized that for the first time in decades, he didn't hate the nickname.

CHAPTER FORTY-TWO

MADIGAN

THE LAST TIME Madigan had been this nervous he'd been driving up this same road from town over a month and a half ago. Back then he'd been worried about the guys, worried if he'd made the right choice by moving them up here, wondering if the beautiful boss of this mountain would accept them as they were, accept him as he was. This time, he only worried about how quickly he could get that beautiful boss alone. Because there were things he needed to say to her, things he needed to *do* to her.

He could see them standing at the window, Davis, Maude Alice, Ashley. He saw Davis's lips move, saying, "There they are!" with her hand splayed out on the window as a huge, heart-stopping smile spread across Ashley's face.

After sliding to a stop, throwing Lydia into park fast enough to make several of the guys yell at him, he hopped out of his truck. He didn't take a moment to look around. He didn't wait to help the men with their bags. The second his feet hit the snow, he glanced up at the lodge window, grinned, and curled a finger at Ashley, beckoning her to come down.

"Hey, beautiful," he said, opening his arms wide at the bottom of the stairs. But a single breath before she reached him, Murphy sailed past her.

Barely keeping his feet as Murphy leapt into his arms, Madigan said, "Hey, buddy," while taking monstrous licks to his cheeks. "I've missed you too, pal. But I need to see your mommy now, okay?"

Dropping back down to all fours, Murphy sat with his tongue lolling out of the side of his mouth, watching Madigan's every move while he closed the distance to Ashley.

"Welcome back," she said.

"It's good to be back," he purred. But then he slowed, because her chin was wobbling, her shoulders tight, her eyes misting. "Ashley, do you need a hug?"

Like she couldn't hold her head up for one more second, her chin fell to her chest. "I really do."

When he opened his arms again, she stepped inside them. Breathing her in, he said, "I've missed you."

Turning her head, her ear pressed right over his heart, she said, "I've missed you too." Then she pulled back, blinking her eyes dry. "When you're done getting the men settled, catch last chair with me?"

He touched his forehead to hers. "I thought you'd never ask."

THEY MADE out for the entire chairlift ride, not saying a single word, too busy kissing and feeling and trying to get as close to each other as possible in their ski gear. Racing back down the mountain, they skied straight to his cabin, no words, only need.

Ashley walked through the door he held open for her, unzipping her coat and hanging it on a hook on the wall. Madigan unzipped his own coat, tossed it over the rocking chair, and then they both stepped out of their snow bibs. Silently, they stared at each other, Madigan on one side of the room, Ashley on the other. When she took a step toward him, as impossible as it was, he backed away.

"Can you sit on the couch?" he asked, adding, "Just for a second," when she pouted at him. "I have something I want to say to you."

"Okay," she said warily, settling onto his couch, pulling off her boots while he pulled off his.

Taking off his hat, he made a quick fire in the stove, then sat down next to her and gathered his nerve. After spending the entire afternoon going through this same exercise with the men, one by one, trying to make things right, he'd realized how much he needed to do this with Ashley too.

Turning to face her, he admitted, "I hurt you. I said hurtful things to you during our fight, and then again when I left without listening to you. And at Little Timber, when we say hurtful things to each other, we have to make up for them by saying something good and true about the person we hurt." He took Ashley's hands in his. "I said a lot of hurtful things to you, so I'll need to say a lot of good things to make up for them."

"I said hurtful things to you too." Her throat bobbed. "This really isn't necessary."

"I think maybe it is." He gazed into her eyes, big and brown and home. "Ashley, there are so many good things about you that narrowing it down was difficult. But I didn't think we'd want to do this all day, so I did my best. Here are just a few of the good and true things I've noticed about you. You have a deeply caring soul. I see it with the men, with Davis, even with Maude Alice. You love and support everyone around you, and because of that, people feel safe to be themselves when they're with you. That is such a gift."

Slowly, her lips parted, her eyes glassy. How long had it been since someone had told her how amazing she was? From this day forward, he wouldn't let her go more than a day without making sure, through his words or his actions, that she knew.

"You also have a vibrant soul. You've had hard things happen in your life, but you still try to spread joy everywhere you can. You have a light inside you. It's irresistible." He brushed her hair back off her shoulder. "I wonder if you got this from your father."

"Madigan, please. Stop," she pleaded, blinking tears down her cheeks.

He wiped them away. "I'm almost done, I promise. You have a warrior's soul. You fight for the things you love. You fight for this mountain, for your daughter, for your mother. You fight to honor and remember your father the way you think he should be remembered. You fought for me, for us." Now tears stung his own eyes, but he reined them in. This wasn't about him. "Because along with everything else, you have a faithful soul. And I love you for it. I love you because you care. I love you because you never give up. I love you because you make me believe that maybe I'm good enough to be with someone as wonderful as you. I love you, Ashley Cooke. I love you for everything."

Gathering her into his lap, he held her close while her body shook. He hadn't meant for this to happen, but he knew better than most that people needed a good cry far more often than they thought they did. "It's all right, Ashley. It's all right." He kissed her hair, rocking her side to side, sliding his hand up and down her back in slow, gentle strokes, wanting to take her to bed and make her forget about everything. Because he also knew that nothing felt better after a good cry than a good fuck.

Lifting her face to his, he kissed her once, then he stood and carried her into the bathroom. After setting her on her feet, he brushed a warm washcloth over her cheeks and eyes, cleaning her tears away. Then he led her back to the bed and slipped her thermal shirt off over her head, placing it on his dresser. Reaching behind her to unclasp her bra, dropping it to the floor, he kissed the line of her collar bone, then down between her breasts as he sank to his knees. Pressing his lips into the feather-soft skin just below her belly button, he hooked his fingers into the band of her underwear and eased them down her legs while she threaded her fingers into his hair.

His gaze moved up her body until he met her eyes, her eyelashes still sparkling with tears. Sliding his hands up her thighs to brace her hips, he said, "Are you ready?"

"Ready for what?" She wiped her eyes. "I don't think I can handle much more openness today."

"Oh, I think you can handle just a little bit more." Licking his grinning lips, he rolled onto his back, taking her down with him.

"What are you doing?" she gasped, up on her knees, straddling his chest with her hands on the couch above his head.

"Making you feel better. Now hold still." Sliding down, positioning himself under her, he pulled her down onto his mouth.

She sighed as he licked her, kissed her, slid a finger inside her. When he felt her sadness dissolving over his tongue, when she started grinding against his mouth, moaning and drenching his beard, he pictured the new tattoo he'd get as soon as he could—a little bit of Ashley living on his skin forever. Apple blossoms.

In no time at all, she shuddered, cried out, bucked against him, and then she slumped onto the couch, making those deliciously sweet mewling sounds she made after she came. He kissed her one last time, then he slid out from under her, hooking one arm under her legs and the other under her arms.

"Madigan," she slurred as he picked her up and carried her to the bed. "What the hell was that?"

Turning to lay her down, he hovered over her and said, "That was just the beginning." And he meant those words with all his heart.

The post-orgasm haze clearing from her eyes, she sat up, pulled his shirt off over his head, kissed his Christmas pendant once, then she slid his underwear down just enough to free his erection. Rolling him over onto his back, she sank down onto him, moving her hips in a slow, perfect rhythm that made his eyes flutter closed. Leaning forward, she kissed his lips and said, "I love you for everything too, Matthew Madigan."

Madigan rubbed his neck, looking around the room, taking in the group of men who all deserved so much better than this hand they'd been dealt.

"We're going to be on TV?" Kev asked. "All of us?"

"Only if you want to be," Madigan said. "But once Chuck finds out we're back on the mountain, calling the press will surely be his next move. If we beat him to the punch—"

"Then we can tell our story instead of his," Clay said, stroking his chin stubble. "It makes sense."

Madigan had spent the rest of the day after Ashley left his cabin trying to figure out how to do this right, how to get the most bang for their human-interest story buck. Luckily, neither he nor Ashley had taken any steps to cancel the concert during their few days apart, and Madigan knew there was no better time for Ashley to take Chuck down than during a big, public spectacle. After he'd met with Ashley, Davis, and Maude Alice, telling them about his plan, making sure to get their consent—especially Davis's since Chuck was her father after all—Madigan called this meeting.

"Davis," he said, "will you please pass out the fliers?"

"Sure, Boss." Davis hopped to her feet.

"Boss, Davis? You too?"

She shrugged. "I could go back to calling you sexy pirate, but—"

"Boss," he said quickly. "Boss is good." A few of the men snorted.

Brian whistled, studying the flier in his hand. "Starflare, Gravel, Chaining Jane, the Makers." He looked up at Madigan. "That's your band, right?"

"Used to be," Madigan said.

"Yes!" Kev thrust a fist into the air. "Mad Madigan back in action!"

"Please," he said tightly, "don't call me that. In fact, none of you call me that ever again."

Ashley coughed, raising a brow.

"Except for Ashley," he amended. He wanted to sound confident, but apprehension crept into his tone. He hadn't seen his bandmates in years, and he hadn't played in front of an audience in over a decade. This entire situation was a massive anxiety bomb ticking away. "This concert, FlannelFest—"

"Woot!" Davis interrupted, cheering for the name she'd come up with.

"—will mark the beginning of what Ashley and I hope will be a long partnership between Bluebird Basin and Little Timber."

Someone whistled, but Madigan couldn't tell who, probably Kev, maybe Davis, could have even been Maude Alice with how happy she looked, staring back at him.

Ashley piped up. "It will also be the best time for us to confront Chuck and make him sorry he ever messed with us."

Tex got to his feet, Shannon rising to hers beside him, everyone else in the room following suit. "Well, then," Tex said, settling his hat on his head. "Enough sitting around, let's get to work."

CHAPTER FORTY-THREE

ASHLEY

ASHLEY'S JAW hit the snow because the stage was phenomenal. The guys, along with some volunteers from town, had worked late every night this past week, building the entire structure with lumber and lights donated by Bud's Hardware. Walking the grounds, she checked on the warming and bar tents, the grill Clay was running with Brian and Maude Alice. She met with and thanked every local vendor who'd arrived with tables full of items to auction for the fund raiser. Smiling up at the professional skiers and boarders Madigan's famous friends had recruited for the event—most of whom had driven for hours and even hopped planes to come demo the terrain park today—a heavy, grief-stricken ache took up residence inside Ashley's chest.

"He would have loved this," Maude Alice said, walking up to stand beside her.

"Dad would have lost his mind over this. He lived to see the mountain shine. In fact," Ashley turned toward her mother, "that's what we should name it. Max's Park."

Maude Alice's hand floated to her chest. "It's perfect," she said, her voice wavering. "It's all so perfect, Ashley. You and Madigan and all the men, all your hard work, this concert, Max's Park... It's perfect."

Resting her head on Maude Alice's shoulder, Ashley said, "It really is."

"And as much as I hate to ruin this perfect moment, I think we've already made enough in ticket sales for you to have this."

Straightening, Ashley glowered at the check Maude Alice handed her, made out to Charles Thompson for $10,000. "I hate that we have to pay him anything."

"Then don't," Maude Alice said hotly. "Don't pay that criminal a single red cent."

"I have to. I refuse to be indebted to him in any way."

Maude Alice huffed. "I still think we should call the police. He drugged five men, and me! And we have the proof. He should be in jail."

"I agree," Ashley said. "But Madigan and the guys think he'll only deny lacing the pies, even with the results from the lab. He'll just shift the blame to Mira or her staff from Glazed and Confused, and they don't want to pull anyone else into this. Also, apparently none of them like getting the police involved in anything."

"I suppose that makes sense. But then Chuck just gets away with it?"

"I don't know about that," Ashley said. The interviews with the local news station about the guys, Little Timber, and FlannelFest in general had gone so well she was a little disgusted with herself for ever thinking she'd needed to hide who the men were in order to protect her mountain. Because who they were *was* her mountain—strong, resilient, humble. But with the press, with their stories being told the way they'd wanted them to be told, Chuck's threats to call them out had been brushed away like snow. "After today, he'll know he's no longer welcome at Bluebird. And if Madigan gets anywhere near him, he might wind up leaving on a stretcher."

"We'll need to keep Madigan occupied," Maude Alice said

soberly. "The last thing we need is a murder on the mountain. Although I do know several good places to bury a body up here."

Laughing, Ashley said, "I'm sure you do," then they both cheered with the crowd as a boarder landed some ridiculous, gravity-defying jump.

"Can you believe this?" Davis shouted, throwing her hands into the air and screaming for Gravel, the all-woman band just starting their final song. "This is amazing!"

Ashley could only agree. She'd never seen this many people at Bluebird. Cars and trucks already packed the parking lot, and they kept coming, concertgoers forced to park down alongside the main road and hike up. The bands had all arrived on time, and watching Madigan reconnect with people from his life, people who obviously loved and missed him, had reduced Ashley to such an emotional puddle she'd had to fight back tears all day.

She spotted Madigan standing by the stage, tuning his guitar, looking nervous. Murphy panted beside him, gazing up at him like an enormous, furry, emotional support groupie.

"I'm gonna go," she shouted back at Davis, tilting her head toward Madigan.

Davis nodded, then grabbed Ashley and kissed her hard on the cheek. "I love you, Mom," she shouted over the music. "I may never talk to Dad again for as long as I live, but I love you so much, and I'm so happy for you."

Ashley had cornered Davis earlier to discuss her plans to not return to school. Davis wanted to stay and help manage Bluebird's nonexistent marketing. Was this the life Ashley would have chosen for her daughter? Probably not. But looking around now, seeing so many people smiling and celebrating, having the best time together, Ashley understood why Davis had made this choice. Bluebird had a way of getting under a person's skin and settling in deep, becoming a home to anyone who needed one. Maybe Davis would settle here, maybe she wouldn't. It was clear either way, though, that she needed a break from school, and Ashley was just going to have to find a way to be okay with that.

"I love you too, honey!" Ashley yelled, kissing her back and nodding at Kev who'd just walked up to watch the show. Slipping through the crowd, she sidled in beside Madigan and said, "Hey. You're pretty hot. Are you in one of the bands?"

Barely even registering her presence, he took his hands from his guitar and shook them out. "Why am I so nervous?"

"Happens to the best of us." A tall, handsome man with silver-blond hair, a jawline for days, and a knowing, crooked smile strode over to them, extending a hand toward Madigan.

Grabbing the man's hand, Madigan yanked him into a hug. Once they pulled apart, Madigan turned to Ashley and said, "This is Cole Sanderson, the drummer for the Makers and one of my best friends. Cole this is Ashley. She runs the mountain, and she's also my..." When he looked at her, his expression was a question mark.

"I'm his girlfriend. Hi, Cole. Welcome to Bluebird Basin." Ashley shook the man's warm hand.

Slapping Madigan's back, Cole said, "Happy for you, Mad. Nice to see you finally leaving the monastery."

In most circumstances, Ashley was the blusher. It was nice to see someone else turn red for a change. Standing on her tiptoes, she kissed Madigan's warm, flushed cheek.

"We're up next," Cole said. "You ready?"

"As I'll ever be," Madigan admitted.

Ashley heard a familiar rumble, turning in time to scowl at the jacked-up truck charging through the parking lot. "He's here," she said as Chuck parked illegally right behind her snowplow. "Asshole still thinks he can park wherever he wants."

"Now we're talking." Madigan grinned. "I've been waiting all day for that prick to show up. Anger almost always cures my anxiety. I feel better already."

While Chuck jumped down from his truck and scoffed at the stage, Ashley raised her face to Madigan and said, "A kiss for good luck?"

He did more than that, sliding his guitar around his back so he could haul her close, slipping her the tongue and grabbing her ass with both hands. She hoped Chuck was watching.

"Now, Mad Madigan, get up there and break some hearts."

Taking her hand in his, he raised it to his lips and brushed a kiss over her knuckles. Then he stepped onto the stage to the roar of the crowd like a teenage dream come true.

As Ashley walked back out into the crowd, Chuck dog whistled at her, and she pretended she'd just now noticed him. Clutching the test results in one pocket, the check from Maude Alice in the other, she strode over to him, smiling the sweetest smile she could force her mouth to make.

"You made it," she said, accepting a kiss on the cheek from the gutless, backstabbing bastard.

His expression was pure condescension. "It's a little much, don't you think?"

"Really?" Ashley turned back to the stage where Madigan had started to loosen up, even smiling at the crowd while he strummed his guitar. "I think it's perfect."

Chuck laughed, a humorless, backhand of a noise. "And your little terrain park is certainly...quaint."

Overwhelmed by a sudden desire to grab his head and drive her knee into his nose, Ashley said, "Thanks. Speaking of the park, I have something for you." She reached into her pocket and pulled out the check. "I wanted to pay you back."

"So soon?" He looked almost disappointed. He'd wanted to hold this over her head for as long as he could.

"Don't put off until tomorrow, am I right?"

Crumpling the check, he pocketed it like it was a piece of trash he'd picked up from the ground. "I couldn't help but notice the ex-cons are back. Or should I call them cons now? They did break the law, after all. I'm actually wondering why they aren't in jail. Maybe someone needs to investigate the situation. Maybe," he stepped closer to her, his voice dropping an octave, "someone is covering for them."

This was the opening she'd been waiting for. He was nothing if not predictable. "You are so right, Chuck. We definitely need to get to the bottom of this situation. Maybe we should call over one of the reporters here to do a story on the concert and tell them all about those drug tests." She kept her expression calm and thoughtful. "Because I had the most fascinating discussion with Mace the other day."

"Who's Mace?" he said, trying for ignorance but the blood draining from his cheeks gave him away.

"You know, Mace, my EMT. The person you gave all those pies too."

"I'm sure I have no idea what you're—"

"Shut up, Chuck," she snapped, whipping the copy of the test results from her pocket and shaking it open, holding it out in front of his face. "This bullshit was beyond low. It was evil. And if you ever try anything like this again, it won't be me you're dealing with. It'll be him." She pointed up to the stage where Madigan, spotting them, raised a hand from his guitar to flip Chuck the bird. "And they don't call him 'Mad Madigan' for nothing."

"Ash," Chuck said with a nervous, guilty laugh, his face as white as the snow he was backpedaling into, "I have no idea what you think is happening here, but it isn't—"

"I know *exactly* what's happening here, and unless you want to spend the next few years of your life behind bars, you can get the hell off my mountain and never, ever show your face here again."

"That's ridiculous! My daughter is here. You can't keep me from seeing my daughter."

Now it was Ashley's turn to look at him like he was a naive fool, and she milked it for all it was worth. "Do you honestly think she wants to see you after this?"

"You told Davis?" His eyes narrowed into slits. "How could you?"

"Because," she said, getting right up in his face, "it's important to know when someone in your life is a lying, cheating, pathetic piece of shit. Davis may never talk to you again, Chuck, that's between the two of you. But you will not come back to this mountain unless you want to be part of the biggest news story this town has ever seen, which I'm sure the CEO of WinterMass won't appreciate. I have his card here somewhere." She patted down her pockets. "I'm sure I do, because you're the one who gave it to me."

"Yo, Chuck!" A delicious growl through the speakers brushed over Ashley's skin, sending goosebumps racing up her arms. *"You have five minutes to get your ass off this mountain before I come over there and kick it down myself."*

Chuck squinted up at Madigan who smiled threateningly at him while the crowd, led by Madigan's friend Cole, started chanting, "Fuck off, Chuck! Fuck off, Chuck!"

"Ash," Chuck pleaded. "Come on, let's be adults about this."

She shrugged. "You heard the man. It was his men's lives you tried to ruin. It's out of my hands now. I think you still have a couple of minutes to get back into your truck if you hurry."

At that moment, Kev, Tex, Sam, Clay, Brian, and all the other guys started marching down the hill to join her, looking like they were not at all messing around.

"You know what?" Chuck cried, stumbling back toward his truck, slipping in the snow when Murphy came charging down the hill at him, growling and snarling. "Fuck all of you. Fuck you all. All of you." His finger pointed wildly at the whole group, the whole mountain. "Fuck all!"

"Gonna need some ice for that burn, bro," Kev sneered sarcastically while Chuck raced to his truck and threw open his door, leaping inside. He tried to peel out of his spot, succeeding only in spinning his wheels in the snow until he screamed and pounded on his steering wheel like a child throwing a fit. Eventually, while everyone else laughed so hard at him they were clutching at their bellies and wiping tears from their cheeks, Chuck let off the accelerator and backed out slowly, like someone's grandmother leaving the grocery store.

Joy, warm and insistent, spread through Ashley's chest as she danced with the crowd while the Makers played, and the sun set behind them. Shannon danced with Tex, his hat perched crooked on her head, while Kev and Davis cheered at the foot of the stage. Izzy had arrived after her shift at Scotty's, and both she and Sam were beaming, swinging a squealing Sara between them, bright red safety earmuffs covering her little ears. Brian winced while his daughters screamed at the tops of their lungs beside him. And Maude Alice and Clay laughed together, flipping burgers and grilling hot dogs for the crowd. Ashley knew it would still take time for the men to heal from what Chuck had done to them, to feel safe on the mountain again, but with the happiness in the air, the music and dancing, she felt the lightness of the moment everywhere she looked.

Madigan's voice pulled her attention back to the stage. "I'd like to dedicate this next song to my girlfriend." Spotting her in the crowd, he winked. "Ashley, this one's for you."

Walking closer to the stage so she could stand right beneath the super-hot lead guitarist, she swooned while he played the opening chords to "Shine Bright." Madigan gazed down at her, smiling as he harmonized with the lead singer, "All the stars in the sky shine dim, compared to you."

Poking her head into Madigan's cabin hours later, after she helped take down the last of the vendors' tents, Ashley said, "Hey, this is pretty nice. Is this where you take all your groupies after the show?"

Madigan sat on the edge of his bed, his eyes wet and red. "No, it's where you come over here and console your overly sensitive boyfriend who can't stop crying into his beard."

"Oh, sweetheart," she said, because he loved it when she called him that. "What can I do?" Sitting down beside him, she ran her hand over his back.

"Hold me?" he said through his tears.

She wrapped her arms around him, rocking him side to side. "Was it hard to see your friends, your bandmates? Did it bring back old memories?"

He sniffed. "I thought it would, but it didn't. It didn't even remind me of how many people we've lost, although there was a bit of that too. Mostly, it just reminded me of how many good people there still are in my life. People I don't talk to nearly enough. But I'm going to try harder to stay in touch with them. Especially Cole."

She kissed his cheek, tasting the salty tang of his tears. "So they're good tears then?"

"Good tears," he replied. "Watching He Who Must Not Be Named In Bed fuck off was pretty good too."

"You can say that again. I didn't realize how cathartic that would be, but it was amazing. I wish you'd been there."

"No, you don't. Trust me." He sat up, rolling his shoulders, and then his neck. "What was the final take?"

"Let me put it this way," she said, crawling into his lap, straddling him, "we won't have financial problems for the rest of this season at least. Thanks to you." Taking his face in her hands, she kissed him. "You are the best boyfriend. But," she sniffed at him, "you need a shower."

"I'm sure I do," he said with a laugh. "I was sweating like a pig." Grabbing her ass with both hands, he hoisted her up and started walking toward the bathroom. "Take a shower with me?"

Kissing his neck, she said, "Absolutely. I'm freezing."

Under steaming water, she washed his body, running her soapy hands over his chest, over the tattoo of Mary, over the compass above his hip, the one that would always remind him where he'd been and where he was going. She washed his shoulders, his arms, his wrists, each of his fingers, over every single tattoo he had. She knew them all now, every bit of ink on his skin, she knew by heart.

Spinning him around, she washed his back, the curves of his ass, sliding her soapy fingers between his cheeks, down over his balls, biting her lip at the noises coming from his throat. She kneeled to clean his legs, and on her way back up she let her hands slide around his hips, clasping them together to run over the length of his shaft, so hard for her already. So perfect.

When he turned around, he dropped to his knees, hooked one of her legs over his shoulder, and licked her until she trembled and moaned and begged him to make her come, almost ripping the shower curtain off its rings. But just before that surge of pleasure rocked her, he pulled away and stood again, lifting her up into his arms and wrapping her legs around his waist.

Their eyes met, and he drove into her in one smooth thrust, sheathing himself fully. After that, she could only hold on to him as he slid her up and down his shaft, bouncing her over him until she came hard enough to accidentally pull out some of his hair. While her orgasm still had her in its grip, he pulled out, spun her around, bent her over, and plunged back in, thrusting into her over and over, wild and fearless, slapping her ass once while he grunted through his own release.

She laughed and moaned and laughed again, worked and throbbing and indescribably happy.

His hands moved up her stomach to cup her breasts, his arms pulling her up so they stood together. She could still feel him pulsing inside her, his chest heaving against her back as he leaned forward to rest his forehead on her shoulder.

Turning her head, she accepted a deep, passionate kiss, then she said with a smile, "Mad Madigan rides again."

TWO MONTHS LATER

ASHLEY

A SEASON HAD NEVER SPED by so quickly. With the bright, golden sun turning the once pristine slopes into ragged lines of wet, grey slush, revealing small patches of rocks and grass that would only spread in the coming weeks, Ashley felt the same strange sadness she felt every year around this time. Only this year it was so much worse.

These last three months had been some of the happiest of her life, working all day, skiing all afternoon, spending every night with Madigan in his cabin. Watching the men come into their own, becoming experts at their positions, becoming strong skiers and boarders who, she hoped, would keep at the sport even after they left Little Timber. Watching Sam teach Sara and Izzy how to ski. Watching Kev and Davis grow closer, developing a deep and intense bond she knew she didn't fully understand. And now everything was about to change.

The men were leaving today, packing up their cabins and heading back down to Little Timber again. Some of them were heading home or on to their new lives, having completed their time with Madigan.

Peering out through Madigan's window, she watched Tex talking animatedly with Shannon while they walked down the path from the cabins, each holding one of his two bags in their hands. She watched Sam carry his bags in one arm and Sara in the other while Izzy walked beside them, laughing, looking happy.

She ran her fingers over the window frame, over the initials Madigan had carved into the wood way back when he'd installed it: M.M. + A.C. He'd never told her he'd done this, and when she'd finally noticed it a month ago, she'd raced to his cabin to thank him for it all night long.

And now he was leaving.

He wouldn't be just down the path anymore. She wouldn't be in his arms every night. Even though they'd made plans to have date nights twice a week, and Madigan had hired someone to watch over Little Timber one night a week for overnights, this still felt like the end of something.

"Are you going to go say goodbye?" Maude Alice asked, coming to stand beside her at the window, chuckling as little Sara threw a snowball at Sam's chest.

"Are you?" Ashley said while Clay rounded the corner, sliding his boots through the slush, one of his bags slung over his shoulder, the other hanging from his hand at his side.

Maude Alice sighed. "This will be hard."

Ashley's breath caught, trapped somewhere in her chest when Madigan finally made his way down the path. He stared longingly into the trees, up at the slopes, like a captain bidding farewell to a beloved ship that was set to sail away from him. "Too hard," Ashley said. She didn't want this. She didn't want him to leave, but what could she do? The work was over. What could possibly allow him and Little Timber to remain up here over the summer? What work could they do? What could...they—

"Davis!" she shouted, her heart suddenly pounding because why hadn't she thought of this earlier?

"What's gotten into you?" Maude Alice said, leaning down to pet Murphy who'd come bolting out from under Ashley's desk.

"Davis!" Ashley shouted again. Murphy barked. "Davis, come to my office!"

Maude Alice stared at her. "Are you all right?"

Laughing, Ashley pulled her mother into a hug. "Maybe it won't be hard. Because maybe we won't have to say goodbye."

"What!" Davis cried out, running into the office. "Why are you yelling at me?"

Letting go of Maude Alice, Ashley vibrated, practically jumping up and down in place as she asked, "Do you remember that brochure I asked you to make last year?"

"Yeah, why? Do you need it or something..." Davis's eyes ratcheted open, realization dawning. "Could we? Do we have the money? Are you even serious right now!"

After the fundraiser, they had enough. Barely, but enough. "We do. I think. Can you go get the brochure?"

"Yes!" Davis shrieked. "I'll be right back!"

Taking hold of Maude Alice's arms, Ashley explained, "The trails, Mother. I think we can do it."

"The trails," Maude Alice repeated, looking out through the window again, her smile growing. "Of course. We'd need lots of workers, wouldn't we? All summer long."

Ashley kissed her mother hard on the cheek. Once Davis returned with the brochure, she snatched it from her hands and bolted from her office, flying down the stairs while Davis and Murphy thundered down right behind her.

"Madigan!" Ashley shouted, trying to run through the slush but slipping with every other step. "Madigan! Wait!" She waved the brochure in the air above her head, running with it like it was the damn Olympic torch.

"Hey, baby. What is it?" he asked, catching her in his arms when she lost traction trying to slow down.

"Don't...go," she managed between panting breaths.

"What?" Madigan frowned at her. "We have to go. Season's over."

She shook her head, still trying to catch her breath. "No...you don't."

Just then, Davis bolted past them and flew into Kev's arms, wrapping her legs around his waist while he spun her around in a circle and asked, "What's going on?"

"I want you to stay." Ashley thrust the brochure at Madigan's chest before leaning over, putting her hands on her knees, too old to be sprinting through the snow anymore. "Please stay."

He scanned the pictures of the downhill mountain biking trails Ashley and Davis had designed last year. "Mountain biking? At Bluebird?"

Finally catching her breath, she replied, "We've been talking about it for years, but we never thought we could pull it off. But now we have the donors and the time." She tried so hard not to cry, but emotion made her chin wobble, blurring her vision. "We just need the men."

He blinked at her, a high-voltage smile breaking out across his face. "Does this mean?"

"We could start on construction in a few weeks. It would take all summer, multiple summers probably to get it as big as we'd want it. And then it would need to be maintained."

His eyes darting between the brochure and Ashley and back again, he dropped his bag into the snow.

"Stay," she said. "Please stay. I love you. I don't want you to go."

Spinning around, he shouted at the men, "Hey, boys! Who wants a summer job?"

"Is that a yes?" Ashley asked, pulling Madigan around to face her again while the men cheered. "Will you stay? I know you wanted to get back to Little Timber, but I can't imagine my life without you up here. I can't imagine your cabin empty." No matter how hard she tried to fight them back, the tears came. "I don't want you to leave. I want you to stay up here with me. I want to be with you forever, always."

He only stared at her, then he pulled her into his arms and kissed her fiercely. "Hell yes, I want to stay up here," he told her after, leaving her breathless. "Will we move into the cabin or into the lodge? When should we get married? The fall? I bet it's gorgeous up here in the fall."

Gazing up into his crystal blue eyes, she asked, "You want to get married?"

He barked a joyous laugh that made her toes tingle. "That was the worst proposal in the history of the world. I take it back. I'll do it again later."

When he held her close, she clung to him, never, ever wanting to let go. With the sun on their faces and the mountain at their backs, Madigan kissed her again, swept her up into his arms, and carried her back to their cabin while the men cheered and Murphy trotted along beside them.

~THE END~

For a steamy (puns) Madigan and Ashley extra scene, click here.

LIPS LIKE SUGAR

Preorder Book 2 in the Bluebird Basin series now!

FAKE DATE. REAL FEELS.

Mira Harlow has finally lost it. Between running her bakery, parenting her 14-year-old son, and taking care of her mom, she's a stretched-thin mess. But kissing a total—and totally gorgeous—stranger before begging him to be her date to the biggest wedding her small town has ever seen so her ex won't think she doesn't have one? That's a whole new level of chaos, even for her.

The last thing Cole Sanderson expects when he drives into the ski town of Red Falls, Montana is to score a date to his best friend's wedding. But since his ex-rocker life in Seattle is stagnating, when the gorgeous, green-eyed bakery owner propositions him to play the role of her long-distance boyfriend, stirring his punk-shenanigans roots to their core, he doesn't hesitate to say, "Hell yes!"

Mira hopes for a fun night with her fake date, but when their wedding weekend turns into a genuine connection, when Cole returns to Seattle and she tries to go back to her normal life, she wonders if she missed out on something real. But Cole isn't done with her yet, and when he finds his way back to Red Falls, she'll have to decide what's more important: clinging to the neat and tidy life she's struggled to maintain, or taking a risk, embracing the chaos, and maybe even falling in love.

ACKNOWLEDGMENTS

There are so many people to thank for this book becoming a book, and I know I will forget many. But I'll try my best. First, thank you to my family. My husband, my son, my dog, my other dog. I couldn't possibly write without your support. Thank you to my brilliant friends who read early versions of this book, cheered me on, and made invaluable suggestions to make Madigan and Ashley's story shine: Angela Crocker, Paul Grealish, Heather Williams, Katy Lapierre, Angelique Migliore, Cass Scotka, Sarah T. Dubb, and Jessa Kaina. Thank you to my mom for helping edit and sending me awkward texts about the sex scenes. Thank you to Katie Golding and J Calamy for never-ending support and friendship. Thank you to all my ARC readers for being so amazingly supportive of this book. Thank you to Aljane Compendio for rocking my character art. Thank you to the 90s, grunge music, mixtapes, Suburbans with wood paneling, flannels, and the late Mark Lanegan for his music, his inspiration, and honest, heart-wrenching memoir.

And lastly, thank you, from the bottom of my heart, to everyone who has taken the time to read this story. It means the world to me.

ABOUT THE AUTHOR

A Montana transplant hailing from the suburbs of Chicago and about twenty other places, Jess K Hardy is a lover of mountains and snow, long nights and fireplaces. She has been a sandwich artist, a student, a horse trainer, a physical therapist, a wife, a mother, and also a writer. She writes contemporary and speculative adult romance.

ALSO BY JESS K HARDY

THE CURSE OF NONA MAY TAYLOR
THE 7 RULES OF MOVING ON
LOVE IN THE TIME OF WORMHOLES
I, BIONIC
THE PRINCESS AND THE BRUISER

www.ingramcontent.com/pod-product-compliance
Ingram Content Group UK Ltd.
Pitfield, Milton Keynes, MK11 3LW, UK
UKHW021034090326
11144UKWH00056BA/3002

9 798988 516309